Wildfire Creek

**Redemption Mountain
Historical Western Romance
Series**

SHIRLEEN DAVIES

**Book Two in the Redemption
Mountain**

**Historical Western Romance
Series**

Book design and conversions by Joseph Murray at 3rdplanetpublishing.com

Cover design by The Killion Group

ISBN: 978-1-941786-12-3

I care about quality, so if you find something in error, please contact me via email at:

shirleen@shirleendavies.com.

Books by Shirleen Davies

Historical Western Romance Series

MacLarens of Fire Mountain

Tougher than the Rest, Book One

Faster than the Rest, Book Two

Harder than the Rest, Book Three

Stronger than the Rest, Book Four

Deadlier than the Rest, Book Five

Wilder than the Rest, Book Six

Redemption Mountain

Redemption's Edge, Book One
Wildfire Creek, Book Two
Sunrise Ridge, Book Three, Releasing 2015

MacLarens of Boundary Mountain

Colin's Quest, Book One
Coming in 2015

Contemporary Romance Series

MacLarens of Fire Mountain

Second Summer, Book One
Hard Landing, Book Two
One More Day, Book Three
All Your Nights, Book Four
Always Love You, Book Five
Hearts Don't Lie, Book Six, Releasing 2015

Description

Wildfire Creek – Book Two
Redemption Mountain Historical
Western Romance Series

"A passionate story of rebuilding lives, working to find a place in the wild frontier, and building new lives in the years following the American Civil War. A rugged, heartwarming story of choices and love in the continuing saga of Redemption Mountain."

Luke Pelletier is settling into his new life as a rancher and occasional Pinkerton Agent, leaving his past as an ex-Confederate major and Texas Ranger far behind. He wants nothing more than to work the ranch, charm the ladies, and live a life of carefree bachelorhood.

Ginny Sorensen has accepted her responsibility as the sole provider for herself and her younger sister. The desire to continue their journey to Oregon is crushed when the need for food and shelter keeps them in the growing frontier town of Splendor, Montana, forcing Ginny to accept work as a server in the local saloon.

Luke has never met a woman as lovely and unspoiled as Ginny. He longs to know her, yet fears his wild ways and unsettled nature aren't what she deserves. She's a girl you marry, but that is nowhere in Luke's plans.

Complicating their tenuous friendship, a twist in circumstances forces Ginny closer to the man she most wants to avoid—the man who can destroy her dreams, and who's captured her heart.

Believing his bachelor status firm, Luke moves from danger to adventure, never dreaming each step he takes brings him closer to his true destiny and a life much different from what he imagines.

Dedication

This book is dedicated to my wonderful readers and fans who continue to encourage me with their amazing support. They inspire me and keep the energy flowing. Thanks so much!

Acknowledgements

Thanks also to my editor, Kim Young, proofreader, Alicia Carmical, and all of my beta readers. Their insights and suggestions are greatly appreciated.

As always, many thanks to my wonderful resources, including Diane Lebow, who has been a whiz at guiding my social media endeavors, my cover designer, Kim Killion, and Joseph Murray who is a whiz at formatting my books for both print and electronic versions.

Wildfire
Creek

Prologue

Bison City, Idaho Territory, 1866

"What do you see?" Luke Pelletier held his position as Dutch McFarlin peeked over the edge of the window, watching and listening to the conversation taking place inside.

Dutch had been with the Pinkerton Detective Agency for well over a year, while Luke had been recruited a month before. It was supposed to be one quick job—in and out. Weeks later, Luke found himself embroiled in a string of events, which threatened to go on for months if he and his partner didn't end it tonight.

"The man I believe to be Flatnose and at least ten of his men," Dutch hissed, trying to keep his voice low. They'd followed the outlaw to the remote hideout after a tip from a member of the local vigilante committee or, as they preferred to call themselves, the citizens committee.

Flatnose and his men were suspected of robbing a series of gold transport wagons, stealing the treasure, and killing anyone who resisted. The death count stood at two confirmed. The trouble was no one had any firm proof Flatnose's gang was behind any of the crimes—and no one could identify the man. The outlaws had been careful to hide their faces behind bandanas and hats pulled low across their foreheads. The only clue to his identity had been a slip by one of his men during a holdup. A guard swore he heard the man call their leader Flatnose.

The good people of Bison City established the citizens committee after the killing of the two guards. It hadn't taken them long to hire the Pinkerton Agency. Dutch arrived a couple weeks before Luke, contacting his friend when it appeared a second agent would be needed and Pinkerton had no one available to send. In truth, Luke had jumped at the chance to get away from the ranch and give his brother, Dax, and new wife, Rachel, some privacy. Besides, Luke needed time to figure out his own future.

If they could find the proof, Luke would be on the road back to his ranch in Montana tomorrow, ending his relationship with Allan Pinkerton and his illustrious agency, at least for the moment.

"Damn," Dutch murmured and dropped down, scooting behind some bushes as two men stepped onto the porch. Dutch recognized Flatnose Darvis from a game of cards at a Bison

City saloon. He heard Flatnose had earned his nickname during a fight when his opponent slammed a shovel into his face. Dutch didn't recognize the second man, who reached into a pocket, pulled out a slim cheroot and lit it, blowing the smoke out in a long stream.

"The committee has hired someone from Pinkerton's to find out who's behind the robberies," the man standing next to Flatnose said. No one knew him by his real name, Frederick Marlowe, or his connection to Flatnose. Few knew he and Darvis were equal partners, and no one, except Flatnose, knew his last name. The men called him Rick.

"Where'd you hear that?" Flatnose asked, turning toward the man and lighting his own cigar.

"The mayor's daughter," Rick answered, recalling how easy it had been to flatter the information out of the naïve young woman. "She said they believe a gang, led by a man named Flatnose, was behind the thefts."

Flatnose let out a string of curses before taking a deep draw from his cigar.

"We should head back to Montana. There's more gold to be had closer to home, without the interference of the Pinkerton men." Rick didn't mention Star Ranch, even though both knew that's where he wanted to go. The property consisted of several hundred acres he and Flatnose purchased after Rick's brief term as a lawman in the Dakota Territory. He'd learned a lot in the job and applied much of it to the robberies they pulled afterwards.

Flatnose looked out over the thick pine forest, finished his cigar, and ground it out under his boot. "Tell the boys we'll leave at first light."

Dutch moved further toward the back of the cabin, where Luke covered a second entrance. He'd heard enough to believe Flatnose and his men were who they sought, but not enough to convict them. They'd need to find the gold or have one of the men confess.

"What now?" Luke asked as Dutch crouched next to him.

Dutch pulled out his pocket watch. "We've got six hours until daylight. That's when they plan to ride out to Montana."

"Not much time to get what we need." Luke pushed his hat further back on his head. "If they're leaving, the gold's got to be here. We need to catch them with it before they ride out."

"You know, the odds are in their favor— twelve to two." Dutch felt the need to point out the obvious since he'd been the one to get Luke involved. Luke and Dutch had served together in the Confederate Army, both ending up in the

Confederate Secret Service Bureau, a covert group made up of men and women from the military as well as private citizens.

"We've got four, maybe five hours before they make their move. We have two choices—ride back to Bison City to gather more men, or stay here and handle it our way."

"Have we ever faced odds like this before?" Luke asked.

"Never."

Luke pulled off his hat, speared his fingers through his dark auburn hair, and flashed a grin at Dutch. "Guess it's time we did. What's life without a little adventure?"

"Not worth living, in my opinion." Dutch smiled back. He checked his revolver, confirming it was loaded, then checked his second gun before picking up the Spencer repeating rifle he'd hidden a few feet away. "What's the plan?"

Luke positioned himself several yards away from where the gang had used a line to string their horses. All had remained saddled. The only item missing for a quick escape was the gold. He could see Dutch crouched at the corner of the rickety house, checking his guns again and stifling a yawn. It had surprised both men to see no guards posted. Luke figured Flatnose had become more arrogant as time passed and their crimes had gone undetected. He'd always believed stupidity played a key role in catching most outlaws.

He glanced up to see Dutch's signal, indicating movement inside. Not a minute later, several men walked out carrying saddlebags, plus small metal boxes balanced on their shoulders. They were silent as they trekked the short distance to their horses and secured their loads. Once finished, they started back inside, not once looking around, even though the early morning light made it easy to see.

As soon as they were out of sight, Luke moved with quiet confidence toward the horses. He checked the saddlebags on one horse, found nothing, then moved to the box. Surprised it had no lock, he lifted the lid to find it filled with gold. He quickly checked one more before signaling Dutch and reclaiming his position behind a stand of bushes a few yards away.

"Hurry up. We need to move," Flatnose's voice boomed through the quiet morning air. He stepped aside as several men walked past him, heading for their horses, and carrying more boxes.

Nine men stood with the horses, including Flatnose. Dutch signaled Luke as the last three men stepped out of the house and onto the porch.

"Hands up, gentlemen." Dutch leveled his pistols at the outlaws as their hands moved for their guns. "I wouldn't try it," he warned and glanced toward Luke, who'd drawn his weapons and pointed them toward the men standing near Flatnose.

"Everyone stay where you are and don't move." Luke made his way toward the cover of a large boulder, where he'd left his rifle, keeping his eyes focused on Flatnose.

No one moved until a laugh broke out from one of the men Dutch had covered—the same man Dutch had seen with Flatnose hours before. "You really think you can take all of us?"

"Doesn't matter. You and Flatnose will be the first to die." Luke's words slipped out as shots blasted near the house. He shifted his gaze from Flatnose long enough to see two outlaws lying motionless. It was seconds too long.

Fifteen seconds seemed like minutes as bullets flew, men shouted, and bodies fell. Later, Luke wouldn't be able to recall how he'd made it behind the boulder with a wound to his head, or how Dutch had taken two hits and still remained alive. When he woke, he found himself face down in the dirt, a small pool of blood under his head.

Luke pushed to his feet, feeling nauseous and dizzy. He didn't stop moving until he found Dutch trying to tie a kerchief around the wound to his leg with his one good arm, the other one hanging useless.

"How many did we get?" Dutch's jaw clenched at the pain ripping through his body.

"I counted six, including the two on the porch."

"Five got away." Dutch rested his back against the house, angry they'd let so many escape.

"Why didn't they stay around to finish us?"

"You don't remember?"

Luke shot a disgusted look at Dutch before lowering himself to one of the porch steps and resting his head in his hands. "I don't remember much after you shot the first ones."

"Not a second passed before you plugged the two closest to you, then spun and hit one more. I hit another before taking shots in my leg and arm as Flatnose and the rest of his men mounted and took off. One of their bullets must have grazed your head."

Luke looked toward the bodies several yards away. "Guess I'd better load them on horses and deliver them to the sheriff, along with any gold the outlaws left behind."

"Then what?"

Luke leveled his gaze at Dutch. "If Pinkerton gives the okay, we follow them to Montana."

Chapter One

Splendor, Montana Territory

Two months later

Water from the falls a mile away could be heard over the rippling creek where Luke Pelletier sat contemplating—he wasn't quite certain about what. No one would accuse him of being an introspective sort, given to long hours of self-reflection. Immediate action had always been the force which drove him, becoming second nature during his youth in Savanah and during his time fighting for the Confederate Army against the Northern Aggressionists.

Several weeks earlier Luke had returned to Redemption's Edge, the ranch he and his brother, Dax, owned. He and Dutch had followed the outlaws into Montana before losing them over the rough terrain. They didn't have any leads. All they knew was Flatnose had a ranch somewhere in the massive territory. It didn't take long for the citizens committee to notify Pinkerton they no longer required their services. Dutch had been reassigned to a case in Denver, while Luke rode home.

He reached down to pluck a flower from the edge of Wildfire Creek, the place he went to relax from the never-ending activities around the ranch. He rolled the stem between his fingers before placing it in the running water to watch it drift from sight.

Ever since Dax had married Rachel Davenport, he'd struggled. A constant state of unease plagued him, causing Luke to doubt his decision to stay in Montana. The restlessness had nothing to do with Dax and Rachel's marriage. He'd encouraged it, been glad when Dax came to his senses and asked her to marry him. Something else troubled Luke, but he had yet to identify the cause.

He watched as a small rock struggled to keep its spot on the edge of a short drop off into the creek. It clung to the spot as the fast moving stream pounded against it, as if telling the stone it didn't belong there. Luke rested his arms across his bent knees and focused on the one rock, finding himself hoping it withstood the water's onslaught. His mind drifted to the last two years and the enormous changes he and Dax had experienced since leaving their Savannah home to search for new lives away from the war's destruction.

He ended his final assignment for the South in a role he'd undertaken numerous times during the war—Southern spy gathering information which could be used to thwart the Union Army. He'd known they'd suspected his intentions, but the Northerners finally accepted him as a Southern boy with sympathies toward the Union cause. It had taken time to build the ruse, using family contacts and friends he and his family had developed over many years in the merchant business.

Although based in Savannah, they'd transported and sold goods throughout the Eastern seaboard. The list of people they called friends had been long and illustrious, allowing them to enter some of the finest homes. Luke even courted the daughter of an affluent New York banker. The war had ended the courtship, as well as life as everyone knew it—especially those from the South.

He focused once more on the small stone, which stubbornly held its spot, refusing to be dislodged. A few yards away, a tree branch made its way through the current, inching closer to the rock. It whirled as the water pushed it one direction, then another before sweeping over the place where Luke's stone clung tenaciously to the ledge. When the branch moved on, the rock was gone, uprooted by the strength of the broken limb. He wondered if he also grasped for something out of his control in an effort to fight off the growing feeling of detachment.

For most of his life he'd distanced himself from Dax, never feeling quite as capable. He loved his brother, would do anything for him, but he always felt as if he lurked somewhere on the edge of Dax's shadow.

When their younger brother, Andre, was born, Luke obtained the status as the middle brother—an almost invisible son in a family made up of individuals with distinct personalities. Their father counted on Dax to continue and grow the family businesses. Their mother doted on Andre. Luke became almost invisible, spending much of his time in the stables, helping train horses while building a reputation as the rascal of the family. He'd come and go at will, solidifying his standing as somewhat of a rogue, although a charming one. Early in life he'd made up his mind he wanted nothing more than to find adventure wherever he could, never committing to the ties of marriage and children.

The sound of voices pulled Luke from his musings. He glanced around and listened intently, rising in a quiet, fluid motion, pulling his Remington .44 from its holster. The voices came again. Most of their Indian neighbors were friendly, even visiting the local doctor when their own medicine failed. Others were hostile. Hunger and what they considered travesties against their people by the white man drove some to raid local ranchers and, on occasion, kill. A couple of years before, a group of eastern Montana Sioux had reportedly taken several white settlers prisoner. They'd never been seen again.

He'd left Prince, his palomino stallion, in a nearby pasture to graze on the thick grass. The voices came from the opposite direction, across the creek from where he stood. He stepped backwards in quiet strides, bending low, taking cover behind a large boulder partially surrounded by shrubs and pines, and waited.

The Indians made their way down the opposite slope toward the stream, stopping directly across from where Luke had rested a few minutes before. He guessed them to be part of the Blackfoot renegade band led by Long Feather. There'd been numerous complaints of missing cattle and the ranchers were quick to blame the renegades. From what he'd heard, Long Feather's band tended to raid and steal from their traditional enemies rather than ignite the wrath of the white man's army. However, desperation could make any man take risks to care for his family.

They stood in a small circle and spoke in quiet voices. Luke guessed they were a hunting party in search of food. One pointed upriver, while another seemed to think they should head downstream. It appeared they'd made the decision to retrace their steps up the hill when Prince let out a loud whinny, followed by another.

Luke glanced toward his horse, then back at the group, who'd stopped and looked around for the source of the noise. All carried bows and quivers filled with arrows. They readied them as they crossed the creek, drawing closer to Luke's hiding place. He raised his gun and fired into the air, hoping they'd stop or turn back. They ignored the warning.

"You're on Pelletier land," he shouted, stepping from behind the protection of the boulder.

The man in the lead stopped for a split second to stare at him, then charged.

He fired another two shots at their feet. It was enough to stop them and give him time to sprint toward Prince and swing into the saddle, tapping his heels against his horse's side. It was all the encouragement the animal needed.

He felt an arrow fly past his face before feeling another pierce his shoulder, a sharp pain spreading down his arm. Luke transferred the reins to his other hand, slumped low over Prince's neck, and glanced behind him. They'd disappeared.

❧

"What the hell?" Bull muttered when he spotted Luke riding in, the sleeve of his shirt covered in blood, an arrow sticking out of his shoulder. "Whoa, Prince." Bull raised his hands, signaling the horse to stop before catching the reins as well as Luke's body as it began to slump from the saddle. "Dax, Rachel, come quick!" He cradled him in his arms and climbed the front steps to the door as Dax pulled it open.

"Rachel," Dax called and directed Bull to a back bedroom, where he positioned Luke on his side.

"What is...?" Rachel's voice faded when her gaze landed on her brother-in-law. She hurried to the bed and began to inspect the injury before turning to Dax. "Get my bag, hot water, clean towels, and whiskey."

"I'll get the hot water, boss." Bull headed toward the kitchen as Dax took the stairs two at a time, heading for their bedroom.

During the war, Rachel had been a Union Army nurse, working in some of the most primitive conditions while trying to keep men alive long enough to provide treatment. Almost a year ago, she'd traveled to Splendor to help her uncle, Doctor Charles Worthington, with his medical practice. Until a few minutes ago, she'd been enjoying a relaxing Sunday with her husband.

Rachel cut Luke's shirt away, careful to avoid pulling the area around the wound. She touched the arrow's shaft, trying to judge if it had lodged against a bone. It didn't budge. He moaned, then began to stir.

Dax laid her bag on a table at the same time Bull walked into the room with a pot of hot water, followed by their resident cook and housekeeper, Bernice.

"Luke, can you hear me?" Rachel asked.

"Uh-huh." His low, strained voice told Rachel the pain was extreme. She glanced at her husband, then back at Luke.

"I need to get the arrow out."

"Yes," he gritted out.

"I'll do the best I can, but the pain will be severe." She picked up the bottle of whiskey and poured a generous amount into a glass before turning him slightly toward her. "Drink this." Dax held his brother's head as Rachel lifted the glass to Luke's lips. "I need to break the shaft to relieve the pressure before I start." She kept her voice low, even. "The arrow is lodged against a bone, which means I must dig it out. You'll need every drop in this glass."

He finished the contents before Dax lowered his head back to the pillow.

"Let's get this over with," Luke said as the alcohol began to dull his senses.

"Bull, I'll need you to hold his legs. Dax, steady his shoulders. Bernice, please go to the other side of the bed with a wet cloth."

"Here. Put this between his teeth." Bull handed Dax a length of leather used for sharpening knives.

"You ready, Luke?" Rachel asked.

He nodded as she broke the shaft a couple of inches from his skin. She looked at Bull and Dax, then nodded as she positioned the knife at the point of entry and began.

She kept a close watch on Luke, noting the perspiration accumulating on his forehead. The third probe into the wound caused him to shudder before his eyes closed and he, mercifully, lost consciousness.

Within an hour, the arrowhead had been removed. Rachel cleaned the wound, wrapped it, then measured out a small amount of laudanum for the pain. He'd stayed unconscious the entire time. As with all wounds, the biggest fear came from infection. If she could keep the wound clean and bandaged, Luke would have a good chance at a full recovery.

Bull removed the water, leaving the extra towels and whiskey on the table.

"I'll sit with him until he wakes up." Rachel straightened, stretching her arms above her head and rolling her neck from one side to the other.

"You take a break. I'll stay." Dax placed a kiss on her cheek.

"What do you think happened?" She brushed strands of hair from her face and stared down at Luke's still form.

"My guess is he crossed paths with a band of renegades—possibly the ones we've heard about from the other ranchers." Dax crossed his arms and looked down at his brother. "An attack is rare, though."

"Perhaps he caught them by surprise." Rachel leaned against her husband, knowing there'd be no real answers until Luke woke. "Do you know where he'd been riding?"

Dax placed an arm around her waist and pulled her close. "My guess is Wildfire Creek. That's where he usually goes when he wants to get away." His eyes wandered over her tired face. "Go rest before you fall down."

Rachel walked out of the room and closed the door behind her. She needed to send someone into town tomorrow to pick up additional supplies from the clinic and bring her uncle out to check on Luke. She'd just stepped into the kitchen when she heard the front door slam open.

"Rachel?"

"In the kitchen, Hank."

"Bull told me Luke was attacked by those Indians who've been raiding the area. That so?" Hank Wilson and his wife, Bernice, had worked at the ranch since the original owner had bought any land which became available. Unfortunately, Pat Hanes' life had been cut short when an outlaw he and the Pelletier brothers had been pursuing gunned him down, leaving the property to Dax and Luke.

"We don't have any details yet. All we know is Luke rode in with an arrow in his shoulder. I dug it out and he's resting in the back bedroom. Dax is with him." Rachel grabbed a cup for tea. "Would you like some coffee?"

"No, thank you. I believe I'll go check on Luke." Hank hurried down the hall and into the bedroom. "I just heard. How is he?" he asked Dax.

"The arrowhead is out and he's resting. With luck, it won't get infected." Dax kept his gaze focused on his brother.

Hearing their muffled conversation, Rachel sat in the kitchen and sipped her tea, thinking about her life since she'd first met Dax.

He and Luke, suffering from a dangerous stomach infection, had pulled into Splendor with a pine box containing the body of their fellow Texas Ranger, Pat Hanes, in the back of their wagon. Rachel had been the first person Dax approached for help. She and her uncle hadn't wasted a minute tending to Luke. In just a little over a day, he walked out of the clinic. He was weak, but alive. A few months later, she and Dax married.

It didn't take her long to learn life around the Pelletiers would never be boring.

Rachel glanced behind her to see Dax approaching. "Is he awake?"

"He drifts in and out, moaning each time. He did mumble something about Wildfire Creek." He grabbed the coffee pot and poured a cup. "I'm going to get Bull and a few others together, see if we can find them." Dax focused on her. "The creek is a mile away from here—too close to ignore."

Although she understood, Rachel didn't like Dax heading out into possible danger.

She'd lived in Splendor a few months longer than Dax, knew about some of the raids on local ranchers, and had treated a few knife and arrow wounds from the confrontations. The only deaths she knew about were a couple who had joined a wagon train heading to Oregon. The party had been attacked by a band of renegades between the territorial capital of Big Pine and Splendor. No one else in the group had been hurt. The deaths sent a clear warning that Montana was still a wild frontier with very real dangers.

"I'll keep watch on Luke for a few days, then I need to return to the clinic. I'd like one of the men to fetch Uncle Charles tomorrow to check on him."

"Good idea. Until we know what's going on, me or one of the men will ride to and from town with you. No sense taking chances."

She wanted to protest, but experience had told her once Dax made up his mind, he seldom changed it.

"You know, it's going to be a long few weeks around here." Rachel glanced at Dax, knowing he understood what she meant.

He gave her a small smile. "Luke's not the best patient. I may need to post Bull by the bed so he doesn't try anything." Dax pushed back his chair and strode toward the door. "I'll speak to Bull," he threw over his shoulder as it closed behind him.

They both knew if Dax gave Bull the order, he'd follow it, no matter how much Luke protested. Although about the same height as Luke, Bull's shoulders were wider. His thick arms and *don't mess with me* stare could stop just about anyone. Those who ignored the warning signs learned to regret it.

Rachel watched the group of riders head out. A part of her hoped they'd find whoever attacked Luke, another part hoped the renegades had moved on. Somehow, she doubted it. She couldn't help wondering if there might be something more to the risks the Indians took. The ranchers traded with the local Blackfoot tribe for hides in exchange for meat. Some had hired men from the tribe to help on their ranches. Overall, there had been good relations between both groups. The increase in thefts vexed her. The oddest part was what they took—eggs, chickens, pigs, and grain. She turned toward the bedroom, thinking of one of their newest ranch hands, a man who'd been injured much like Luke.

The day of her wedding to Dax, a man had ridden into Splendor, slumped over his saddle, an arrow protruding from his back. Travis Dixon had traveled alone from Tennessee with no destination in mind, leaving behind a depleted horse breeding ranch to start a new life in the west. He'd made it to Big Pine, then decided to continue to Splendor. He'd heard about a family from the South, the Pelletiers, who'd recently taken over a thriving cattle ranch and were breeding horses.

A small band of renegades attacked him a few miles from town. He'd been lucky to survive. Once recovered, Dax and Luke had offered him a position as a wrangler and ranch hand. In the few short months he'd been at Redemption's Edge, he'd turned into one of their best workers. Quiet and unassuming, he'd shared little of his past.

As far as Rachel knew, there had been no other attacks since—until Luke.

"Damn it, Dax. I need to get out of here. You try being cooped up and see how you feel." Luke had reached his limit. A week in bed, followed by Bull trailing him everywhere for the last ten days had caused more than a few rifts between the brothers. Dax hadn't budged, even though both knew Luke was free to do what he wanted.

"The doc was real clear about trying to do too much before your shoulder is healed. We need you at full strength." They stood in the barn, Dax grooming Hannibal while Luke tended to Prince. "I don't know why you're so fired up to work. Used to be you'd do anything to get out of it." Dax knew it wasn't quite true. Luke could work as hard as anyone—if he chose to. That was before the war and the changes it brought to everyone.

Luke dropped his brush in a nearby bucket and turned toward Dax. "You remember the Ramsey sisters?" A broad smile broke out on each of their faces at the mention of the beautiful young women in Savannah. "I swear their daddy would've killed both of us if he had any idea what his daughters let us do."

"Thank God he never found out. I heard they hightailed it up north to live with their momma's parents in Boston." Dax led Hannibal to his stall and closed the gate.

"Do you remember the time—" Luke stopped at the sight of Rachel entering the barn.

"I thought I'd find you both in here." She didn't notice the look which passed between the two as she stopped next to Dax, then glanced at Luke. "Uncle Charles just pulled up. He came to look at your shoulder."

"Guess I better go see him." He put Prince in his stall and took off at a slight run.

"Appears he's anxious to get out from under Bull's watch and throw away the sling."

"We both know he hasn't been using it most of the time. Says it feels better to work the muscles." Dax draped an arm around Rachel's shoulders as they followed Luke outside.

"You understand Uncle Charles told him that knowing his instructions would be ignored, right? I think he has a pretty good understanding of Luke."

They climbed the steps onto the porch as Luke dashed out the front door, all smiles.

"Doc said I'm healed and ready to get back to work." He rotated his arm in a wide arc, grimacing at the remaining stiffness. "I'm riding out to join the men."

They watched as he entered the barn. Ten minutes later, he rode out on Prince, heading toward the herd.

"We may not see him for days," Dax joked as they continued inside.

Luke headed north before taking a sharp turn to the west and Wildfire Creek. Dax and the men hadn't been able to find any trace of the band of renegades. They'd searched most of the western property line without success. The entire incident bothered Luke, until he'd convinced himself the renegades were looking for something other than cattle or horses. They were on foot, following the creek as if trying to decide which way to go—perhaps hunting something other than game.

A small herd of Pelletier cattle grazed in a pasture a few hundred yards away with just three men on guard, the same as on the day of the attack. It would've been easy for the band to distract the men and disappear with a steer.

He slid off Prince close to where he'd encountered the Indians and walked toward the creek. It had been several weeks since the attack. He didn't expect to see anything, yet he still felt the need to inspect the area. An hour later, after finding nothing, he rode north toward the rest of the herd, convincing himself it had been a random event.

Luke's recuperation had done nothing to lessen the apprehension he felt. It had haunted him throughout his recovery. Although the injury had taken his mind off his sense of unease, he still felt it weighing him down, like an anchor from one of the merchant ships his family had owned in Savannah. Cold, heavy, and indiscriminating as to what might be taken down with it during the descent into the unwelcome salty water.

Luke could see the herd a mile ahead and reined Prince to a stop, pulling out his canteen to take a long drink. He turned in the saddle, checking behind him and to the sides, shaking his head at the melancholy which seemed to envelop him. It was time to shrug off whatever haunted him.

"Hey, Luke. The doc give you the okay to come out this way, or did you run off?" Bull reined up beside him.

"I'm clear to work. What's Dax have you doing?"

"We're moving the herd to the south pasture, the one closest to the house. We've been changing locations every few days with five men watching the herd at night. Dax doesn't want to take any chance of the renegades coming for the herd. Some of the men are going into town tonight. You ought to join us. Been a long time since you got off the ranch."

"I've been thinking the same all the way out here. Count me in." He put the canteen away as Bull turned toward the herd. An evening at the Wild Rose might be just what he needed.

Chapter Two

"Over here, Luke." Bull waved toward the table where several of the ranch hands played cards.

He took a seat, scanning the saloon.

"If you're looking for Ginny, she took a break. Her sister's sick so she needed to check on her." Ellis scanned his cards and threw down a couple. He'd been with Pat Hanes before Dax and Luke took over the ranch and, along with Rude and Bull, was one of their most trusted men.

"Anyone with a whiskey will do," Luke lied. He *had* been looking for Ginny, hoping to see the pretty barmaid who'd captured his attention when she'd first come into town. Everyone had been warned by Amos Henderson, owner of the Wild Rose, that Ginny's job included serving drinks and nothing more. She wasn't part of the "upstairs social club", as he liked to refer to the women who offered more than whiskey.

It didn't matter. Luke had no interest in anything other than conversation. Her sweet disposition, free of the jaded attitude of the women who worked upstairs, made her a favorite of all the men. Besides, he was too much of a free spirit to ever settle down and have a family. Ginny was the type of woman you'd marry.

"What's wrong with her sister?" Luke asked.

"Stomach pains from what Amos said." Bull tossed a card down and waited.

"Deal me in the next hand." Luke walked to the bar, ordering a drink from the bartender while continuing to check the door.

"She ain't here, Luke." Al wiped down the bar as he spoke, keeping watch on the patrons.

"Bull said her sister's sick."

"That's what I heard. Fever, stomach pains. Ginny took her over to see the doc." Al moved further down the bar.

Luke downed his whiskey in one swallow and walked toward the entrance, ignoring the amused gazes of the boys at his table.

He crossed the street, pushed open the clinic door, and walked to the back where the doctor saw patients.

Charles barely looked up from examining Mary, a worried Ginny standing next to the table, holding her sister's hand. Luke knew she had little money and would fret about paying Doc Worthington.

"Luke. What brings you in here?" Charles asked.

"I heard Mary was sick and thought I'd come over to check on her—and Ginny."

"It's a stomach infection. Not much different from what you had when you first came to town." Doc straightened and looked toward Ginny. "Best to leave her here tonight. I'll keep watch over her, make sure the fever's going down."

"I'll stay," Ginny said, her hand tightening on Mary's.

"Well, then, you'd better let Amos know you won't be back to work." Doc used a damp cloth to wipe Mary's forehead and neck.

Ginny glanced at Luke, then back at Mary. He knew she felt conflicted. Even one night without working would be a major issue for them. She worked a couple days a week for Suzanne Briar at the boardinghouse where they lived. Luke had heard that, plus the money she earned at the Wild Rose kept them in a room and put food on the table, but not much more.

"I'll let him know, Ginny. Amos will understand." Luke took off across the dirt street, already deciding what he'd say to the saloon owner. "Where's Amos?"

Al looked over from pouring a round of drinks and nodded his head. "In the back."

Luke spent a few minutes with Amos, then stopped at the table where the boys still played cards, noting a slight smirk on Rude's face.

"How's your girl?" Rude asked.

Luke glared at one of their most experienced ranch hands, surprised he'd been the one to ask what he knew the others were thinking. "She's not my girl. Just a woman trying to make it without selling her soul." The bite in his words wasn't lost on the others.

"How's her sister?" Bull asked, tossing back his drink.

"Like you'd expect. Ginny refuses to leave her, so you boys are on your own if you want another drink." He turned toward the doors, pushing them open as Gabe Evans, the town sheriff, came up the steps.

"Leaving already?" Gabe asked. They'd become unlikely friends within weeks of the ex-Union colonel's arrival in Splendor to visit his good friend, Noah Brandt. He'd volunteered to take on the role of sheriff until the town could hire someone else. So far, there'd been no takers.

"Ginny's sister is over at the clinic. I'm going to check on them."

"Is it serious?"

"I don't believe so, but doc wants her to stay overnight."

Gabe pushed open the saloon doors before turning back to Luke. "Say hello to Ginny for me." He shot Luke a knowing grin.

Hell, did everyone think he'd set his sights on Ginny? Luke shook his head and crossed the road. Even though Splendor seemed small, it had grown over the years and now had as many people as other large towns in Montana. They had one main street anchored by Noah Brandt's livery and the school at one end, and the church and bank on the other.

"Her fever breaking any?" Luke asked as his gaze landed on Ginny sitting next to the exam table where Mary slept.

Ginny glanced up, her tired eyes red around the edges. "A little. What did Amos say?"

"He said to tell you to take care of Mary and come back when you can." At least that was a fair summary of the conversation Luke had with him.

"Amos is a good man," she muttered, then shifted her gaze back to Mary. She laid her head on their joined hands and prayed, glancing up at the feel of Luke's warm hand on her shoulder.

"She'll make it. The doc won't let anything happen to her."

His calm words reassured her, even though the fear she felt at loosing Mary almost choked her. She'd promised—*promised*—her parents she'd keep her safe. Their mother and father hadn't survived the wagon trip west, but she and Mary had. Ginny would not lose her now.

"Ginny?"

The weak, raspy voice wasn't much above a whisper, yet it pierced Luke's consciousness. He opened his eyes, surprised he'd fallen asleep in the uncomfortable chair. Ginny lay quiet, her head propped on her folded arms next to Mary.

"Ginny?" The voice sounded stronger this time, more determined.

"It's all right, Mary. Ginny's right here." Luke looked down at the little girl. Her color had returned and, although tired, her eyes weren't as red as they'd been earlier. He felt her forehead. No fever.

Ginny jolted at the sound of Luke's voice as he leaned over Mary.

"Mary." Relief flooded through her. She took her sister's hand and held it to her face. "How do you feel?"

"Thirsty."

"I'll get the doc." Luke walked out, took the few steps to the doctor's house in back, and pounded.

"Coming," Charles called, then pulled the door open.

"Mary's awake."

He moved past Luke and walked toward the clinic. When he saw Mary, he smiled. "Well, you look much better. How does your stomach feel?"

Mary looked at Ginny, who nodded. "Good," she said in a small voice and turned her head back toward her sister.

"That's wonderful." He glanced at Ginny. "The fever is gone and her color is much improved. I see no reason why you can't take her home."

A radiant smile broke out on Ginny's hopeful face. She looked at her sister. "Are you ready to go home?"

"Yes." Even as tired as she looked, Mary clearly wanted to leave.

Ginny grabbed her reticule from a nearby chair. "How much do I owe you, doctor?"

"Don't concern yourself with it now. We'll discuss it after you've had a chance to rest and Mary is fully recovered."

"All right. Thank you." She felt her face heat up, knowing she had almost no money and nothing to trade. She reached for Mary's blanket to see Luke already wrapping it around her sister, pulling it tight.

"Will you let me carry you home?" Luke asked in a soft, calm voice.

Mary's gaze moved up to look up at the tall man and nodded, reaching her arms up to wrap around his neck.

"I can take her."

"No, ma'am. All you need to do is show me where you live and we'll get her back to bed." Luke turned toward the doctor. "Thanks, doc. I'll be in touch."

Charles nodded, opening the door for the three to pass into the early morning light.

Ginny walked toward the boardinghouse a few doors from the clinic, Luke following with Mary. She stepped around back and through a door leading to a narrow staircase.

"Upstairs?" Luke asked.

"No. We're behind the stairwell." She kept her words quiet, yet Luke could hear the hint of awkwardness behind them.

He glanced around the staircase and narrowed his eyes before sending her a questioning look.

"Here." She opened a door not more than two feet wide hidden behind the stairs, and stepped aside.

Luke walked past her to see one narrow bed, a dresser, and wash basin. It couldn't have been more than an eight foot square with one window at the top for ventilation. He didn't say anything as he lay Mary down.

Ginny pulled another blanket from under the bed and bent down to drape it across her sister, feeling her forehead once more. She watched as Mary's eyes closed and she dropped off to sleep.

"Will you be all right in here?" He looked around, noticing a few clothes hung on hooks, a small satchel against one wall. A brush and mirror sat on the dresser next to a small pitcher.

Ginny stood and rested fisted hands on her hips as her face turned red. "Of course. This is our home."

Luke held up his hands in surrender and took a step backwards. "I didn't mean anything by it, Ginny." He kept his gaze on her until her anger began to fade and she let her hands drop to her sides. He needed to get out of there. Something about being this close to her, with no one else around, unsettled him more than he wanted. He had the wildest urge to reach out and pull her toward him. Yes, it was definitely time to leave.

"I'd better go." He walked around the stairwell to the back door.

"Luke?" He turned to look at her. "Thank you."

Ginny took a deep breath, closed the door, and turned to check on Mary. Tucked under two blankets and rolled up into a ball at the head of the bed, her sister appeared so tiny and fragile. At five years of age, she was considered small. Most thought her to be closer to three—until she started to talk.

Suzanne Briar had taken to Mary right away, encouraging her to talk and read the children's books that had belonged to the daughter she'd lost in a snowstorm years before. Ginny could see the comfort Suzanne got when she was around Mary, and she felt fortunate the three had become friends. Suzanne provided a room and meals in return for Ginny helping in the kitchen and cleaning rooms.

She'd told Amos that Suzanne needed her just three days a week. In truth, Ginny helped clean each morning and worked in the kitchen at dinner. Several days each week she helped Mary with school lessons until her shift at the Wild Rose started in the late afternoon. Some days all she wanted to do was drop down on the bed and sleep. When those days came, she'd pull out the wooden box from under the bed and count the twenty dollars she'd already saved since their arrival several months before. She knew it wouldn't seem like much to most people but, to her, it felt like a fortune.

Ginny sat on the edge of the bed and rubbed her eyes. It wouldn't be long before she'd have to grab the cleaning bucket and start upstairs. Just two rooms needed cleaning today—a light load. Then she'd start helping Suzanne in the kitchen. In between, she'd check on Mary and make sure she ate something.

Careful not to disturb her sister, she lowered herself back on the bed, rested an arm across her eyes, and thought of Luke. She didn't know him well. Besides tonight, the only other times she'd been around him was at his brother's wedding, the times he came into the Wild Rose, and once or twice at the boardinghouse restaurant. He'd been friendly, never crossing any boundaries, and told her if she needed help with anything to let him know. Suzanne said he and Dax were just that way— willing to help those who needed it. She didn't know why he'd taken such an interest in Mary's illness, but she wouldn't dismiss his kindness. Ginny just wished she didn't find him so attractive. In all her life, she'd never been attracted to a man. Not until Luke.

She'd never had a beau, had never even wanted one, and now was not the time to start. The responsibility of raising Mary sometimes seemed overwhelming. Over the months in Splendor, she'd come to the realization there'd be no man in her life, which suited her just fine. At five, it would be a long time until Mary was old enough to start her own life. By then, Ginny would be well past the marrying age. She'd be a spinster, but Mary would be all right.

From what she'd heard about Luke, he worked hard and played harder. More than once, the girls upstairs at the Wild Rose had commented about what a shame it was that he never took them up on their many offers. Instead, every few weeks, he traveled to Big Pine for a few days. Ginny hadn't thought much of it until Belle, one of her friends at the saloon, explained the reason for his trips. Or at least what the girls chose to believe. Why he traveled to Big Pine still held no real interest to Ginny.

On her sixteenth birthday, her mother had informed her that men had needs. Before marriage, they satisfied it with willing women. Afterwards, the wife took on the responsibility. Her mother spoke as if it were just another chore, rather than something a woman would enjoy. Ginny had never put much stock in marriage after that. Being a spinster didn't bother her a whit.

Luke still fascinated her, though. She'd heard he sometimes worked for the Pinkerton Agency and had spied for the South during the war. Both sounded dangerous, as well as exciting. Ginny would like to get to know him better just to hear his stories. She figured there must be some wonderful tales tucked away in his head.

"I don't understand it. More flour and sugar are missing, as well as another chicken." Hank tossed his hat on a nearby chair and took a seat next to Rachel in the kitchen. "The shed is locked and no one's heard any commotion from the horses or chicken coop. How is someone able to slip in without us knowing?"

"You're certain we haven't used more than you counted?" Rachel sipped her coffee and grimaced. No matter how much sugar or milk she added, the bitter taste still assaulted her.

"I am. I've been keeping track ever since supplies started to go missing a couple weeks ago. Besides the foodstuff, they've taken three chickens, plus I don't know how many eggs."

They both looked up as the back door pushed open and Luke entered. "Coffee?" He looked at the stove and, seeing the pot, grabbed a cup.

"Nice to see you decided to come back," Hank said, still cranky over the missing supplies.

Luke narrowed his eyes, taking a seat next to the older man and not responding.

"How's Mary doing?" Rachel asked and saw Luke's confused expression. "Bull told us about her and Ginny. He figured you were staying at Uncle Charles', so he put Prince up at Noah's livery."

"I figured it must have been Bull. Noah found me walking around this morning and flagged me over." He tasted the coffee, then set his cup down. "Mary's better. The fever's broken and her color's improved. At least it was when I carried her to their place at Suzanne's." Luke settled back and let his long legs stretch out in front of him. "They live in a small room at the boardinghouse."

"Yes, I know. She's come to the clinic a couple times when either she or Mary haven't felt well. I worry about them sometimes." Rachel rinsed her cup and set it next to the sink.

"Why?"

"She's real stubborn. It's hard for her to accept help. And God forbid anyone should offer money or take care of a debt for her."

Luke grimaced. *Well, what Ginny doesn't know won't hurt her...or me*, he thought as he stood to leave. "Guess I'd better find the others and get busy."

"There's a few with each herd. Some of them are breaking horses behind the barn," Hank said. "I believe I'll check everything once more. Make sure I didn't make a mistake." He stepped outside and started for the shed.

"What's he talking about?" Luke asked.

"Flour, sugar, and another chicken are missing. It's got him confounded. You know how meticulous he is about keeping track of all the supplies and amounts needed for a ranch our size."

"He have any ideas?"

"He didn't say. I'm wondering if the Blackfoot, or possibly Sioux, are sneaking in at night. It might explain why they were on our land when you got injured."

"We're a little too far west for the Sioux, and I'd be surprised if the Blackfoot would steal when they know we'll trade with them. Besides, most Indians tend to steal cattle, not supplies." Luke shook his head. "All the same, I can't think of anyone who might be stealing. I'd best be going."

Rachel heard the door slam shut. Dax had ridden out to the herd earlier, leaving her a Saturday to do whatever she wanted. She never had much chance to socialize with other women. Maybe she'd ride into Splendor and check on Mary, then visit with Ginny and Suzanne. It wasn't any of her business, of course, but Rachel had a strong urge to talk with Ginny and learn more about the young woman and her thoughts about Luke.

Chapter Three

"I thought I'd find you up here." Gabe Evans, Splendor's sheriff, slid off his horse and walked toward the unfinished cabin his friend, Noah Brandt, had been working on for weeks.

Noah looked up from preparing the window frame. "Lots to do before the weather sets in. I expect about three weeks of fair weather before the first snow."

The warm winds of summer had already given way to chilly nights and brisk breezes. As he took off his coat and threw it across a tree stump, Gabe guessed three weeks might be optimistic.

"What do you want me to do?"

Noah shot a look at his closest friend, a man he'd known since childhood. Gabe had been a colonel in the Union Army during the war, while Noah had risen to the rank of major. They'd planned to open a business together in their hometown of New York after the war, yet neither felt quite ready when Lincoln announced Lee's surrender at Appomattox. They'd wandered out west, Noah settling in Splendor a year before Gabe made his way back to the small town and, out of exasperation and guilt, accepted the sheriff's position.

"Help me frame out the last two windows, then we'll finish chinking."

They worked alongside each other for hours, stopping for an occasional drink of water or to swallow down some hardtack and jerky. Noah sometimes brought more substantial food. Today, and for as long as the weather held, he planned to work hard, taking little time to eat. As the day wore on, the men stepped back from the house and looked it over, gauging the workmanship and what needed to be fixed.

"You've done a fine job." Gabe clasped Noah on the shoulder. "She'll love it."

Noah shot him a look. "Who?"

"Miss Abigail. That *is* who you're building this for, isn't it?"

Noah snorted at the thought. Someone as fine and beautiful as Abigail Tolbert wouldn't think of setting foot in a cabin such as his. The young woman who'd so completely captured his heart would never be his. Her father, owner of the biggest ranch in this part of Montana, would never allow her to marry a mere blacksmith. No. She'd marry some fancy gentleman from Big Pine. At close to twenty thousand residents, she'd have quite a few to choose from, and all more financially successful than him.

"This cabin is for me. No woman will ever cross the threshold." He stalked toward the bucket of water and took one more drink. "You ready to ride back?"

"Let's clean up, grab supper at Suzanne's, then see what's happening at the Wild Rose."

"Sounds good." Noah mounted Tempest, the horse he'd owned since before the Civil War. He looked over his shoulder once more before following his friend toward Splendor.

The cabin had been built on several acres not too far from town. It stood on land the Pelletiers had given Noah in thanks for his part in freeing Rachel, Doc Worthington, and two neighboring ranchers from an outlaw gang determined to kill Dax and Luke. Without the quick and accurate work of the ex-Union sharpshooter, Rachel and the others may very well have become victims. Instead, Noah's expertise had been the deciding factor in their victory.

Dax and Luke had offered to help him build his cabin, providing him whatever he needed. He'd refused flat out, giving no explanation. In fact, until today, he'd waived off Gabe's help. He wouldn't have accepted if the weather wasn't about to change.

"Did I tell you some of my supplies have turned up missing?" Noah asked about halfway to town.

"You mentioned jerky missing."

"When I got to the cabin this morning, a blanket, a tin of hardtack, and a tin of jerky were gone."

Gabe thought this over. He'd had complaints of food missing from Frank and Hiram Frey, widowed brothers who lived a few miles from Noah's land. Dax had mentioned stolen chickens, eggs, and supplies. The three properties shared a common boundary and all rested against the base of Redemption Mountain. For years, Noah's land had been known as Sunrise Ridge, due to the magnificent sunrises visible from the site. The location gave him good southern exposure and protection from the strong northern winds.

"The Freys and Dax have mentioned missing supplies. At first I thought it might be a Blackfoot raiding party."

Both rode in silence the rest of the way...Gabe considering who could be behind the stolen items, and Noah absorbed in thoughts about Abigail Tolbert. In his mind, whomever she married would be getting a prize—a beautiful, delicate flower. He'd never have her, and that's the real reason he spent so much time building his cabin at Sunrise Ridge. Once she married, he knew he'd need a refuge, somewhere he could go to be alone. From then on, he'd let his dreams sustain him.

"I'm so glad you came to town." Ginny gave Rachel a quick hug. "With my work and caring for Mary, I don't have much time to visit." They sat in Suzanne's kitchen, drinking tea and munching on cookies. Ginny knew she should start getting ready for her shift at the Rose, but she wanted to squeeze in as much time with Rachel as she could.

"From what Uncle Charles said, Mary had a pretty high fever. She seems much better now."

"Oh, she is. I won't let her get out of bed for a few days, at least until she feels like eating regular food, but the difference from last night is incredible."

"Luke mentioned he helped you bring Mary home." Rachel averted her eyes, not wanting to appear too interested in the answer.

"He's been very kind. I could've handled Mary myself, but I couldn't refuse the help." Ginny finished the last bite of her cookie and wiped her hands on her apron.

"Luke is a good man, as is Dax. It's been fascinating to watch how they work together.

Sometimes it's as if they read each other's thoughts. If Luke does decide he ever wants to settle down and marry, the woman will be very lucky."

Ginny chuckled at the thought. "I can see Dax settled, but Luke? He seems the type of man who'll go through life without commitment, other than to you, Dax, and the ranch. I doubt he'll ever put down roots with a wife and children."

"Why do you say that?"

"I don't know. He's always on the move, looking for his next escapade. I'm sure he'd make a wonderful friend. Not so sure he'd want to be a husband and father, or be tied down." Ginny glanced at Rachel, hoping she didn't read too much into her words. "It doesn't matter to me. I've no intention of ever marrying and being tied to a man. I'll raise Mary. She'll be my family."

Rachel watched Ginny's face as she spoke. Although the words were clear, she doubted the young woman had a lot of conviction behind them.

"You're still so young. Who knows what will happen?"

"I know everyone believes I'm still a girl, but the truth is, I'm almost twenty-one. By the time Mary is old enough to move out, marriage will be out of the question for me." She pushed up from the table and grabbed the two cups. "Besides, I'm not like other women. I just don't think I'd make a good wife."

Rachel let the comment settle between them without response. In her mind, Ginny would make a wonderful wife and mother. She also knew each person had to make the choice for themselves.

"Well, it's time I left for home. I'll check on Mary once more, make sure she's still resting peacefully. Be sure to get in touch with Uncle Charles if anything changes."

"I will." Ginny gave Rachel one more hug. "Please be careful riding home, and thank you for coming in to check on Mary."

The sun still hovered above the mountaintops as Rachel left town. She rode past the school on the left and Noah's livery on the right. She saw no one inside, an unusual occurrence before Dax and Luke gave Noah the land. In her mind, the man spent too much time in the livery, working in the heat produced by his forge. It was good to see him taking time away to concentrate on something besides his work.

The road forked not far from the edge of town. Going right would take her toward King Tolbert's ranch, while going left would take her home. She'd heard little from the rancher since her marriage to Dax. At one point he'd indicated an interest in courting her. All other men, including Tolbert, faded into the distance the more time she spent with Dax. The attraction between them had been instantaneous, even though it took time for Dax to come to the conclusion he couldn't live without her. She believed the same pull existed between Luke and Ginny.

No matter how much the young woman denied it, Rachel believed she had a strong interest in him. The same held true for Luke. As the ranch house came within view, Rachel wondered how long the two would suppress their feelings. Both were as stubborn as any two people she'd ever met, so it might be a long while.

"You're not going into town with the boys tonight?" Dax asked as they finished supper.

"Not tonight." Luke finished his pie and pushed the plate away.

"I checked on Mary today." They'd discussed ranch business all during supper, leaving Rachel no time to speak of her visit to town.

"That so? And how's she doing?" Luke asked, not wanting anyone to detect his true level of interest. The main reason he had decided to stay home on a Saturday night was to avoid Ginny. He just didn't like the way his body responded to her.

"She's on the mend. I told Ginny to be sure and contact Uncle Charles or me if anything changes. She also mentioned how much she appreciated your help," Rachel added, noting something pass over Luke's face. Perhaps surprise that Ginny had spoken of him?

"I didn't do anything someone else wouldn't have offered."

"You may think that, but not everyone would have spent the night at the clinic with her, then carried Mary home." Rachel stood to help Bernice gather the empty plates, then stopped and looked at Luke. "Did you know Ginny is almost twenty-one? I would've sworn she couldn't be older than eighteen." She disappeared into the kitchen, leaving Luke, Dax, and Hank to themselves.

"The woman's not much younger than you." Dax's off-handed comment hit a nerve.

"Doesn't matter to me. It's not as if I'm courting her. Hell, I've no interest in courting anyone." Luke stood and stomped toward the front door, leaving Dax and Hank to watch his retreating back.

"I don't believe that boy knows his own mind," Hank said, sitting back and crossing his arms over his chest.

Dax's brows furrowed as he heard Luke slam the front door, then looked at Hank, one side of his mouth lifting in a wry grin. "I believe you're right."

Luke stopped on the porch, breathing in the cool night air, focusing on the almost full moon and brilliant stars. He didn't understand why he got so edgy when anyone mentioned Ginny. She was nothing like the type of woman he'd want, if he were looking. He liked tall women with full figures, not overly slim and petite. She couldn't be much over five feet, four inches and willow thin, as if a strong wind could carry her away.

He raked a hand through his hair before settling his hat on his head and resting his hands on the railing. What he needed was a weekend in Big Pine, playing cards, drinking, and doing whatever he pleased without the watchful eyes of the citizens of Splendor on him. The town had grown at a rapid rate since he and Dax arrived almost a year before. The gold mines around Big Pine had attracted thousands to what was now the territorial capital. Some of those who hadn't struck gold traveled on, many deciding to make Splendor their home. They opened stores, purchased land, and began to build new lives. All the same, it still seemed small and any amount of gossip traveled fast.

"Hey, Luke, you sure you don't want to ride into town with us?" Bull led his horse out of the barn, followed by Rude, Ellis, and several other ranch hands.

He straightened, pushed his hat back from his forehead, and shook his head. "Not tonight. You all have a good time and try not to lose too much of the pay we handed out."

"You know where we'll be if you change your mind." Bull saluted before turning his horse toward Splendor.

Luke watched them ride out, not feeling the regret he'd anticipated. Most times he'd be the one leading the pack, wanting to cut loose and enjoy some time away from the ranch. Although he didn't regret his decision to stay, there were times he needed space, separation from Dax and Rachel. He'd contemplated approaching Dax about building a place of his own with a view of Wildfire Creek. Something about the rolling waters against the base of

Redemption Mountain soothed him, helped him forget some of what he'd seen during the war.

Unlike Dax, he hadn't been on the battlefields for long. He'd been separated out, asked to join the Confederate Secret Service Bureau, a covert agency. The organization ran espionage and counter-intelligence operations in Washington and throughout the North. The work had been challenging, exciting, and somewhat dangerous. He never knew where they'd send him, or which group or organization he'd be required to infiltrate.

The one problem had been over-zealous agents, his counterparts who extracted information in ways he felt were cruel and inhumane. There weren't many, but enough to see some innocent people harmed and others, who were guilty, escape.

His short stint helping Dutch and the Pinkerton Agency was more his style. Little bureaucracy, freedom to pursue leads, and agents who didn't worry about jurisdictions. As non-government officials, their ability to make arrests fell outside normal boundaries. When they'd parted ways several weeks before, Luke let Dutch know if Pinkerton ever had another need in either the Montana or Idaho territories to contact him.

Luke heard the front door open and close, followed by approaching footsteps. He didn't turn. He didn't need to in order to know Dax stood a few feet away.

"You going to tell me what's bothering you?" Dax asked, leaning a hip against the porch railing.

He turned and mimicked Dax's stance, resting a hip on the rail. "I'm thinking of building a place next to Wildfire Creek."

Dax narrowed his eyes at his brother, wondering what had triggered his desire to create a different home. "You do whatever you need to. Just know that Rachel and I like having you here."

"It's got nothing to do with you and Rachel. I've been thinking about this for months, and the appeal of having my own place keeps gnawing at me. I figure it's time I did something about it."

"Snow will be coming in a few weeks." Dax looked up at the clear sky. Those who hadn't spent a winter in this part of the territory had no idea of the treacherous weather. He and Luke had seen the end of last year's weather. This would be their first full season on the ranch.

"I figure to have maybe three weeks if I start now. If not, I'll have to wait until spring." He looked at his brother. "That's too long, Dax."

Dax pushed from the railing and took a breath. "All right. We'll talk to the boys tomorrow, figure the supplies, and get what you need out to the site. I figure we can spare three or four men at a time." He paused a moment, thinking through what Luke would need. "You do have a spot picked out, right?"

Once more, Luke took off his hat, this time tossing it on the nearby swing, relieved and thankful Dax hadn't fought him on this. "I do."

Dax nodded, clasping Luke's shoulder. "Good. We'll talk more tomorrow."

Bull picked up his cards and glanced around the room, looking for one of the girls to fill his glass. He spotted Ginny as she walked in from the back and waved. The expression of friendly recognition on her face faded as she marched toward the table he shared with several others.

"Where is he?" Ginny's words were calm, although her hands were fisted on her hips and her eyes sparked.

Bull glanced at the others, then back at Ginny. "Where's who?"

"You know darn well who I mean. Luke. Where is he?" She looked around the room, hoping to spot him at another table.

"He didn't come in with us tonight."

"Coward." Her mumbled response could just be heard over the noise in the saloon.

"You got a problem with him, Ginny?" Bull asked. He'd never seen her so angry. She'd get irritated with some of the more insistent customers, but over the months, she'd learned to deal with the drunks and obnoxious ones.

"I sure do, and I'm certain he knows it or he would've come in tonight." She blew out a breath and turned toward the bar to grab a bottle of whiskey before walking back to the table. She poured drinks for those who held up their glasses, then set the bottle on the table. "You tell Luke I need to speak with him." She'd calmed a little, but not much. When no one responded, she added, "You understand?"

Bull kept his face impassive, although he was mighty tempted to grin. Compared to Luke and most of the men, she was a slip of a thing, yet she had no problem holding her own against any of them. He understood Luke's attraction to her, even if his boss wouldn't admit it.

"Yes, ma'am, I sure do."

She brushed a strand of hair from her face and stared down at Bull. "I'd better see him in here soon." Ginny stalked off, stopping at a couple of other tables and smiling as if nothing unusual had happened.

"Never seen her quite like that," Ellis said as he sipped his whiskey.

"Don't bode well for the boss," Rude added, still keeping his eyes on Ginny. "Wonder what he did."

"Guess we'll find out." Bull picked up his whiskey and tossed it back.

Chapter Four

"Isn't this close to the spot you took the arrow?" Dax asked, wondering at the location Luke had chosen for the house.

Several of the men gathered in the study with the brothers, discussing Luke's plans to build a cabin. It was Sunday morning, the sun had only been up for an hour, yet everyone seemed focused and alert.

"It is. I figure no matter where I build, if the Indians want to find me, they will."

His home would sit about a mile from the main ranch house. Distant enough for privacy, yet close enough to go back and forth with ease.

Dax looked over the materials Luke listed, some of which would need to be ordered, including a cook stove. "Are you planning to stay there this winter?"

"If I can. I'll travel to Big Pine next week to get some of the supplies. I figure it'll take less time." Luke glanced at the other men peering down at the rough sketch he'd drawn. "What do you think?"

"If we start today, there's a chance it'll be ready in a month. Three weeks is pushing it. It just depends on how much time we can take away from the herd." Out of all of them, Bull had the most experience in construction. His father had owned several businesses in Cincinnati, one of which built many of the buildings in the city and along the river bordering the large town. He'd grown up working alongside the men.

"How many men are needed to get it done within three weeks?" Dax asked.

"You give me five men, plus Luke and me, we'll have it ready in three weeks." Bull's eyes never left the drawing as his mind worked through what needed to be accomplished.

"Ellis and Rude, I need you with the herd. Bull, you tell me which five men you want and I'll speak with them." Dax picked up the supply list and handed it to Luke. "I guess you plan to head into town tomorrow to get what you need?"

"I do."

"Have Hank go with you. He's become friends with Jenks at the lumber mill."

Luke nodded. Any help with supplies was welcome. "Appears we'll be ready to start tomorrow then."

"Hell no. If you want it ready in three weeks, we start today." Bull started for the door. "I'll grab the other men. No use wasting any more time."

Other than the few men already with the herd, everyone else volunteered to ride the short distance to the site and help lay out the foundation. Stakes and rope were used to identify exterior walls, location of the porch, and a stable large enough for Prince and his tack. The house would be two stories, with just the bottom floor finished. Come spring, Luke would build a barn, dig a well, and finish as much as he could of the second floor. For now, his horse would be fine in the three-sided stable, and he'd haul water from the creek, storing it in large barrels.

The men worked until the sun shone bright overhead, taking a break when Rachel and Bernice arrived with food.

"We can't do much more on the house until we get the wood." Bull took a drink from his canteen. "There are a few hours left. If you men are still up for it, I think it'd be best to clear a path to the creek from the back of the house."

"Count me in," Tat Whalen said as he finished off his fried chicken. He and Johnny Grove had almost died during a stampede the previous spring. They'd become close friends during their recuperation at the ranch.

"Same here." Johnny stood and stretched his stiff muscles.

No one left, not even Rachel and Bernice. They were as curious as the men about Luke's plans. Truth was, even though it appeared to be work, helping someone erect a new home brought a satisfaction they didn't get herding cattle.

Although the front of the house would face the creek, the meandering water would come close to the back walls at one point, making it a short distance for hauling water until Luke dug a well. They finished clearing a wide path to the creek, a spot where the shoreline widened, creating a calm pool a few feet deep, perfect for hauling water or dropping in a fishing line. When done, everyone except Luke and Bull walked toward their horses.

"I almost forgot to tell you. Miss Ginny was looking for you last night." Bull straightened, holding the sickle he'd been using to cut the brush. "She was *not* a happy woman."

This got Luke's full attention. "Did she say anything else?"

"Not a word. I have to tell you, something set her off. None of us had ever seen her so angry." Bull wiped a sleeve across his brow. "Up to you, but it may be wise to give her a few days to calm down."

"Thanks. I appreciate the warning." Luke had no idea what would set Ginny off to the point she would approach Bull. She might be stubborn, but it was rare when she let her good nature and sense of humor be dampened by anger. He'd have to speak with her sometime— it might as well be tomorrow.

"Anything else?" Silas Jenks asked as they loaded the last of the wood Luke needed. They'd brought two wagons, both filled to the point that nothing else would fit.

"No, that's it. What do I owe you?"

Silas did some quick calculations and named a figure, watching as Luke pulled out the money and handed it to him.

"Pleasure doing business with you, Luke."

They shook hands before he climbed onto the wagon, waiting for Hank to get settled in the second wagon, then decided he'd make a slight change in plans. He jumped down and walked toward Hank.

"I need to talk with someone before heading back. Why don't you go on? I'll catch up when I'm finished."

Luke shoved his hands in his pockets, not looking forward to the conversation with Ginny, even though he had no idea what bothered her. He figured she'd be working at the boardinghouse at this hour, either cleaning rooms or helping Suzanne prepare dinner. From what he knew, she worked every day for Suzanne and took Sundays off at the Rose, but only because Amos closed the saloon on the Sabbath.

He walked the short distance across the main road to the boardinghouse entrance and pushed open the door, noting Gabe at one of the tables.

"Morning, Gabe. Have you seen Ginny?" He glanced around once more, not seeing either her or Suzanne.

"I believe she's in the kitchen." Gabe nodded toward the back as Suzanne approached with a pot of coffee and an extra cup. She set it down in front of Luke and filled it, then topped off Gabe's.

"Good morning, Luke. Did you come into town to see Ginny?" Suzanne asked.

Irritation bubbled inside him. "Why would you ask?"

Suzanne chuckled. "Might be because she's been fuming for a few days. Appears something you did set her off. I'll let her know you're here, but you'd better be prepared."

Luke watched her retreat, wishing he had an idea of what he could've done.

"Doesn't sound good." Gabe sipped his coffee as Suzanne disappeared into the kitchen.

Luke shook his head and picked up his own cup, bringing it to his lips as the kitchen door flew open. Ginny headed straight for him, not glancing at the one other couple in the restaurant.

"We need to talk." She glared at Luke, not acknowledging Gabe. She nodded toward the back and began to walk away.

"Guess I'd better go," Luke said to Gabe before setting his cup down and following Ginny.

She walked through the kitchen and toward the back where she and Mary lived, then stopped in the small space near the stairs.

"Where's Mary?"

"I let her go to school today." She hadn't turned to face him.

"Do you want to tell me what's got you so upset?" Luke asked, touching her shoulder, applying enough pressure so she'd look at him. He didn't like the fiery look in her eyes as she locked her gaze on his.

"Did you tell Doc Worthington you'd take care of Mary's medical bill?" She almost spit the words out.

"I—"

"And did you pay Amos for the days I took off?"

"I—"

"Don't deny it, Luke. I'm certain you did."

"Look, Ginny, I—"

"How could you do it? I'm not your responsibility and neither is Mary. She's mine."

This time Luke stayed quiet, deciding it would be best to let her get it all out before he tried to explain. He set his feet shoulder width apart and crossed his arms, looking down at her with narrowed eyes, waiting.

She blew out a breath and turned away, walking to the end of the hall, then rotating to look at him. "I don't need your help. I've done fine without anyone since our parents died and I won't start taking charity now—from anyone. The doctor refuses to take anything from me, and Amos won't discuss it at all." She paced to within a foot of him. "That leaves you, and I *will* pay you back every cent."

Luke held his silence a few more moments until he felt certain she'd finished, then dropped his arms to his sides. "I don't expect you to pay me back."

"If you don't want money, what do you want?"

He tilted his head at her, not comprehending what she asked. "I want nothing from you."

"I don't believe you. My experience with men may be lacking, but I do know they don't do something for you unless they want something in return. Well, all you'll get is money—nothing else."

His anger surfaced as her meaning became clear. He couldn't believe she'd think that of him and the more he focused on it, the hotter his temper flared. His expression turned to stone as his gaze bored into hers.

"You think I want to bed you in exchange for the money?" His deep, calm voice held an edge she'd never heard before, causing Ginny to take a step backward. He moved forward until her back hit the wall and he stood inches away, towering over her. "Is that what you think?" he asked again. He trapped her against the wall with a hand on either side of her head. She had nowhere to go.

Ginny swallowed the lump in her throat and shifted her eyes away.

He'd have none of it and captured her chin between his thumb and forefinger, turning her to face him. "Well?"

Tremors swept over her at his closeness and her heart beat so hard, she thought it might burst from her chest. She could feel heat washing over her cheeks. They stood in a small, confined area. Ginny felt certain the temperature had risen well above normal as dampness formed on her skin. She tried to squirm from his grip without success. She lifted her chin in defiance and locked eyes with him.

"Yes."

Luke cursed under his breath and released his grip, pacing a few feet away as he speared a hand through his hair. He shook his head, then spun toward her, his face impassive.

"First, I would never expect what you're thinking from *any* woman. If a woman is in my bed, it's because she wants to be, *not* because I forced her. Second, if a woman was what I wanted, I'd find one. You're not much older than a child."

The moment the words passed his lips, he could see the hurt they caused and he regretted being so blunt. However, he knew no other way to get Ginny to understand he wanted nothing from her. He may be attracted to her, want to bed her, but it would never go that far.

She pushed away from the wall, trying to regain what dignity she could, and clasped her trembling hands in front of her. She'd never fooled herself into believing she was attractive like other women. Her figure seemed more like a boy's than a girl's, and she dressed in whatever she had, never caring much about fancy hairstyles or rouge. Even so, the truth of his words stung. Of course he'd want someone beautiful and charming, someone who would turn men's heads. That wasn't her.

Ginny cleared her throat, her face emotionless as she met his stare. "All right. Then I will find some way to pay you back." She walked past him, not letting Luke object.

He watched her disappear into the kitchen, realizing that instead of the anger he experienced moments before, he felt hollow, as if she'd taken a part of him with her.

Chapter Five

A week passed, then another, bringing cooler days. There'd been no snow, although it had threatened a few times.

Luke, Bull, and the others worked from dawn to dusk. By the end of the second week, they'd completed as much of the first and second stories as possible without the last of the supplies. Luke and Bull planned a trip to Big Pine the following day for whatever they could get.

Tat and Johnny built shutters for each window opening until glass ones could be found. At least the shutters would help ward off some of the cold. Luke planned for three stoves. One for each of the rooms they'd been able to lay out—kitchen, front living area, and bedroom. He might decide to remove one later, but for now, he'd rather have too many than not enough.

While Luke and Bull were gone, the men planned to chop wood, finish the front porch, and install counters in the kitchen. The trip would take three days—one day to Big Pine, one to pick up supplies, and a third to return.

Every night after supper Luke fell into bed exhausted, yet feeling better about his decision as each day passed. He could almost envision his future, something he hadn't been able to do for months. He'd work the ranch each day, then retreat to his place, fish the creek when possible, and take on the occasional Pinkerton job. Dutch had already sent him a telegram about a potential assignment in Big Pine. Luke responded, saying to count him in as long as it happened after a few more weeks. By then, he felt he'd be tucked in at his cabin and ready for another job.

"Are you leaving at first light?" Rachel asked when she poked her head into the study after supper. She took a seat next to Dax, who slid an arm over her shoulders as he nursed a whiskey.

"We are," Luke said. "Neither of us want to get stuck in Big Pine if a storm comes through. I don't plan to spend more than three days away. I'm ready to finish the last of it and get back to pulling my weight here."

"The work is getting done. Don't worry about it for a couple more weeks. We should be good until then." Dax had noticed the change in Luke over the past few weeks. He seemed more at peace, as if a load had been lifted from his shoulders. At first Dax hadn't been comfortable with him moving out, especially with the thefts. Now he believed it would be a good move for him.

"Is there a chance you might have room in the wagon for medical supplies?"

"We'll make room. What do you need?" Luke asked.

"There isn't much. I'll get my list."

"Have you heard anything from Pinkerton?" Dax waited until Rachel left before asking. He knew she didn't care for Luke taking off for weeks at a time, more out of worry than the effect his absence had on the ranch.

"Dutch sent a telegram. There's a chance a citizens committee in Big Pine may hire the agency to check into the theft of gold during transport. I thought I'd talk with Sheriff Sterling while I'm there, find out what he knows."

"I doubt he's too supportive of vigilante groups. Most lawmen believe they're as bad as the people they chase." Everyone had heard of the group further north in Montana who, a year before, had lynched several men without trial. They hadn't even taken time to hear the men's side of the story. As ex-Texas Rangers, neither he nor Luke approved of this type of frontier justice.

"Dutch believes bringing in the Pinkerton agents helps cut down those types of reactions. Usually the town steps back, for a while anyway, and lets us do our job. At least with the agency, the people we arrest get a trial."

They looked up as Rachel walked back in and handed a slip of paper to Luke. "Here you are. I hope it's not too much."

He scanned the few items. "We should be able to find room." He stood, folded the paper, and shoved it in his pocket. "Guess I'd better get some sleep. See you in the morning." The stairs to his room seemed steeper tonight, as if he had to lift his legs higher to hit each step. Perhaps a few days away from building would be good for both he and Bull.

"You ready?" Luke asked Bull as he climbed onto the wagon. Bull would ride ahead, keeping watch for intruders and trouble along the trail.

"Ready, boss."

The sun had yet to rise, although most of the men were up and preparing for their day. Dax and Rachel stood on the porch and watched the two men disappear, hoping their journey would be safe and they'd return without incident.

The last year had seen an increase in Indian raids along the trail between Big Pine and Splendor. The worst occurred when a group of Sioux renegades killed a couple who fell behind in a wagon train. The Indians disappeared with the wagon before most of the settlers realized what had happened.

They cut across a trail north of Splendor, then dropped into the flatlands before connecting with what had become the main road to Big Pine. Bull kept up his pattern of riding ahead, then cutting back to check on Luke. Halfway to their destination, he pulled up alongside the wagon and motioned for Luke to stop.

"A group of settlers are stopped a mile up the trail. The wagon master hopes to reach the outskirts of Splendor tonight." Bull wiped a sleeve across his forehead. "They saw what he believes was a Sioux scouting party a couple of hours outside of Big Pine."

"They didn't approach the wagons?"

Bull shook his head. "Just sat up on a ridge, watching."

Luke reached for his canteen, took a long swallow, and handed it to Bull. "We'll stop and talk with them. I want to know more about what they saw."

He pulled to a stop alongside the lead wagon and jumped down, watching a man he thought to be the wagon master walk toward him. He nodded at Bull, then looked at Luke and exchanged introductions.

"Your man tells me you're heading to Big Pine."

"We are. He says you spotted a band of Sioux not far from here. I'd like to know more about what you saw."

"Not much to tell. Looked to be about a dozen of them on horseback, sitting on a northeast ridge about five miles back. They didn't try to hide and made no move to approach us. My scout is Sioux. He started to ride out and talk with them, but they disappeared back over the hill."

"Have you heard of any recent attacks between Big Pine and Splendor?"

"That where you're from?"

Luke nodded, then broke eye contact long enough to scan the horizon.

"I spoke with Sheriff Sterling when we first arrived in Big Pine. He knew of a couple instances of settlers making camp and having a horse or other supplies disappear. A few weeks ago the bodies of three cowhands were found a few miles from town. Appeared to be the work of Indians." He pulled off his hat and scratched his head. "All I can figure is we've got a decent-sized group of people in the wagon train. Maybe they decided it was too great a risk. If they'd been looking to trade, I don't know why they'd ride off the way they did."

"We'd better all get moving. Don't want to be stuck out here after dark." Luke shook the man's hand. "Maybe we'll see you in Splendor."

"Maybe so. Good luck to you."

Luke and Bull kept going, spotting a small group of riders who appeared to be Sioux. As with the wagon train, they didn't approach. The two had no idea what it meant.

By nightfall, they'd entered Big Pine, found hotel rooms, and had spoken with Sheriff Sterling. He told them nothing more than what the wagon master mentioned. There was one bit of information he did share which caught Luke's interest. Three gold transport wagons had been attacked over the last two months.

"Good evening, gentlemen. What can I get you?"

"Hello, Miss Ginny. Whiskey for all of us," Ellis said, leaning back in his chair.

She walked to the bar and watched as Al poured their drinks, then carried them to the table, setting a glass before each man.

"It's a little quiet in here tonight." Ellis dealt the cards while glancing about. Saturday was usually the busiest day all week, yet the tables were half-full and the bar almost empty.

"I heard King Tolbert is having a shindig at his place. Most of the town was invited." She looked toward the doors as Gabe and Noah walked inside. She guessed not everyone decided to attend.

"Good evening, Ginny. How are you doing?" Gabe asked, acknowledging the men around the table as he and Noah took seats nearby.

"Good, Sheriff. Can I get you each a drink?"

"That'd be great. Thanks." Gabe watched her walk toward the bar, noticing the gaze of most of the men following her. They all knew her agreement with Amos and most respected it. When someone didn't, one of the men set him straight real quick.

"You want to join us?" Ellis asked Noah and Gabe as he prepared to deal another hand.

"Not me. Maybe later." Noah paid Ginny for the drinks and took a slow sip. "Luke and Bull not with you tonight?"

Ginny's ears perked up at the mention of Luke. She took her time wiping down a table close by, trying to listen without being obvious. She hadn't seen him since their talk at the boardinghouse weeks earlier. The disappointment at not seeing him for so long surprised her. He'd been gone weeks at a time in the past and she'd barely noticed, but his disappearance this time left an unpleasant and unwelcome emptiness Ginny hadn't expected.

"They went to Big Pine for supplies. We expect them back tonight or tomorrow." Ellis threw down his cards and settled back in his chair.

"The house is coming along then?" Gabe asked.

"Almost finished. Guess he'll be talking to you soon about more hardware and locks, Noah."

Until tonight, Ginny hadn't heard a word about Luke building a house. She didn't know why the information surprised her, except she'd assumed he'd live with Dax and Rachel until he met someone, which she believed would be a long time coming.

"Your cabin almost finished?" Rude asked Noah.

"It will be by tomorrow. I would've stayed up there tonight, except I left some tools in town. Hey, Ginny, can you get me one more?"

"Sure, Noah." She wanted to hear what else they said, but she still had to work. Since telling Luke she'd pay him back, she'd saved an extra fifteen cents. It would be slow going, but she'd not stay indebted to him.

Everyone looked up as the front doors swung open and Bull walked in, followed by Luke. Both men looked exhausted and thirsty.

"A couple of drinks, Ginny." Bull grabbed a seat next to Ellis.

"Sure, Bull," she replied, but her eyes never left Luke as she walked toward the bar. The flutter in her stomach, which started the moment he walked in, irritated her. Ginny didn't want to have *any* feelings for him, especially attraction. She liked him, his smile, the way he laughed, and even the way he made fun of himself. Everyone enjoyed his company. Her mother would have said he was the type of person who attracted others. Magnetism was the word her mother used to describe an actor she'd once seen on stage. Ginny believed Luke had the same trait.

He spotted Ginny the minute he stepped into the saloon. She didn't offer her usual smile. Instead, he saw a cautious look in her eyes, which she normally reserved for saloon customers who made her uneasy. A tinge of regret passed through him although, looking back, he wasn't certain he would've done anything different. It hadn't occurred to him she'd take his actions of paying the doctor and Amos so wrong.

"How'd it go in Big Pine?" Ellis asked, dealing Bull and Luke into the game. Luke held up his hand to decline, then pushed his hat back on his forehead.

He didn't feel the normal desire to talk with the men or focus on a game of cards. One drink and he'd be back on the road toward the ranch. Tomorrow they'd unload the supplies and continue working. He stood and nodded at Noah and Gabe as he took a seat at their table. He wanted to let Splendor's sheriff know what he'd learned in Big Pine about the gold thefts, plus what he considered to be strange behavior by the small band of Indians who'd tracked them much of the way home.

"Here you are." Ginny set a glass of whiskey in front of Luke, then turned to walk away.

"Good evening, Ginny," Luke said, trying to catch her gaze while offering a sincere smile.

"Hello, Luke." She didn't meet his eyes, deciding instead to check on a group of gamblers at a nearby table. Two of them were familiar, both cowhands at Tolbert's ranch.

"You're not at your boss' party tonight?" she asked and picked up their empty glasses.

"It's pretty tame. Besides, after a week working, it's time to get away. How about another one?" The cowhand nodded at the glass on Ginny's tray.

Luke followed her retreat toward the bar. She'd always been friendly toward him, standing by his chair on occasion, watching him play his cards, and laughing at his jokes. On some nights, after the bar quieted, she'd even taken a seat at his table. She said little about her and Mary, although he knew their parents died on the way west. He also knew the responsibility of raising her young sister weighed heavy and how serious she took her obligation.

"Saw your brother and his wife at Tolbert's tonight, Luke," the cowhand called toward Luke's table. "The boss asked about you."

"They mentioned his party earlier in the week. Bull and I were in Big Pine."

"You didn't miss anything," the man laughed and resumed his card game.

"You two didn't go?" Luke asked Gabe and Noah.

"We spent the day finishing Noah's cabin. It's looking good." Gabe sipped his whiskey, glad his friend had let him help again. "You ought to come by and see it."

"I need to finish up at my place, then I'll ride over. The offer of help still stands, Noah."

"I appreciate it, Luke, but you and Dax have done enough."

"Not nearly when you think we could've lost Rachel and the doc." The encounter with outlaws at the Frey ranch a few months back had been too close.

Noah let the compliment pass. "The place is about done. I'll haul up a few more tools tomorrow. By Friday, I'll be staying at the place when I can."

Luke's eyes kept drifting toward Ginny as she moved from table to table, talking and laughing. He'd give it time. Maybe there'd be a way to regain the friendship they'd started.

"You hear any news in Big Pine?"

Gabe's question pierced his mental ramblings and he leaned forward, not wanting everyone in the saloon to hear what he'd learned. A couple minutes later, he sat back, having provided Gabe all the information he knew about the gold thefts.

"I'd gotten a telegram from Sheriff Sterling. He's heard of the mines near Splendor and suggested caution. I rode out to tell the miners, but so far I haven't heard about any thefts. The wagon master stopped by a couple days ago. He told me about meeting you and what he knew.

The train camped not far from town until this morning. A couple families ended up staying.”

Luke wondered if the families intended to ranch, farm, or open a store, but let the thought pass. There were more urgent issues to discuss. “What do you make of the band of Sioux? I don’t have enough experience to guess what’s going on.” Luke knew neither Gabe nor Noah had been in the territory long, yet they’d both been in the territory while he and Dax had been Rangers in Texas.

“From what you said about the band who attacked you, and their actions lately, my guess is they’re looking for something or someone. It’s as if they’re searching—except for the missing supplies and livestock. Even Noah’s had some jerky and hardtack taken from his cabin.”

“That so?” Luke looked at Noah. “Hank’s been complaining about missing supplies for weeks now, but we can’t catch them.”

“Small stuff. Like Gabe said, hardtack and jerky. One oddity is the sickle I use for clearing brush. Last week I found it leaning against a different wall from where I keep it, and it still had brush wrapped around it.”

“Appears someone borrowed it. At least you got it back.” The news left Luke more perplexed than ever. He pushed his hat down and stood. "I'm taking off. I'll be by to see you, Noah."

He took a couple of steps toward the door before taking one last look at Ginny. She leaned against the end of the bar near the back door, trying not to make it obvious she watched him. He tipped his hat at her before walking out, letting the doors swing behind him.

Chapter Six

"That's the last of it, Luke." Bull wiped his hands down his trousers and stepped a few feet away to look at the home. It had turned out well and all the men were pleased, but no one more so than Luke.

He walked from one man to another, shaking hands and thanking them. Even though they were paid for all the work, it hadn't been what they'd signed up for when they hired on, yet he'd never heard any of them complain. Bull had picked the right men.

"I'm riding over to Noah's to check out his place. I'll see you all at the Wild Rose tonight. Drinks are on me."

All except Bull mounted their horses, ready to clean up for a night in town.

"Mind if I ride along, boss?" Bull asked.

"Let me put these tools away and we'll get going." Luke stored what he'd brought from the house, including food supplies, and closed up. Noah had provided locks for the doors and windows, the type he'd built for his cabin. Of course, if someone wanted to get in, all they had to do was break out the windows. At least nothing much of value was inside. He doubted anyone would haul away a stove, table, or chairs.

He walked around once more, noting the tall stack of wood the men had cut. It would be enough to last through the winter. A stable for Prince had been constructed on one side of the house. He'd asked Travis Dixon to handle it and the man had done a fine job building and installing a front gate, using a lock from Noah. Luke had thought it would be temporary and he'd just tear it down once he erected the barn next spring. Now he wasn't so sure.

Luke's only real concern centered on Prince, the horse he'd trained before the war and who'd served him well after the surrender. He was as much a partner to Luke as Dax.

"Let's go." Luke swung onto Prince, took one more look around, and headed toward a small trail opposite the one he used to ride back and forth to the ranch. It followed the creek much of the way to Noah's land.

They hadn't ridden long when Luke spotted something odd hanging on a branch near the creek. He stopped alongside it, reached down, and grabbed what appeared to be a scrap of cloth.

"What do you have?" Bull asked.

"Looks like an old piece of fabric." He turned it over. It couldn't have been more than an inch square, frayed all around, and dirty. They took a few minutes to circle the area, riding across the stream, then up and down several yards before meeting back where they'd started. They found nothing.

"You know, it could have been on the bush for years." Bull continued to look around. He had the sense they were being watched, but didn't see or hear anything.

"Guess so." Luke slid it into his pocket, paying more attention during the rest of their ride.

An hour later the roof of Noah's cabin came into view. They could hear someone pounding as they approached, finding him securing a water barrel on the side of the cabin.

"Need any help?" Luke asked as he and Bull slid from their horses.

"Got it done. Thanks." He set down his hammer and stood, stretching his arms above his head. "Come on. I'll show you the inside."

It didn't take long. Noah had built his cabin on a twenty-four by twenty-four foot foundation using two twelve foot squares with a large opening between the two. This made it close to twice the size of similar structures Luke had seen. A cooking and living area were in the front, his bedroom in the back.

"You've done a fine job." Unlike Luke's home, which was made of cut timbers, Noah had built his home out of logs. He scanned the notches Noah had made in each log to connect the corners. They were perfect.

"Someday I may add more rooms," he said, pointing to areas where he'd used vertical logs to board up openings for passageways if he ever expanded. He walked to a stove, grabbed cups, and poured coffee. "Come on."

They followed Noah outside and leaned against the front porch railings.

"Anything else turn up missing?" Luke asked.

Noah let out a low groan. "A bucket, my last blanket, and a tin of hardtack from Suzanne at the boardinghouse. There has to be someone living up in the mountain, maybe in one of the caves not far from here. Similar caves exist near your place on Wildfire Creek."

"The caves where the Mayes gang hid before they took Rachel and the others captive." Luke sipped his coffee, remembering those days several months before.

"That's my guess. You missing anything?" Noah asked.

"Not the last few days, but I've been staying there at night." Luke reached into his pocket and pulled out the piece of fabric. "We found this on the trail over here."

He handed the scrap to Noah. He turned it over a couple times, then gave it back to Luke. "No telling what it's from or how old it is," Noah commented.

"It's not much, but I may get some men together and start searching the caves before the snow starts, see if we can find the culprits and stop the aggravation."

"Another round, Ginny," Luke called over his shoulder, oblivious to the tempestuous glare she shot him.

The men who'd helped build the house, plus all the other ranch hands who weren't with the herd on Saturday night, crowded around three tables in the Rose. They'd been drinking, playing cards, and celebrating the completion of Luke's house for four hours with no sign of slowing down. She didn't blame them. From what she'd heard, it had been a huge undertaking for this late in the fall.

Noah and Gabe had joined them for a while before taking off to get supper at the boardinghouse. How Ginny wished she were there and not forced to watch as Luke pulled one saloon girl after another onto his lap. It seemed innocent enough, even though each of the women would have liked more. Although he never gave any of them an indication he wanted to follow them upstairs, the entire scene still irritated Ginny. What really irritated her was that she had no idea why she cared so much.

"Here you go." She almost slammed the drinks on the table, spilling more than a small amount out of Luke's glass.

"Hey, Ginny, watch what you're doing." Luke grinned as he looked up at her, a somewhat loopy expression on his face.

She almost smiled, then stopped herself. If he didn't slow down, he'd be spending the night in the back of a wagon or anywhere he could find a bed. She grimaced at the thought, knowing any of the ladies would be glad to take him upstairs, even in his drunken state.

"May I get you anything else, Mr. Pelletier?"

Luke didn't take his gaze off her. Her smile seemed forced and a little too sweet, which bothered him more than he liked. He knew she thought he was drunk, but in truth, he had a long way to go before he wouldn't be able to walk out of the Rose on his own two legs. During the war he'd spent many nights drinking with those who had information he needed. Not once had he not completed his assignment.

"No. I think we're fine for right now." Luke watched as she turned from him, and on impulse, reached out to grab her wrist. "Why don't you sit for a while? Amos won't mind if you take a short break."

The feel of his hand on her skin sent a strange tremor up her arm, which wasn't so different than when he'd been within inches of her in the confined boardinghouse hallway. His nearness had caused the same pulsing sensation through her body, as well as heat to creep up her neck and face. She looked down at him, wishing she could sit next to him and talk the same way they had before Mary's illness. Their friendship had been less strained and more relaxed then.

"I'd better not." Her voice sounded thick, even to her. She slid her wrist from his grasp and walked away.

Luke forced his gaze back to the cards he held, a part of him wishing they could've had time to talk, another part glad she didn't take his suggestion. Tonight was about him, the men, and the hard work they'd put in over several weeks. It had nothing to do with mending fences with someone who wanted nothing to do with him.

Ginny stood at the bar, continuing to scan the saloon, looking for those with empty glasses. Amos paid her not just to deliver drinks, but to encourage the men to order more until they needed to be strapped to their horse to get home. Tonight they might need to tie more than a few onto their saddles.

Tat and Johnny were already falling off their chairs, while Ellis and Rude were a drink away from passing out. Travis had nursed one drink throughout the night. He'd come into the Rose a handful of times since he'd arrived in Splendor. Like Luke, he never accepted any of the offers from the ladies and gambled on a rare occasion. He'd be able to get back to the ranch just fine.

Several others looked as if they would require help out the door. Bull had disappeared a while back, and she assumed he'd decided to cut the night short. When her gaze landed on Luke, she saw his eyes lock with hers. He didn't motion to her or indicate in any way he wanted her to join him. He simply stared, one corner of his mouth curved upward.

For the first time in her life, Ginny wished she knew more about men. She didn't like feeling at a disadvantage to anyone, especially Luke.

"Ginny? Would you mind picking up the empty glasses. I believe we're about ready to lose a bunch of drinkers." Al nodded toward the swinging doors as Bull sauntered in, a wide grin splitting his face. He nodded at Luke, then walked straight toward Ellis and pulled him to a standing position.

"Come on, Ellis. Outside with you."

Luke stood and did the same with Rude, then followed Bull outside.

A few minutes later, they walked in again and did the same with Tat and several men at the other tables, Travis taking their cue and hauling a couple out as well. Others, those able to stand and walk on their own, didn't protest, just followed everyone out. Bull walked in once more and headed for Johnny, the last of the men. As he leaned down to help him stand, Johnny reared his arm back and tried to land a punch to Bull's face. He might have succeeded if his actions hadn't been so slow and sloppy.

"Whoa, Johnny. I'll fight you some other time," Bull chuckled and wrapped both arms around his friend, who stood five inches shorter and weighed at least forty pounds less.

Ginny watched, fascinated with the way Luke, Bull, and Travis had cleared the saloon of over a dozen drunken cowboys without triggering a brawl. She walked to the door and peered out to see a wagon loaded with at least five men, several others hanging tight to their saddle horns and pulling another horse along. Luke had begun to climb onto the wagon when he looked up to see Ginny watching them.

"Hold on a minute, Bull."

He jumped down and took the steps two at a time to catch her before she disappeared inside. He crossed his arms over his chest and swept his eyes over her, noting the tired expression and lips that had been drawn into a thin line.

"I'd better finish cleaning up." She began to turn.

"Is this it, Ginny? Our friendship's over because I tried to help you?"

Her heart stopped and she felt her stomach tighten. At that moment, Ginny knew she needed to mend the rift between them. She turned back toward him and searched his face.

"I hope we're still friends." Her voice came out in a whisper before she worried her lower lip with her teeth.

He dropped his arms to his sides as his eyes warmed on her face.

"Good. I'm glad to hear it." He held her gaze a couple more seconds until she smiled at him, then he turned to head home. Luke didn't understand why a friendship with Ginny seemed so important to him, but it did. He thought of her on the ride home, glad he'd approached her and grateful for the response. Now his life could get back on track—new home, work he enjoyed, and a friendship he valued.

"What are you thinking, Rick?" Flatnose asked as they sat on the porch, deciding their next move. They'd stolen three gold wagons over several weeks, stashing the gold in a location no one would ever find. The fact the gang had killed a couple men on the last raid didn't bother him as much as it did Rick. His partner had warned him several times there would be no killing and to keep his bullets in his gun. He'd followed Rick's orders the first two attacks. On the third, movement from one man triggered a deadly response. Something about sending a man to his grave was more temptation than Flatnose could resist. It sent a thrill through his body, even if it did incur Rick's anger.

"Another wagon is supposed to move within the week. Lansdon to Big Pine. I want to take it, then lay low awhile." Rick lit a rolled cigarette and inhaled deeply.

"The same guy who told us about the last shipment?"

Rick nodded. "He mentioned it when I went to Lansdon this morning."

"How many men will we need?"

"The ones here will do." Rick flicked the end of his cigarette onto the dirt. "He expects this one to have two additional armed guards."

"Six?"

"That's what he says." It had been a good decision to plant his own man in the mining town of Lansdon. He didn't just hear about shipments from the local mines, but also news of other transports from camps miles away. As a precaution, he hadn't shared the man's identity with his partner.

Until this morning, Rick had been thinking of laying low, maybe leaving the area until spring. They'd stashed away enough gold to make them all rich. Each man could start over someplace far away from the Montana Territory where no one would connect them to the robberies or deaths of the two guards—killings that still weighed heavily on Rick.

He'd met a lady, a widow who lived near Big Pine. It was at least an hour's journey, but she was worth it. The information he'd been given today had him reconsidering. One more job, then he'd get a place near Big Pine so he wouldn't have to ride so far to see her.

It'd been years since his wife and son were gunned down by that posse in Nebraska. The sheriff had thought Rick belonged to an outlaw group who'd terrorized the local area, stealing and killing at will. At the time, he'd been trying to carve out a living like everyone else. He knew a couple of boys in the gang, but had refused to take part.

The ten man posse had ridden in, ignoring the commands of the sheriff to stop shooting. Rick shouted at his wife to stay put, but she'd run outside, trying to talk some sense into the sheriff's men. His eight-year-old son had followed her. When it was over, his family lay dead and he'd been arrested.

The trial would have been a farce, except the killing of a woman and child didn't sit well with the inhabitants of this God-fearing town. A group of them hired a lawyer to defend him. Rick had been acquitted and released with an apology. He'd thanked his neighbors, taking their condolences with the good intentions that were meant. Yet his future had changed. It now stretched before him like the desolate, parched earth of his miserable farm. That day he made his choice and, except for a brief stint as a lawman, he'd followed a path outside the law ever since. The one man keeping him from making a final decision to move to Big Pine was the sheriff—Parker Sterling. The man had a reputation for sniffing out those who broke the law, making them pay. Rick had no intention of being one of his casualties.

"You planning to go see that lady friend of yours?"

Rick shot a look at Flatnose. The man had an uncanny and unwelcome ability to read his thoughts. He almost didn't respond, then thought better of it. "Thinkin' about it."

"You want to take off for a while after this next job, go ahead. I can keep enough men here to run the herd this winter. No reason for you to stick around for months when your woman's in Big Pine. Most of the men have nowhere else to go anyway, and I've got Stella here with me."

"I'll consider it." Rick walked toward the barn. He'd been contemplating riding toward Big Pine, surprising Felicity, and taking her to church. She was a churchgoing woman, same as his wife had been, while not being quite like any churchgoing woman he'd ever known. When they'd first met, he'd introduced himself as Frederick, never mentioning the nickname he used with Flatnose and the other men.

Heading to Big Pine would give him a chance to learn anything new about local reaction to the three transports his gang already stole. He didn't want to run into another vigilante situation like the one in Bison City. Or worse, learn they'd hired the Pinkerton Agency to stop the thefts. He'd start out well before dawn, take Felicity to Big Pine for church, then stay in town a few hours before taking her home. He'd learn what he needed, spend time with her, then head back to the ranch to wait for his man's signal.

Chapter Seven

"I'm riding to town, Father. Is there anything you need?" Abigail Tolbert, King Tolbert's only child, poked her head into his study and continued inside at his nod.

"Is there anyone riding with you?" It had been a few months since he'd begun to loosen the grip he held on all her activities, and he still found it difficult to provide her with the amount of freedom she wanted. It wasn't in his nature to relinquish control.

She smiled at him, knowing he loved her, and also understanding she had to be the one to push the boundaries if she were ever to rule her own life. "Everyone's busy. Besides, I ride to town without escort all the time."

"Weather's changing." He offered no other argument.

"It will be—just not today." Her eyes crinkled at the corners, although her face remained impassive as she waited for her father to come up with another excuse. Patience was her friend in these negotiations. He would relent. Besides, there was someone in town she wanted to see, without the prying eyes of anyone from the ranch.

"You'll be back before supper." It wasn't a question.

"Of course." She stepped closer and looked at the paperwork on the desk. She wished he'd allow her to help with the bookkeeping. He'd refused so far. She longed to be useful at something other than planning meals and making sure the housekeeper did her job. Perhaps someday, if she married and had children, she'd feel different. For now, she needed more.

"I want you home before dark."

She walked around the desk, leaned down, and kissed his cheek. "I'll be back before you've had a chance to miss me." She left without a backward glance, eager to get started and wanting to leave before he came up with another excuse or request.

King watched his daughter close the door, already feeling a slight tinge of regret at her riding out alone. It had been a long time, but memories of his niece and her accident years before still haunted him. He'd been busy, eager to close another business transaction. She'd asked permission to ride alone to town and he'd agreed without thought for the time of day or weather. It never occurred to him he'd never see Francine again. He'd promised his sister if anything ever happened to her and her husband, he'd take care of their daughter. King had failed miserably and still berated himself for his lack of judgment.

He put his hands on the desk and pushed up from his chair, walking to the window as Abby rode out of the barn. She glanced his way, saw him standing there, and waved. Panic seized his chest and he had the strongest urge to ride after her. Instead, he walked to a nearby table, grabbed a glass, and poured a drink, tossing it down his throat in one quick movement.

King needed to focus on finding her a suitable match. He'd arranged the last shindig in order to invite several potential suitors to the ranch. Of course, neither Abby nor the young gentlemen had any idea the reason behind the party. Although several indicated an interest in his daughter, three asking him if they'd be allowed to call on her, she'd refused to see any of them. He suspected she wouldn't spurn the attention of one young man in particular who had not been invited, nor would he be if King had his way. Gil Murton might be a hard worker and an honest man, but his lack of wealth and social standing would never be worthy of Abigail Tolbert.

"Come on, Willie," Abby urged. "Can't you move any faster?" she whispered under her breath, trying to press the animal on.

The person she sought hadn't come to their party, even though she'd made an extra trip to town to deliver his invitation. She'd been disappointed to find his place closed up tight. Even the store he'd opened a few months before was being run by a young man she'd never met, and he wouldn't tell her anything other than his boss was away for a couple days.

She hoped to find him today. Even though it sat at the other end of the main street through town, Abby could hear the church bells chime twelve o'clock. Her destination was at this end and she could already see the smoke from the livery forge. She rounded the corner by the lumber mill, passed the tack and saddle shop, his other business, and reined Willie to a stop in front of the livery. She could see him inside, heating a piece of metal, then pounding it to the desired thickness. Abby sat there, mesmerized by his strong form. He'd taken off his shirt and the muscles of his back were damp with perspiration. She drew in a deep breath and dismounted, hoping he'd take time to talk with her.

She took a few steps inside, feeling the heat coming at her in waves as the breeze fanned it about. A bucket a few feet away caught her attention and she walked over to pick it up. It appeared more oversized than most she'd seen and Abby wondered if it would be used for a special purpose. She fingered the metal rings, knowing Noah had made them. Her own thoughts encompassed her to such a degree, she didn't notice the pounding had ceased or that Noah had walked up behind her.

"Something I can do for you, Miss Tolbert?"

She jumped, dropping the bucket, a hand flying to her heart as she turned around. "You startled me."

She began to bend down toward the bucket when a large hand moved in front of her and grasped the handle. Abby straightened and looked up into the face of the man she'd come to love. She didn't believe he felt the same, and she knew her father would never approve, but God help her, she couldn't stay away.

Noah watched her face turn from alarm to embarrassment to discomfort. He could stare at Abby's face all day, every day, and never tire of it. Wisps of fiery red hair framed her cream-colored skin, highlighting the splattering of freckles he found so attractive. She may seem frail and waiflike, but something in Noah told him she'd be no man's doormat.

Her discomfort grew as he stood in front of her, saying nothing more. "I, uh...came to town to see you, Mr. Brandt." She felt like an idiot. How long had she known him and she caught herself stumbling over her words?

"Noah," he said. They'd agreed to call each other by their first names months before. For some reason, though, both had a hard time doing it.

"Noah." Her voice sounded breathless, as if she were winded. Abby reminded herself of why she'd come to see him. "You didn't come to the party. Didn't you get the invitation I left with your man at the saddle shop?"

He set the bucket down and looked at her, his face impassive. "Yes, I got it. I had work to do."

He noticed the bright light in her eyes dim a little and regretted being so blunt. One of them had to face the truth. No matter how he felt and regardless of what he saw in her eyes each time he looked into them, King Tolbert would never allow Abby to marry a blacksmith.

"I heard your father invited several people from Big Pine." Men of means from what the Tolbert ranch hands had said.

She clasped her hands in front of her, trying to decide how best to word her response. Winning him over would be hard. He was also more stubborn than any five men she'd ever known. Of course, she'd known virtually no men, except those in town and her father. She'd gone to boarding school in Philadelphia, been surrounded by other girls her age, and had never once been courted. Since coming home, she'd had no desire to be courted, except by one man...the one standing before her.

"He did. A couple of ranchers, a banker, and a lawyer, all quite boring and, well...quite taken with themselves." She glanced up at him, a slight smile curving the corners of her mouth.

"Boring, huh?" Relief he shouldn't be feeling washed over Noah.

"The rancher from England had some interesting stories, but he had to be as old as Father."

She crinkled her nose and walked past Noah toward the forge. On one wall he hung his finished work, which always fascinated her. She looked over a few pieces before turning back to him. "Is the saddle shop doing well?"

He watched her move from one object to another. He wished she'd leave, give him some relief from the desire he felt whenever she came around. Didn't she understand he was not the right man for her, could never give her the life she deserved?

"I'm sorry. What did you say?" He'd been lost in his own thoughts, but her curious stare caught his attention.

"The saddle shop... Is it doing well?" She tilted her head to one side, wondering what had captured his interest.

"Yes, it is. The mining tools sell good, as does the tack. Some days it does better than the livery." His voiced reflected his pride in the store.

"Who is the young man working for you?"

Noah's eyes narrowed on hers and he wondered if perhaps Abby might be attracted to Toby. "Toby Archer. He came in with the same group of settlers as Ginny and her sister."

"Oh. I never saw him before I stopped by to invite you to our party."

"Would you like me to introduce you, Abby?" He hoped she'd say no, because even though Toby didn't come from wealth, he had a cleaner soul than Noah. "He isn't married."

Her eyes shot to his as color began to creep up her neck. "What makes you think I care one way or another about him being married? I have no interest in him or anyone else, except..." She clamped her mouth shut.

"Except?" Noah prodded.

"Hello, Abby, Noah."

They both turned at the sound of Rachel's voice. Abby was glad for the interruption, but Noah wished he'd been able to hear her response.

"Hello, Rachel. I'm so glad you were able to attend the party." Abby had made several friends since coming back home, and even though Rachel was several years older and married, she considered her one of the closest.

"I had a wonderful time, as did Dax." She looked at Noah. "We missed you there."

He cleared his throat, feeling as if he'd been cornered. "Gabe and I were working on finishing my cabin. It took longer than I thought." Truth was, he'd never intended to go to the party and neither had Gabe, each for separate reasons. Noah wanted to distance himself from Abby, especially once he'd learned the purpose of the party had been to introduce her to prospective suitors. Gabe just didn't like King Tolbert, even if most considered him to be the most powerful rancher in the area.

"You're building a cabin?" Abby's head snapped toward Noah.

"On the land I got from Dax and Luke."

"For saving our lives," Rachel added. She'd always be grateful for Noah's quick actions that day.

Abby's gaze stayed fixed on Noah, whose eyes were trained on the ground. He never mentioned what he'd done at the Frey ranch and didn't comment when others brought it up. It seemed as if he wanted to forget it and move on, the same as his service during the war. He never discussed what he'd done as a sharpshooter in the Union Army, but Abby believed the experience weighed on him.

"Would you have time to join me for dinner?" Rachel asked Abby.

"I'd love to." She glanced up at Noah. "It was good to see you, Mr. Brandt. Perhaps someday you'll show me your cabin."

He stifled a groan. "Perhaps."

Noah watched as the women locked arms and walked across the street toward the boardinghouse. If Abby ever made it out to see his cabin, he believed it would be over her father's dead body—or his.

"Good afternoon, ladies," Suzanne greeted as Rachel and Abby walked in, giving each a warm hug. "How was the party, Abby?"

"Very nice. I wish you could've come."

"You know how it is with the restaurant. Ginny works at the Rose on Saturdays, so it was just me."

"Next time we'll plan it so you can come." Abby had known Suzanne for years. As a little girl, she'd follow her around the boardinghouse kitchen. Then her father made the decision to send her to boarding school in Philadelphia. Suzanne had become a surrogate mother after Abby's had passed away years before.

"Two specials?" Suzanne asked.

"That would be perfect," Rachel replied as she slipped off her coat. Although the sky remained clear, the temperature had dipped over the last week. "How is Noah doing?"

Abby glanced out the window and across the street at the livery. "You know more about him than I do," she sighed. "He's always polite and friendly, but..." She let the words fade when she caught a glimpse of him moving toward the forge.

"You would like him to notice you?"

The question brought Abby's gaze back to her friend as heat crept up her face. "Well, yes," she answered, embarrassed to say it out loud. She clasped her hands in her lap and lowered her eyes.

"Noah is one of the finest men I've had the privilege to know. I can see why you'd find him attractive."

"You can?" Abby's eyes had grown wide at Rachel's comment.

"Of course. He's smart, attractive, and works hard. Maybe too hard with having the livery, his store, and building a cabin a few miles from town. He doesn't boast about himself like some men are prone to do, and from what Dax and Luke say, he'd rather walk away from a fight than be drawn into one. Someday I'm sure a clever young woman will snatch him up."

"Do you think—" She clamped her mouth shut when she spotted Ginny walking toward their table.

"Hello, Ginny," Rachel said.

"Hello, Mrs. Pelletier, Miss Tolbert." She set plates heaped with food before the women and stepped back.

"I wish you'd call me, Rachel," she requested.

"And please, call me Abby," Abigail added.

"All right." She began to turn toward the kitchen, then stopped. "How is Luke doing with his house?"

Rachel had wondered if Ginny would ask about him. "He stays there most nights. You ought to go out and see it sometime."

"Oh, I could never take time from work. Besides, I don't have a horse or wagon." She fidgeted as if the conversation were moving in an uncomfortable direction.

"I'd be glad to take you," Rachel offered.

"We could all go out. I'd like to see it as well," Abby said.

"You don't work on Sundays, Ginny. I'll ask Luke if it would be all right if we ride out after church."

"Oh, no. I'm certain he wouldn't want to be bothered," Ginny protested, wishing she'd never asked about him.

"Nonsense. I'm sure he'd be pleased we're all so interested to see it."

"No. Absolutely not." Luke glared down at Rachel as she finished preparing supper.

His adamancy amused her and had her wondering why he had such a strong reaction to her request. "Why ever not?"

He paced a few feet away, then turned toward her. "I built it to get away, not because I want visitors. You, Dax, Bernice, and Hank...fine. Bull and a couple others would be all right. Noah and Gabe are always welcome. But no other women."

"Ginny and Abby just want to see what you've done. I told them how hard you and the men worked to get finished before the first snow. It would be wonderful to bring them by after church this Sunday."

"Perhaps I haven't been clear. *No.* They are not invited to the house. You and Dax are welcome after church, but that's it."

She opened her mouth to protest once more before a look from Luke silenced her. Rachel knew the time had come to accept his decision and inform her friends. She winced as he slammed the door and headed toward the barn. *That had not gone too well*, she thought.

"Was that Luke I heard?" Dax walked in through the back door, walking into the front room. Rachel followed a few feet behind.

"I made the mistake of inviting Ginny and Abby to visit his house, thinking Luke wouldn't mind."

Dax looked out the front windows in time to see his brother mount Prince and ride away at a brisk pace. He then turned his gaze to Rachel, casting her an amused grin.

"What do you find so humorous?"

"He built the house to get away and find solitude, not to entertain. Did he set you straight?"

"Oh, he certainly did." She strolled across the room, then looked back at Dax. "It makes no sense to me. Who would spend all that time building a home and not want people to visit?"

He watched her retreat toward the kitchen and shook his head. However, he did make a wager with himself. He'd bet any amount of money the first woman to set foot inside his home, besides Rachel, would be Ginny Sorensen.

Chapter Eight

Luke finished grooming Prince and closed the gate to the stable. He'd been staying at his place for over a week, finding he preferred the quiet solitude after a long day working cattle and being surrounded by the other men. Most days he'd stay at the ranch long enough to visit with Rachel and Dax before riding out, but Rachel's surprise announcement had him eager to get away.

He walked up the steps to the front door and turned to survey the area. The sun had set over the mountains. If not for the few kerosene lanterns he'd placed around, everything would be covered in darkness. He'd loaded each of the stoves with wood before he left that morning and had already started the one in the kitchen, which was where he headed to check on the extra stew Rachel had put aside for him the day before.

As he stirred the contents of the black pot, Luke felt a tinge of regret about his response to Rachel. Her intention had been good—show off his new place to her friends. He wondered if it would've bothered him if she'd wanted to show it to her Uncle Charles or someone other than Ginny.

"Ginny..." The whispered name slipped from his lips without thought. Ever since the night he and Bull had hauled the others from the saloon, the same night he'd realized her friendship had become important to him, her image often appeared.

Luke realized the magnitude of his feelings when the last image he would see as he fell asleep was Ginny. She was the first person he thought of each morning for the past week— longer if he were being honest. The reason he'd stayed away from the Wild Rose, and Ginny, had everything to do with the understanding of how much he wanted her, but not as a wife. He honestly believed he would never marry, and that was the danger. He had too many travels in his future to settle down with one woman.

He grabbed a bowl, ladled up a healthy portion of stew, and took a seat. The aroma floated through the air as he dug in, taking one bite after another until the bowl was empty. He'd just pushed away from the table when Prince let out an ear-piercing whinny.

Luke drew his gun and dashed to the front door, pushing it open an inch, then further, until he had a better view of the outside. He'd left two lanterns burning on the porch, and the moon shown through the clouds, adding enough light to cast the area in a solid glow. He saw nothing.

He could hear Prince prancing in the stable before letting out another whinny, this one less forceful. Luke crouched low and made his way to the end of porch, then swung over the railing to land in front of the stable.

"What is it, Prince?" Luke opened the gate and stroked his horse. Prince shook his head, then began to calm as Luke continued to talk in a low, calm voice. "Is there someone out here?" He'd just gotten the words out when he heard the sounds of breaking twigs, as if someone rushed through the bushes.

He took off running in the direction of the noise, stopping several times to listen. Again, he heard the rustling of shrubs near the creek and started in that direction, hearing water splashing as he ran. Luke stopped at the water's edge, looking up and then down the creek, but saw nothing. He thought of going across the stream, rejecting the idea when he realized it would be impossible to find anybody in the dense forest.

Luke holstered his gun and began the short trek back to the house, glad he'd left so many lanterns burning. In the morning he'd make a full sweep of the area. Perhaps he'd find boot tracks or another piece of cloth, anything to help him figure out who was hiding in the mountains, and possibly behind the missing supplies.

"Perhaps he'll change his mind." Abby and Ginny stood at the back of the church, listening to Rachel's news. They wouldn't be going to Luke's.

"Maybe. With him, it's hard to say. It may be smart to let him enjoy his time alone for now and hope we receive an invitation in the future." Rachel could see the disappointment in Ginny's face. She wondered if her feelings for Luke were as obvious to others as they were to Rachel. "Have you seen him in town lately?"

"Not since the men finished his place and they all came to the Rose to celebrate. I'm certain you see him quite often. It makes no difference to me if he comes to town or not. He's just another customer at the saloon." Ginny's voice became more resolute with each word, doing her best to convince herself she truly didn't care one way or another about him.

Abby shot a curious look at Rachel. She hadn't thought about Ginny having feelings for Luke and wondered if he returned her interest.

"Of course, you're right. You must serve them at the boardinghouse, then at the saloon in the evening. All the men must run together in your mind," Rachel said.

Ginny shook her head. "That's right. None holds any more interest to me than another."

"Good morning, ladies."

The women turned at the rough voice to see Frank Frey walk up with his brother, Hiram. Rachel gave them both a hug. When the Frey brothers, along with her and her uncle Charles, were held captive by outlaws several months before, the Pelletiers, Gabe, Noah, and Cash Coulter, a friend of Dax's and Luke's from before the war, had rescued them, killing the outlaws in the process.

"It's so good to see both of you." Rachel knew the brothers didn't come to town often. "I believe you know Miss Abigail Tolbert and Miss Ginny Sorensen."

As greetings were exchanged, Abby spotted Noah a few yards away, glancing in her direction as he carried on a conversation with Gabe. She wanted to break away to speak with him, but noticed her father near the front of the church, speaking with Reverend Paige. She was about ready to walk toward him when she saw Noah turn in her direction.

"Hello, Hiram, Frank." He held out his hand to the ranchers.

"Noah. How are you doing with your cabin?" Frank asked.

"It's finished. I stay there most nights." Noah cast a look at Abby, hoping they'd have a few minutes to talk. If nothing more, he enjoyed the sound of her voice, her open and animated expressions. She could make him smile with a few words.

"Any chance you've noticed anything missing—supplies, food, tools?" Hiram asked.

He focused on the brothers. "As a matter of fact, I have. Not much, mainly hardtack, jerky, and other food. A bucket went missing a couple weeks ago."

"Hmmm..." Hiram rubbed his chin between his thumb and forefinger. "Sounds like what's been happening at our place."

"You don't say." Noah thought on it a minute. "How far would it be for someone to travel between your place and mine?"

"If they're riding a horse, it's a few miles. By foot, you can cut through the trees and brush, cutting off some of the distance." Frank glanced at his brother, who nodded.

"A few hours?" Noah asked.

"Maybe a couple hours by foot if they keep moving. You don't think someone's camped up in the mountain, do you?" Hiram asked.

"Could be. Luke's been noticing the same as us. I'm guessing it's about a two hour distance on foot between his place and mine."

"With good weather, a body could travel between all three places in a day, then head back to where they're hiding." Frank thought about it a moment. "Harder in the winter. Plus, they'd be carrying what they stole. I'm guessing there's more than one person doing the stealing." He looked up at the darkening sky.

"Did you find any tracks?" Noah asked.

"Nothing. We're guessing it's Indians. Maybe the band of Blackfoot that have been camping north of the Pelletier ranch. Could be a small party from their village."

Rachel, Ginny, and Abby listened with rapt attention to the conversation. No one wanted trouble with the Blackfoot. Most would look the other way if small amounts were taken, but the way the men spoke, it seemed the thefts had increased and spread from ranch to ranch. Few could afford to let the thievery go on for long.

"Hank's been grumbling about supplies missing from our place," Rachel said. "I thought he'd made an error in his count. Listening to you, though, perhaps not. We've also lost a pig and several chickens. You know, Luke's place is only a mile from the main ranch house."

"Four places that are being raided." Frank shifted from one foot to the other as he considered all the information.

"That we know of." Noah crossed his arms, not liking what he'd been hearing.

"If it continues, we'll need to get a group together and search the caves." Frank and Hiram had been through this a few years back. They found a man and his young son holed up in a cave with little food and water. They'd brought them to their ranch and put the man to work. He was still one of their best wranglers and the brothers helped with schooling the boy.

"It's time to leave, Abigail."

Everyone turned at King Tolbert's booming voice several feet away. He made no move to walk forward and greet anyone, just stood erect with his gaze fixed on his daughter.

Abby stared at him, uncomfortable with the way he treated many in the town. She'd mentioned it to him once or twice. He'd cut her off each time, saying she had no business telling him how to act toward others. Her eyes darted to Noah, who looked as disappointed as she felt because they'd have no time to talk.

"Coming, Father." Abby said her goodbyes before joining him at their buggy. It was an unpleasant end to an otherwise wonderful morning.

"We missed you at church today." Rachel set the plate of roast beef on the table. She'd been taking over more of the cooking from Bernice, who'd fallen ill a few weeks before. She seemed to be over the sickness when, without warning, a relapse sent her back to bed. Bernice hadn't been able to regain her strength. She and Hank took meals in their place near the bunkhouse—meals Rachel made and carried over.

"Too much to do. I'll make it next week." Luke passed a bowl of potatoes to Dax.

"You need any help at your place before the snow comes?" Dax asked.

"Everything is closed up, wood's stacked, and I have plenty of blankets."

"And food?"

Luke smiled at Rachel's question. "Figured I'd be here for supper most nights. I'll take over eggs and a slab of bacon when I need it. My coffee tin is full and I have a bottle of whiskey. What else does a man need?"

She laughed at the self-satisfied look on his face. "I guess there isn't much else."

They ate in silence a few minutes before Rachel brought up the question they'd all been avoiding. "What happens if Bernice doesn't pull through?"

Dax set down his fork and settled back in his chair. No one wanted to contemplate the ranch without Bernice—or Hank without his wife.

"Does Charles think she won't pull through?" Dax asked.

Rachel's Uncle Charles was a wonderful doctor and cared a great deal about the people of Splendor. He held out more hope for patients than most doctors she'd worked alongside during the Civil War. Even so, she could sense his hope weaken regarding Bernice's chance of recovery.

"He hasn't said it in so many words. It's what he *isn't* saying that has me wondering if she's fading more than he's letting on."

"She and Hank will always have a place here, even if she can no longer cook and clean for us. They can stay in their place out back." Dax looked toward Luke and saw him nod.

"I can continue to cook and clean until we know if she'll improve."

"That's fine for a couple more weeks, then we have to make a decision. You're doing enough here, along with going to the clinic most days. Even before she got sick, I'd been thinking of hiring someone to help her. We have twice the men we did when Luke and I took over the place. It's too much for one person."

"You have someone in mind?" Luke asked.

"No, but I'll give it some thought. Do you know of anyone looking for work?"

"No one comes to mind. Just asking. Besides, it's your decision since you'll be around the person more than me. I just want someone who can cook well enough to keep the men from grumbling about their food."

"I'll ask around when I'm in town," Rachel said. "There are a few young women who are of an age to move out of their family's home and start to work."

"I'm not certain that's what we want. A mature woman who the men won't be inclined to follow around and moon over would be best." Dax didn't care to imagine how the men would respond to a young, pretty woman.

She scrunched her face a little and looked at Luke. "Do you feel the same?"

"I do." He didn't elaborate. Dax had said it all. He stood and walked toward the window, looking up at the blacking sky. "I'd better head back. Appears as if a storm may be coming and I don't want to get caught in it."

"Why don't you stay here tonight?" Dax asked. Luke's room at the ranch would always be his and he saw no reason for him to ride out into approaching weather.

"Another time. Looks like whatever is coming is moving at a slow pace and I want to get the house heated before I turn in. I'll see you in the morning."

Dax stood at the front window, an arm around his wife's shoulders, and watched Luke ride off. Although his brother seemed more at peace than he had in a while, Dax couldn't squelch the feeling that the tranquility Luke felt now would begin to unravel...and soon.

"That's the last of it." Flatnose swung up on his horse and stared down at the guards standing with their hands in the air.

Rick looked around at the men and the surrounding hills, seeing no sign of anyone watching them. Each man had stuffed their saddlebags full of gold. He didn't want to take the wagon back to the ranch, preferring to tie up the guards and take off.

Flatnose glanced at two of his men. "Collect their guns, tie them up to the wagon wheels, and set the horses loose. We need to get moving."

The men worked at a quick pace, not wanting to prolong their stay. Gold wagons moved within a tight schedule. When the gold didn't appear as planned, a search group would be formed to find it. They wanted to be as far away as they could by then.

"Let's go." Rick didn't wait to see if the others followed—he knew they would. He headed toward the brush and a small deer trail hidden from the road. It would take longer to reach the ranch, but it would make tracking them almost impossible.

They'd ridden close to an hour when Flatnose edged up beside him. "We're being watched." He nodded toward the ridge above and ahead of them.

Rick lifted his gaze to see a band of Indians, he assumed Sioux, sitting astride their horses, making no move to come closer.

"How long?"

"They've been following for a few miles. My guess is they saw us steal the gold and are waiting for the right spot to attack."

Flatnose continued to watch as they kept pace with them. They had little trouble with the various tribes who lived throughout the territory. A few stolen cattle and missing supplies. He'd heard rumors a small band of renegades had been robbing gold shipments north of here. Perhaps they'd moved south. He held up his hand, signaling for his men to stop.

"Stay close. We're a mile from where the trail splits and we head to the ranch. If we make it to that point, they'll have a hard time getting down the ridge and picking up the trail before we head up the creek to the property." Flatnose glanced up to the ridge. The riders still sat motionless, watching.

"What do you think they're up to?" one of the men asked.

"Could be watching to see what we do and where we stash the gold." Rick turned his horse back to the trail and glanced over his shoulder. "Keep together."

They'd get to the ranch, unload the gold, post guards, and wait. After they'd split the gold with the men, he and Flatnose would stash the remaining bags in an underground room they'd built in the house.

Rick had thought more and more about this being his last job. Getting a place near Big Pine and Felicity appealed to him more and more, as well as leaving the life of an outlaw behind. They'd taken enough to allow him the luxury of never working again. He'd still find something so as not to make people wonder. Maybe he'd even see about being one of Sheriff Sterling's deputies. Rick smiled at the thought. What better way to push suspicion away from him than being a lawman? It just might work.

Chapter Nine

"When are you leaving?" Ginny asked as she set a drink down in front of Luke. She'd heard him mention to the men at the table he'd be traveling to Denver on business. When Bull asked why so far, all he'd said was a friend needed his help, then went silent. She guessed it had something to do with his Pinkerton work.

"In two days." He took a good look at her, the first one he'd allowed himself since walking into the Rose. Luke hadn't seen Ginny in weeks, purposely avoiding the saloon and the conflicting emotion he felt whenever they were close. Each time he saw her, she seemed more beautiful than the time before. No matter his resolve, he couldn't control his body's response to the woman he wanted as a friend and nothing more. At least that's what he'd been telling himself for weeks as he sat in his place, alone, wishing he could figure out why she muddled his mind.

"Isn't it a bad time of year to be traveling over the mountains? The odds are good you'll be hitting snow." Bull threw his cards on the table. "I'm out."

"I'm meeting up with someone in Big Pine, then we're riding to Denver."

Ginny glanced at him and wondered if the "someone" he referred to might be a woman, then mentally shook herself. She had no business thinking about Luke and other women, especially since she was almost certain he had someone in Big Pine he saw every few weeks. At least that's what Belle had said, and her friend knew just about everything there was to know about the men in Splendor.

"Whatever it is, it must be important to have you traveling so far this time of year," Ellis muttered.

"Are you making some kind of point, Ellis?" Luke asked. The oldest ranch hand never said much, so when he did, Luke tended to listen.

"Nothing in particular, 'cept we don't have much time to get the work done before the bad weather starts. You haven't been here a full winter and don't know how bad it can be. Dax is going to need everyone."

"And you're saying that includes me?" As an equal owner in the ranch, Luke knew the men were hesitant to bring up any of their opinions about how to run the place, which made what Ellis implied worth considering.

"All I'm saying is you haven't experienced a Montana winter and neither has Dax. They can be brutal enough to cause even war-hardened men like the two of you to take notice." Ellis threw down his cards. "It's been a long week. Think I'll head back."

Bull and the other men followed Ellis' lead and stood.

"You coming, Luke?" Bull asked.

"I'll follow in a bit." He watched them leave, then turned toward Ginny, who'd already begun to pick up the empty glasses. "What do you think?"

She stopped to stare at him. "About what?"

"Am I making a mistake leaving for Denver?"

Ginny's eyes widened. She couldn't have been more stunned at his question. "You're asking my opinion?"

Luke stood, downed the last of his whiskey, and placed the empty glass on her tray. "Yes, I'm asking what you think."

"Well—"

"Ginny," Al called from behind the bar. "Why don't you finish up and go home?"

"Thanks, Al." She glanced at Luke.

"Finish and I'll walk you home."

He waited outside, wondering why he'd offered. She walked the short distance to the boardinghouse by herself each night after work. Tonight he realized he didn't like it. Of course, he'd asked her about leaving for Denver. Luke wanted her opinion, although he didn't understand why it mattered to him.

"All done." Ginny walked outside, slipping into her coat. Luke moved behind, her, helping to pull the tattered wool over her shoulders. "Thanks," she mumbled, confused and curious about his actions tonight. "Why are you going to Denver?"

"A telegram arrived from Dutch McFarlin, a Pinkerton agent. He needs help finishing a job in Denver. There's an agent in Big Pine he's worked with before who'll also make the trip." Luke slipped her arm through his, telling himself the dirt street looked rutted and treacherous this time of night.

Ginny glanced up at him, surprised at the simple courtesy. "It must be a big job."

"Guess so. He didn't say much about it in the telegram."

They walked to the back entrance. Luke opened the door, then stepped aside, allowing her to pass by him. He could smell the scent of her hair. *Roses*, he thought as he followed her.

They stood outside the room she shared with Mary, Ginny's arms crossed in front of her chest.

"I *do* want to know what you think of me leaving."

"You mean leaving Dax and the others to handle the ranch?"

"Ellis doesn't say much about how we manage the place, so his comments tonight got me thinking maybe it isn't such a good idea." He shoved his hands in his pockets, feeling a slight amount of discomfort at needing to hear her thoughts.

"I don't know much about this area or what's needed to keep cattle safe during the winter. It does seem as though there'd be a lot more work, so every man would be needed. Suzanne says storms can arrive with little to no warning, and the temperatures can drop to below freezing in minutes."

Like the last time they stood together in the tight space, Ginny began to feel heat flow through her body as her heart rate picked up. She began to shrug out of the old coat, letting Luke pull it from her shoulders.

"Does it seem hot in here to you?"

Luke watched her drape the coat over an arm and pat the back of her hand against her forehead before looking up at him. Her soft green eyes drew him in as his gaze locked with hers. In the span of one breath, he used his forefinger to lift her chin. He hesitated when he saw her eyes widen and bottom lip tremble, yet she made no move to step away.

He lowered his head, brushing his lips against hers in a soft caress, then once more. When she made no move to back away, he stepped closer, cupping her face with his hands before increasing the pressure. Luke couldn't remember ever feeling anything as sweet as the feel of Ginny's lips as his mouth moved over hers. He'd kissed many woman, yet the incessant thundering in his chest warned him this was new territory and to proceed with caution.

He let his hands fall to his sides and stepped back, watching as her eyes opened. Her dazed expression mirrored his own confused state. Luke cleared his throat and put a few more inches of space between them before reaching up to tuck a loose strand of hair behind her ear.

"I'd better leave." The thickness of his voice surprised him. "Thank you for your thoughts."

Luke watched as her eyes cleared and she took her own step backward.

"I didn't offer much." Her voice sounded shaky, unnatural.

He nodded, not trusting himself to say anything else or stay in the small space with her any longer. "Goodnight, Ginny."

"Goodnight, Luke."

She watched him leave, her heart pounding as her breathing slowed. *So that was a real kiss*, she thought as she let out a deep breath and turned toward her room. From the comments her mother had made years before, Ginny never thought she'd enjoy the feel of a man's lips on hers. Her mother hadn't.

At first she had no idea what to do, so she'd stood still, enjoying the feel of his warm lips, the unexpected sensations. She hadn't wanted him to pull back and end the contact.

Ginny opened the door a crack and peered in at Mary, fast asleep in bed. Suzanne read her a story and tucked her in each night after finishing with her supper customers. Mary would sit in the kitchen, watching everything Suzanne did, drifting off at the table with her head cradled in her arms. The routine had worked for several months now, but Ginny knew she couldn't rely on Suzanne's generosity forever.

She sat on the edge of the bed and touched a finger to her lips, which still tingled from Luke's kisses. Ginny didn't know what it meant when a man kissed you. She knew it meant nothing to the ladies who worked upstairs at the Wild Rose, and suspected it meant nothing to the men, either. She wondered if Luke had felt the same jolt she had, and if he'd wanted it to last longer, like she did.

Ginny fell back onto the bed and stared at the ceiling. She knew it would be folly to believe the kiss meant more than it did. A man such as him might dally with a girl like her, but would never take it seriously. As Belle had told her, Luke Pelletier had his pick of women, and it wouldn't be some poor girl who worked in a saloon.

Luke loaded the last items in his saddlebags and tied them down. He'd meet Dutch's associate in Big Pine, then travel to Denver. Who knows? The trip might help him get over the constant thoughts of Ginny and what had happened the night he'd walked her home.

He derided himself again for his rash action as he checked Prince's cinch, then walked into the house, checking for anything he may have missed. He'd done this twice already. Each time he walked back outside without remembering what he'd gone inside to do. Luke felt his common sense slip away and knew the cause had to be Ginny.

"You ready, boy?" he asked Prince as he swung into the saddle, looked around once more, then headed for the ranch house. He'd say goodbye to Dax and Rachel before hitting the northern trail for Big Pine, careful to avoid riding through Splendor.

"You taking off?" Bull asked as Luke reined Prince to a stop and slid to the ground.

"Just need to speak with Dax and Rachel."

"Dax already took off with Ellis toward the north pasture, but Rachel's still inside. Have a safe trip." Bull shook Luke's hand, mounted his horse, and headed out with Rude and the rest of the men.

"Rachel, it's Luke," he said as he headed inside and towards the kitchen, following the smell of fresh brewed coffee.

"Good morning." Rachel reached up and pulled down a second cup, filling it to the top and handing it to Luke. "You ready to go?"

"I'd hoped to speak to Dax. Bull said I missed him."

"Something happened with the cattle and he rode out with Ellis to check it out." She saw the concerned look on Luke's face and knew he struggled with his decision to leave. "It'll be fine. Dax and the men can handle everything while you're gone." She offered a vague smile. In her heart, she didn't want him to leave at such a difficult time of year.

"I could send a telegram to Dutch, tell him I just can't make it."

"And regret it within a few days? I'll tell you what I believe Dax would say. *Go. Get the job over with, then decide if it's the last one.*" She gave him a hug, then turned toward the hall. "I need to ride to the clinic. Do you mind some company?"

"Of course not." He finished his coffee as she walked back into the room, slipping into a heavy coat. "Dax says it looks like a storm coming today or tonight. I sure hope you miss it."

"Something tells me this trip is going to be nothing but bad weather. You ready?"

Rachel narrowed her eyes at Luke. Of all of them, he could be counted on to see the adventure in everything. She wondered from where his dark mood had come.

"I'll check to see if one of the men saddled Dancer for me."

Dax had given her the beautiful pinto mare as a wedding present. She was the sweetest horse Rachel had ever owned, with good spirit and exceptional lines.

"I saw Tat bringing her out when I rode up." Luke glanced upward as they walked toward the horses. For the moment, a cloudless blue sky covered the ranch. The one hint the weather could change in an instant was the brisk, cold wind starting to move over them. "You sure you want to ride to town today?"

"I told Uncle Charles I'd be available. I'll come back early if it looks like snow."

The wind picked up as they rode closer to Splendor. When they came upon the trail Luke had intended to take, he made a quick decision to stay with Rachel and make certain she arrived at the clinic. Even this close, a freak storm could let loose, reducing visibility to a couple of feet within minutes, which was what happened a quarter-mile from the edge of town.

"Move closer to me," Luke said as the storm picked up and visibility lessened. He grabbed his rope and looped an end around Rachel's saddle horn, securing it tight. "Stay low and hold on tight. We'll ride to the livery. Watch for the fire from Noah's forge." His voice became a shout as the wind howled around them. At least they could still see the trail well enough to guide them the last part of the trip.

Within minutes they spotted the outline of the schoolhouse on the right. Looking left, the lumberyard had all but disappeared, while the livery's fire shown bright through the thickening snow.

Luke rode into the open doorway, Rachel right behind, the rope still secured to her saddle horn.

Noah raced toward them, taking Dancer's reins from Rachel and walking him to a nearby stall. He reached up and helped her down, then uncinched the saddle, laying it and the blanket over a rail before picking up dry rags to wipe down the horse. He glanced over his shoulder to see Luke mirroring his actions with Prince.

"I was just thinking of closing the doors, but decided to hold off a few minutes. Glad I waited." Noah wrung out the soaked rags and laid them on the railing beside the blanket. "Stand next to the forge, Rachel, and warm up."

"I should check on Uncle Charles—"

"No!" Luke and Noah said in unison.

"I'll check on him," Luke said. "You stay here."

The storm hadn't let up. In fact, the wind had increased since they rode into the livery, whipping gusts of snow around so fast it stung his face. He pushed his hat low and drew the collar of his coat up as he ran across the open lot between the livery and Western Union office. He poked his head inside to see Bernie Griggs, who ran the post and telegraph office, slipping into a coat.

"Are you all right, Bernie?" Luke asked.

"I'm not closing if that's what you mean. This storm will blow over. Not worth going home and losing business."

Luke nodded, although he doubted anyone would be sending a telegram in this weather. He moved on past the saloon to the jail. Gabe stood by the window, watching the storm as Luke pushed the door open, then slammed it shut, warm air enveloping him.

"Hell of a storm for starting up so quick." Gabe wore long sleeves and a heavy vest, the fire in the stove going full force. He grabbed the coffee pot and a cup, poured it full, then handed it to Luke. "Drink this."

"I rode in with Rachel. The storm came through so fast, we only made it as far as Noah's. I offered to check on Doc Worthington."

"I saw him walk into the clinic not long before the storm started. Give me a minute and I'll head over." Gabe snagged his coat from a hook and slipped an arm inside before Luke stopped him.

"No need, but I appreciate it." Luke stepped outside, closing the door behind him. The clinic stood across the street from the jail—a small storefront with the doc's house in back. Rachel had lived with her uncle when she and Dax first met. Luke tried the front door. Finding it locked, he dashed around back, beginning to feel the cold seep through his thick, wool coat. He pounded on the door and waited a moment before pounding once more. The door flew open.

"Come in and get out of this storm. Is Rachel with you?" He glanced behind Luke, then shut the door.

"We made it as far as Noah's. She's holed up inside by the fire, keeping warm. We thought it best someone check on you."

Doc motioned Luke to follow him to the kitchen and waited while he handed him a cup of coffee. "Drink this, then we'll go get Rachel."

Luke used the cup to warm his cold hands, not too interested in drinking more of the hot liquid.

"Doc, you stay here. I'll let Rachel know everything is fine. As soon as there's a break in the storm, I'll make certain she gets here." He handed the still full cup to Charles, slipped on his gloves, and reached for the door as someone pounded from the outside. He threw it open to see Ginny shivering, her lips turning blue.

"What the hell are you doing out in this storm?" Luke's words came out hard and tight as he grabbed her arm and pulled her inside. "Where's Mary?"

Even though she could hardly speak for being so cold, she ignored his questions, lifted her chin in a defiant gesture, and turned toward the doctor. "Suzanne is hacking something fierce. She holds her chest and can't draw a full breath. Can you come check on her?"

"Hold on a minute while I get my bag and coat." Charles disappeared toward the back, leaving Luke and Ginny alone.

She moved a couple of feet away, her anger subsiding as her body's response to Luke increased. Her heart had slammed into her chest the moment he'd opened the door. He looked windblown, cold—and annoyed at her. She'd confided in Belle about what happened between her and Luke a couple nights before. She'd gotten an earful from her friend about what she could expect from him, which was nothing. Belle said men thought of kisses the same way they thought of holding hands or having a woman slip an arm through theirs. It meant little, if anything. More than likely, he'd probably forgotten about it within seconds of walking out the door.

"Don't you own anything warmer?" he asked, taking in the thinning wool coat and threadbare cap she'd pulled over her head.

"No, I don't. And it's no business of yours anyway. Aren't you supposed to be on your way to Denver?" She glanced toward the hall, wondering what was taking the doc so long.

"At the moment, I'm right where I want to be. Anyway, I plan to make sure you and the doc get to the boardinghouse safe."

"It's three doors down. Nothing will happen between here and there." At least her teeth weren't shattering any longer. She almost hated going back outside, but there was no help for it.

"You ready, Ginny?" the doctor asked, walking back into the room, pulling a woolen cap over his head.

"I'm coming along. Hope you don't mind." Luke opened the door and stepped aside.

Charles looked at the sky and noted the visibility had deteriorated even more. "Good idea. I'm sure Rachel is safe at the livery."

Chapter Ten

Ginny fumed. She had enough on her mind, with Suzanne being sick and Mary seeking her attention, without dealing with her confusing feelings about Luke. Ignoring him didn't seem to work. He captured her thoughts without saying a word. As Belle said, the chance he had actual feelings for her were slim.

She glanced over at Luke and thought of the money she owed him. Today would be a good time to give him what she'd set aside.

"I'll get coffee," Ginny said as they walked into the boardinghouse. She'd prepared breakfast for the one guest, then closed the restaurant, telling the man to seek her out when he wanted another meal. If the storm cleared, she'd check with Amos to see if he needed her at the Rose. She'd heard customers were slim when the larger storms blew through.

Charles made his way to Suzanne's bedroom while Luke found a seat in the front sitting room. He'd never had reason to use this room before and found it comfortable. His mother would have called it "cozy".

"Here you are." Ginny handed him a cup and stepped back. "You don't need to stay. I'm certain the storm will pass soon."

"I'm staying. Rachel is safe in the livery with Noah." He set the cup down and stood. "Is your need to get rid of me because of the other night?"

She raised her chin to stare up at him. "I don't know what you mean."

He chuckled before his expression sobered. "All right, but if it is, don't worry about it. It was just a kiss and it won't happen again."

She lowered her eyes, disappointment flooding through her. Even though she had no intention of ever falling in love and marrying, her fantasy about him enjoying the kiss as much as she did was now blown to dust, as so many of her dreams had been. Once more, Belle had been right.

Luke saw the conflicting emotions flash across Ginny's face and wondered at her thoughts. Had she liked the kiss, enjoying it as much as he did? Had remembering kept her awake as it did him? Regardless, it wouldn't happen again.

He looked at the open doorway to see a small head poke around the corner, then duck back out of sight. "I believe we have company," Luke whispered to her.

Ginny shot a look toward the hall and walked to the opening. "Mary, come in and say hello to Mr. Luke." She took her hand and guided her into the room, stopping in front of Luke, who crouched in front of the little girl.

"Good morning, Mary."

"Hello, Mr. Luke." She fidgeted a little and grabbed hold of Ginny's skirt, clutching it in her small hand.

"You look much better than the last time I saw you."

She glanced up at her sister, her face scrunched in confusion.

"Remember when Mr. Luke carried you home from Doctor Worthington's clinic? You were sick." Ginny placed a hand on Mary's shoulder.

She looked back at Luke and shook her head. "I was sick."

Luke smiled, glad it all worked out so well. Colds could turn into a major illness within hours. He stood as Charles walked into the room.

"Well, good morning, Mary. How are you doing?"

"Good." She shook her head again. "Can I go outside and see the snow?" she asked Ginny.

"We'll have to wait until it clears. You can watch from the window, though."

Mary raced to the settee in an alcove in front of a window, climbed up onto her knees, and peered out.

"Suzanne should be fine in a few days, although keeping her down could be an issue. She wanted to get up as I left, but I told her she was to stay in bed at least two days. I'd better get back to the clinic. Let me know if she starts to worsen."

"Can I get you some breakfast before you leave?" Ginny asked.

"No, I've had mine. I'll see you both later." Charles pulled up his collar and walked into the storm, which hadn't let up since they'd entered the boardinghouse.

"Guess I'd better take off, too. I need to let Rachel know her uncle is fine and get her to the clinic." Luke drained the last of his coffee and handed the cup to Ginny.

"Are you still leaving for Big Pine today?"

"If the storm passes. If not, I'll ride with Rachel back to the ranch and leave tomorrow. Regardless, I need to be in Big Pine in two days."

"I guess you won't be back for several weeks?"

"Maybe. I have no idea how long I'll be gone." He buttoned his heavy coat before settling his hat on his head. "Take care of yourself, Ginny." He leaned down and placed a chaste kiss on her cheek. Even the brief contact caused his body to react. He backed away, not wanting to act on his impulse to wrap his arms around her and claim her mouth—which is what every instinct screamed for him to do.

Ginny recovered from the brief contact just as he reached the door. "Wait." She turned and disappeared down the hall, returning a minute later holding a hand out to him. "This is for you."

Luke looked at her in confusion, then stretched out his arm and opened his hand, watching as Ginny dropped coins into it.

"Part of what I owe you." She met his gaze, a look of triumph on her face.

Luke could feel the heat creep up his face as his jaw clenched. Ginny saw his reaction and took a step backward, not liking his expression. Luke grabbed her wrist, opened her hand, and dropped the coins back into it.

"Save enough to buy yourself a decent coat. I won't take a penny from you until then." He turned on his heels before he said something he'd regret.

Ginny looked at the coins, swallowing a lump in her throat as he opened the door to let in the cold wind. "Take care of yourself, Luke."

His gaze locked with hers a moment before he nodded once and stepped into the storm.

"He should be on his way to Denver by now." Bull settled into a chair at the usual table the men claimed for their card game.

Ginny walked up as the men shook off their coats and draped them over the back of their chairs. "Are you talking about Luke?"

"Yep. He left the day after the storm. Man's got a wanderlust something fierce." Bull began to shuffle the cards.

"You ask me, he's got no business leaving the ranch this time of year," Rude grumbled, then glanced up at Ginny. "Whiskey for me."

"Well, no one asked you. It's his and Dax's business what the two of them decide. You know he wouldn't have taken off if Dax objected." Ellis felt the same, but he'd had his say a few nights before. It didn't change the decision.

"Did he say how long he'd be gone?" Ginny asked, even though she knew it would be wise to keep her mouth shut.

"He didn't tell you?" Tat asked.

Her eyes darted to the young cowhand. "Tell me what?"

"He's thinking of staying there. Maybe never coming back." Tat grinned until a hard kick got his attention. "Hell, Bull. What'd you do that for?" He bent down to rub the lump already forming on his shin.

Bull had watched Ginny's eyes grow wide and her shoulders slump at Tat's news. "Tat is fooling with you, Ginny. Luke will be back. He's just not sure when."

She let out an audible breath, even though she knew it shouldn't matter to her whether he returned or not. "It doesn't matter to me one way or another. I was just curious, that's all."

Bull and Ellis exchanged glances, both knowing a lie when they heard one.

Tom Horton secured his saddlebags, checked the cinches once more, then mounted his horse. After fighting for the Union Army, he'd signed on with the Pinkerton Agency over a year before, wanting to put the war behind him. He'd been in Big Pine two weeks, checking into the gold thefts north of town, when he'd received Dutch's message. Tom hadn't been pleased with being asked to leave just as new information had come to his attention, but when headquarters sent an order, you followed it.

"You about ready?" Tom asked Luke.

Luke finished securing his belongings, then swung up onto Prince. "Let's go." He glanced at Tom, then lowered his hat over his forehead to shield the sun.

They rode in silence through the town of Moosejaw, keeping a continuous watch of the hills and sky. Their route would take them through the Dakota, Nebraska, and Colorado territories in an attempt to avoid the snow storms they'd heard were already moving over the Rocky Mountains. Dutch had suggested taking the stagecoach, but neither he nor Tom wanted to be without their horses. Besides, they could travel over trails a stage couldn't.

The first two days were uneventful—good weather and no Indian sightings. Luke spent most of his time trying to stay warm, thinking of Ginny, wondering if she and the rest of the citizens of Splendor were safe from the marauding Sioux. It seemed unlikely they'd attack a town when travelers were easier targets.

He worried about Ginny making it through a full winter with the meager clothing she and Mary owned. If she'd let him, Luke would buy them whatever they needed. It still burned him the way her pride pushed her to not accept his help, yet a part of him understood it. She had a hard life in front of her. All he wanted was to make it easier.

The thought brought a wry smile to his face. The day before he and Tom had left Big Pine, he'd made an impulsive decision. Walking past a dress shop window, he'd noticed a dark tweed woman's coat with a small collar and six large black buttons, hanging next to a woolen dress. The coat was meant to be worn over a full skirt, not the cotton calico dresses common on the frontier. He pictured Ginny and knew the coat would hang to below her knees. Luke noticed the black fur banding of the sleeves and collar as he pushed the door open and walked inside. It took less than ten minutes for him to purchase the dress and coat, arrange for it to be sent to Suzanne's boardinghouse, and make payment. A part of him wanted to be there when she opened the package. Another part, the part focused on self-preservation, was glad he'd be far away. By the time he made it back home, she might still be mad, but he'd wager she'd be wearing both.

The thought of returning home had his mind shift directions to a conversation he had the day before he'd left.

Gabe confided in him that an investor from Big Pine had purchased the vacant lot between the clinic and land office with plans to build a saloon in competition with the Wild Rose. When Luke questioned Gabe, the sheriff said the local banker who'd made the loan, Horace Clausen, wasn't allowed to divulge the owner's name until the saloon opened. The owner had plans to hire a number of men to build the saloon, with orders it must open prior to Thanksgiving. Luke found himself wondering how a second saloon would impact the Rose and Ginny. She relied on the income, and a loss of business might put pressure on Amos to make changes.

Nearing sundown on the third day, Tom spotted a small group of what he guessed were Sioux riding along a bluff. They had been attacking soldiers and settlers near Fort Karney in Wyoming, stealing horses and killing as many whites as they could. Luke and Tom had hoped to slip through the area unseen.

"We'd better keep moving." Tom picked up the pace and continued southeast.

They rode long into the night, not stopping, putting as much distance as possible between them and the raiding party. The freezing wind whipped around them, penetrating their clothing, hindering their progress until they were forced to stop just before dawn and take refuge within a thick stand of trees.

By midmorning they were ready to ride again and headed south toward Denver. In three or four days they'd reach their destination.

"What do you think, Al?" Ginny asked as she watched the men working sixteen hours each day, except Sunday, to complete the building across the street. Amos had pitched a fit when Horace told him the news, but nothing could be done. The town had grown and the new owner felt it could accommodate two saloons—the Rose and his place. It was a belief Amos shared, except he'd hoped to be the one to open the second establishment.

"Don't know. Amos had been talking with Horace Clausen about purchasing the land. Looks like someone beat him to it." Al continued to wipe down the counter and glanced about the saloon. The evening card players were trickling in, while other patrons were headed home. Everyone speculated about who owned the place, what it would be called, and how it would be different from the Rose.

"Does anyone know who the owner is?"

Al looked at Ginny and shook his head. "From what I hear, just Clausen, and he's not talking."

"I know Rachel and the doc aren't too happy about it being right next door to the clinic."

"And with the doc's house at the back of his property, it's going to be kind of hard to ignore the noise on a Saturday night. At least *we've* never had complaints about it." Al listened to the pounding of nails and men yelling at each other. They worked across the street and three doors down, yet he could still hear the conversations as if they were right in front of him.

"Maybe because we're right next to the jail?" Ginny asked, amusement in her voice. It wouldn't be long before the Rose would be filled with cowboys celebrating the end of another week. The men from Redemption's Edge should be coming in at any time—they always did on Saturday nights. She wondered if they'd have news of Luke.

As if her thoughts had conjured them up, the doors swung open and Bull walked in, followed by several of the men. She nodded a greeting, watching them take their seats, then walked over to the table.

"Let me guess. Whiskey all around?"

"That'd be great, Ginny." Ellis pulled out a deck of cards and watched the expression on Johnny's face turn from amusement to awe in a split second. Following the man's gaze, Ellis noticed a pretty, young woman walking down the steps in an emerald green dress.

"Will you look at that?" Tat stared along with his friend.

"She must be new." Bull never paid much attention to the women of the Rose. Although he wasn't immune to their charms, he'd never had an interest in seeking them out. Looking suited him just fine, but this woman had a different aura about her, drawing all eyes her way.

"Who is she, Ginny?" Johnny asked as she returned with their drinks.

She glanced over her shoulder. "Her name's Dinah. She arrived on the stage today, walked in here, spoke with Amos, and walked out with a job."

"Upstairs?" Bull asked.

"Yes." She watched his expression change from fascination to acceptance. Belle told her he and Luke were impossible to entice upstairs. Belle didn't understand why, but Ginny thought she knew. Neither seemed to have an interest in announcing their private lives to the town, much the same as Gabe and Noah. If any of those men had ever been upstairs, Ginny sure didn't know about it.

The night dragged on. Ginny's mind jumped between two subjects. First, a small house not far from the lumberyard, near Noah's tack shop. She'd noticed it months before and always wondered if anyone lived in it.

Suzanne told her it had been built by an old widower who'd since passed. No one had ever shown an interest in buying it, so it sat vacant and unattended. She thought it had one small bedroom, a front area, and tiny kitchen. As far as Suzanne knew, the old furniture still sat in the place. She'd offered to go with Ginny to see Horace Clausen at the bank, but Ginny had refused. She'd keep it as a dream, something to focus on for her and Mary—a home of their own.

As quickly as the image of the house slipped from her mind, another image appeared. Luke. She wondered if he'd made it to Denver. No matter her decision to never marry and just make a home for her sister, she enjoyed his company and wanted him as a friend. Pushing the thought of their kiss aside, she accepted he wanted nothing from her except friendship. Ginny could give him that.

She felt warmth envelope her at the thought she'd made so many friends during her few months in Splendor. Luke, however, was special. She'd never had a male friend. When he returned, she'd work at being one he could depend on. She knew she could depend on him, and he would never want anything more from her.

Chapter Eleven

Luke shot straight up, drenched in sweat, blankets twisted around him, his eyes darting around the room. He and Tom had arrived in Denver, taking rooms at a boardinghouse Dutch recommended before grabbing supper, then collapsing in their rooms.

He yanked the covers away and swung his legs over the side of the bed, scrubbing his hands over his face. Gripping the side of the bed, he tried to remember what he'd been dreaming of when he'd jolted awake.

Ginny. He'd been in bed with her in his house on the ranch. They'd been making love, clinging to each other. She'd pulled away and smiled up at him, a guileless expression filled with warmth and love.

His heart hammered in his chest as the dream-induced images played across his mind. Where the hell had they come from? He paced to the dresser and poured water into a glass, finishing it in three big gulps. In all his life he'd never once dreamed of a woman. Never. Why now? And why Ginny?

Luke walked to the window, forced it open, and peered onto the street below, sucking the cool air into his lungs. The sun had begun to rise. At this hour the town seemed eerily quiet, as just a few lone wagons made their way from one end of the long block to the other.

He turned away from the window and speared his fingers through his hair. The image of him and Ginny tangled together danced across his mind, causing slight beads of moisture to form on his brow. He shook his head in a desperate attempt to eradicate the vision.

"Hell," Luke muttered, grabbing his trousers and shoving his legs into them. He needed to get out of there and into the fresh air, into the openness where he could clear his head. Strapping on his gun belt and grabbing his hat, he walked down the stairs to the dining room, the aromas of coffee and bacon drifting from the kitchen. Strong coffee and food would clear his head and wipe images of Ginny from his mind. It had been just a dream after all, not some forecast of the future.

He took a seat at a table by the window, accepting the coffee set in front of him.

"Bacon, eggs, flapjacks, and lots more coffee." He didn't even look at the lady taking his order. Instead, he focused his gaze outside while taking a couple of deep, slow breaths. Luke and Tom would meet with Dutch, firm up what needed to be done, then he'd find a solution to whatever dogged him. He'd been without a woman too long. Perhaps it would be as simple as finding a willing companion for an evening.

"You're up early." Dutch pulled out a chair and signaled to the server. "Have you seen Tom this morning?"

"No. I just got downstairs myself."

"Don't take offense, but you look about as useful as a man recuperating from a three day drunk. You want to talk about it?" Dutch thanked the lady for the coffee, then focused his attention on Luke.

He'd known Dutch long enough to accept the man could sometimes read his mind, a disquieting ability when all Luke wanted was to rid his thoughts of a certain woman.

"There's nothing to talk about besides finishing the job you started and getting out of Denver." Luke's words were terse, devoid of the usual charm Dutch had come to expect from his friend.

"Good morning, gentlemen." Dutch and Luke glanced up as Tom approached and took a seat. "Have I missed anything?"

"Not a thing." Dutch shot a look at Luke, not believing for a minute Luke wasn't troubled by something, but he let it go. "I'll tell you about it while we eat."

The reason for Dutch's request they help him became clear as he explained the assignment. In Luke's mind, Pinkerton should have sent additional men long before now.

"The rustling had been going on for months before Gus Salter and his son, Elgin, gave up trying to find the culprits on their own and contacted Pinkerton. I spoke to everyone on the ranch, the local sheriff and his deputies, plus anybody else who might have ideas on who is behind the thefts. What I found has not been discussed with Salter or anyone else." Dutch sipped his coffee, his expression grave as he guessed what Salter's reaction would be when he explained his conclusions.

"Who do you think is behind the rustling?" Luke asked.

"His foreman, Bob Bray, along with some of Salter's men. The man's been with him for over twenty years."

"Shit," Luke mumbled. "I hope you have a good amount of proof before approaching the old man."

"I do, including the testimony of Bray's lady friend."

Tom and Luke glanced at Dutch, wondering how much they could rely on her story.

"She's reliable, if that's what you're worried about. Her name's Nell Deeds, and she works for Salter as his cook and housekeeper. Been there a few years. She and Bray have been seeing each other a while, but Salter knows nothing of it. Seems Bray got careless and began confiding in her."

"About the rustling?" Luke asked.

Dutch nodded. "It took her some time, but she finally told me what he'd confessed to her." Dutch signaled to the server for more coffee, crossed his arms, and leaned back in his chair. "Messy business."

"How many men is he using, and how do you want to proceed?" Tom asked.

"I believe it's a small group. A few men from the ranch and maybe a couple others. They cut out small groups and drive them to a predetermined location. There, the buyer uses his own men to rebrand the same night. They're not just stealing from Salter. Bray and his men are hitting the neighboring ranchers, just not in the same numbers. It's been quiet as of late, which makes me think they're due to hit again soon. I want to ride out today and let Salter know what I've found and introduce you two. This is what I have in mind."

Splendor, Montana

"They took at least one chicken, dried beans, and flour. Don't know how one person could carry it all." Hiram Frey tossed his hat on Gabe's desk. He and his brother, Frank, made the journey into town to seek the sheriff's help after two more weeks of missing supplies. So far, from what they could determine, the thief hadn't taken any livestock. The brothers believed they'd eventually lose cattle and horses if the culprits weren't stopped.

"You heard anything from Noah or Luke? Those boys missing stuff, too?" Frank paced back and forth in front of Gabe's desk, none too happy they had to take a day away from the ranch and ride to town.

"A few days ago, Noah told me a sack of beans and a shovel were missing. Luke left for Big Pine almost two weeks ago, but I'll ride out and check his place. Did either of you see any tracks?"

"Nothing. Whoever they are, they're like ghosts. No noise, no tracks, just missing supplies." Hiram grabbed his hat and settled it on his head.

"I'll ride out to Luke's place. We'll need to get a group of men together from your ranch and the Pelletier place to search the area."

"Let us know what you need. We want this stopped." Frank stepped outside, followed by Hiram, and headed straight for the livery to speak with Noah.

Gabe watched them leave, baffled by the strange thefts. No cash or other valuables were missing, which meant whoever did this needed the food. All of it pointed to the Blackfoot camp north of Pelletier land.

He guessed the village consisted of less than a hundred people and, for the most part, they lived in peace with the neighboring ranchers. Their chief, Running Bear, would oftentimes seek to trade for what his people needed.

A group led by a renegade warrior splintered off over a year ago after a dispute with Running Bear. Long Feather had no use for the whites. He and his band were suspected of attacking settlers and wagon trains in the northern part of the territory over the past year. They'd swoop in, steal what they could, kill the men, and capture the women and children. There had been no survivors on more than one attack. If Long Feather's band needed anything, it wouldn't be a bag of beans or hardtack. They'd steal cattle or horses, not basic supplies.

Gabe grabbed his coat and hat, then walked outside toward Blackheart, the stallion he'd had for years. He'd ride to the Pelletier ranch, talk with Dax, then go to Luke's place and check around. He hoped to avoid making a trip to Running Bear's camp, but would if needed.

He was so lost in his own thoughts, he almost missed the small child who ran out in front of his horse. Gabe reined the large stallion to a halt with a quick move and looked down to see a frightened Mary staring up at him, wide-eyed.

"Mary!" Ginny ran from the boardinghouse, Suzanne right behind her, and grabbed her sister by the collar, pulling her away from the horse. "I'm so sorry, Sheriff. She knows better than to run out like that." She glared down at Mary, who shook under her grasp. Ginny's heart still pounded from the fear at seeing Mary run toward the huge animal.

Gabe slid to the ground and knelt in front of the frightened child. "Are you all right, Mary?"

She didn't speak, but nodded once. He could sense how scared she felt and didn't want to upset her even more.

"I'm sure Ginny has told you how dangerous it is to run out into the street, right?"

She nodded again, trying to hide behind her sister's skirt.

"You won't do it again, will you?" Gabe asked in a low, calm voice.

Mary shook her head.

Gabe stood and glanced at Suzanne, then Ginny. They walked to the side, away from the passing wagons and horses.

"Appears she'll be fine." He looked down the street toward the new saloon. They'd made considerable progress in a short time. Gabe figured it would be open for business in another week. "What do you think of the new place?" He directed his question to Suzanne, nodding toward the building as he continued to watch the men work.

She took a breath, her heart settling down from the scare. "To tell you the truth, I'm not real comfortable about it since no one seems to know who owns it."

"Horace Clausen does, but he isn't talking."

"I understand Horace has to honor the owner's wishes. All the same, it doesn't seem right. Besides, who's going to work there? He'll need at least one bartender, serving girls, and well...you know." Suzanne did wonder if he planned to have the same upstairs services Amos offered. "You don't think King Tolbert is behind it, do you?"

"Could be. Clausen did say the owner is out of Big Pine and Tolbert owns considerable property around there." Gabe turned his gaze back to Suzanne and Ginny. "Guess I'd better get going. Hiram and Frank have had more thefts, and I need to find out if Dax or Luke are missing anything."

"Is Luke back from Denver?" Ginny hadn't heard anything about him returning, yet her heart skipped a beat at the mention of his name.

"I doubt he'll be back for several more weeks. It's a long trek from here to Denver." He swung up on Blackheart and tipped his hat at the ladies before heading north toward the Pelletier ranch.

"You know the empty building at the end of the street, next to the general store?" Suzanne asked Ginny as each took one of Mary's hands and walked toward the boardinghouse.

"Yes."

"A new restaurant is opening in there within a week. One of the settler families who came in when you did has been working on it." Suzanne's voice sounded cautious and weary.

Ginny stopped as her gaze flew down the street, surprised at the revelation. "I haven't heard anything about it, or noticed anyone working inside. Who is the family?"

"Percy Slater and his wife. Gabe mentioned it to me a couple weeks ago. They've been working nights, and since all the stores down at that end of town close up by sundown, no one noticed what they were doing—except Gabe. He spotted them entering in the back during his rounds. Slater told him they plan to serve breakfast and dinner at first, maybe add supper service if the others go well. I'm telling you this as I don't know how the place will affect my restaurant."

A knot formed in Ginny's stomach at the thought that Suzanne might lose business. Perhaps enough to impact Ginny's job.

Suzanne saw the concern on Ginny's face and reached out to touch her arm. "I'll let you know if I need to make changes. For now, don't worry too much about it. I just thought you should know."

The words didn't ease Ginny's fear. First a new saloon and now a new restaurant. Both could impact her and Mary. She couldn't afford to lose even one hour at either place. Well, she'd just have to wait, like Amos and Suzanne were doing, and pray all would go well.

"I'll ride with you." Dax didn't like what Gabe had told him about the continued thefts at Noah's place and the Frey ranch. There'd been no time to ride over to Luke's as he'd planned. Now he had no choice.

Hank had told him about the change in the daily egg count. Every few days he'd find no more than a dozen eggs when he expected to see three times as much.

They covered the short distance from the ranch house to Luke's place in little time. Both men reined to a stop fifty yards from the porch at the sight of the front door standing open and what appeared to be a broken window.

Gabe pulled out his pistol as he slid from Blackheart. "Better check it out."

"I'll circle around back." Dax moved behind the shrubs and trees surrounding the house. He guessed whoever had entered would be long gone by now.

Gabe climbed the three steps and stopped next to the open door. He glanced around, seeing Dax make his way to the back.

"Anyone here?" It didn't surprise Gabe when he got no response. He repeated his question, then entered, taking in the sparse furnishings in the front area, then moving toward the kitchen. Nothing caught his attention, except a cupboard standing open at one end of the room. He turned to check the bedroom when Dax entered through the back door.

"What have you found?"

"Cupboard doors are open, but I can't tell if anything is missing." Gabe walked to the bedroom to see sheets, blankets, and pillows missing. He holstered his gun before returning to the kitchen.

"Luke brought over sugar, flour, beans, coffee, and some fruit Rachel had put up. I don't find any of it on the shelves." Dax closed the cupboard doors.

"Bed's been stripped. There might be some clothes missing, but you'd have to check to be sure."

Dax walked through the rest of the house. Foodstuff, bedding, and a few clothes were all he found missing. The answer seemed obvious.

"Someone's living up in the caves."

Gabe took one more look around. "That's my guess. I'll need some of your men, along with some from the Frey ranch. If I can get enough help, we might be able to cover a good-sized area in two to three days."

"Blackfoot?" Dax asked.

"Hell if I know. We'd better check around outside, see if we can find any tracks. Neither Hiram nor Frank have found anything, but they're certain it's more than one person. Noah believes the same. By the looks of what's missing here, I'd say they're right. No one person could carry all that's missing from each place."

They circled the house, then concentrated on the path the men had created to the creek. A few feet wide, it contained enough loose rock to hide most tracks.

"Look at this," Gabe called as he crouched down.

Dax squatted next to him. "They dragged something along here."

"Some kind of tool. Strange there aren't any boot prints." Gabe glanced at Dax, knowing they both had come to the same conclusion.

"It has to be a group from Running Bear's camp."

"Or Long Feather's band, although they're quite a ways north. I've never heard of them taking much besides cattle and horses." Gabe stood and looked around. "Guess I'd better talk to Running Bear."

"I'd hold off on it until we've had a chance to search the caves. Bull knows where a good number of them are located."

"So do Hiram and Frank," Gabe added.

"Good. When do you want to start?"

Chapter Twelve

Big Pine, Montana

"It's lovely, Frederick." Felicity walked around the house Rick had purchased at the edge of town. The place had been vacant for months, allowing him to get it at a cheap price. It stood a few blocks from her home.

After the last job, Rick took Flatnose up on his offer to run the ranch while he spent time in Big Pine. He hadn't yet told his partner of his decision to quit the life they'd started a few years before. Rick had as much gold as any man needed and he wanted out, away from the constant dread Flatnose would lose control and kill again.

He planned to return to the Star Ranch one more time—to pick up his share of the gold.

"I still need furniture, and there's some repair work that needs to be done from standing empty for so long." He walked to a window, pulled back the curtain, and looked out. The lots were large, allowing for more privacy than the smaller homes built close together near the center of town. He turned toward Felicity, admiring her beauty, wondering at her attraction to a man like him.

He watched as she moved from the front living area toward the parlor, then the study. She opened the door and stepped back.

"Oh, they left all the books." She walked straight to the massive bookshelf, ran her fingers along the spines until her eyes locked on one and she pulled it out. "Look, Frederick. The first volume of *Great Expectations* by Charles Dickens." She opened it reverently, turned a few pages, her expression bright and excited. "I wonder if the other two volumes are here." She scanned the shelves again, finding them after a few minutes of searching. "Have you read these? They're wonderful."

Her enthusiasm over something as simple as a book touched Rick, and he found his breath hitch as her broad smile flashed at him.

"Uh...no. I've never read it." He had no intention of falling in love again or trying to reclaim the life he'd lost to the murderous posse years before. Meeting Felicity had changed him and he found the hope he thought was lost. "I'm going upstairs. Take as much time as you want, then join me."

Rick strode up the stairs at a slow pace, admiring the wooden banister, recalling the night he and his wife had laid in bed and spoke of the day they'd be able to afford a home such as this. It had been a silly dream back then, both knowing he'd never earn enough for anything more than what they already had, yet it had been a good dream. One that had turned into a nightmare a few days later.

He walked to the end of the hall and pushed open the door to a large bedroom, furnished with an ornate four-poster bed. The first time he'd seen it, Rick found himself conjuring up an image of he and Felicity tangled together under the sheets. He wanted the image to become reality.

"Here you are." Felicity walked up beside him, her eyes wide. "What a beautiful bedroom." As she'd done in the study, she walked around, running her fingers over the furniture, noticing each small detail. "You've found a wonderful home. I'm sure you'll be quite happy here." She looked at him without expectations, simply enjoying the fact he'd found what he wanted.

She stopped in front of an oil painting of a stallion and studied it. Rick walked up behind her, wrapped his arms around her waist, and pulled her to him, nuzzling her neck.

"You could share this with me," he whispered.

He heard her sigh, then nervous laughter as she turned in his arms and pushed back a little to look up at him.

"Marry me, Felicity." Rick hadn't expected to ask her today, maybe never. He watched as her gaze moved from him to the ground. Her hesitation already signaled the answer.

"I care about you a great deal, Frederick. It's just, well... I'm not ready to remarry. I need more time." Her husband died a few years before, leaving her comfortable, if not wealthy. She lived a simple life, had become involved in the community, and was well-liked. He knew she had no reason to be tied to a man.

"I'll give you as much time as you need." He kissed her, then stepped away. "I'm finished here. Let me take you to dinner."

She let out a breath, her relief at not being pressured obvious. "I'd like that."

He helped her into the carriage he'd purchased the day before and drove to a restaurant she'd mentioned wanting to try. As the town's population swelled from the discovery of gold, the number of good restaurants, hotels, and theatres expanded, allowing residents to have a choice not enjoyed in most frontier cities.

Rick placed his hands on her waist to help her down, then wrapped her hand around his arm as they entered. A man dressed in a black suit approached.

"May I help you?" the steward asked.

"A table for two, please." Rick looked behind the steward to see a room half-filled with people, then went still at the sound of a man's voice behind him.

"Excuse me. I'm sorry to interrupt, but I'm to meet Sheriff Sterling. Is he here?" The question was directed at the steward, but the voice sliced through Rick as if it were a knife piercing his heart. His grip tightened on Felicity's hand, causing her to let out a gasp before he let her arm drop from his and turned slowly. The man's look of surprise mirrored Rick's as their eyes locked.

"Sheriff Duncan." Rick's voice held distinct disdain. He didn't hold out his hand, keeping his arms rigid at his sides.

"Marlowe. I haven't seen you since..." Ezra Duncan's eyes clouded as if he'd been gripped by a memory from his past—one which haunted him.

"Nebraska, I believe." The chill in Rick's voice remained, but he made no further comment to the man who led the posse that killed his wife and son.

A cough from behind Rick had both men looking up at the steward standing a few feet away, his eyes on Ezra. "When you're ready, I'll show you to the table where Sheriff Sterling is seated."

"Excuse me," Ezra said to Rick. He looked as if he wanted to say more, but stopped himself and followed the steward to his table.

"Who is he, Frederick?"

He glanced down at Felicity's worried expression, his lips forming a thin line. "Just a ghost from my past. One I'd like to forget."

They ate in silence, Rick's gaze darting between Felicity and the table where Sterling and Duncan sat. He wondered at the lawman's presence in Big Pine, as well as the reason for his meeting with Sterling. He tried not to let it affect his time with Felicity, but found it hard to keep the hate from his mind as he watched the man who ruined his life sitting so comfortably across the room.

Duncan had been steadfast in his condemnation of Marlowe, certain he'd been a part of the gang which terrorized the small Nebraska community. To his credit, he had apologized for the killings of Marlowe's family, but his belief in Marlowe's guilt remained firm. Only when two of the gang members, arrested for their part in brutalizing the residents, testified Rick had no part in any of their activities had Duncan relented, finally admitting they'd been after the wrong man.

"Would you care for anything else?" the steward asked.

"No, we're finished here," Rick replied.

The steward moved to the next table as Rick laid his napkin down. He had to get away from Duncan and memories of the past. He'd take Felicity home, change clothes, then ride to his ranch where he could put the man's face behind him. By the time he retrieved his gold and returned, Ezra Duncan would be gone from Big Pine and out of Rick's life once again.

Denver, Colorado

"You believe they'll strike again tonight?" Gus Salter asked, hands on his hips and irritation in his voice. They'd said nothing to convince the rancher his head man for over twenty years was responsible for the rustling.

Although Dutch had told Gus and Elgin Salter he had a reputable informant, he hadn't confided the identity of the person who'd supplied the details. Neither knew Nell Deeds, their cook and housekeeper, was privy to the foreman's plans.

"Yes, sir." Dutch leaned over a map of the local area. "From what we know, they plan to drive cattle from this pasture to the property line here." He indicated a spot on the boundary between Salter land and an adjoining ranch. "Luke and Tom will be at this location, along with the sheriff's men. I'll follow Bray."

"We'll go with you." Gus glanced at Dutch.

"It would be better for you and Elgin to stick with Luke and Tom. It's easier to spot three men tracking you than just one. We don't want Bray to get suspicious."

Salter cut a look at Dutch. "I'll stay with your men, but Elgin will ride with you."

Dutch glanced at Luke and Tom, who both nodded.

"All right." He looked at Elgin. "I expect they'll start out around midnight."

"I'll be ready," Elgin said. The idea Bob Bray led the group of rustlers still ate at him. Bray was like a second father to him. He found it hard to believe the man he'd grown up around would betray them like this.

"How long would it take to drive cattle between the two locations?" Luke asked.

"If they keep moving? An hour, maybe a little longer." Gus paced to the window, watching Bray with a group of ranch hands. Bob was his closest friend, his ally. Sadness and disbelief engulfed him as he kept his gaze fixed on the group outside, wondering what had changed between them.

He turned back to the others. "We set?"

"I believe we are, Mr. Salter. I'll be back after supper. I suggest you meet Luke and Tom in town later tonight."

The three walked to their horses, glancing at Bray and the other men near the barn. Salter had introduced them as businessmen from St. Louis, and Bray hadn't indicated he believed otherwise. If it weren't for Nell, Luke wouldn't have guessed the foreman to be the gang leader. He couldn't imagine learning any of the Pelletier men were involved in rustling cattle.

Dutch glanced over his shoulder as they rode from the ranch. "We need to meet with the sheriff, make sure we're ready for tonight."

"I'm concerned about Salter." Luke didn't like the look on the rancher's face when they left.

"How so?" Dutch asked.

"Someone needs to stick close to him so he doesn't do anything rash."

"Such as take a shot at Bray?" Tom asked.

"He's been adamant Bray's not involved. I think we need to be prepared for a reaction from Salter when he learns he's been deceived by his closest friend." Luke rested a hand on the butt of his gun, wondering how he'd take the news. An image of Bull crossed his mind. He and the ranch hand had become close over the last months, at least as close as Luke would allow himself to get to one of their men. If Bull ever did what they suspected Bray of doing, Luke would be outraged enough to confront him and take matters into his own hands. He hoped Salter's reaction would be different.

"One of you needs to stay near him, make sure he keeps his temper under control." Dutch agreed with Luke and expected either Salter or his son to go after Bray once they'd confirmed the truth.

It had been a long few weeks. Luke had hoped to be heading back to Splendor by now, surprised at how much he missed the ranch. If all went well tonight, they'd be on the trail within a couple days.

Dutch and Elgin positioned themselves behind a group of boulders about a half-mile from the smaller of the two bunkhouses. Only the foreman and a few ranch hands slept in the building, while everyone else occupied the larger one. According to Nell, every man where Bray bunked was involved.

If their information proved correct, Bray and his men would have to pass right by Dutch and Elgin to get to the herd.

"Riders coming," Dutch said, indicating with the end of his rifle.

"They're too far away to make out their faces," Elgin murmured, still hoping Bray wouldn't be among them. His hope faded as they rode closer. He recognized Bray's horse and the set of the man's hat—full brimmed and cocked to one side. He let out a mumbled curse at the realization.

"We'll let them get ahead of us before following." Dutch hoped they'd get through the night without anyone getting hurt.

Within an hour, they'd followed Bray and his men to the herd. Even though the rustlers kept a steady pace, it took another hour before the cattle approached the spot where Luke and the others were supposed to be waiting. Dutch hoped his men and the sheriff were in place, ready to arrest the rustlers.

Luke heard the cattle approaching before he saw them. They'd guessed Bray would be moving under a hundred head. He and Tom had scouted the area, locating the buyer and his men waiting in a nearby valley. The sheriff had sent a few men to keep watch on them while everyone else stayed put, ready to close in on Bray.

"Can you tell if one of them is Bray?" Luke asked Salter as the herd drew closer.

"It's Bob all right. No mistake." The resignation in the man's voice signified how his friend's betrayal wounded him.

"We'll let them pass by, then follow behind. We want them to reach the buyer and his men before making our presence known," Luke said as the sheriff and Tom joined them.

"Looks to be Bob Bray all right." The sheriff had been as adamant as Gus Salter in his defense of the ranch foreman. "He's the last person I'd have thought would do this to you, Gus."

Salter didn't respond. No words could describe the confusion and pain he felt at learning the truth.

As the herd approached, Luke could hear Bray yelling orders, making sure not a single head was lost in the transfer to the buyer. He looked toward the front of the herd as it approached the valley, spotting riders moving forward. He guessed those men worked for the buyer.

"Let's move behind them," the sheriff said, wanting to close off any retreat Bray might have. His men would approach from the other side, making a tight circle around the cattle, as well as the rustlers. He hoped they'd surrender without a shot fired. No one needed to end up dead tonight.

As Luke, Tom, Salter, and the others closed in, a shout came from behind them. The men turned to see a rider approaching at a quick pace, his gun drawn. Luke recognized Elgin Salter. Gus yelled at his son to stop, but his words had no impact on the young man, who flew toward Bray.

The noise of the herd muffled Elgin's shouts until he was almost upon Bray. He raised his gun to fire as a shot rang out, the bullet catching Elgin in his shoulder, toppling him from his horse. Within seconds, shots rang out across the valley, causing the herd to stampede first one direction then another as the wild-eyed animals tried to avoid the gunfire.

Luke kept the barrel of his rifle locked on Bray as the man pulled his gun and aimed at the sheriff.

"Don't do it, Bob. Give up!" Gus yelled, trying to be heard over the sounds of gunfire and cattle. His warning fell on deaf ears.

Bray brought his horse around and redirected his aim at Salter. Before he could get a shot off, a lone bullet ripped through the night, catching Bray square in the chest. He dropped his gun, clutching at the wound, then fell from his horse.

Salter shot a look at Luke, nodded once, then rode straight to his son, who lay on the ground. He slid from his horse and let out a breath as he confirmed the bullet had only grazed his son's shoulder.

"What the hell were you thinking, riding in like that?" Anger and relief tinged Gus' voice as he pulled off his shirt, using it to stop the bleeding.

Elgin closed his eyes, not knowing how to answer. He hadn't planned to ride at Bray. The anger and bewilderment he felt boiled to the surface when he saw the other group of rustlers moving toward the herd. Something snapped and he'd felt powerless to contain his rage.

"Why would he do it, Pa?" His voice was strained and Gus could see tears form in his son's eyes. The older man felt a slice of pain rip through his chest.

"I don't know, son. I just don't know."

Dutch joined them, kneeling down next to Elgin. "Looks like he'll be all right." When Gus didn't respond, he continued. "A few rustlers got away. The others who survived are under arrest. You may want to check on Bray. He's hanging on, but probably not for long."

Gus pushed from the ground and walked in slow strides toward Luke and the sheriff, who knelt beside Bray. He looked down, knowing Bob wouldn't make it. He pulled off his hat and ran a shaking hand through his hair before dropping to his knees.

Luke motioned to the sheriff. Both stood and walked away, leaving Salter and Bray alone.

Bob's labored breathing turned into a series of wracking coughs. His eyes opened to slits, landing on Gus, who fought to control his emotions.

"Why'd you do it, Bob?" Gus choked out, grabbing his friend's hand when he reached out to him.

"For Nell..." he managed before the pain gripped him again.

"Nell? I don't understand."

Bray forced his eyes open. "Home... She wants a home." His voice had turned reedy, his words faint.

"I don't understand. What home?" Gus implored, trying to understand the motivation behind the actions.

Bob opened his eyes once more, but nothing else came before his head rolled to the side and his body stilled.

Chapter Thirteen

Nell sat before Gus and Elgin, wringing a handkerchief between her hands. Sobs shook her small frame as she tried to explain what she knew about Bob's decision to steal from his friends—men he'd always considered his family.

"Bob wanted to build a house...for me. He'd never saved much, never believing he'd marry." She took a breath, trying to control the tears. "He needed land and couldn't figure how else to get it. I begged him to go to you, but he refused. I told him I'd tell you myself, but he said you'd never take my word over his."

"Hell," Gus blurted out as he stood and paced the room. "I would've given him the land and built him a house. Why didn't he come to me?"

"Pride." She wiped tears from her face. "It's my fault. If I hadn't said I'd marry him if we had a home, none of this would've happened."

Elgin, his wounded shoulder bandaged, took one of her hands in his. "Don't blame yourself, Nell. The decision to steal our cattle was Bob's choice. He could've spoken with Pa or gone to the bank for a loan, but he didn't." Elgin helped Nell stand, then escorted her to her room where she could grieve in private.

Dutch, Tom, and Luke stood a few feet away, watching and listening to the heartbreaking conversation. Nothing excused Bray's actions. Still, it was hard to hear what transpired and remain unmoved.

Luke found himself wondering if any of the men he and Dax trusted would make the same decision if they needed money. He ticked off the names in his head—Rude, Ellis, Tat, Johnny, Bull. He couldn't comprehend any of them making the same choice as Bray.

Dutch walked up to Gus and extended his hand. "I guess our time here is over. We wish it had ended different."

Gus locked his gaze on Dutch. "I didn't believe any of it, right up until I saw Bob ride up with the cattle. You boys were right." He accepted Dutch's hand. "Be assured I'll let Pinkerton know."

The three rode back to town in silence, each lost in their own thoughts. By all standards, the assignment had been a success, yet each felt the sting of the void left at the Salter ranch where no one seemed to come out a winner.

Dutch planned to stay in Denver until new orders arrived. Tom and Luke would begin their return trip to Big Pine the following morning—Tom to resume his search for those who stole the gold, while Luke rode back to Splendor. Each expected it to be a more treacherous journey than their ride south. Several storms had passed over the mountains since their arrival. They'd also learned of an attack on a new fort under construction in northern Wyoming. They could avoid the fort, but it wouldn't be as easy to find a way around the snow, and each anticipated the trip to take twice as long.

They grabbed breakfast before Luke stopped at the telegraph office to send a message to Dax, letting him know of his return. He couldn't believe how much he looked forward to getting back to his own place, the peace and quiet of the house tucked up against the forest and facing Wildfire Creek. As much as he enjoyed the occasional Pinkerton assignment, the daily routine of ranch life, his family and friends, and the serenity of his home would always be what drew him back.

Splendor, Montana

"I understand, Amos. Of course you have to make some changes." The knot in Ginny's stomach formed as soon as she arrived at the Rose. Al told her Amos needed to speak with her right away.

The new saloon had opened two weeks before, drawing considerable attention, enticing customers away from the Rose. Amos had weathered the first Saturday night with less than half the normal business. When the second Saturday came and went with an even larger drop, everyone knew he'd have to do something. The first, and most obvious choice, would be to let Ginny go. After all, the women upstairs could serve drinks, plus provide services she was unwilling to offer.

"I'm sorry, Ginny. I just don't have a choice." Amos held out a small pouch. "There's enough there to keep you going for a week or so. It's not much, but..." His voice trailed off.

She took the pouch, stuffing it into her reticule and then into the pocket of her new, and quite warm, coat—the one which had arrived several weeks before, along with a beautiful wool dress from a store in Big Pine. Even though a note hadn't been included, no one had to tell her who sent them. At first, she'd been furious, feeling the same sense of indebtedness as when Luke paid Doc Worthington and fronted her missed pay at the Rose. As the days passed and the temperatures dropped, she became grateful for the gift. Suzanne had told her Luke wouldn't have sent it unless he believed she needed it, and he'd expect nothing from her. Now, weeks later, she kept it close, day and night, sometimes wrapping it around her for warmth at night.

"Thank you. It's more than I expected." Her voice cracked as she offered a weak smile to her former boss. At least she had work at the boardinghouse until she could find another job. She had no idea where, though. The increase in settlers deciding to make Splendor their home made it harder to find work than when she'd first arrived. She turned to leave, then stopped at Amos' words.

"If I can, I'll hire you back."

She would've thanked him again if her throat hadn't chosen that moment to close up. All she could do was nod before walking out. Ginny didn't stop and talk to any of the friends she'd made at the saloon, although all of them watched as she left. She could feel their eyes on her and knew each understood what had happened, thanking God it hadn't been them.

When Ginny had walked into the Rose, the sun had already dropped behind the nearby mountains. As she walked out, the night had turned dark, the only light provided by kerosene lamps shining through the occasional window.

She glanced across the street at the new saloon. From the look of it, there must be a hundred lamps burning inside. The sounds of a piano drifted through the doors, almost taunting her, and Ginny found herself drawn toward it. She hadn't allowed herself a peek inside since they'd finished building. It opened with little fanfare, the owner still a mystery.

The bartender and several saloon girls, young and alluring, showed up by stage a few days before the first drink was served, stepping onto the dirt street as if they were royalty. Belle and the other girls at the Rose had snickered, telling each other they were much prettier than the new arrivals and doing their best to believe they had nothing to worry about. As the nights passed, more men were drawn toward the lively new addition—all except the men from Redemption's Edge. They stayed loyal to the Rose.

Ginny crossed the street, then walked the last few feet to the edge of one of the saloon windows. No one stood outside and she made the decision to take one quick look, then leave. She peered through the sparkling clean glass. All tables were filled, patrons sitting elbow-to-elbow at the bar. The stairs were ornate with red carpet leading to the second floor, and a huge chandelier hung from the high ceiling. She counted six girls, two more than at the Rose, all in glittering dresses of various colors. Ginny recognized most of the men and a sadness washed over her at how easy it had been to leave the Rose behind.

"May I help you?"

Ginny jumped at the deep voice behind her. She swung around, a hand to her chest, to face a tall, wide-shouldered man dressed all in black, except for a thin, red ribbon tie under his shirt collar. The patch over his left eye being his most distinguishing characteristic.

"I...uh...," she stammered, partly from being caught and partly from the intimidating man before her. She cleared her throat and tried again. "I was just walking past and heard the music."

"You're Miss Sorensen, correct?"

Her eyes widened in surprise. "How do you know my name?" She took a step back, almost tripping before strong hands reached out to steady her.

"Careful there." His deep chuckle held no malice. "I've heard your name mentioned by some of the customers. Not many saloons hire a girl who doesn't work upstairs. I got curious and came by to see for myself, much like you're doing tonight."

"You came by the Rose?"

"I wasn't dressed quite like this at the time, but yes, I stopped by to check on what I'd heard, and try to convince Al to come work for me."

Al had never mentioned being offered a job. "He obviously turned you down."

"Flat. Didn't even ask how much I'd pay him. So, why are you here, Miss Sorensen?" He stepped a couple of inches closer, crowding her space. For the first time Ginny felt a flicker of unease.

"No real reason, except curiosity. Well, I'd better get home. It was nice to meet you, Mr..."

"My apologies for not introducing myself sooner. I'm Nicholas Barnett." He made a slight bow as he tipped his hat.

"Do you own the saloon?"

"It's called the Dixie Saloon."

"You're from the South?" The name surprised her. His voice held no hint of a southern accent. She'd guessed him to be from New York or Boston.

He cocked his head, as if deciding whether or not to answer. "My partner is."

"I see." She pulled her coat tighter, feeling her face chill in the cold air. "It's nice to meet you, Mr. Barnett."

"The pleasure is mine, Miss Sorensen. I hope to see you again." He stepped back, watching as she made her way toward the boardinghouse, where he already knew she lived with her sister, Mary. Nick had learned quite a bit about the young woman and decided he admired her. He had no idea why he hoped she'd never be forced through circumstance to offer services other than serving whiskey or food.

Ginny shivered at the cold wind, which had picked up as she approached the boardinghouse. She pushed the door open, seeing Suzanne's brows arch in surprise as she poured coffee for a couple at a table near the front. Ginny shook her head in a slight side-to-side motion and held the palms of her hands out. Suzanne nodded once, letting her know she understood the silent message, then returned to her customers.

Ginny shrugged off her coat, her mind wandering to thoughts of Nicholas Barnett as she walked down the hall to her and Mary's room. It had taken a while for her heart to settle down after he'd startled her. Everything about him intimidated and fascinated her. He knew too much and offered little in the way of answers. At least she'd learned the Dixie belonged to him and his partner.

She tossed her coat on the bed, then walked to the kitchen where Mary sat at the table. She ruffled her sister's hair and gave her a quick kiss on the cheek as Suzanne came in from the dining area.

"What can I do?" she asked, humbled at the hectic pace Suzanne kept up each day until the last customer walked out the door.

"Grab four plates and add potatoes and vegetables." Suzanne sliced thick pieces of roast and set one on each plate Ginny held out to her. "They're for the four people at the corner window."

Ginny made quick work of delivering the meals, then returned to the kitchen as Suzanne cut six pieces of pie.

"I get them ready early as most of my supper customers order it."

The routine continued for another hour until Suzanne locked the front door. She poured a cup of coffee and took a seat next to Mary, watching as Ginny dried the last plate.

"Tell me what happened tonight."

"Amos decided he could no longer afford me." She sat on the other side of Mary and folded her hands in her lap. "He gave me a week's worth of pay, which he didn't have to do."

"Well, it's something anyway. The new saloon must be having a big impact on his business."

"You should see how few men come in now that the Dixie is open."

Ginny needed to bring up the subject which most worried her. "I know you don't have enough work to use me more than you already do. I'll start looking for another job right away."

Suzanne took a deep breath, wishing her situation were different than Amos'. "I wish I did have enough work to pay you cash. Suppers are still busy around here, but since the other restaurant opened, my breakfast and dinner customers have dropped quite a bit. The new place serves a variety of meals, and I just offer one choice for dinner and one for supper. I don't think I can manage adding more, and I can't afford to hire anyone to help."

Her situation had been perfect. Ginny worked for room and board. The cash she made came from Amos, which now meant there'd be nothing available to pay for the doctor, clothes, or the house she hoped to buy someday.

"There must be some way to make the change. I'd be happy to help you add more menu items until I find another job."

"Let me think about it."

Ginny sat forward and set her arms on the table. "I met the owner tonight."

Suzanne cocked an eyebrow. "Of the Dixie Saloon?"

"Yes. Have you met him?"

"I heard the owner hadn't come to town. There's a manager who arrived before the saloon opened. Tall, wears a black hat, has an eye patch. A little rough-looking."

Ginny smiled at the description. "That's him. His name is Nicholas Barnett. When I asked about the saloon's name, he said his partner is from the South."

Suzanne thought over this information. Being from the South would leave out Tolbert as a partner, or anyone else she would have guessed. "How did you meet him?"

Ginny stroked Mary's hair as her sister placed her arms on the table and lowered her head. She glanced up at Suzanne, still a little embarrassed at being caught peering into the Dixie. "I heard the music from their piano as I left the Rose and decided to look through one of the windows. The saloon was full, not even any space at the bar. I didn't hear him come up behind me."

"So tell me what you thought of him."

"I'm not sure, we didn't talk too long. He seemed curious about me, although he already knew my name and that I worked for Amos." Ginny thought a moment, trying to decide her feelings about the man. "He's somewhat intimidating."

"I saw him in the bank, meeting with Horace Clausen, but didn't actually meet him. He appeared to be about the same age as King Tolbert."

"You may be right." Ginny stifled a yawn. She hadn't realized how exhausted she felt. "I'd better put Mary to bed."

"Goodnight, Ginny." Suzanne poured another cup of coffee, not yet ready for sleep, even though her body protested the long hours. Over the years, since her husband and daughter died in a massive snowstorm, she found peace could only be achieved by working long hours. She pushed herself until exhaustion took over, leaving little time for the nightmares. Besides the boardinghouse, her one other solace had come from Ginny and Mary.

For a while, between the time Abigail Tolbert's mother died and King sent her away to school, he'd allow his daughter to visit Suzanne in her kitchen. Abby's departure to the school back east had created another void in her life. With Ginny losing her job at the Wild

Rose, something told Suzanne she should begin emotionally preparing for another change.

Chapter Fourteen

"I'm afraid she's not improving. At least not enough to resume her duties at the ranch." Uncle Charles sat in the kitchen with Rachel and Hank after examining Bernice. As always, the doctor had presented a positive front to his patient, although he saw the doubt in her eyes. The illness had taken a tremendous toll on the older woman.

Rachel filled cups with coffee and took a seat. She'd been afraid of this ever since his last visit. At least Bernice hadn't gotten any worse.

"Is there anything more I can do?" Hank asked, wrapping both of his calloused hands around the warm cup.

"You're doing all you can. I've no doubt she'll improve given time and rest. I just don't believe she'll ever be able to handle the same workload as before." He looked at Rachel. "I'd suggest you start looking for a replacement, unless you plan to handle all the duties here, as well as your work at the clinic."

"Dax and I have discussed it, and decided to try and find someone from town. Are you aware of anyone who may be looking?"

"Well, now, I did hear a rumor that Amos had to let Ginny go."

Rachel's eyes widened at the news. "Did Ginny tell you that?"

"No. I had breakfast at the boardinghouse before coming out here. Suzanne mentioned it."

"She'd be perfect, except I know Ginny trades her work at the boardinghouse for room and meals. I doubt Suzanne would want to let her go."

"I think it would be wise for you to speak with Suzanne. From what I gather, the new restaurant has cut into her breakfast and dinner business, even though her rooms are filled most nights. The boarders eat there, but many of her regular customers are switching between her and the new place. Having another room available might help her out."

Rachel's mind raced at the news. Ginny would be ideal, except for one factor...Luke.

"I'll speak with Dax tonight, and if he agrees, I'll talk to Suzanne right away. I don't want to approach Ginny until I know Suzanne can afford to lose her."

"I think you may be making too much of it, Dax. Why would Luke object to Ginny taking over Bernice's job? She's a hard worker, and according to Suzanne, a good cook." Rachel couldn't believe her husband's negative reaction on approaching Ginny. Everyone knew how much Amos appreciated having her at the Rose and what a good job she did for Suzanne.

"I'm telling you, Luke will have stronger objections than what you're hearing from me." Dax thought the idea of hiring Ginny both perfect and insane. He turned to Hank, who'd been listening to him and Rachel going back and forth on the idea. "What do you think?"

"Well, I don't know Ginny, so it's hard to answer. From what I've heard, she'd do a good job, and I believe she and Bernice would get along just fine. Of course, Luke did have powerful objections to bringing your friends to his new house, Rachel. I doubt his thoughts have changed."

"Yes, but I asked about visiting his *home*, not about her working here at the ranch. Besides, he's the one who said we should hire the person we think best. He said it should be our decision since he no longer lives here." She refused to back down, her instincts shouting she'd found the perfect solution to their problem. She focused her attention on Dax. "He'll only be around her if he stops by for supper—"

"And when we meet in the study, and when he stops by in the mornings or during the day, and—"

"Fine. I understand you believe Luke wants nothing to do with her, and perhaps you're right. My concern is finding someone who can handle all Bernice's work and is used to sharing space in a busy house." She pushed an errant strand of hair from her face, then crossed her arms. "Do either of you have a better suggestion?"

"Isn't there anyone older who'd be interested? Someone who won't turn the men's heads?" Dax asked.

Rachel dropped her hands to her sides and lowered herself into a nearby chair. "I don't know. Perhaps. Do you honestly believe Ginny's presence here will disrupt the work?"

Dax stood, then walked over to sit next to Rachel, taking her hand in his. "It's Luke I'm concerned about. I've never known him to intentionally put distance between himself and a woman, which he's doing with Ginny. It tells me he either can't stand her, or he's fighting how he feels about her. Which do you think it is?"

"From the few times I've seen them together, it's obvious he's quite attracted to her. At the same time, he's made it clear he has no intention of following up on his feelings. If that's his decision, he should have no problem with her being here."

Dax pinched the bridge of his nose between his thumb and forefinger, accepting he'd already lost the battle. "If you believe this is the best solution, I won't try to stop you. Talk with Suzanne and also with the reverend's wife. Everyone seems to confide in Ruth Paige. Maybe she'll have some suggestions."

Rachel flung her arms around Dax's neck. "Thank you."

"Keep in mind, you'll be the one doing the explaining to Luke."

She dropped her arms, her mouth tilting into a smile. "Why, General, I never thought of you as a coward."

"Hell yes, I'm a coward when it comes to what you're proposing. Remember, I've been on the receiving end of Luke's anger and I don't recommend it."

Rachel couldn't contain a chuckle, picturing two of the most stubborn men she knew going head-to-head. "Fine, just send him to me and I'll battle it out with him." She turned toward the door.

"Where are you going?"

"To town, of course. I don't want to miss an opportunity."

"These are wonderful ideas, Ginny. Preparing one soup and adding a second meat dish each night will give my customers as many choices for dinner and supper as the new place. I'm so glad you persuaded me to listen to you." Suzanne read over the list Ginny prepared once more, adding her own notes.

"Badgered, you mean." She'd finished the last breakfast plate and stacked it with the others. "You were smart to build the root cellar."

"Each time it snows, I pack as much ice as possible in buckets and carry down chunks of ice from the frozen stream. A few of the boys come by after school and help out. I pay them what I can, but they usually just want a slice of pie. In the summer, I can't keep meat for more than a few days without salting it, even though it stays cool down there."

"Hello. Anyone here?"

Suzanne hurried to the front to see Rachel slipping off her hat and coat.

"What a nice surprise. Have you come for breakfast or dinner?" Suzanne asked as she gave her a hug.

"Actually, I hoped you might have one of your cobblers for me to take back to the ranch as a surprise for Dax."

"I have a cherry and an apple. You can have your choice."

"Cherry would be wonderful. I'll buy you a cup of coffee if you have a few minutes to talk."

Suzanne laughed. "I'd love to. It's not often someone buys me a coffee." She walked to the kitchen, emerging a minute later with two cups. "Ginny is getting the cobbler ready for you. Have you heard from Luke?"

"Dax received a telegram a few days ago. Luke said he'd be leaving Denver the following day and hoped to be home within a couple of weeks."

"He must be anxious to get home," Suzanne commented. She knew Ginny would be glad to see him.

"You never know with Luke. He works hard and would never leave if Dax needed him. At heart, though, I believe he craves the excitement of working with Pinkerton." She sipped her coffee, deciding to go ahead with the reason for her visit. "I know you need to get back to work, but I have something important to ask you."

Suzanne sat forward, resting her arms on the table. "I have time now." She listened, without interrupting, as Rachel explained her request.

"I won't approach Ginny if you need her. Please, be honest with me."

Suzanne knew this time would come. Ginny and Mary had been a gift. Now the time had come to the let the gift go and share it with others.

"The truth is...the new restaurant has cut into my business more than I thought it would. As much as I've come to love them, Ginny needs a job where she can earn enough money to save for a place of her own, which is what she wants. It'll take years, but I've no doubt that girl will do it. I can't think of a better place for her to live and work than at your ranch." Although the words were sincere, it didn't stop the ache of regret she felt at losing them. "Would you like to speak with her now?"

Rachel reached across the table and squeezed Suzanne's hand. "Yes, as long as you're sure."

"I am." She stood and walked toward the kitchen as Rachel paced to the front window.

Since she'd entered the boardinghouse, a light snow had begun. She watched the flakes drop to the ground, hoping it wouldn't get worse and compel her to spend the night in Splendor with her uncle.

"Hello, Rachel. Suzanne said you wanted to talk to me." Ginny stepped closer, hands clenched in front of her. "It's not about Luke, is it?"

Rachel saw the worry in her eyes and hurried to answer. "As far as we know, Luke is fine. I've come to speak with you about something else."

They sat at a nearby table, Rachel noticing Ginny still clasped her hands tight.

"Our cook and housekeeper, Bernice, has been ill for quite some time. The doctor believes it will take a while for her to recover, and even then, she'll never be able to do the same amount of work as before. We've made the decision to look for someone to take over her duties, then work with her as she recovers. I understand you may be looking for more work, and thought you might have an interest."

Ginny's expression changed from one of uncertainty to surprise as Rachel spoke. The tension Rachel noticed earlier seemed to ease, replaced by a look of hope.

Ginny cleared her throat, not wanting to anticipate too much. "What would you expect me to do?"

"To be truthful, she does quite a bit for us. Keeps the house clean, makes meals for us and the men, does our laundry... It's a lot for one person."

"I can do it," Ginny blurted out, then sat back, wishing she hadn't been quite so bold.

Rachel's chuckle eased the tension. "Dax and I are certain you can. I help sometimes, and Bernice will be able to help a little as she recovers."

"Would you want me to stay after she gets better?"

"Of course. If all goes well, you'd have the work as long as you want it."

Ginny's mind spun at what Rachel suggested. She had so many questions and she didn't know which one to ask first.

"Would you expect Mary and me to live at the ranch?"

"Yes. We have extra bedrooms downstairs, along the hall to the kitchen. You'll take your meals with us and earn a wage for the work." Rachel fixed her gaze on Ginny, wanting to be sure she fully understood. "It won't be easy. The ranch is growing and we keep adding men. Bernice provides breakfast and supper every day for everyone. She makes dinners for those who are out with the herd, and makes a hot meal at noon for those at the ranch. The laundry isn't much as it's only Dax, Luke, and I."

Luke. Ginny hadn't thought about him being there. Perhaps this wasn't the opportunity she'd first thought.

Rachel could see her expression change at the mention of Luke and hoped it wouldn't cause her to decline the work.

"You don't have any problem working with Luke around, do you?"

Ginny's back straightened and she lifted her chin. She would not let anything, or anyone, stand in the way of this job. "Why should I?"

Rachel wondered if she should voice her thoughts, then decided it best to keep them to herself. "No reason."

"What about Mary's schooling? I don't have a horse or wagon to get her back and forth to school, although I could teach her what I know." Ginny's mother had insisted on her attending school, and she felt fortunate to know how to read, write, and do her numbers. She didn't know if she could do all the work Rachel expected, as well as school Mary.

"Most days I come to town to help Uncle Charles. She's welcome to ride with me. On the days I don't, I'm happy to work with her—if it's agreeable with you."

She'd never dreamed of anything such as this happening. Ginny swallowed the lump in her throat. "I accept, Rachel. When would you want me to start?"

"When would you like to begin?"

"Tomorrow, if someone is available to take us to the ranch," Ginny said, then paused, not believing she hadn't thought of this sooner. "Does Suzanne know?"

"I hope it was all right, but I spoke with her earlier. She has no objections. Someone can be here tomorrow morning to bring you and Mary to the ranch." Rachel walked around the table and pulled Ginny into a hug. "I'm thrilled you want to work for us."

"Your offer is a gift, Rachel. It's what I've prayed for." She stepped back, her eyes misty. "I'd better tell Suzanne and Mary. We'll be ready in the morning." Ginny turned to leave, glancing over her shoulder once before disappearing into the kitchen.

As promised, Ginny and Mary sat in the parlor of the boardinghouse, their two bags packed and ready, as Dax pulled the wagon to a stop. He jumped down, then helped Rachel, who walked inside to see two bright smiles greeting her.

"We're ready!" Mary jumped up and down, excited with the idea of living on a ranch.

"I see you are, Mary," Dax said and picked up the two bags. He looked around, quirking a brow. "Anything else?"

"Just those two bags." Ginny buttoned the top of her coat, wondering if Rachel and Dax had any idea Luke bought it for her. She'd used her small amount of cash to purchase a new coat for Mary, which she buttoned all the way up. "Are you ready to go?"

"Yes, yes!" Mary ran outside and stopped next to the wagon.

They'd already said their goodbyes to Suzanne, who now busied herself in the kitchen. Ginny knew their departure was difficult for her, even though Ginny promised they'd visit often.

They'd brought the larger of their two wagons, this one boasting a seat wide enough for three adults. Dax leaned down to Mary. "Would you like to ride on Ginny's lap or in the back?"

She turned toward her sister. "Can I ride in the back, Ginny? Please?"

"All right." Ginny smiled at Mary's uninhibited enthusiasm. She'd been afraid her sister would miss her friends in town. She needn't have worried.

"Just hold on. The ride will be bumpy." Dax lifted her up and over the side. "Sit with your back against the seat and let me know if you want to move up with us." Once he felt certain Mary would be fine, he helped Ginny and Rachel up, then took a seat next to his wife. "We ready to head home?"

Home, Ginny thought, realizing she wanted one more than anything.

They'd had several storms since Luke left Splendor. Nothing seemed to melt, just added to the existing amount of snow already piling up on the ground. Without the snow, their trip would take less than thirty minutes. Going home today took a bit longer.

"Look, Mary." Ginny turned in her seat while pointing ahead, indicating the big ranch house in the distance.

"Is that our house, Ginny?" the girl asked, her voice full of wonder.

"It's not *our* house, but it's where we'll be living."

Rachel glanced at Dax, her eyes sparkling, knowing they'd made the right decision to hire Ginny.

Chapter Fifteen

Eastern Range, Wyoming

Luke lay huddled beneath his blanket as Tom stoked the fire. They'd found what appeared to be a cave. Instead, it turned out to be no more than six feet wide, a few feet deep, and about six feet high, enough for the two of them and a fire, but not the horses.

They'd made the decision to take an even longer route back after hearing of continued hostilities in the western part of the territory. It would take twice as long to reach Big Pine, even though the snowfall had been more moderate in this region.

"Two, maybe three more days and we should reach Big Pine." Tom tossed aside the stick he'd been using. "You still interested in helping find those responsible for the gold thefts?"

"Yes, if you can get Pinkerton's approval. I need to ride on to Splendor first, make sure all's well."

"Understood. I still have more inquiries to make based on information provided by Sheriff Sterling. What do you think of him?"

"Sterling? Seems capable enough. From what I've heard, the citizens of Big Pine respect him, and he's hired experienced deputies. Why?"

"No reason. I just like to know with whom I'm dealing." Tom pulled his blanket around him.

"Whenever you're ready, let me know. Sounds like a job for more than one man. Of course, Dutch may be available by then."

Luke stared at the fire and thought of the ranch, wondering if they'd even thought about him much during his absence. He knew winters in this area were brutal...not just some years but every year. Dax's attention would be focused on the cattle, not on his absent brother.

Luke let his mind wander to Ginny. He wondered how she'd reacted to the gift he'd sent her. Not well, he guessed. He didn't know when he'd ever met such a stubborn woman. Well, he'd done what he could for her, and whether or not she appreciated it, he felt good about it. Luke doubted he'd see much of her while in Splendor. He knew there'd be too much to do, and the journey into town and back would take at least twice as long as other times of the year. Besides, with two jobs, he guessed she'd have little time to socialize, and he sure as hell didn't want her to take his friendship as anything more than that. Keeping his distance from her would be best for both of them.

He closed his eyes, ready to return to the familiar, unchanging faces at the ranch.

"Real good breakfast, Ginny. Thanks." Bull stood, washed his plate in a bucket, and stacked it with the others on a shelf near the bunkhouse door. Over the last year, as they'd added more men, Bernice prepared the food, then some of the men carried it in large bowls to the bunkhouse.

Ginny watched the men devour everything she'd made. She'd pick up the empty bowls later, after Mary and Rachel left for town.

"You need to finish your breakfast so you can ride to town with Miss Rachel. Hurry up now," Ginny said, walking back into the house and seeing Mary fidgeting with her food.

"I'm not hungry, Ginny." Mary gazed up at her and yawned.

"Well, eat what you can. It's a long ride to town, and I'm certain Miss Rachel will want to leave soon." Ginny hurried into the kitchen to get the food she'd prepared out to the men who'd be with the herd all day, then she'd begin preparing dinner for those working closer to the house. She'd been up since well before dawn, never once sitting down, yet the hectic pace suited her.

"How are you doing, Ginny?" Dax asked as he walked into the kitchen to grab one more cup of coffee before riding out with the men.

"Quite well. I believe the men enjoyed the food."

Her harried smile told him more than her words. So far, she enjoyed the work. Time would tell if they'd placed too much of a load on her, although he doubted it.

She laced up the canvas sack of food.

"I'll take it." Dax grabbed the bag, flung it over his shoulder, and dumped his unfinished coffee in the sink. "Hank will be around if you need anything."

Ginny watched him walk down the hall, then heard voices as he spoke with Rachel a moment before leaving.

"Mary, are you ready to leave?" Rachel asked.

"Yes, Miss Rachel."

"Let's get you in the wagon and start for town." She turned as Ginny came out from the kitchen.

"You be good for Miss Rachel." She gave her sister a hug. "I'll see you tonight."

Mary waved as she ran out the front door. Hank helped her into the wagon, then waited to help Rachel, even though he knew she had no problem climbing up on her own.

"Watch the weather, Rachel. Looks to me like it may turn early." Hank stepped back.

"We'll stay at Uncle Charles' house if it gets too bad." She slapped the reins, noting the white clouds against the clear blue of the sky and wondering how Hank could be so accurate in predicting coming storms.

Ginny stood on the porch and waved, knowing Mary wouldn't notice.

"What do you think?"

She looked at Hank, who now stood beside her. "Um...about what?"

"The ranch, the work." He shrugged, as if his question was obvious.

"The work is what Rachel described. I hadn't realized how many men work for Dax and Luke. I thought I knew most of them from working at the Rose, but there are several I don't recognize."

"Well, now, some like to stay put and play cards or read. I never saw much reason for riding into town after spending all day in the saddle."

"I'm going to head out now, Hank." They both looked at Travis Dixon, who doffed his hat. "Ma'am."

She recognized him from the couple times he'd been at the Rose, although he'd spoken little, other than to introduce himself.

"How are you, Mr. Dixon?"

"Fine, ma'am. Breakfast was mighty good. Thank you." He looked to Hank. "Anything you need me to tell Dax?"

"We spoke before he left."

"Then I'll be taking off." He tipped his hat to Ginny, then walked toward his saddled horse.

She'd never noticed his limp before and wondered how he'd been injured.

"Where's he from, Hank?"

"Tennessee, I believe. Real quiet. If I recall, he fought for the South. That's how he hurt his leg. You might recall he's the one who rode into town with an arrow in his back the day of Dax and Rachel's wedding."

"I'd forgotten. I've seen him at the saloon a couple times. He plays cards, then leaves." Ginny's gaze followed him as he rode off. "Guess I should get started on dinner and cleaning. There's so much, I'm not certain where I should start." Her nervous chuckle belied the worry she felt.

Hank placed a hand on her shoulder. "You'll do just fine, Ginny."

Star Ranch

"All I'm saying is the men are getting restless." Flatnose chewed on the end of his cold cigar. "They want to take another gold wagon." He glanced over at his partner who stood with his arms crossed, leaning against the porch rail.

"It's a bad time to pull another robbery. Sheriff Sterling hired more deputies, and the citizens committee hired one of those Pinkerton men. We need to lay low." He pushed from the railing and dropped his arms. "Truth is, I've been considering putting this behind us. We each have more than enough money stashed away. We don't need to take any more chances."

Flatnose flicked the dead cigar out onto the dirt and leaned back in his chair, balancing the front two legs off the floor. "You thinking of taking up life as a gentry with that woman of yours?" His smile came out as a sneer, letting Rick know what he thought about the idea.

"We've pulled enough jobs. There's no need to put ourselves in danger, and that includes

Stella. If someone does connect us with the holdups, they'll come straight here. My idea is to move the gold, sell the ranch, and start over in something legal."

"Legal, huh? You've been a farmer and lawman. You gonna put a badge on after all this? I worked for my pa on his place, served time in the Union Army before coming west. What the hell would I do?" Flatnose asked, his voice moving from disbelief to anger.

"You don't have to do a damn thing. Retire. Enjoy what you have. Make Stella an honest woman and have children."

Flatnose snorted at the idea of marriage. "She's not the marrying kind and you know it. Besides, I have no use for children." He tipped the chair down and stood, pushing his hands into his pockets. "I guess if we sell the ranch, I'd head to California."

"And leave Stella?"

"I'd give her plenty of money, make sure she'd be all right. Maybe even buy her a place in Big Pine."

"You don't think she'll talk?" Rick asked. He had the same fears about the men. Even though they had nothing to gain and everything to lose by exposing other members of the gang, some men were none too bright and one wrong word could bring the law down on all of them.

"She'll say nothing. Got no reason to." Flatnose pulled another cigar from his shirt pocket, cut off the end, and lit it.

Rick thought about this. No one had anything to gain by talking. Their best course would be to take their gold and leave the area, build new lives as far away from Montana as they could. It would certainly be best for him since Ezra Duncan had arrived in Big Pine.

He now had to consider the house he'd bought—the one he hoped Felicity would agree to share with him someday.

He'd already moved his gold to a place no one would ever find it. He knew a buyer in eastern Montana, and had traveled there before buying the house, selling some of the gold and banking the cash. As far as the man knew, Rick had a mine north of Big Pine, and would be coming in every few months to exchange what he'd discovered for cash. Over the next few years, he planned to sell all his gold in amounts that wouldn't draw too much attention, leaving no trail for anyone to follow.

"We'll tell the men before I ride back to Big Pine. Give them time to make plans and leave, then sell the place—livestock, furniture, everything. I don't want the men around when the new owner arrives." Rick felt certain he'd made the right decision.

"You sure about this?" Flatnose asked, still not convinced they couldn't rob at least one more wagon.

"I am. It's time to get out before anyone suspects us. The added law makes more raids too much of a risk. One I'm not willing to take." Rick didn't say he also wanted no part in any more killings by Flatnose. He couldn't count on his partner to keep the bullets in his gun. From what Rick had seen, the man had an almost perverse need to watch others die. Rick wanted to place as much distance between himself and Flatnose as possible.

"All right. We'll tell them they need to ride out by the end of the month." Flatnose let out a puff of smoke, cut off the burnt end, and laid the cigar on the top porch rail. "Stella and I will be out of here soon after."

Splendor, Montana

"Everyone ready?" Gabe asked the men who'd gathered to search the caves. They'd met at the Pelletier ranch and planned to start north of Luke's place, then ride south toward Noah's cabin and the Frey brother's ranch. Frank and Hiram Frey had brought one of their wranglers, Walt Jones—a man who'd lived in one of the caves with his son for a few months before the ranchers had discovered them.

"Hold up," Dax called and pointed to Noah.

"Sorry about being late. King Tolbert gave me a job and wanted to wait for it." He shrugged at the implication the man always expected to immediately get what he wanted, no matter the inconvenience to others.

"Guess we're ready." Gabe nodded at his friend as he and Dax took up the lead, heading toward the mountain on the other side of Wildfire Creek. They'd been fortunate. The last storm passed through without adding much more snow.

As they approached the base of the mountain, they split into groups, each one taking a different path to check the existing caves and other places someone could hide.

"Don't waste time riding up higher onto the mountain. If people are living in the hills, they'll most likely be hiding lower to the base, where it's easier to get in and out during the winter," Gabe called over his shoulder as he started up a narrow ravine with one group. Dax led another, while Hiram and Frank led the third. They'd meet back at their starting point within an hour, then move south.

Six hours passed without finding a trace of anyone living in the caves. A few showed signs of habitation, but nothing indicating they'd been lived in within the last several months.

"Come up here and check this out."

Dax looked up ahead to see Walt Jones motioning behind a large group of boulders partway up the mountain.

"What is it?" Dax rode up, Bull reining to a stop next to him.

"Looks like someone's been here recently." Walt walked into a grotto within the rocks, large enough for several people. "My guess is whoever lived here has been gone a week, maybe two." He pointed to a fire pit, an empty tin with a lid, and what looked like chicken bones in a pile against one wall.

"I wonder if the Freys or Noah would recognize the tin." Bull picked it up and pulled off the lid, noting the crumbs inside. "Looks like it may have held hardtack."

"Take it with you." Dax bent to pick up a rock, which had been chiseled to a point. He'd seen others similar to this in Running Bear's camp when he and Luke visited last summer.

"What'd you find?" Walt asked.

"An arrowhead." He laid it flat in his palm for Bull and Walt to examine while he glanced around. A few feet away, Dax spotted a smaller one, and slid both into his pocket.

"Blackfoot?" Walt asked.

"I don't know." Bull took another quick look around before walking outside. "Odd they'd leave arrowheads behind. Takes a good while to make one of them."

"Maybe they left in a hurry and missed them. At least we now have some evidence someone's been living up here, and not too long ago." Dax swung up on Hannibal and started down the hill to join the others.

"Find anything?" Gabe asked as Dax, Bull, and Walt joined the rest of the men.

"Look at this." Bull handed the tin to Noah.

"Where'd you find this?" Noah turned it over in his hand, recognizing it.

"There's a small grotto up in those boulders." Bull pointed toward the large rock outcropping halfway up the hill. "Appears someone lived there until recently. You recognize it?"

"Suzanne packed biscuits in this for me a few months back. I realized it was missing maybe six or eight weeks ago." Noah slid it into his saddlebag.

Gabe looked up at the darkening sky. "Guess we'd better start back."

"You think it's Running Bear's people?" Noah asked Dax as they rode toward the ranch.

"Either them or some of Long Feather's band. The only way to find out is to ride to Running Bear's village and speak with him."

"We'd best do it soon." Bull didn't like heading so far north this time of year. He'd hoped the thefts would have stopped by now, eliminating the need to track down the culprits. The damage at Luke's place indicated otherwise.

"It might be best to head north tomorrow and wait to search again until Running Bear has looked at what we found. Bull and I can ride up," Dax said.

"I'll go with you." Gabe wanted this settled before it created further tensions between the ranchers and local Blackfoot tribe. Or worse, escalated into violence if cattle or horses came up missing.

"Be at the ranch at sunup and we'll head out."

Chapter Sixteen

Moosejaw, Montana

"Maybe we'll be able to head out tomorrow." Luke let go of the curtain in the front window of the hotel. They'd been stuck in the eastern range of Montana for three days, waiting for the storm to pass. The last few hours had been the first signs it might be letting up. It would take at least two days to reach Big Pine, then one more for Luke to make it to Splendor.

Tom looked up from the piece of paper he held in his hand—a telegram from Sheriff Sterling. "At least we made it here before the worst of it started." He handed the message to Luke, who read through it.

"No more robberies since you left. Maybe the gang has moved on." Luke folded the message and tossed it on the table.

"Perhaps, or they may be laying low, waiting out the winter."

"Except gold must be moved all year, not just when the weather's clear. You would think a gold wagon, moving in thick snow, would be a prime target. Whatever the reason, I'd wager they'll start up again, unless they've left Montana." Luke's words triggered a memory of Flatnose Darvis and his gang targeting gold transport wagons. They'd mentioned a ranch in Montana, but not the town. Could there be a connection between the robberies in Bison Basin, Idaho, and those near Big Pine? "Did you get a response from Dutch?"

Tom had sent a message to Dutch, wondering if he'd gotten a new assignment or still sat in Denver, as they sat in Moosejaw, biding his time.

"He's waiting to hear from headquarters. Gus Salter offered him a job, taking over for Bob Bray."

"Dutch, a ranch foreman?" Luke smiled at the thought of Dutch moving from Confederate spy to Pinkerton man to head wrangler. "I don't see him working cows all day."

Tom chuckled at the vision it made. "He turned Salter down."

"Salter's offer is positive in one way. Seems as if the family is moving on." Luke thought of the stricken look on Gus' face as he watched his friend die.

"He's a tough one. My gut tells me they'll be fine, including Nell." Tom stood and walked to the window, looking on to the main street.

"You're right. Seems to be clearing up. It might be we can head out at first light."

"We'll need to wait until the telegraph office opens," Luke said.

"Why's that?"

"I need to send Dutch a message. It may be Pinkerton will want him to travel to Big Pine."

North Boundary of Redemption's Edge

Dax sat atop Hannibal, using his field glasses to look down onto the Blackfoot village below. He'd been watching a band of Running Bear's warriors on the opposite ridge. They'd been following him, Gabe, and Bull for the last hour, making no move to approach.

The three started out at dawn, stopping only to rest the horses as they headed toward the Blackfoot village. Dax and Luke had met Running Bear once. The meeting had been cordial, the chief impressive, and the village filled with women and children. They'd been told the warriors were out hunting. Running Bear's English had surprised Dax and Luke, neither expecting to be able to communicate with the chief. They'd been wrong.

"What do you see?"

Dax handed Gabe the field glasses. "Take a look."

"The village looks quiet. Mainly women and children." He handed the glasses to Bull, who took a quick look before giving them back to Dax.

"It's not as large as I thought." Bull shifted to look at the warriors, who still watched from the opposite ridge.

"Time to head down." Dax nudged Hannibal forward.

When they were within a hundred yards of the village, Bull glanced over his shoulder to see the group who'd been following them closing in, forming a semicircle so there'd be no retreat unless the chief allowed it.

Children began to run toward them, drawing the attention of their mothers and the elders of the village. A pretty, young woman Dax recognized as Running Bear's daughter walked to a tipi, opened the flap, and stepped inside. Within moments, Running Bear emerged and walked toward them in slow, measured strides, his head held high.

Dax, Gabe, and Bull slid from their horses, handing the reins to the children who crowded around. They waited in silence as the chief approached. He stopped before Dax, his face unreadable.

"It is good to see you again, my friend."

"It is good to see you, Chief Running Bear. These are my friends, Gabe Evans and Bull Mason. We have come to speak with you about an important matter."

The chief nodded, motioning for them to follow him. He spoke rapidly to the young warriors who'd followed them to the village, then continued on to his tipi and stepped inside.

"It seems we're to follow him." Dax stepped into the tipi behind Running Bear. Gabe and Bull followed, as did two elders from the village, everyone taking a seat on the ground.

Dax waited, uncertain of the etiquette for bringing up the reason for their visit.

Time passed without a word being spoken, Blackfoot or English, as each man took in the others, until Running Bear decided the time had come to speak.

"You say you have come to speak of an important matter, my friend?"

"Yes," Dax replied.

The chief motioned with his hand to continue. It didn't take Dax long to explain what had been happening, careful not to accuse the tribe of anything. He said they sought answers, nothing more. He pulled out the arrowheads and handed them to Running Bear, who turned them over in his hand, then gave them back to Dax.

"Do you know if they are from your village?" Dax asked as he slipped the arrowheads back in his pocket.

"There is no way to know." Running Bear stood, motioning for Dax to follow him outside, while Gabe and Bull remained inside with the elders. "We will walk."

They followed a path toward the creek, which ran to the west of the village. Running Bear stopped at the edge of the water, clasping his hands behind his back before breathing in the cold winter air.

"There is one who might have the answers you seek."

"Who is this man?" Dax asked.

"Long Feather."

"Yes, I know of him. How do I find Long Feather?"

"My braves tell me his people are camped to the north, a long way from here."

Dax thought of the distance, thinking it made no sense unless a renegade group had splintered off, no longer camping with Long Feather's band. Perhaps he'd exiled them. If they'd been unable to hunt or catch fish, they would be driven to steal.

"Does his village have many people?" Dax asked.

"Not so many as my people. There are few women and children."

Dax heard nothing to provide answers about who could be stealing from the local ranchers. The one certainty seemed to be the innocence of those in Running Bear's village. The chief knew them all and no one had vanished.

"Thank you, Running Bear. I will seek answers elsewhere."

He followed the chief back to where Gabe and Bull still sat, cross-legged, inside the tipi.

"Let's go." Dax turned toward the horses. He reached into each saddlebag and took out several bundles, handing them to Running Bear. He'd watched Rachel pack fabric, tobacco, dried beans, and bread. At the last moment, she'd slipped in a handful of candy purchased from the general store.

Running Bear handed the packages to the women, and in return, offered Dax necklaces and bracelets of elk teeth, and a club with a stone head.

Dax, Gabe, and Bull rode out, again followed by the same group of young braves. They didn't know any more now than when they rode in. As they rode, Dax explained what little Running Bear knew of the thefts and his suggestion of finding Long Feather.

"So far, nothing makes sense." Bull rode next to Dax, puzzled by the lack of information. "No one from Running Bear's village is missing, yet there were clear signs whoever is stealing is from one of the tribes."

"Searching for Long Feather's camp would gain us nothing. He's not a friend of the whites. Running Bear has chosen to try to live alongside us, while Long Feather wants to rid us from the territory." Dax looked over his shoulder, noting Running Bear's braves no longer followed them. "His camp is miles away from our ranch or the Frey's. They'd search for food closer to their village, not this far south."

"We can continue to search the mountain." Gabe wasn't at all convinced they'd be able to locate the thieves before the worst storms began. "You, the Freys, and Luke can post men to keep watch on the supplies. Noah doesn't have that option."

"Hank is moving all the supplies into our root cellar, including the beans and grains. I don't see how we can post an extra man at Luke's. We'll have to find another answer until the thieves are caught."

"Do you want to continue the searches?" Bull asked.

Dax reined to a stop and slid off Hannibal, checking the cinch as he weighed the needs of the ranch against the small amount of supplies they'd lost.

"No. We'll need every man to help with the stock, and I don't see any real threat other than the loss of supplies."

"You're right, except you never know what anyone will do if they're hungry and confronted by someone who has what they want." Gabe pushed his hat further down and pulled up his collar to ward off the increasingly cold air.

"Luke should return soon. Once he does, I'll speak with him. Maybe convince him to bring back anything of value and stay at the ranch over the winter." He mounted Hannibal and turned toward home.

"Don't count on it. He can be one stubborn cuss," Bull chuckled, willing to bet Dax would have no luck talking Luke into moving back to the ranch house—especially with Ginny now living under the same roof.

Big Pine, Montana

"How do you know Frederick Marlow?" Sheriff Sterling asked Ezra Duncan, who'd agreed to become his newest deputy a couple of weeks before. He'd been introducing Duncan around, giving him his thoughts on the various citizens—good and bad.

Ezra hung his coat and hat on a rack near the front door and took a seat across from the sheriff, not wanting to bring up a subject which had haunted him for years. He still woke in a cold sweat, remembering the bodies of Marlowe's wife and son. His own marriage had suffered due to his insistence on Marlowe's guilt. When the verdict arrived, exonerating the man, his wife had taken their two children back east, unable to forgive him for the senseless death of a woman and child who'd been her friends. Had he not been so stubborn, so vocal about the man's guilt, perhaps they could've worked through the horror. Instead, he'd clung to his belief, at one point implying it had been their own fault for running out of the house toward the posse.

"We lived in the same town in Nebraska."

Sterling watched the man's expression change, his gaze remote as if he were trying to block something painful from his mind. "Anything you want to tell me about the man?"

Ezra's gaze shot to the sheriff. "I'm not sure what you mean."

"I didn't ask the day at the restaurant, but you two didn't appear to have a cordial exchange."

Ezra stood and walked to the window, looking out at a darkening sky. He didn't look at the sheriff as he spoke.

"We have a history. All the evidence pointed to Marlowe as being part of a gang terrorizing the area. My facts were wrong and a jury found him innocent. For me, the verdict came too late. I'd made a series of bad decisions, one ending in the death of his wife and son."

"Shit," Sterling muttered, trying to understand how the deaths of two innocents could've happened.

"A witness claimed Marlowe was part of a group of raiders who'd been stealing and killing for months. I selected the first few men who volunteered to ride out with me to Marlowe's ranch. Turned out, they had no intention of listening to my orders and were more inclined to shoot first, then ask questions." Ezra turned from the window and fixed his troubled gaze on the sheriff. "Their deaths were senseless, and I was to blame."

"Appears you still blame yourself."

"You can never reverse the deaths of two innocent people. Nothing you ever tell yourself makes it right or erases it from your mind." Ezra grabbed his hat and coat, then grasped the door handle. "Unless you have an objection, I'll make the rounds."

Sterling shook his head and watched him leave. He'd heard about the troubles in Nebraska, the reason Duncan had quit his job as sheriff and left the territory. He hadn't known the family's name, or that a woman and child had been killed.

When he'd realized Duncan knew Marlowe, Sterling hoped he'd be able to learn more about the man and how he'd come upon what seemed to be considerable wealth. He'd paid cash for a home which had been abandoned, furniture and all, by the previous owner. According to the banker, he hadn't balked at the price. He'd wired for funds from a bank in Moosejaw, and the home had been his within days, then Marlowe had disappeared.

Sterling hadn't seen Marlowe for a couple of weeks after the purchase. He'd returned to show the house to Mrs. Felicity Baker, the widow of one of Sterling's good friends. The sheriff discovered Marlowe had been courting the pretty, and quite wealthy, widow. He felt he owed his friend to learn as much as he could about the newcomer before Felicity made a mistake, such as marrying the man. Now at least he had some information about Marlowe, albeit slim.

Sterling pulled out his pocket watch and checked the time. It had been a long day, a storm threatened, and he still hadn't eaten. He slipped on his heavy coat, grabbed his hat, and turned toward the door, nearly getting slammed in the face when Luke Pelletier pushed it open. He stepped out of the way as he and Tom Horton walked inside.

"Evening, Sheriff." Luke shrugged out of his snow-covered jacket and walked toward the stove in the corner, rubbing his hands together.

"Pelletier, Horton. You just get back into town?"

"Came in from Moosejaw. I'll tell you, the weather's getting worse, fast." Tom followed Luke to the stove, hanging his hat on a hook.

Sterling shrugged out of his coat and settled behind his desk, curious as to why the jail would be the men's first stop. "Your business in Denver work out?"

"It did. If you have time, Luke and I want to talk about the gold robberies." Tom sat in a chair opposite Sterling and stretched out his legs. "Any more of them since we left?"

"Not a one. It's been quiet, as if maybe the gang has moved on. Why?"

"You heard of Dutch McFarlin?" At Sterling's nod, Tom continued. "As you know, he and Luke worked similar gold transport robberies in Idaho. They got some of the gang, but the leader and several others got away and headed for Montana."

Sterling glanced at Luke. "You told me all this before. What's it have to do with the robberies here?"

"From what Tom has learned, Dutch and I believe it's the same group, headed up by a man named Flatnose Darvis."

"I remember the name. Why do you think they're connected?" Sterling asked.

"The raids in Idaho were by a gang of between six and twelve men. All used black bandanas. They'd tie the guards to the wagon wheels, unload whatever gold could be carried in their saddlebags, and take off, leaving the wagon, guards, and everything else behind. The raids here don't appear to be much different from the thefts in Idaho."

Sterling leaned forward, placing his arms on the desk, and focusing on Luke. "How does this information help us find this Flatnose fella?"

"It doesn't...yet. Once Dutch arrives, we may be able to figure it out," Luke answered.

"McFarlin is coming here?" Sterling asked.

Tom glanced at Luke, then looked back at the sheriff. "It seems the local citizens committee has been in contact with Pinkerton. They've asked for another agent on the job."

"Damn citizens committee." Sterling shot from his chair and paced toward the front windows, staring out as snow began to blanket the street. "I don't know why they keep me around when they make decisions without informing me."

"We expected they would've let you know." Luke felt for the seasoned lawman. The committee in Idaho had kept the sheriff informed of their actions, even when they knew he'd disagree. The men heading up the committee in Big Pine saw Sterling as a man at odds with their goals. They accepted his experience, even as they ignored his recommendations and kept him out of their discussions.

"I believe most of them might make other decisions if it weren't for the man leading them." Sterling walked back to his desk and rested a hip against the edge.

"Who is that?" Luke asked.

"You don't know?" Sterling's expression showed his surprise at Luke's question.

"No... Should I?"

"It's King Tolbert."

Luke's face hardened at the news. "Tolbert? What the hell is he doing in charge of the committee in Big Pine?"

"The man has substantial property in this area, including several businesses. He also owns part of at least two gold mines. Both have lost shipments to the outlaws. To be honest, I'm surprised he hasn't hired his own gunmen to go after the gang. Of course, it doesn't mean he won't."

"I haven't met the man. You know him, Luke?" Tom asked.

"I do. His ranch in Splendor shares part of our eastern property line. He did his best to run Dax and me off when we took possession of our place." Luke found it hard to keep the disgust out of his voice.

"I'll be meeting with the committee again tomorrow. Why don't you come with me?" Tom directed his question at Sterling.

"I might do that. It won't matter, though. Tolbert sends his demands by telegraph to the committee and they do what he tells them."

Luke stood. "Good luck to both of you."

"You're not staying?" Sterling asked.

"I'm heading back home tomorrow. It's time I helped Dax with the ranch." Luke shook hands with both and walked outside, looking up at the sky as he pulled his collar up. He headed toward the hotel, deciding that no matter the weather, he'd be on his way home at first light. He looked forward to his first good night's sleep in weeks.

Chapter Seventeen

"I expect we'll be back after dark." Dax slipped into his heavy coat before grabbing leather gloves and walking up to Rachel. "Stay in town if a storm starts up. I don't want you caught in it." He leaned down, placing a quick kiss on her lips. "It wouldn't surprise me to see Luke in a day or two."

Rachel thought about Luke arriving to find Ginny working for them. "It might be best for you to be here to explain about Ginny."

"Sorry, darlin', but I'm leaving the explaining part to you. In fact, I plan to be as far away from the house as possible when Luke learns who the new cook is." He sent her a look, letting her know he still felt Ginny's presence might create some major problems once Luke learned she lived at the ranch.

"I believe you're underestimating him. He'll see it as a good opportunity for her, and a perfect solution for us." As Rachel spoke the words, her mind told her Dax might be right. After all, he knew Luke better than anyone. "I'd better get started for town." She gave him a hug before they headed down the stairs. "Mary, are you ready to leave for school?"

"Yes, ma'am." She skipped toward the front door as Rachel watched, wishing she had the same kind of energy so early each morning. She'd stayed in bed longer than usual, feeling exhausted, as if she hadn't slept at all. The same fatigue had plagued her all week. Rachel thought it might be time to mention it to her uncle.

Ginny followed them outside, noticing the dark clouds approaching from the east. It didn't bode well for the rest of the day. Still, she felt fortunate. Her job left her inside most days—cleaning, cooking, and doing laundry, which she hung from rafters in the attic. Most days she ventured outside only to collect eggs, or go down into the root cellar.

"We'll be home right after school. I don't want to take a chance of getting caught in the storm." Rachel nodded toward the horizon, noting the same dense, black clouds as Ginny. "Fact is, I may pull Mary out sooner, if needed."

"Whatever you think is best." Ginny waved as they drove away in the wagon, then hurried inside, shutting the door against a gust of cold air. The last few days had been frigid. Hank expected the heavy snows to start any day, making travel to and from town difficult.

Ginny looked around the kitchen, deciding what to do first. Dinner would be easy because Dax hadn't left any men behind, preferring to have every available hand with the herd. It would be just Hank, Bernice, and her. She'd clean the house first, fix dinner, then start on supper.

She started upstairs, grabbing extra bedding, then stripping Dax and Rachel's bed. She did the same with the beds downstairs, stuffing as much as could fit in the washtub Hank had placed in the kitchen. Her thoughts turned to Luke as she worked the sheets in the warm water. She wondered if he'd made it to Big Pine, if he was safe, and when he'd be home.

As often happened when she thought of Luke, she felt butterflies invade her stomach. She knew the reaction had everything to do with her concern about how he'd react when he discovered her at the house—an employee at the Pelletier ranch. The notion stung a little, but not enough for her to walk away from the chance to take care of Mary and save for their own home.

Ginny still had her mind set on the abandoned house in town. Suzanne had spoken to Horace Clausen at the bank, learning it was for sale and that he'd be willing to make a good deal to anyone willing to clean it up. He, as well as most of the business owners, saw it as an eyesore. Stan Peterman at the general store even mentioned tearing it down, a comment which made Ginny even more determined to save every cent she could.

Sometimes at night, she'd pretend it belonged to her and Mary. She'd often force her mind from thoughts of Luke, and her conflicting feelings toward him, by focusing on the house and how she'd fix it up, make it her own. The fact she'd need a job in town didn't deter her fantasies. Even now, as she scrubbed the bedding and planned for what needed to be done for supper, she let her thoughts drift to the house and what she dreamed would be her future.

Luke pulled his collar up against the chill. He'd left Big Pine well before dawn, taking advantage of a lull in the storm. He made several stops, letting Prince rest and feed on grain Luke kept in his saddlebag. A couple of miles before Splendor, he took the trail north, avoiding the town and riding straight toward home. If the weather held, he'd be at the ranch well before supper. He'd stay at the ranch tonight and catch up with Dax, work with the men tomorrow, then head to his own place. His mouth curved into a slight grin at the thought of his house. He wondered how it had fared since he'd left weeks before.

The sky began to turn an ominous gray-black as he approached the ranch. He didn't detect any movement until he approached the barn and saw Hank inside, sitting on a bench, holding something in his hand. He lifted his head and set down what he'd been working on when he saw Luke rein to a stop.

"Wondered when you'd decide to come back." Hank took Prince's reins, allowing Luke to brush off the trail mud and stretch. "You don't look so bad, considering you've been gone for weeks."

"Feels like longer."

"Go on inside while I take care of Prince. Should be coffee on the stove."

"Is Bernice inside?" Luke asked.

"She's resting at our place." He nodded in the direction of the foreman's house behind the main house. "Doc says it'll still be a while before she's able to get about much. Rachel's at the clinic, and Dax is out with the rest of the men, tending the herd."

Luke nodded and headed toward the house. Hank watched him take the steps two at a time and open the front door, glad he'd made the decision to say nothing about Ginny. Better to let Luke find out for himself and decide how he'd handle it.

Ginny grabbed one more piece of wood. She'd made four trips outside to gather as much as she could for the stoves before the snow started. Several days before, Rachel had watched her do the same, noticing the thin cotton dress Ginny wore under the heavy wool coat. She'd rummaged through a trunk, pulling out a pair of trousers and shirt, and handed them to Ginny, explaining they'd be more practical for outside work during the cold weather.

At first, Ginny had balked, not wanting to wear men's clothing, but Rachel persisted, telling her no one at the ranch would care one way or another. Since then, Ginny had worn them each day she worked outside. They made a big difference against the frigid wind.

Climbing the back steps, she pushed the door open and stepped into the kitchen, kicking the door closed and dropping the wood next to the stove. She removed her gloves and unbuttoned her coat, letting it fall open, then reached up to check supplies in the cupboard. If needed, she'd make a trip to the root cellar before taking off the coat and replacing the trousers with a dress.

Luke shrugged out of his coat at the same time a noise came from the kitchen. He glanced out the front window to see Hank still working in the barn. Bernice was at their place and everyone else was gone. Who the hell was in the house?

He moved toward the kitchen in time to see a man, or boy, reach up into a cupboard and pull something down. In a slow, silent move, he drew his gun from its holster, pointing it at the intruder.

"Hold it right there."

Ginny froze, not recognizing the deep growl coming from behind her.

"Put your hands up and turn around."

She did as he asked, her heart pounding, wondering if someone had slipped by Hank to come in the front door. Slowly she turned, raising her eyes to meet those of the man holding a gun on her. Her breath caught at the sight of Luke, his face hard, his mouth in a thin line. She could see the instant recognition dawned. He lowered the gun in a quick motion and slammed it into the holster.

"What the hell are you doing here? And why are you dressed like that?"

She swallowed the hard lump in her throat and took in a shuttering breath, anger replacing the fear she'd felt. "You scared the daylights out of me," she hissed and pulled the hat off her head, exposing soft brown wisps of hair which had escaped the loose bun.

He held his ground, taking in the sight of her in men's trousers, a too big shirt haphazardly tucked inside and held together by a wide leather belt. The coat he'd given her covered the ridiculous outfit. He let his gaze wander over her, his eyes softening at the same time his body tightened—a reaction he was powerless to control.

"I asked what you're doing here, sneaking around the house. Stealing?"

"I am *not* stealing," she threw back at him. "I work here."

"What?" His voice took on a hard edge as his eyes narrowed, signaling his disbelief.

"Dax and Rachel hired me to take on Bernice's job."

He took a step forward, then thought better of it, crossing his arms over his chest, planting his feet shoulder width apart. Frustration warred with the desire he felt toward her. This was not what he'd expected to come home to—Ginny living at the ranch. It slammed into him that he'd see her every day, obliged to be around her, and forced to fight his constant attraction toward her. His jaw hardened as he processed the implication of her new position. He didn't like it. Not one bit.

"We'll see about that." He turned and stormed from the room, walking into the study, slamming the door behind him.

Ginny took a deep breath and tried to calm her heart from the relentless hammering she'd felt since he'd pointed his gun at her. As she relaxed, his words began to register. Did he mean to force Dax to let her go, return to town, and try to find work elsewhere? No, he wouldn't...would he? The look on his face told her he might. He'd been as angry as the time she'd suggested his kindness toward her required some form of gratitude. An accusation he'd set her straight on real quick.

She glanced around the kitchen at the items she'd taken from the cupboard, understanding why he'd thought her an intruder. Now he meant to send her away. Well, for now, she had a job to do, and she'd do it the best she could until Rachel and Dax returned.

Ginny disappeared into her room, changed clothes, and grabbed a shawl to ward off the chill she felt, even though the house remained warm from the stoves in several rooms. She'd make a fresh pot of coffee, refill the stoves and fireplace, then start supper. She'd do whatever it took to keep her mind off what Luke intended, and pray his attempts to make her leave failed.

Luke paced the study, stopping at the cupboard where the whiskey sat, calling to him. He pulled it down and poured a good amount into a glass, downing it in one swift motion. His head pounded and fatigue overwhelmed him. He poured another measure of the deep amber liquid into his glass and lowered himself into one of the large leather chairs, stretching his long legs in front of him. Taking slow sips, he pondered what he'd come home to.

He thought of the panicked look on Ginny's face when he implied he'd do what he could to send her away, and regretted the careless words, even as he wanted her gone. He'd get no peace as long as she worked at the ranch. Whatever drove him to seek a life without entanglements still burned hot within him. It wasn't that he didn't find Ginny desirable. Hell, he wanted her with an intensity he'd felt for no other woman. What he didn't want was to change his life, be tied to one person with all the commitments and responsibilities it implied. He liked his bachelor status, even if he wasn't the rake some believed.

If he were being honest, Ginny scared him more than anyone he'd ever known. She threatened all he believed about himself and his future. He liked the freedom of coming and going at will, answering to no one except himself and Dax. The Pinkerton assignments provided excitement, and his house near the creek offered peace. His life felt perfect, except for the woman in the other room. He set the empty glass down and closed his eyes, letting exhaustion overtake him.

Luke didn't know how much time passed before he heard the soft knocking. He rubbed his eyes, stood, and walked to the door, pulling it open. Ginny stood in front of him, a cup of coffee in her hand.

"I thought you might want this." She held it out to him, a look in her eyes he couldn't quite decipher.

"Thanks." He took the cup from a hand that trembled, and started to close the door when she took a step forward.

She looked up at a face devoid of emotion and tried to boost her courage, even as her heart hammered in her chest. "I want to thank you for the coat and dress." She swallowed and clasped her hands tight in front of her. "They're wonderful."

The sincerity in her words shook Luke. It took every ounce of willpower he had to not reach out and pull her to him. "You needed them." He stepped back, trying to put a safe distance between them.

"You're right. I did. I used the money I'd saved to buy a coat for Mary, but I will pay you what I owe."

He locked his eyes on hers. "You owe me *nothing*, Ginny. Save your money for whatever you want—just don't offer it to me."

"Do you mean to send Mary and me away?" she blurted out.

He had started to turn away, then stopped at her question. Is that what he intended?

"What happened to your job at the Rose?"

"Amos couldn't afford to pay someone who couldn't...or wouldn't..." Her voice trailed off as she thought of Belle and the others at the saloon.

She didn't need to explain. Luke understood what jobs in a saloon included and said a silent thanks Ginny had refused to go along with it.

"The new saloon is pulling a lot of business from the Rose, and the boardinghouse is suffering from people going to the new restaurant. Suzanne would've let Mary and me stay, but there'd be no money for necessities. The offer from Rachel and Dax was a miracle."

Luke listened and felt like the worst type of scoundrel for wanting to talk Dax into sending her away. His reasons would be selfish—protecting himself from the intense feelings she produced. He took a deep breath, struggling with the realization he'd have to learn to live with the decision Dax had made.

He walked to the desk, rested his hip against the edge, and took a sip of coffee, making the decision to ride to his place when he heard laughter coming from outside.

The front door flew open and a breathless Mary ran into the study, coming to an abrupt stop when she spotted Luke.

"You remember Mr. Luke, right, Mary?" Ginny asked as her sister continued to stare.

"Hello, Mary. How was school?" Luke asked, trying to ease the apprehension he saw in the little girl's eyes.

"Miss Rachel came and got me."

"Because of the snow?"

She nodded, then turned as Rachel came up behind her.

"Well, you're finally home." She smiled and walked up to Luke, giving him a hug. "It's good to have you back."

"I'm glad to be home." He shot a quick look at Ginny, once again regretting his reaction to her presence. "Ginny just explained what happened at the Rose."

"Amos did what he had to, and it certainly turned out well for us. Ginny's been a blessing."

Luke pushed away from the desk. "Guess I'd better get going."

"Won't you at least wait for Dax and stay for supper?"

"Another time. I'm anxious to see my place. Dax and I can talk tomorrow."

"Um...Luke..." Rachel began, worry on her face.

"What's wrong?" A knot formed in his gut.

"Whoever is stealing broke into your place and took food and bedding. Dax and Gabe boarded up the broken window, but the new one he ordered hasn't come in from Big Pine yet." She saw the expression on Luke's face turn from worry to anger and wished Dax had been the one to tell him. "It's not as bad as it sounds. Other than the window, Dax said whoever did it didn't damage anything else."

"Did they take anything besides food and blankets?"

"Dax and Gabe couldn't tell. You'll have to look around to see what else is missing. Why don't you stay and talk with Dax? I can pack up blankets and food, and Dax can follow you over in the wagon after supper."

"No sense waiting for Dax to return. I can pack up what's needed and drive the wagon over myself. I'll bring it back in the morning." Even as tired as he felt, he needed to see the place and figure out what else had been taken.

"All right. I'll pack food and bedding while you get the wagon ready." Rachel walked past Ginny, who hadn't moved from her spot near the door. Ginny waited for her to disappear into the kitchen before taking a few tentative steps toward Luke.

"Can't you stay for supper? I've made pot roast and a pie. There'll be nothing for you at your place."

He looked down at her, a vague sense of regret washing over him. She was right. He had nothing of real value at his place. It was a wooden structure meant to bring him a sense of independence. Although he preferred being close to the creek, his own house had yet to become a real home. An image of Ginny, standing at the sink in his kitchen, flashed across his mind, sending a brief wave of panic through him. He shook it off before it took hold.

"I need to see the house for myself. Rachel will send food along for tonight." He grabbed his coat and hat, then headed toward the wagon, determined to put some distance between him and Ginny. He did want to check the house. What he wanted more was to get as far away as he could from the temptation she posed.

He finished tying Prince to the back of the wagon as Rachel and Ginny approached, their arms full of bedding and supplies.

"There's meat, biscuits, and pie for tonight. You know, Dax is going to be upset you didn't stay." Rachel placed what she'd packed in the wagon and stepped back as Luke climbed up and settled on the seat.

"He'll understand. I'll be back early tomorrow." He picked up the reins, then turned his gaze on Ginny. She hadn't said a word to him since he'd left the house. He opened his mouth to speak, then stopped, tipping his hat to her before slapping the reins.

"Stubborn man," Rachel mumbled as she turned toward the house.

Ginny watched Luke disappear into the fading light. She had such conflicting feelings about him. She'd worried every day he'd been away, had been glad he'd returned in one piece, and disappointed in his reaction to her being at the ranch. Although it shouldn't have surprised her. As much as he seemed to want her friendship, his actions toward her said much more than his words. He would tolerate her working at the ranch for the sake of peace between him and Dax. She knew if it were up to him, she and Mary would be gone, shuttled back to town without any regret.

She followed Rachel into the house, making up her mind she'd stay until Bernice recovered, then find a job in town. Before Rachel offered her the job, she'd been considering another possibility, one that would provide her with more than enough money to support her and Mary, and allow her to save for the house. It would take more time to think it through, and she'd have to discuss it with at least one other person, but with Luke back, the idea made more sense. By the end of winter, after the last storm, she'd make her decision. For now, all she needed to do was stay out of Luke's way.

Chapter Eighteen

Walking around, Luke surveyed the damage, noting a couple other missing items. It could've been worse—might have been if Dax and Gabe hadn't discovered what happened and boarded up the place.

He made up his mind he'd build shutters for the windows and get Noah to make locks. He'd heard Gil Murton had a way with dogs. Not many people bred them, believing they weren't of much value on a ranch. Gil felt different. It'd been said he could train a dog to do anything. Luke wanted a dog to guard his place when he was away.

Luke unpacked the wagon, unwrapping the cold meat and biscuits, and pulled up a chair in front of the stove in his bedroom—the only one he'd had time to light. Even cold, the roast tasted mighty good. He finished it and the biscuits before unwrapping the pie. As much as he liked Bernice's cooking, Ginny's pie had to be one of the best he'd ever eaten.

Luke stoked the fire, tossing more wood inside the stove before closing the door. He fell back on the bed, not bothering to remove anything except his boots, then rested the crook of his arm over his eyes. An image of Ginny standing on the porch, tossing a look at him over her shoulder, a broad smile on her face flashed across his mind. He could feel his body tighten at the fantasy being created. As he drifted off, he briefly wondered if the image might be more real than he wanted to believe.

Early the next morning, Luke pulled the wagon to a stop next to the barn and jumped down. The storm had dumped at least a foot of snow during the night, making the short trip from his place to the ranch house more hazardous. The wind had picked up, blowing frigid air across the drifts, which came to three feet in some places. There'd be a lot more on the ground before spring replaced winter.

He spotted Bull coming out of the bunkhouse and nodded in acknowledgment, getting a dubious look in return as the ranch hand walked up next to him.

Bull grabbed Prince's saddle and blanket from the back of the wagon, tossing them over a rail of one of the stalls, and turned toward Luke. "Dax had a few harsh words about you not staying around long enough to talk with him yesterday."

"I had to check the damage at my place." Luke tried not to read too much into Bull's warning. He knew Dax would get over his initial irritation.

"Who do you think is doing it?" Bull asked.

"It's got to be Indians. Who else would be up in those mountains this time of year?"

"Dax, Gabe, and I visited Running Bear while you were gone. He told Dax no one from his village has disappeared." Bull told him of finding the arrowheads and Noah's biscuit tin.

"Then it's another tribe or a band of renegades. Doesn't matter. I just want to stop them." Luke explained his plan to build shutters and talk to Gil Murton about a dog.

"I've heard the same about Murton. It's said he's equally as good with horses. Too bad he's got his own place because he'd be a good addition to the ranch." Bull grabbed his own tack and started for the corral in back.

Just what I need, Luke thought as he strode toward the house, *another young, single ranch hand to draw Ginny's attention*. He stopped and shook his head, wondering where that had come from. He didn't care a whit if Ginny found one of the wranglers attractive, as long as it didn't affect her work. And if she fell in love, it would suit him just fine. He didn't need visions of her clouding his mind and keeping him awake at night. The sooner she met someone, the sooner he'd find peace and get on with his life.

Luke trudged up the front steps, wondering why the thought of Ginny with another man left a hole in his chest. He let the thought pass as the front door swung open, Dax standing in the opening.

"I heard you'd gotten back. I would've felt better about it if you'd stuck around for supper." Dax stepped aside, noticing Luke's grim expression. He wondered whether it had to do with the thefts at his place or their new cook.

"Rachel told me what happened at the house. I needed to see the damage for myself." He walked into the study and tossed his hat on the desk before sitting. "Thanks for taking care of boarding the windows up."

"Gabe helped. I saw you talking with Bull. Did he tell you of our visit to Running Bear's camp?"

"He did. Doesn't make sense that it's not someone with his village or another tribe. Perhaps it's a brave who had a disagreement with Running Bear, the same as Long Feather." He scrubbed a hand over his face and glanced outside, noticing Ginny coming out of the chicken coop with a basket in her hand, wearing the trousers he'd seen her in the day before. She didn't walk back to the house. His gaze followed her as she stopped next to Travis, pointed to something and laughed. Travis laughed with her, causing a knot to form deep in Luke's stomach.

"She going to be a problem?" Dax asked.

"Who?" Luke's eyes never left her and Travis. They continued talking before she nodded toward the house and walked away.

"Ginny. Is her working here going to be a problem?"

Luke turned his attention back to Dax. He'd been wondering the same since he'd found her in the kitchen, dressed in men's clothing. "Why is she wearing trousers and a man's hat? Doesn't she have enough clothes of her own?"

Dax stared at him, wondering why men who'd met their match in a woman continued to deny their feelings. Not too long ago he'd done the same with Rachel, and Luke had been the one to set him straight. He'd keep his mouth shut about it—for now.

"The weather. Some days it's too cold and windy to walk outside. All she owns are thin cotton dresses, except for the wool coat and dress some anonymous person sent her from Big Pine." Dax cast a knowing look at Luke. "Rachel found the pants and shirt in a box and thought they'd fit. I'm guessing they belonged to Pat Hanes." Pat owned the ranch before them, fought alongside the brothers as a Texas Ranger, and died from an outlaw's bullet. He'd left the ranch to Dax and Luke. "Now answer my question. Is Ginny living here going to be a problem for you?"

Luke grabbed his hat, shoved it tight on his head, and walked to the door. "I'm heading out to the herd."

"You'll stay for supper tonight." It wasn't a question.

Luke glared at Dax, nodded, then left without another word.

Dax leaned back in his chair, watching as Luke mounted Prince and took off toward the north pasture. His brother might come across as relaxed and charming with a slow temper, but Dax knew the other side of him. He could be coiled as tight as a piano wire and as angry as a frustrated bull, but no one would notice—except Dax. Luke had an uncanny ability to hide how he felt about a situation and continue toward the goal he had in mind. A skill which served him well as a spy for the Confederacy and an agent for Pinkerton. However, Dax doubted it would help him much with Ginny.

Noah pointed his pistol into the air and fired off one shot. "Stop before I put a bullet in you," he yelled as the slim figure disappeared into the trees. He knew the threat wouldn't stop the thief, just as he knew he'd never shoot someone in the back.

He'd spent a long day at the livery before stopping by Suzanne's to pick up the food he'd ordered for his cabin. The heavy snow made his trek to the cabin long and cold. He knew each day would get worse until winter turned to spring, then summer. Darkness cloaked the trail the last several hundred yards, and if it weren't for the lantern, he wouldn't have suspected anything. At least until he'd gone inside.

Noah saw the light, jumped off Tempest, and ran toward the front door, kicking it open. A crash from the kitchen was followed by flames from a broken lantern. He glanced out a window to see the intruder running away from the cabin, then worked to douse the fire, accepting there'd be no finding the thief tonight.

He let out a muffled curse before slamming the gun into its holster. He wished he'd gotten a better look at the thief. "Short and slender" wasn't much to go on. He hadn't even gotten a good look at the clothes.

Noah let the damage inside the cabin wait until he'd unsaddled Tempest and placed him in the lean-to he'd built in back. He dropped an armful of hay in front of the horse, then used rags to wipe him down, thinking of the incident in the cabin. Something seemed off, but he couldn't figure out what. He tossed the rags aside, grabbed his saddlebags, and headed into the cabin, removing his coat and hat. Reaching up, he hung the coat on a hook, then stopped. Even though he hadn't gotten a good look, he swore the thief hadn't worn a coat or hat. He shook his head, realizing it would be madness for anyone to venture out on a frigid night without wearing warm clothing. He'd check for tracks tomorrow. Tonight, he'd clean up the broken glass, eat, and get some sleep, hopeful his mind would clear enough by morning to recall a better image of the thief than the one he had tonight.

Big Pine, Montana

"What the hell are you thinking, coming here?" Rick Marlowe glanced outside before slamming the door shut and turning an angry glare at Flatnose. Although early morning, anyone could've seen the man ride up. "We agreed you'd get a message to me if you wanted to talk and we'd meet up outside of town."

Flatnose ignored the tirade and walked toward a table where glasses and a bottle of whiskey sat, waiting for him to help himself. He poured a good measure and downed it in one gulp.

"The news I have couldn't wait."

The hairs on the back of Rick's neck danced as Flatnose drank another shot, set down the empty glass, and turned toward him.

"Word has it a large shipment of gold will be heading out within a few weeks. Bigger than any we've ever gone after."

"I don't see how that's important to us. We made a decision to lie low and let everything blow over."

"*You* made the decision to lie low, not the rest of us. The boys are restless, tired of keeping watch on the herd and sitting around as wagon after wagon moves from the mines to town."

"They may not like tending cattle, but it's a lot better than coming against the Pinkerton man the town hired or the sheriff and his deputies. I can tell you they haven't stopped looking for us or believing we'll hit again. Now's not the time to draw their attention."

Flatnose looked around the room, noting the fine furnishings and expensive paintings.

"You're just growing soft, living in a place like this."

Rick snorted at the comment. "You've got as much stashed away as me. Probably more, now that I've used part for this place."

"It's not enough," Flatnose sneered. "I want more. The men want more. You're holding us back."

Rick didn't like the tone in his partner's voice. He took a couple of steps forward and planted his feet, ready to pull the gun holstered on his right.

"What you're talking about is folly. Wouldn't surprise me if the committee is setting this shipment up to draw us in. Have you thought of that?" The look on Flatnose's face told Rick he hadn't. "They're serious about doing whatever is needed to find us. If they do catch even one of us, they'll find everyone else. None of the men will go to their deaths without talking."

"Maybe so, or it might be they've already decided we've given up and left the area."

"Then why have they sent for a second Pinkerton man?"

Flatnose's eyes flew to Rick's. "Where'd you hear that?"

"Felicity is friends with the sheriff. Sterling told her the citizens committee approved a second agent to partner with Tom Horton. That news doesn't tell me they believe we've packed up and left." Rick pulled back the curtains from a front window and glanced around before letting them drop. "You need to leave. Anyone could've seen you come in."

"We're not done with this, Rick. You check on the new agent, and I'll see what more I can learn about the shipment." He swung the door open, then turned back. "The men aren't done and neither am I."

Rick watched him leave, a sick feeling building in his chest. He'd hoped his outlaw days were over so he could distance himself from his association with Flatnose. The man wouldn't be satisfied with what he had, knowing there'd always be more gold out there ready to be taken.

What disgusted Rick the most was his partner's belief they shouldn't let any of the guards live, even if they did cover their faces. He'd been able to hold him off since the killing of the last two guards, telling Flatnose it made no sense when they couldn't identify any of the gang. However, he knew he couldn't hold him off much longer. The man's need to kill had to do less with his desire to protect their identities and more with his own need for blood. If ever a man existed who enjoyed the act more, Rick hadn't met him.

He walked to the kitchen and tossed out his cold coffee, filling the cup again and taking a sip, contemplating his next move. He had no intention of riding with the gang again. Rick knew Flatnose had no desire to stop the raids, so an idea began to form in his mind. It would be risky and require much more thought, but it might be the answer he'd been seeking. A way to get out of the outlaw life for good.

Redemption's Edge Ranch

"Are you certain you don't want me to ride along?" Rachel asked as Ginny climbed onto the wagon seat.

Ginny glanced down at her friend and employer, knowing the information she sought would be better obtained alone. She raised her eyes to the clear sky, devoid of clouds, and shook her head. "I'll be fine. Besides, it will be a quick trip. I need a few items from the general store, and I need to pick up a book I left behind at Suzanne's. It will give me a chance to see how she's doing. Thank you for letting Mary stay here with you."

Rachel watched Mary running after a group of chickens and chuckled. "She's no problem at all. I sure don't know where she gets her energy." She wrapped her arms around her waist, holding the wool coat tight. "Go ahead. Stay at Uncle Charles' if the weather turns bad." She stayed on the porch until the wagon had disappeared, then walked toward Mary.

Rachel undid then retied the bonnet under her chin and shivered. She hadn't slept well again last night and now couldn't seem to get warm. She had to talk about her symptoms with her uncle. Maybe he'd have some idea of why she'd been feeling so poorly. Even with her extensive nurse experience, Rachel knew her skills lay in healing the wounded and not sick patients.

"Come on inside." Holding out her hand, Rachel clasped Mary's smaller one and turned toward the house. Everyone except Hank and Bernice were with the herd. Bernice had improved since Ginny arrived and even gotten out of bed, letting Hank walk her to the big house a couple of times. Her energy didn't last long, though. Within minutes, he'd wrapped an arm around her waist and helped her back to their place. At least she seemed to be feeling better.

"I saw a boy today." Mary's comment almost escaped Rachel's notice.

"What boy?"

"The one who comes in the morning." She said it as if everyone knew him.

They took the front steps, then walked inside. Mary pulled her hand free and worked to unbutton her coat. Rachel hung both coats on hooks, then headed for the kitchen.

"Tell me about the boy, Mary," she said before filling a kettle with water, placing it on the stove, and sitting down at the table.

"You know...the boy who hides with the chickens." She climbed on a chair and sat next to Rachel, grabbing a tin filled with biscuits.

"Do you see him every morning?"

Mary shook her head as she fumbled with the metal lid.

Rachel reached over, removed the lid, and took out a biscuit, handing it to her. "Do you want some jam?"

She nodded. "Yes, please."

Rachel pulled jam from the cupboard, cut the biscuit, and slathered a generous portion on each side. "Have you ever spoken with him?"

"No. I can't find him when I go outside." She took a large bite of the biscuit and grinned.

Rachel leaned back in her chair and wondered what to make of Mary's comments.

Was it the imagination of a little girl who had no one else to play with, or had she truly seen a boy hiding in the chicken coop? She waited until Mary had stuffed the last bite in her mouth, then stood.

"Come outside with me. I want you to show me where you've seen the boy."

Mary slipped into her coat, dashed down the steps, and ran toward the chicken pen, pointing toward the door to the coop. "He hides in there, Miss Rachel."

"What does he look like?"

"He's bigger than me." She held a hand above her head.

"Taller than Mr. Dax?"

"No," Mary giggled. "Like Ginny."

"Do you remember what he wears?"

Mary grabbed Rachel's hand, pulled her into the house, and pointed to a pillow Bernice had made with deerskin Running Bear had traded them for meat.

Deerskin, Rachel thought. It seemed as if the men were right about the thieves being Indian. Few white men wore deerskin.

"If you like, you can help me start supper."

Mary ran toward the kitchen. Rachel trudged along behind her, feeling tired while looking forward to speaking with Dax and Luke. They'd be most interested in what Mary had seen. Perhaps now they could catch the culprit and stop the pattern of stolen supplies.

Chapter Nineteen

Nick Barnett finished dinner, nodding when Suzanne walked up with a pot of coffee. "Sure tasted good, Mrs. Briar." He held his cup up, noticing again the attractive boardinghouse owner. He knew she'd lost her husband and daughter years before, and had heard the stories of her refusing any offers of marriage since.

"Thank you, Mr. Barnett. Can I get you another piece of pie?" Suzanne offered a broad smile to the saloon owner. A week before he'd come to her, asking if there might be an extra room at her place, one he could rent for an indefinite period. At first she'd been hesitant, knowing he had a place at the Dixie, then she listened to his reasons. After years of owning and living above saloons, he'd grown tired of the noise and lack of privacy. He wanted a quiet place to rest at night, and one where he could leave his personal belongings without worrying about them.

"I'd better not. At least not until tonight after supper," he said, giving her a quick wink. He looked around the empty restaurant and nodded toward a chair. "Why don't you sit a while, keep me company until I finish my coffee."

Suzanne seldom stopped to take a break, as the work at the boardinghouse seemed never to end. She'd start each day preparing breakfast for boarders and guests, then clean rooms and do laundry while she baked pies and started dinner. After the noon meals were finished, she'd start supper. Her normal day lasted from before dawn to well into the night. More than six hours of sleep felt like a luxury.

She took a quick look around as Nick stood to pull out a chair. "Thank you. Sitting sounds real good."

Nick waited for her to sit, pushed in the chair, and walked to a shelf on a nearby wall. He grabbed a coffee cup and filled it for Suzanne.

"Now I won't feel so awkward sitting alone." He sat and wrapped his hands around his own cup.

She let her eyes wander over him, realizing how little she knew about the man. In truth, she learned little about any of her boarders, most staying a week, two at the most, then moving on.

"How long have you owned this place?"

She blinked at his question, feeling embarrassed at being caught staring. "I bought the boardinghouse years ago when the owner wanted to move south."

"Did it always have a restaurant?" He stretched out his legs and relaxed, letting her warm, rich voice wash over him.

"Only large enough for the boarders. When Splendor began to grow a few years ago, I added space and opened it up to others." She sipped her coffee, looking over the rim of her cup at Nick, wondering what had happened to his left eye to require the use of a patch. Someday she'd find the courage to ask him. "Have you been in the saloon business long?"

"Too long, I'm afraid. My mother worked in a saloon when she had me." He held her gaze, watching for the look of pity he'd come to expect when others learned where he'd grown up.

Instead, the corners of Suzanne's eyes crinkled in amusement. "I guess that would qualify you to run a saloon." She offered a warm smile—not what he'd expected.

"That's the same response I got from my partner when I told her."

"Your partner is a woman?" The information surprised Suzanne. She assumed he'd be partnered with a man.

His mouth tilted up at the stunned look on her face. "And quite a woman at that."

"Your wife?" Suzanne wished she could yank the question back as soon as it escaped her lips.

Nick almost spit out the coffee in his mouth. "No, not my wife," he managed to choke out. "It's business only."

Suzanne felt an unexpected feeling of relief knowing he wasn't married. "Never married?"

"Never. I came close a couple of times before realizing I'd make a horrible husband and an even worse father."

"I find that hard to believe, Mr. Barnett."

"What kind of life could I offer a woman with me spending most of my days and nights in a saloon? It would take a special woman to want to get tangled up with me."

Nick looked up and Suzanne turned at the sound of the front door opening. Both stood to greet Ginny as she walked toward them, Suzanne wrapping her in a hug.

"I thought you'd never come for a visit," she said and dropped her arms.

"This is the first chance I've had to get away. Dax and Rachel keep me quite busy." Ginny turned her head toward Nick. "Good afternoon, Mr. Barnett."

"Miss Sorensen. It's a pleasure to see you again."

"Have you eaten? There's still plenty left in the kitchen." Suzanne could see by the look on Ginny's face she hadn't. "I'll be right back." She walked toward the kitchen, leaving Nick and Ginny alone.

Nick pulled out a chair. "Join us. We were just finishing our coffee."

She took a seat and clasped her hands in her lap.

"How is your job at the Pelletier place?"

"Busy. It's much bigger and they have more men than I expected."

"Must be a lot better than working at the Rose." He crossed his arms over his chest and sat back.

"In most ways."

"Oh?"

"Dax and Rachel are wonderful. I'm just not certain it's the best place for me."

Nick narrowed his eyes, fixing them on Ginny, wondering what she meant.

"Here you are." Suzanne set a plate in front of Ginny. "There's pie when you're done."

She inhaled the wonderful aroma of Suzanne's stew, glad to be eating someone else's cooking for a change. "It smells great."

"Same food as always."

"It's time for me go. Miss Sorensen, I hope to see you again and learn more about your work for the Pelletiers."

"I hope to get back into town more often, Mr. Barnett."

He made a slight bow to Suzanne and left.

Suzanne's gaze followed Nick, feeling a tug in her chest—unlike anything she'd felt in years.

Ginny finished the last bite and set her fork down, watching Suzanne's reaction. "Does he come in here to eat often?"

Suzanne swung her head toward Ginny, feeling her face heat. "He rents a room here. So, yes, he takes his meals here every day. Tell me how it's working out at Rachel's."

Ginny explained the work, the rooms provided to them, and the men who worked there, carefully avoiding any mention of Luke. "The days are long. Sometimes I fall into bed without the energy to even slip out of my dress."

"Mary's happy?"

"Yes, she loves it there."

"It sounds perfect." And it did, except Suzanne didn't see the sparkle she expected in Ginny's eyes. "And Luke? I heard he returned from his trip."

Ginny let her eyes fall to her lap, then looked up. "He has."

"And he's not too happy about you living at the ranch."

"How did you know?"

Suzanne admired Ginny's determination to provide a life for Mary, build a friendship with Luke, and assert some independence. Few women her age would make the same choice, preferring to find a man to take care of them. Unfortunately, Ginny seemed unaware of the struggle Luke felt between his own need for freedom and the obvious affection he held for her. Suzanne doubted either recognized or accepted the strong feelings each had for the other.

"It's hard for men to become friends with a woman. No matter their intentions, he'll eventually want something more, or the struggle will be so great, he'll decide to walk away."

"What struggle?" Ginny leaned forward, placing her arms on the table.

"Ginny, it's obvious he's attracted to you. He's also made it clear he isn't content to settle down. You're a temptation he doesn't need."

Ginny let Suzanne's words play over in her mind, trying to understand their meaning. She started to speak, then stopped, as if everything had suddenly become clear.

"You think he likes me?" Ginny's astonishment amused Suzanne.

"Yes. I believe Luke likes you very much. Too much, given the plans he has to work the ranch and for Pinkerton. He craves his independence. Luke believes he can't be tied to one woman, no matter how attracted he is to her. Of course, he might change his mind. For now, all he can do is push you away and avoid being around you."

"If what you say is true, I'm coming between him, Dax, and Rachel."

"I don't believe that's true or Rachel wouldn't have offered you the job. I'm sure he spends time with Dax on ranch business and working the herd. He may not choose to stay as often for supper, but that's his choice. Don't blame yourself for how he decides to deal with your presence there."

Ginny didn't respond as she thought through Suzanne's words, trying to come to some decision about her and Mary's future. She could stay and continue to be a wedge between the brothers, or begin to search for another solution. The need to look for something else didn't come as a surprise. She'd already felt her only option was to leave, allowing Luke to feel comfortable and welcome once again. He wouldn't as long as she and Mary lived at the ranch.

She reached across the table and took Suzanne's hand, squeezing it lightly. "Thank you."

"I don't know as I've helped you much."

"You've helped a great deal. Now I must decide what to do." Ginny pushed her chair back and picked up the empty plate.

"I'll take it. I'd feel better knowing you're on your way back. You never know when the next storm will blow in, making the ride impossible." She took the plate from Ginny's hand and walked her to the door. "Don't stay away so long next time."

Suzanne stood at the door, watching as Ginny climbed up onto the wagon seat.

"I'll see you soon," Ginny called as she slapped the reins.

I hope so, Suzanne thought, and walked back into her quiet restaurant.

"No argument, Rachel. I'm taking you to see Charles tomorrow." Dax sat next to her at the supper table, watching her pick at food she'd normally devour. He'd always marveled at the uninhibited way his wife ate, sometimes consuming almost twice his portion.

"I can go myself, or have Ginny ride with me. You don't need to take time from the herd."

"What good is being an owner if I can't take my wife to see the doctor?" he asked.

"He's right," Luke said, casting a look at Rachel. "He'd be useless to us with his mind on you anyway."

"I don't know why you two are making an issue of this. I'm just a little more tired than usual and not as hungry."

"And you've been nauseous the last few days, the same as Bernice when she started getting sick. I have business with Horace Clausen at the bank anyway. I also want to talk with Noah and Gabe, find out if anyone else has spotted a young boy running wild." He still didn't quite believe Mary's story of seeing a boy in the chicken coop. They'd posted a man the last few nights and he'd seen no one. Of course, Hank hadn't noticed anything missing during that time, either.

Ginny came into the room, carrying the beans she'd prepared, setting them on the table. "Is the meal all right?" She could hear the nervous tremor in her own voice. Luke had stayed away since his return from Denver, deciding to take supper at his own place. Tonight, Dax and Rachel both got on him. He had yet to say a word to Ginny.

"The meat and potatoes are excellent," Dax said, picking up the bowl of green beans and scooping up a large portion. "Why don't you join us?"

"Oh, no, but thank you. Mary's working on the lesson Rachel gave her today. In fact, I'd better go check on her." She turned toward the kitchen, wanting to get out of the room and away from Luke's intense stare. He wouldn't speak to her, yet he'd kept his eyes trained on her since coming in from the barn.

"You know you're going to have to speak to her at some point." Dax shot a look at Luke.

Luke grunted, but didn't respond.

"I had the impression the two of you were friends. Was I wrong?" Rachel asked.

He knew they'd continue to bedevil him about Ginny until he answered. "Sure. We're friends." He glanced at Rachel. "She has a job to do here. It's better if I keep my distance and let her do it." Luke stood, tossing his napkin on the table. "Thanks for supper. I'll be back in the morning before you leave for Doc Worthington's."

Dax's curiosity increased as he watched Luke walk away, grab his coat, and disappear out the door. They had no plans to send Ginny back to town, and Luke had no desire to ease the tension between them. He had to admire

Ginny, at least she made an effort to speak with him. Dax never thought he'd believe it, but the truth was, Luke didn't seem to be man enough to meet her halfway.

"Do you think he'd act this way if he had no feelings for her?"

"No, he wouldn't." Dax stood and walked toward the front window in time to see Luke ride off. He took the trail skirting the bunkhouse and disappeared, but not before he shot a look over his shoulder at the house. Dax shook his head and turned to Rachel. "There's nothing we can do. He's going to have to figure it all out for himself, the same as I had to."

Luke reined Prince to a stop and reached back into a saddlebag for his gloves. Slamming his hands into them, he picked up the reins and guided Prince toward the house. It wasn't a narrow trail. The use of the wagon to haul supplies to the site had necessitated cutting back brush and tree limbs, opening a clear path from the ranch house to his place. Some nights the ride seemed to fly by. Tonight it felt as if he'd ridden for hours.

He'd school himself all day to relax around Ginny, treat her the same as before she'd come to the ranch. Nothing had changed between them since he'd left for Denver.

The change had happened before he left—the kiss outside her bedroom at the boardinghouse. He'd meant it to be quick and meaningless, but the way he'd felt taking her in his arms and pressing his lips to hers shocked him. The sensations were more powerful than anything he'd ever experienced, alarming him to the point that all he could do was walk away. He found keeping his distance didn't help.

His thoughts of her were constant, creating images that seemed to control him. It didn't matter if he were at the ranch, in Denver, alone, or with others, remembering the feel of her haunted him. He wanted more than the kiss they'd shared. What scared him was the thought he might not be able to walk away if he ever held her again.

Chapter Twenty

Doc Worthington walked from the exam room to the area out front where Dax paced back and forth. He refused to let him in the room while examining Rachel, which had caused a strong response from Dax. Regardless, Charles insisted he leave the room.

Dax swung around at the sound of the door opening and glared at the doctor. "Well?" His harsh, one word question emphasized how he felt at being relegated to the waiting room.

Charles walked up and placed a hand on his shoulder. "Come on in. Rachel needs to speak with you."

Fear gripped Dax as he nodded and followed Charles into the exam room. He'd fought battles, commanded hundreds of Confederate soldiers, seen unimaginable carnage, yet the thought of something happening to Rachel shook him like nothing else he'd experienced.

She finished fastening the last button on her dress, a grim look on her face, as Dax stepped beside her. He could feel the large lump in his throat and worked to swallow as he waited for her to tell him what they faced.

"I'll be in the house." Charles closed the door to the walkway connecting the clinic with his place in back.

Dax steeled his expression, preparing himself for whatever Rachel had to tell him. She didn't say a word as she picked up her coat and slipped her arms inside, allowing Dax to draw it up over her shoulders. She turned to face him, reaching for his hands, holding them tight as her gaze fixed on his.

"We'll need to do some shopping."

Dax stared at her, not comprehending her words. "Shopping?"

"Of course, we can wait a while for what we need—about seven months."

Dax blinked, then grasped Rachel's arms. "You're...?"

She smiled. "Yes. We're having a baby."

"A baby..." he breathed out before pulling her tight against him.

She threw her arms around his neck, not believing the mixture of relief and excitement she felt. In minutes, her uncle had figured out what had troubled her for weeks. She'd been stunned into silence when he said she was two months pregnant. Even as a nurse, she'd missed the signs. The reality of it had sunk in one piece at a time until her uncle had ushered Dax into the room and she told him the news.

Dax pulled back, placing a kiss on her lips. "I suppose we should go speak with your uncle before going home. I hope he has some words of wisdom for us."

"He's a doctor, but also a bachelor. Something tells me we'll need to look elsewhere for advice." Rachel grasped his hand, pushed open the back door, and walked the few steps to the house. Before she entered, Dax pulled her to him.

He tried to speak, finding the words wouldn't come to express how he felt. Instead, he just said, "I love you."

"Can I help?" Mary asked as she and Ginny headed toward the barn.

"You can grab the stool and bucket for me, then talk real nice to Bessie."

Mary shook her head and tried to run in the heavy leather boots Ginny bought on her last trip to town. She slipped once and landed on her back, laughing as she jumped and continued toward the barn.

Ginny followed her toward the back where Hank had everything ready. He'd asked her to take over milking the three cows twice each day, a job he'd been doing since Bernice became ill.

She'd started just after dawn before gathering the eggs and preparing breakfast. Her parents owned one cow, which she milked twice daily. Three took considerably longer.

Mary grabbed the stool and one bucket, placing each where Ginny needed them, then stepped away. She giggled as Ginny washed the underside of the cow with warm water, used a rag to dry the skin, then wrapped one hand, then another around two teats. She worked in a practiced motion as milk began to flow into the bucket, falling into a familiar rhythm within seconds. As the milk slowed to a stop, she changed to the two remaining teats, glancing over her shoulder at Mary, who stood mesmerized.

"Mary, could you come over here?" Ginny asked. Mary stopped next to Ginny's shoulder, not taking her gaze from where her sister's hands gripped the cow. "Look here." Ginny nodded toward her hands. As Mary leaned in closer, Ginny shot a stream of warm milk at her face, eliciting a shriek, then a string of giggles.

Luke leaned against the barn entrance, arms crossed, watching the antics inside. Mary's laughter increased as Ginny shot one more stream at her, causing the cow to shift and cast a look over her shoulder. Luke started forward, then stopped as she calmed the cow and resumed the milking. He settled back against the barn entrance, watching as Ginny's hands worked one teat, then the other in slow, steady motions. He imagined the feel of her hands on him, groaning as his body responded to the image he created. He forced himself to look away, uncomfortable in body and mind at the direction his thoughts had taken.

"Mr. Luke!" Mary shouted and ran toward him. "Did you see what Ginny did?"

"Yes, I did," Luke replied, keeping his eyes focused on Ginny.

Ginny froze, glancing over her shoulder when Mary called Luke's name. He'd told Dax he'd be at the house for supper. She just hadn't expected him this early. She finished filling the bucket, placed it aside, and stood, untying the cow and walking her to a pen outside. As she turned toward the second cow, she felt someone come up behind her.

"I'll get her." Luke reached in front of Ginny, taking the second cow from the pen and walking inside, securing her before grabbing an empty bucket. He swept his gaze over her before stepping out of the way, knowing the best decision would be for him to leave.

Instead, he crossed his arms and leaned his shoulder against a stall.

Ginny didn't speak as she pulled the stool beneath her and repeated the process. She stopped more than once to wipe an arm across her brow, confused at the warmth sweeping over her. At one point she stood, shrugged off her heavy coat, and tossed it over the top rail of a nearby stall.

"Hot?" Luke asked, knowing he felt the same warmth as Ginny. Except he knew it had nothing to do with the temperature in the barn.

"Yes. It must be the heat from the cow."

"Maybe," Luke answered, his voice husky.

She finished the second, then the third cow, letting Luke swap the animals. Ginny picked up one bucket as Luke grabbed the other two and walked toward the house.

"Mary, please get the door for us."

Dashing ahead, she threw the door open and ran toward the kitchen, reaching for a tin filled with cookies.

"You'll have to wait until after supper," Ginny said as she and Luke set the buckets on a table.

"May I have just one, Ginny? Please?"

Ginny wiped a hand across her forehead as she looked down at Mary. She hadn't started their supper, which would take at least a couple of hours to prepare. "One small one."

Luke took the tin from Mary's hands, opened the lid, and let her reach inside. She selected the biggest one she could find and ran out before Ginny could notice.

"She took a big one, right?"

"Of course. Wouldn't you?" Luke chuckled as he replaced the tin on the counter. He turned his attention to Ginny as she strained the milk through a porous cloth and into a stoneware crock, then placed a clean cloth over the top and set it aside. "These are good." He took another bite of the cookie he'd pilfered before putting the tin away.

"You think I'd bake bad cookies?"

"I didn't know what to expect." He grinned as he tossed the last bite in his mouth. "I might have another."

She leaned over and slapped his hand away from the tin, trying to hide a smile. "Those are for after supper."

"If I don't grab mine now, Dax may not leave me any."

"I'm sure he wouldn't take them all."

"You didn't grow up with him. Mother would bake a cake or pie and set it out to cool. Within minutes, he'd snatch it and dash into the woods behind our house, laughing."

"He didn't eat it all, did he?"

"Every bite."

"I hope you don't believe the hogwash he's feeding you."

Luke and Ginny turned to see Dax and Rachel standing behind them.

"You mean you didn't steal your mother's cakes?"

"Oh, they were stolen all right, but it was Luke doing the taking."

She shot a hard look at Luke. "You lied to me."

"The story itself is true."

"But the thief was you." She shook her head, not surprised at his ability to turn a tale in his favor. "You all need to get out of my kitchen so I can start supper."

"I'll help–" Rachel started.

"No, you'll rest, just as your uncle ordered." He turned Rachel toward the stairs, then looked back over his shoulder at the two anxious faces. "She's pregnant."

Luke's jaw dropped at the same time Ginny let out a scream and ran to hug Rachel. "That's wonderful news," she said. "Do you need help with anything?"

"I'm just tired right now. Uncle Charles says I have seven months to go. I'm certain there will be much to do before then." She cast

Ginny a weary smile and headed upstairs, Dax right behind her.

Ginny watched as they disappeared into their room, then she walked back into the kitchen. "That's wonderful news, isn't it, Luke?"

"Yes, wonderful." His voice lacked the enthusiasm Ginny anticipated.

Dax had spoken of the future when he and Rachel would have children. It had seemed so far off. At the time, Dax had mentioned his concern about delivering a baby in Splendor. Even with the medical care Charles could provide, pregnancies were risky. Luke had seen the fear on his brother's face.

"You don't sound too happy about it."

Luke glanced over to see her perplexed look as her brows drew together. He heard no censure in her voice, just confusion at his somber statement.

"No? Well...I am. I'm just concerned." He glanced at the kitchen window at the soft flakes beginning to drop. "I'd better finish up a few chores before supper. Unless you need help in here." He wanted to prolong the conversation and stay longer, the same as he had the night they'd walked to the boardinghouse from the Rose. The night he'd kissed her. He pushed the thought from his mind and strode from the room.

"You'll be staying then?" she asked as he stepped outside.

He should say no. He'd already accomplished what he planned by riding to the house early—restore some level of friendship with Ginny. Luke didn't need to stay. From the moment he watched her in the barn, he'd fought the urge to pull her to him and repeat the kiss which burned in his mind. He needed to know if the same searing sensations would consume him a second time, if his body would respond as before, and if she'd gaze up at him with the identical passion he felt.

Luke turned back toward her, seeing the expectant look. In an instant, he lost all of his hard-earned self-control. He strode back inside, and in a few long, purposeful strides, stood before her. She looked up and blinked in confusion as his hands grasped her shoulders and pulled her to him. He'd stop if she tensed or backed away. She didn't. He lowered his head and touched his lips to hers—once, twice, then claimed her mouth the way he'd wanted for weeks.

He loosened his grip, moving his arms around her and splaying his hands on her back. Her hands slid up his arms in slow movements to his shoulders, until she'd wrapped them around his neck. He shifted, deepening the kiss as she moaned, pushing closer to him, setting off waves of heat coursing through his body. The intensity of her response surprised and encouraged him. He shifted once more, moving his hands to her head, holding her in place as he continued to explore her mouth.

A cough from behind Luke had him dropping his arms and stepping away as Ginny jumped back. He could see a hint of red move up her neck to her face, and he turned toward Dax, blocking his view and hiding her embarrassed look.

"I, uh...wondered if there might be any coffee left," Dax said, noting the calm expression on Luke's face. A sharp contrast to Ginny's deep rose color.

She swept a hand over her hair, slipping loose strands behind her ear, clearing her throat. "Yes... I mean no, but I can make some." She turned toward the stove and grabbed the empty pot.

Luke crossed his arms, not showing any remorse at being caught. "How is Rachel doing?"

One corner of Dax's mouth curved upward. "She fell asleep within minutes of lying down. Charles says she's doing fine and all her symptoms are normal."

"She's a smart, healthy woman," Luke said, noting the anxious look on his brother's face. "She knows what's coming and what to do." He clasped Dax on the shoulder. "Relax. It will all turn out fine."

"I helped my mother with Mary's birth," Ginny said as she stoked the fire in the stove.

Dax and Luke shot surprised looks at her. The news of Rachel's pregnancy was so fresh, it hadn't occurred to either that Ginny might be of help.

"Weren't you pretty young?" Luke asked.

"I'd just turned sixteen when Mother learned she was pregnant. By then, she was older and scared. The doctor taught me what to do, in case he couldn't get to the farm in time. He got there—after Mary was born." She handed each a cup filled with coffee. "He checked her and Mother, decided both were fine, and left." She turned her back to them, removed the cover from the milk, and began skimming off the top layer for butter, unaware of Dax's relief.

"You wouldn't mind helping with Rachel, would you?" he asked.

She didn't take her eyes off the task as she answered. "Of course I'll help. Whatever she needs."

"See, big brother. It's all going to be fine." Luke took a seat and sipped his coffee, still trembling from his body's reaction to Ginny. If Dax hadn't appeared, he wasn't sure how much farther he would've taken it. He'd almost lost control, something that never happened. The realization sobered him. There had never been a woman who affected him like Ginny. He glanced at her over the rim of his cup, feeling as if he'd sprung a trap he might be unable to escape.

"You have time to help me in the barn?" Dax asked Luke as he set down his empty cup.

"Sure." He took one more look at Ginny, letting his eyes wander over her and feeling his body tighten, before following Dax outside. He closed the buttons on his coat, feeling as if his head had been clamped in a vise, creating a pressure he didn't want or need.

He stopped inside the barn, watching as Dax looked up toward the rafters and the partial second floor. "Somewhere up there is a cradle Pat built years ago."

"A cradle? Pat was married?" Luke asked. They hadn't known Pat long before his death, but he'd never mentioned a wife or children.

"Bernice told Rachel he married about the time he started the ranch. His wife died from an infection a few months before giving birth. He had Hank store it up there. Said he never wanted to see it again." He shook his head, hoping the fate of Pat's wife didn't befall Rachel.

"I guess we should get it down." Luke climbed up the ladder, and pulled aside a few items before spotting the cradle. "Here it is. I'll need to hand it down to you."

Dax stood on the second rung and grabbed the cradle, then set it on the ground and stepped back. Made of pine, the wood needed refinishing after years of being neglected. The workmanship appeared flawless, and a lump formed in Dax's throat at the knowledge Pat had built this in hopes of it gracing his baby's room.

Luke jumped down from halfway up the ladder, landing next to Dax and the cradle. "You think Pat made this?"

"I'm certain of it."

Luke picked up the cradle and set it on a nearby workbench. He grabbed a rag, doing his best to clean off years of dust and cobwebs, then ran a hand over the wood. "He did a fine job."

"Yes, he did." Dax stared at the cradle, trying to decide if it were best to clean it up for his baby, or put it aside to let it rest as Pat wanted.

"It's not an omen, Dax. The tragedy Pat faced was his, not yours. We can clean it and fix what's needed." Luke glanced at his brother, then back at the cradle. "If you don't want to work on it, I will." He thought Dax would refuse his offer. As a ship's captain before the war, he had more experience working with and fixing wooden objects—and more superstitions.

"If it will keep you here a little longer each day, then fix it up." Dax ran a few fingers over one end, then drew his hand away and crossed his arms over his chest. "You and Ginny?"

Luke's jaw worked as his eyes shot to Dax's. "What you saw meant nothing."

"It didn't look that way, and I don't believe it meant nothing to Ginny."

Luke exhaled a deep breath and scrubbed a hand over his face. "Hell. I don't know what happened back there. I just know I don't want anything from her."

"You sure? Because you looked mighty comfortable."

"It has nothing to do with Ginny. She's beautiful and smart. She has more guts than most men I know, taking on the responsibility of her sister and doing whatever she can to provide. Any man would want her."

"Just not you." Dax didn't believe a word Luke uttered. Still, his brother had to make the decision on his own.

"No, not me. Maybe someday I'll be ready to marry and have what you and Rachel do. Not now."

"And if some other man enters her life?" Dax asked.

"I'd wish them good luck."

"And walk away without regrets."

"That's right." A pain, sharp and piercing, cut through him at the image of another man holding Ginny. He ruthlessly pushed it aside. Luke knew what was best for him and it wasn't Ginny Sorensen—or any other woman for that matter.

He loved the ranch and was committed to making it a success, but he also craved the freedom to take on assignments with Pinkerton. Dax understood this and allowed for it. There wasn't a woman alive who'd go along with his coming and going at will. Luke just couldn't commit to a woman knowing he might not make it home.

"If you're certain, then you'd best stay away from her. Something tells me she feels differently than you, and like you said, she's real special. Too special to dally with."

Luke heard the warning in Dax's voice. This was no request. It was a stern statement from someone who held high standards of conduct, just as Luke did.

He nodded. "What you saw won't happen again."

"Good. I'll hold you to that." Dax left Luke standing alone, knowing their conversation would gnaw at his brother for days. Luke had fallen in love. He just hadn't accepted it and would fight it for as long as possible. Dax had no problem with it, as long as Ginny didn't get hurt. There'd be hell to pay if she did.

Chapter Twenty-One

"You saw someone run from your cabin, didn't get a good look at him, but he appeared to be slim." Gabe turned his attention from Noah to Dax and Luke, who sat across the desk from him. "The two of you tell me Mary Sorensen says she's seen a boy coming out of your chicken coop early in the morning, but no one else has seen him. Sound right?" They nodded. "Frank and Hiram Frey swear they saw two people dash from behind their house a week ago, carrying a bag. They said both were slim and not too tall. Unfortunately, no one has gotten a good enough look at any of these apparitions."

"What are you saying, Gabe?" Noah asked.

"Is it a man or a woman? Could it be a child, or a short adult? No one's seen any tracks to follow, meaning they must be wearing moccasins. We assume they're castoffs from one of the tribes, but which one? The Blackfoot village north of Redemption's Edge makes the most sense. If that's true, why doesn't Running Bear know anything about them?" Gabe tossed the pen he'd been holding on the table and leaned forward. "All we know for certain is whoever is doing this lives in the mountains somewhere. In a cave we haven't found. The only way to find them is to search every inch of the mountain. Do you want to do that with Christmas a week away and the snow already above our waists?"

"Damn." Noah understood the frustration Gabe felt.

"You see the problem. I'll do whatever is needed to find them, but it will take a lot of men and more time. You have to let me know if it's what you want to do now, or if you can wait until spring when our chances for success increase."

"Did you discuss this with Hiram and Frank?" Dax asked.

"No. I hadn't heard from the three of you when I spoke with them. I do know they plan to move everything into their root cellar and post men to watch the chickens and pigs. I'd suggest the same for you Dax. I don't know what to suggest to you two." He nodded toward Noah and Luke. Their situation didn't compare to the others, and each could choose to remove anything of value over the winter. Noah could stay in his place in town, and Luke with Dax and Rachel.

"There isn't much at my place. I've been taking most of my meals at the ranch and I don't keep animals," Luke said.

"What about Prince?" Gabe asked.

"They haven't taken any cattle or horses that we know of. It appears they're after food supplies, eggs, and small animals," Luke replied.

"I agree with what Hiram and Frank are doing. We'll move what we have into the root cellar and post men to watch the chickens at night. In the spring, we'll mount a full search and find whoever is stealing from us. What about you, Noah?" Dax asked the one man who had yet to say a word.

"I've been staying most nights in town. Too much work to close early enough to make it to the cabin. I ride up on Saturday mornings and take what I need with me." Noah shot a quick look at Dax. "I agree with you. Wait out the winter and flush them out in the spring."

"Desperate people act in desperate ways."

"What do you mean, Gabe?" Luke asked.

"What happens when they can't get the supplies needed to survive? They'll starve or maybe harm others to get what they need."

"Are you suggesting we let them take the food?" Dax couldn't abide a thief, but he'd hate himself if his decision caused women or children to starve. He'd seen enough of that during the war to last his entire life.

"Not quite. I think there's one other possibility." Gabe folded his arms across his chest. "If there's nothing at Noah's or Luke's, and the Freys lock up their supplies and post men, the one place left for them to go will be your ranch."

"Which means our place becomes a trap. It will be the closest place for them to find food." Dax could see the possibilities in Gabe's idea.

"We'll post guards each night, rotate them in four hour shifts. Sooner or later the thieves will appear and we'll grab them," Luke said.

"And get them to show you where they've been living," Noah added.

"What do you think, Dax?" Luke asked.

"It's a good plan. With any luck, we'll catch them before Christmas." Dax slapped his hands on the desk and stood. "It's time we head back. Hank swears we're due for a big storm, and he's been accurate so far. Don't forget Christmas supper at our house." Dax looked at Noah and Gabe. "Rachel won't accept any excuses."

"I'll be there," Gabe said.

"So will I," Noah said, "and tell Rachel thank you. I wonder what Suzanne is doing?"

"We asked her this morning. She'll have boarders to cook for and a few others who always come in on Christmas." Luke buttoned his coat and opened the door to see Abigail Tolbert standing outside. "Good morning, Miss Tolbert. You here to see the sheriff?"

"Actually, I wanted to speak with Mr. Brandt." Abby looked around Luke to see Noah standing next to Gabe, watching as his eyes widened in surprise before he recovered and walked toward her.

"Abby, come inside before you freeze." He grasped her elbow and drew her toward the stove, brushing off the accumulated snow on her coat and ignoring the looks of the other men. "Are you in town alone?" His eyes narrowed on her as she fidgeted with her gloves.

"Of course I'm not alone. Father asked one of his ranch hands to accompany me." Her indignant tone did nothing to calm Noah's concern at her flushed face and lips, which had turned a deep blue. "I stopped at the livery and when you didn't appear, I asked Toby where you might be." She looked behind him at the amused looks on the men's faces, realizing she'd probably said too much in front of them. "Your tack shop is quite nice, by the way." Abby flashed her sweetest smile.

Noah fisted his hands before settling them on his hips, taking a settling breath. He glanced behind him, not pleased at the expressions on his friends' faces. "Would you mind giving Miss Tolbert and me a minute?"

"Certainly." Dax opened the door, letting Luke and Gabe walk out ahead of him, then tipped his hat at Abby. "Good day, Miss Tolbert."

"Mr. Pelletier," she responded, watching as he closed the door, leaving her alone with Noah.

"All right. Tell me why you came to see me at the livery."

"If you haven't eaten, we could go to Suzanne's and talk there."

He shook his head, feeling as if he were sinking into a deep pit with no way out. "Abby, you know your father wouldn't approve of us sharing a meal. If he found out, he might not let you come into town for a long while."

"Well, we just won't let him find out, will we?"

"Where's the man who brought you to town?"

"Loading the supplies from the general store, then he's handling some errands for my father until I'm ready to leave. I'm certain we have time."

"If you're sure, then I'd be honored to accompany you to dinner." He again took her elbow, then stopped. "I'm warning you, though, do not try to pay for the meal. You are my guest."

She smiled up at him, stunned he'd agreed, and nervous at the prospect of openly sharing time with Noah. Her father would learn of this, of that she had no doubt. Abby knew she should be concerned about his reaction. Now, however, her excitement overcame her concern. She wrapped a hand around the arm he offered, feeling wonderful and certain this would be the best meal of her life.

Big Pine, Montana

"Good to see you, Dutch." Tom shook the agent's hand, then grabbed his bag from the stagecoach driver. "I'll show you where we're staying."

"I could use some sleep. Longest stage ride I've ever taken. It broke down twice, once before Moosejaw and once after we left."

"He must have made up the time because you're here when the stage master said to expect you." Tom entered the hotel, signed Dutch in, then took the stairs to their rooms.

"Nice place." Dutch looked around the spacious room. "How'd you get Pinkerton to go for this?"

"It's the same as any of the hotels. The town's booming with the gold mines, and rooms go for a good sum, if you can find one. The only way we got these was from the pull of the head of the citizens committee. He owns the hotel."

"Who's that?"

"King Tolbert. His ranch is outside Splendor, where Luke has his place, but the man owns property and businesses here. He also owns part of at least one gold mine. Get some sleep, then we can talk."

Dutch masked his surprise at the mention of Tolbert. "Let me clean up and I'll meet you downstairs." Dutch opened his one bag and rummaged through it as Tom left. He pulled out a wanted poster Gus Salter had gotten from a man who'd come by his ranch. He'd been looking for a suspected murderer and had reason to believe the man had worked with Salter's foreman, Bob Bray, at some point.

Dutch washed his face and changed shirts before slipping the poster into his coat pocket and heading downstairs to meet Tom.

"I could use some food, then a drink."

They walked down the main street, Tom pointing out businesses owned by men on the citizens committee, until he stopped in front of a restaurant.

"This is the best place in town. It's also where many of the men on the committee eat their noon meal."

"Understood," Dutch said as they walked inside and were shown to a table.

Tom glanced around, nodding to a couple men he knew. He expected either or both to head toward their table before leaving. They'd been anxious to get the second agent in place.

They ordered, then Tom wasted no time telling Dutch what he knew.

"The committee...or rather, King Tolbert...is certain the thieves haven't left the area. He believes they're biding their time, wanting us to think they've moved on, possibly north of Splendor where new claims have been discovered. Tolbert and the committee have set a trap, hoping to lure the gang out with one large gold transport to Big Pine."

"Sounds as if this Tolbert fella is running the committee." Dutch stopped as the server set plates in front of them, then walked away.

"Might as well be." Tom looked around the room, then back at Dutch. "This is one of the businesses he owns. He wanted a nice place to eat when he came to Big Pine. The man provides a lot of jobs in town and makes sure the citizens know it. He's not shy about his wealth or what he wants, and doesn't hesitate to push his considerable power. One person he's been successful at keeping out of his way is Sheriff Sterling."

"Tolbert doesn't trust Sterling?" Dutch asked.

"Tolbert doesn't trust anyone, but I don't believe that's his motivation. He knows Sterling is against the committee. The sheriff believes they use their power as a license to hang anyone they believe to be guilty, with or without proof or a trial."

"I've heard of citizens committees acting worse than some of the outlaws they're after, especially north of here."

"It's true," Tom confirmed. "One of the mining towns up north has a tree they've named the Hanging Tree. Last year, ten men were hung within days, without a trial or a chance to tell their side. One was a deputy. A member of the vigilantes swore he was part of the gang robbing their gold shipments. His innocence was proven a week after the hanging. Even his senseless death didn't stop them from hauling in others."

"And you believe Tolbert agrees with the 'hanging tree' solution?" Dutch took another bite, pondering Tom's words and how they might handle similar actions.

"I believe he wants those who've robbed the gold wagons to be captured. Beyond that, well… I just don't know."

"When is this big shipment supposed to happen?" Dutch asked.

"A couple weeks after Christmas. I'm keeping Sterling posted. He's brought in more men with good experience."

"Any of them impress you?"

"It's hard to tell, as I haven't seen them take on any of the robbers. One is a mystery. Does his job and stays to himself. His name is Ezra Duncan. There's something about the man that doesn't add up." Tom glanced away, keeping watch on the comings and goings in the restaurant. "He was a sheriff in Nebraska for a while before something happened and he quit. Moved around and ended up here. Sterling believes there's some bad blood between him and a wealthy citizen in Big Pine."

"A member of the committee?"

"I don't know. His name is Frederick Marlowe. Came into town about the time Luke and I went to Denver, and bought a big house in a prominent area. I haven't been able to learn much about him."

"I can contact headquarters to see if they can learn anything about Marlowe. It could take a while, but it's worth a try. When is the next committee meeting?"

"Tomorrow night."

Dutch pulled the wanted poster out and handed it to Tom. "Have you ever heard of this man?"

Tom glanced at the name and studied the image, then shook his head. "Parnell Drake. Says he's wanted for murder. Where'd you get this?"

"Gus Salter. A man named Cash Coulter is tracking Drake. He came by Salter's place a day or two after Bob Bray's death. Two of the men Drake rides with were arrested the same night, part of the outfit buying the cattle from Bray and then moving the herd out of the area. Drake wasn't with them. Both men refuse to talk, but this Coulter fella is certain he's the leader of the gang buying the cattle from Bray."

"The poster says Drake is wanted for murder." Tom's brows knit in question.

"Coulter told Salter he's wanted for the murder of a family in Louisiana and is suspected of other killings."

"Why'd he give this to you?" Tom asked.

"Salter wants us to be aware of Drake since he's implicated in the thefts at his ranch. He has this notion Drake may have blackmailed Bray into stealing the cattle."

"Making excuses for Bray's actions?"

"It's more as if he's trying to come to terms with his friend's death. Who knows? Maybe he's right and Drake was blackmailing Bray. Regardless, Coulter told him Drake worked for a ranch in Splendor last spring. He disappeared with two others when there was evidence he'd tried to kill some men at a neighboring ranch. Any guess who he worked for?" Dutch asked.

"Who?"

"King Tolbert. And the neighboring ranch is owned by Luke and Dax Pelletier."

"Shit," Tom mumbled.

"Nothing we can do now, except be aware of Drake and his connection to both Tolbert and the Pelletiers."

Tom tossed money on the table before they left. "It's a strange business we're in," he said as they headed toward the sheriff's office.

"That it is, Tom."

Chapter Twenty-Two

Splendor, Montana

"How does it look?" Ginny asked, stepping away from the pine wreath she'd rested against the back of a chair.

"It's beautiful. Did your mother teach you how to make them?" Rachel stood back, admiring the wreath adorned with dried berries, nuts, and ribbons. Two more lay on the floor—one for their door and one for the bunkhouse.

"Mother loved making Christmas ornaments. She'd work on them all year, along with a neighbor who came to America from Germany. She taught Mother what she knew and encouraged her to try new decorations. For many nights before Christmas Eve, Mother would read a poem her family had sent her years before from their home in New York. *The Night Before Christmas*. Mary loves the poem. I don't have a copy, although I do remember much of it."

"My mother used to read it to me, too. It's wonderful."

The door flew open, letting a dusting of snow into the entry as Luke and Dax carried in armloads of wood.

"I'll leave mine in here." Dax placed his by the fireplace in the living room.

Luke continued into the kitchen, noting the smell of spice coming from the oven. He dropped the wood, stacked it next to the stove, then grabbed a towel Ginny used to open the oven door and peeked inside.

"Close that right now." Ginny walked up beside him, pushed the oven door closed and glared up at him. "They're not ready. Besides, they're for after supper tonight."

"They smell wonderful. What are they?"

"My mother called them jumbles. She used to make them for Christmas." She grabbed the towel from his hand, noting he hadn't moved. "Don't you have to help Dax with something?"

He watched the expression on her face change from irritation to amusement to frustration within seconds. Luke knew his efforts to distance himself from her since Dax saw them in the kitchen confused her. Hell, the conflicting emotions he felt for Ginny confused *him*.

He'd stayed for supper several evenings and they'd spoken a few times, but neither mentioned what happened between them. Luke had no desire to sort through and bare the internal conflict her touch created. Even if he could form the words to explain what he saw as his future, she wouldn't understand. Most important, he had no desire to hurt her.

There'd be hell to pay if he didn't figure the best way to handle her presence at the ranch. The same intense desire assaulted him each time he saw her, and it took all his willpower to do what he'd promised Dax—*What you saw won't happen again.* He surely hoped he could keep his vow because his feelings for her hadn't faded. No matter what he told himself, each day brought more doubt about what he thought to be his future.

"I want you to tell me what possessed you to accept an invitation from Mr. Brandt." King Tolbert's temper had simmered since learning of the meal Abby and Noah shared at the boardinghouse a few days before. "You won't accept any of the men I've put before you, yet you'll spend time with someone as common as the local blacksmith. I won't have it, Abby." He paced back and forth across the room, glaring at her between steps.

Abby sat with her back erect, hands in her lap, chin lifted in a defiant pose. "Why not?

You've told me what a fine man Mr. Brandt is and how you admire what he did at the Frey ranch."

"Killing men who threatened to murder others has nothing to do with a public display such as the one you put on with him."

"We simply took a meal in the middle of the day at Suzanne's. There certainly was no 'public display', as you suggest."

"Anyone could have seen you, assuming he had my blessing to court you—which he does not. He is no match for you and I won't have the town think he is."

"Who in Splendor would care? This isn't Big Pine, Father. It's a small town with good people who like Noah." Every impulse pushed at her to rise and walk over to her father. She ignored them, knowing he needed to work through his anger. "He's a good man, Father."

"I'm not questioning whether or not he's honorable. What I'm saying is you are not to spend any more time with him."

"You're forbidding me from seeing him?" Her voice rose along with her temper.

He stopped his pacing to turn toward her. "I am. I will not have you leading him on, thinking he has a chance when you and I both know he doesn't."

"I know no such thing." She jumped up from her chair, her eyes burning with the fury she felt at her father's ultimatum.

"What are you saying?" His voice took on a calm, which didn't bode well for their discussion. She knew what to expect when he vented his anger openly.

"I'm saying I don't understand why he shouldn't have as much chance with me as any man."

"Because the man isn't good enough for you, Abigail. He's a blacksmith. A foot soldier who fought in the war—"

"An ex-*major*, Father. He was an officer."

"A sharpshooter. He killed people on command and ordered others to do the same." He turned his back to her as he walked around his desk, trying to understand how his daughter could be attracted to a man with no money and a grim future.

"It was his duty." She walked up to stand on the other side of his desk, resting her hands on the top. "Would you feel differently if he'd been in the cavalry or infantry?"

King knew he wouldn't. No matter his role in the Union Army, the man's status did not compare to his or Abigail's and never would.

"You are not to see him again. There will be consequences if you defy me on this, and they will not be pleasant."

"What? Do you plan to beat me?" The strength of her anger and the fact she'd chosen to stand up to him surprised Abby. She took a step back and clenched her hands at her sides.

A pained expression crossed his face. "Do you truly believe I'd beat you?" His words were soft and controlled, as if the idea hurt to even think about.

"No, I don't," she breathed out.

He lowered himself into his chair and leveled his gaze at her. "All I want is what's best for you. Being associated with Mr. Brandt is unacceptable, and I'll do whatever is required to make certain his attentions are not directed at you."

"You don't plan to speak with him, do you?" Abby didn't want to involve Noah in the dispute she had with her father.

"Not if you agree to stay away from him."

"I refuse to ignore him or be rude, Father."

King thought on his, knowing it would be impossible for his daughter to be discourteous to anyone. "You'll do nothing to have others believe he is courting you. Understood?"

"Yes, I understand."

"Good."

Abby swallowed, feeling as if she'd won a small, yet significant victory.

"And, Abby. The consequences I mentioned... Don't think I won't make good on them."

She nodded, knowing she'd have to take particular care to be discreet. He believed her to still be a child, in need of his constant guidance. She wasn't. Abby knew her heart, and she wanted Noah Brandt. She'd let nothing stop her—not even her father's threats.

As Luke and Dax rode off, Ginny hung the last wreath on the front door and finished the strands of nuts, dried berries, and popped corn she'd made. The men stayed as long as they could, bringing in armloads of wood and doing what they could in preparation for Christmas. She wanted to speak to Luke, try to figure out how he felt about what happened between them, yet embarrassment and fear stopped her. Embarrassment at being caught by Dax and knowing he'd told Rachel, and fear of how Luke would respond.

She'd felt her world explode when his body aligned with hers, pulling her close. She hadn't wanted him to stop creating the intense emotions which overtook her at the touch of his lips on hers, his arms encircling her back. It had been nothing like her mother had said. She'd made it sound as if nothing wonderful came from physical contact with a man. In fact, she'd implied how unpleasant the experience would be. Ginny felt otherwise, admitting she didn't know what came next. Perhaps that was what her mother tried to warn her about.

The startling sensations had stayed with her all day and into the night. They'd plagued her as she lay in bed, keeping her from sleep as she replayed everything in her mind. She'd hoped he'd pull her aside, explain his feelings. He hadn't. Now he acted as if nothing extraordinary had occurred, making her even more unsure of herself and her future at the ranch.

"It all looks beautiful, Ginny," Rachel said, using a broom to brush up the loose pine needles.

"Let me do that." Ginny reached for the broom, dropping her hand when Rachel pulled it from her reach.

"You have other chores waiting. Besides, I need to keep busy. It's six months before Uncle Charles believes the baby will come, and I won't sit around doing nothing."

"I do need to milk again and start supper. Would you mind gathering the eggs?"

"Not at all. Where's Mary?" Rachel asked.

"She dashed outside a while ago, headed for the chicken coop. I believe she's trying to catch the boy hovering about."

"Odd no one has seen him. Dax and Luke think their plan to force the thieves to come to our ranch will succeed. It just may take a few days or weeks. It all depends on how much they've stored up from their other raids."

"Do you believe it's Indians?"

"I do. Given the arrowheads and lack of tracks, nothing else makes sense. Regardless of who it is, Dax and Luke will help them. They just want the thieving stopped."

They slipped on their heavy coats. The wind had picked up along with the snowfall, whipping snow against their faces.

"I should probably find Mary before starting with the cows."

"I'll look for her. You go ahead and get finished before the storm becomes any stronger." Rachel walked toward the henhouse, a basket slung over an arm, and watched for Mary. As suspected, she found her huddled in a corner, keeping an eye on the chickens, as well as the door. "Any sign of the boy?"

She shook her head. "No."

"Don't lose hope. I expect he'll come back once he's eaten the eggs he's already taken.

Besides, who has better eggs than us?" She checked each spot, filling her basket.

"Nobody."

"That's right."

"Where's Ginny?"

"Milking the cows. Would you like to go help her?"

Mary jumped from her hiding place and pushed open the door. "Come on, Miss Rachel. You can help, too."

"Stand still you miserable cow," Ginny grumbled, as the two walked into the barn. The wind howled, causing the skittish animal to shift, almost tipping her off the stool at one point.

"Are you finished?" Mary shifted from one foot to the other as Ginny released the last cow and picked up a bucket.

"I am. Can you carry the other bucket, Mary?"

Mary used both hands to lift the half-full container. She made it to the first step, set the bucket down, then lifted it to the next step, until Rachel opened the door to let them inside.

"Can I go watch for the boy, Ginny?"

"You can watch from the study. The storm is getting bad and I want you in the house."

Ginny washed her hands, brushing stray hair from her forehead, and looked out the back window. The storm had increased since they began the chores outside. From the looks of it, this storm threatened to be significant.

"I believe I'll lie down for a while." Rachel trudged up the stairs, leaving Ginny alone to her own thoughts.

She fought with herself over the decision she felt needed to be made. She wanted to help Rachel as much as she could during her pregnancy. She just didn't know how long she'd be able to stay at the ranch, working around Luke and feeling constantly vulnerable to her emotions. She hadn't expected anything more to happen between them. He'd made it clear the encounter at the boardinghouse wouldn't happen again, yet it had.

She now accepted her feelings for Luke, even as she knew the future depended on her ability to take care of Mary, a responsibility few, if any, men would want to take on. The fact Luke had said little to her the last few days, never mentioning what had happened, was a stark reminder of how little it meant to him. She had no idea how she'd do it, but she had to find a way to accept it as nothing more than a brief display of affection. Perhaps her mother had been right when she told her men didn't fall in love. Instead, they found someone who'd be a partner, and Luke certainly didn't need a female partner.

She sliced potatoes while letting her thoughts dance between Luke and what she saw as her future. Or rather, what she'd need to do to secure her future. It was far from settled. She still must speak with the person who could permit or stop her plans. Her hands dampened at the prospect of the discussion ahead. She reassured herself it would be the right decision by imagining her life with Mary in their own house, secure in a life which couldn't be taken away.

"Looks as if you might be staying a few nights."

Luke tossed his saddlebags on the floor of the barn and unsaddled Prince. "Hank swears this will be a major storm. After our decision about the thieves, I figured I might as well stay here a while, see what happens."

Dax narrowed his gaze at Luke, wondering if he meant the weather, the thieves, or Ginny. He'd seen how Luke's eyes rarely left her, following her as she served the meals, yet saying little. He'd watched her expectant look change to resignation as the days wore on and

Luke kept his distance. At least he'd kept his word to Dax.

"This storm may keep the thieves away."

"If they have enough food to last through it." Luke closed the stall where Prince fed on hay. He saw no sense in staying at his place when Dax needed the help. Even with the extra men they'd taken on, there never seemed to be enough time in the day to get all the chores done. Come spring, they'd be busy with repairs, expanding the herd, and if all went well, adding another two hundred acres to the south—land the Frey brothers had offered them at a good price.

"Have you heard any more from Pinkerton or Dutch?" Dax hoped Luke would turn down the next assignment. He'd never intended to shoulder the burden of the ranch on his own. Although he understood his brother's determination to combine his role at the ranch with the Pinkerton assignments, Dax didn't believe it could last much longer. They'd need to have a talk after Christmas, figure out what would work for both of them, especially with the knowledge there'd be another Pelletier coming into the world.

"Tom sent a message about Dutch arriving in Big Pine. He doubts they'll get approval for a third agent, so it appears nothing will be coming soon. You may be stuck with me for a while."

"I have no problem with that."

They stomped their snow-encrusted boots on the back step, slipping them off, and hanging their coats in the mudroom they'd built a few months before. Luke had come to expect the inviting aroma of Ginny's cooking. Although he admired her, he'd never thought her capable of handling the growing amount of work around the ranch with cooking, cleaning, milking, and other chores. He'd been wrong.

"Smells good, Ginny," Dax called as they cleaned up.

Luke noted the jumbles she'd baked earlier sitting on a counter and snapped one up before Ginny caught him. He tossed another to Dax, who caught it and took a bite just as the two women walked into the kitchen.

"Luke Pelletier," Ginny scolded. "I told you those were for after supper."

He held his arms in front of him, palms out. "Guess I forgot." He tried to reach for another before she shooed him away.

"You may have to seal those up before these two take them all." Rachel shot a smile at Dax.

"I'm going to tell both of you now. You'd better not get into the pies I'm baking tomorrow," Ginny warned. "They'll be for Christmas Day supper and not before."

Luke's mouth tilted up at the implied threat. "And just what would you do if a pie disappeared?"

She fisted her hands, rested them on her hips, and lifted her chin in a defiant gesture Luke found even more amusing. "Are you certain you want to find out?"

His eyes crinkled at the corners, thinking how beautiful she looked with her cheeks flushed and eyes blazing. He knew her threat was in gest, yet the game he'd started had turned on him, igniting a desire which startled Luke into taking a step away. He placed a hand over his heart.

"Your pies are safe from me, Ginny. Of course, I can't speak for Dax."

She shifted her gaze from Luke to Dax, who chuckled. "Don't worry, Ginny. I don't want to upset the person cooking my Christmas meal."

"Good. Then let me finish supper or you won't eat for hours."

Rachel ushered them from the kitchen. "I want to show you what Ginny did."

The men had entered through the back, missing the decorated wreaths on the front door and window, as well as the strands of dried berries, nuts, and popped corn hanging around the room. The last time Luke saw such a display had been years before when his mother spent days fixing up the house, making it a place where everyone wanted to congregate for the holiday. The memory brought a lump to his throat.

He glanced at Dax, noticing a similar look on his face. Their parents and younger brother had died during the last years of the war, leaving them with an inactive business and a home destroyed by Sherman's army. Christmas had meant little to them since losing their family.

"Isn't it beautiful?" Rachel asked, having no idea how the simple act of decorating for the holiday impacted them.

Luke cleared his throat, not taking his eyes from the decorations. "Yes, it is," he muttered in a hoarse whisper. He glanced over his shoulder toward the kitchen, knowing he should thank Ginny and let her know how much her efforts meant. Instead, he shot a quick look at Dax. "I need to do something before the storm worsens."

Rachel stepped next to her husband as Luke closed the door. "Is he all right?"

Dax wrapped an arm around her waist and pulled her close. "Yes, I believe he is."

Chapter Twenty-Three

"Why are you bringing a tree into the house, Mr. Luke?" Mary's eyes grew wide as she watched him walk past. She didn't wait for an answer before running to the kitchen where her sister and Rachel piled food into serving bowls. "Ginny, come see what Mr. Luke did."

The women turned at Mary's excited voice.

"Come see," she repeated before running back to where Luke worked to place the tree upright in the stand he'd made of wood.

"I suppose we should see what she's talking about." Rachel placed the pot of vegetables aside and wiped her hands on her apron. She stepped into the front room and stopped, blocking Ginny's view. "What a wonderful idea, Luke."

"What is it, Rachel?" Ginny asked from behind her. Rachel stepped aside, allowing her to see the tree he'd placed before the front window.

Ginny looked between Luke and the tree, her brows knit together in confusion.

"Haven't you ever seen a Christmas tree?" Luke asked.

Her eyes widened in surprise. "Yes, in a store window. I've never seen one in a house."

"Our mother made sure we had a tree each Christmas. She spent hours threading berries and nuts, like you have, and hung them on the tree. Every home we visited in Savannah at Christmas had a tree much like this one."

She walked up and touched a branch, noting the dampness still clinging to the needles, then turned toward him. "Is it all right if I make more strands to decorate it?"

"I hoped you would."

"What's all the commotion about?" Dax asked before spotting the tree. "This must be the 'chore' you mentioned."

"What do you think?" Luke asked.

"It may not be as big as the ones Father brought in for Mother, but it will certainly do." Dax's mouth curved into a grin.

"Especially when Ginny gets done fixing it up." Luke tilted a brow at her, looking for agreement.

Ginny flashed him a dazzling smile. "I'll start right after supper."

His gaze fixed on her as she walked toward the kitchen, the sway of her hips adding to the punch he'd felt in his stomach at her smile. Each day brought more uncertainty to his determination to distance himself from Ginny, continuing the path he'd followed for years. He enjoyed the freedom his single status provided—until recently.

Each night he fell asleep with images of her rolling through his mind, then woke with an uncomfortable ache in his body each morning. He felt his resolve crumbling, wondering if he should abandon what had guided him for years to see if there'd be any chance Ginny could fit into his life.

Luke didn't know how long he'd stood in place, immobilized by the effect she had on him, before Dax placed a hand on his shoulder.

"Good idea."

Luke hesitated, momentarily disconcerted, and wondered if Dax read his mind. "About?"

"The tree." Dax dropped his hand and narrowed his eyes. "Are you all right?" he asked, already having a good idea of what tormented Luke.

He recovered, offering the infectious grin that had pulled him through many uncomfortable situations. "Of course. Guess I'll clean up and get myself presentable." He ignored the knowing look in Dax's eyes and hoped he could conceal his confusion over Ginny a while longer.

"If you and the boys are set on it, then go ahead. I won't be a part of another raid." Rick's jaw clenched at the knowledge Flatnose and the men were determined to go after the gold wagon rumored to be the biggest haul in months.

"You'll be missing out on a lot of gold."

"Maybe. But if I'm right, the citizens committee is setting a trap and you'll be riding right into it." Greed and anger had blinded Rick in the past, ever since the deaths of his family. He no longer wanted to be the man he'd become over the last few years, giving in to the destructive emotions which had driven him for too long.

Flatnose didn't like the reminder he might be wrong about the wagon. What troubled him even more was his partner's refusal to be a part of the raid. He thought he could sway him. Rick's flat refusal stunned him as much as the change he saw in a man he believed he knew. The clothes were part of it—fancy suit, ruffled shirt, and expensive pocket watch. The biggest difference was the dead calm of his decision to walk away—not just from the gold, but from him and the gang. Rick had made it clear he wanted no further association with any of them. Flatnose believed you either stayed a part of the gang or signed your own death sentence. No one walked away unless everyone did.

"Guess we'll just find out who's right on this. The wagon is scheduled for the middle of January. Let me know if you change your mind."

"My decision stands. I won't be riding with you on this raid or any others. I'm done." Rick walked to the door and grasped the handle, indicating their meeting had ended. "I hope you and the boys know what you're doing." He stood aside as Flatnose stepped into the predawn night.

"Don't worry about us. Something tells me this will be the take of a lifetime."

Rick hoped the wagon didn't turn out to be a trap. If it were nothing more than an increased load, they'd take their loot and leave the area. Except he'd still be at risk if Flatnose or one of the others were ever caught and implicated him.

He walked to his desk, opened a drawer, and reached into the back, pulling out a small leather pouch. He poured out the contents and reached for a slim gold band. He held it up, remembering the day he'd placed it on his wife's finger, a stab of regret coursing through him. Rick knew he'd never love another woman, not even Felicity, the way he had her.

And he believed, without question, he'd never father more children. The gut-wrenching pain of losing a child wouldn't be repeated.

Rick knew he could find happiness with Felicity. He cared for her a great deal. Perhaps, in time, he would come to love her. He no longer wished to isolate himself, depending on others who lived outside the law, always feeling the need to look over his shoulder. His desire for a respectable life increased with every day he stayed away from Flatnose and the ranch.

Now he must make a critical decision. If successful, his future would be secure. If it failed, he'd be on the run again, leaving Felicity and his knew life behind.

He would spend Christmas with Felicity, not thinking of the decision he must make, enjoying whatever time he had with her. By the end of December, his choice would be determined and he'd be forced to wait for the outcome.

Splendor, Montana

The storm receded as the sun rose Christmas morning, leaving several feet of snow and ensuring there'd be little chance of Gabe or Noah making it to the ranch for Christmas supper. Even so, Rachel held out hope they'd find a way to join them.

"I'm so glad you brought Uncle Charles to the ranch early." Rachel finished dressing, fumbling with her buttons until Dax walked up and took over.

"How are you feeling?" He knew she'd already lost what little remained in her stomach. She'd declined going downstairs to breakfast, preferring to stay in bed. He'd brought up a plate anyway, sitting patiently while she took three or four bites, then rushed to the basin on the dresser. He knew his refusal to leave Rachel alone the last few mornings when she'd become sick embarrassed her, but Dax didn't care. Although common, Rachel had hoped to avoid the experience. Now she prayed for it to be over soon.

"I'm feeling much better. This should last a few more weeks, at most. You don't need to stay with me each time." She grabbed a brush and drew it through her hair, fighting the tangles until Dax's hand clamped over hers and he took over.

A few minutes later, he set down the brush, leaned over and kissed her cheek. "I need to go out with the men. We'll be back in plenty of time to help with whatever you need before supper."

They walked downstairs together, smelling spices intermingled with coffee. Dax inhaled, enjoying the aromas, while Rachel clutched her stomach, wishing she were over the dreaded illness.

"You ready?" Luke asked, handing Dax his coat and hat. "I asked Bull to select two others to stay here. I'm not comfortable leaving the women alone knowing the thieves may come back at any time."

"Agreed. I suspect they won't last long in this weather with no fresh eggs or meat. Is there anything left at your place?"

"No food or supplies. Unless they need a stove or furniture, the house should be safe enough." At least Luke hoped so.

"Did you speak with Ginny this morning?"

Luke shifted his eyes to Dax. "Just to say hello. Why?"

"No reason. Just wondered." Dax looked toward the group of men ready to ride. "Let's go." He waved them forward, the same way he used to as a general in the Confederate Army.

The deep snow made their work harder than normal. It had been a wise decision to move the herd to within a half-mile of the house and double up on feed they'd hauled out the day before. Today, they'd loaded two wagons, hoping to finish and be back home by early afternoon.

Bull, Travis, and Tat watched them ride out. Everyone had put in long hours the last couple of weeks. Tonight's supper would be a real treat for all of them.

"Let's get the tables and benches." Bull trudged through the snow toward the shed behind the bunkhouse. He'd grabbed a key and used it to open the lock Noah had made, letting the thick chain fall away.

The men gathered the furniture and Bull kicked the shed door closed. It didn't take long to place the furniture in the house as Rachel directed, then they started on their other chores. They'd just finished when Ginny called them in for dinner. Afterwards, they busied themselves in the barn fixing tack, milking cows, and organizing tools until Dax, Luke, and the rest of the men returned.

"We'll take care of them." Bull and Travis reached for Hannibal's and Prince's reins.

Dax and Luke trudged up the back steps, the enticing smell of fresh baked bread mingled with roasting meat assaulting them as they entered the house. Neither had eaten anything since breakfast and went on a hunt for whatever Ginny had ready.

When they entered, she didn't lift her head from where she worked over the sink. Instead, she indicated to a pot on the table with the spoon in her hand. "The stew is still warm, and biscuits are in the tin. I already left a pot for the men, so go ahead and finish what's there."

They wasted no time, each taking two servings, emptying the pot.

"I hope you saved room for supper." Again, she didn't glance their way, focusing on the job in front of her.

"You don't have to worry about that." Dax strolled from the room in search of Rachel, guessing he'd find her resting upstairs.

"Do you need help with anything?" Luke carried the bowls to the sink and washed them out.

"I may need more wood for the stove," she tilted her head toward the diminishing amount they'd brought in earlier. "I'm going through it faster than I thought. There isn't much else, other than making sure the fireplace is fed. Oh, and could you check on Mary for me? She should be in the study or someplace where she has a good view of the chicken coop."

"The chicken coop?"

She shot him a warm smile, catching Luke unprepared. He could live on one of her smiles for days. "She's determined to catch the boy who's been stealing our eggs. I told her he might not come back until the storm passes—"

"Which it has," Luke interjected.

"And that is why she's keeping watch. You'll find her all dressed and ready to run outside as soon as she spots him."

"Then I guess I'd better go look for her. Don't want her dashing outside without any of us knowing," Luke said, although he didn't move from his spot near Ginny. She finished the vegetables and filled the pot with water before grasping the handles to carry it to the stove. "I'll get it." He placed his hands next to hers, feeling the warmth and wanting to intertwine his fingers with hers. Instead, she responded by pulling her hands away, gripping the folds of her apron and stepping back.

He set the pot on the stove, tossed more wood into the firebox, then turned to face Ginny. "We should talk about what happened the other day." He lifted a hand to brush back strands of hair falling loose about her face.

Ginny shivered at the touch of his fingers, not wanting to hear his excuses. It had just been a kiss, nothing of real consequence—at least she's certain that's what Belle would say. She'd thought a great deal about her feelings toward Luke, realizing he'd never be able to provide the life she wanted for Mary. His free spirit and charming ways fit a life more suitable to adventure and travel, not the life of someone who dreamed of settling down with a family. He'd work the ranch, fulfill all his obligations to Dax, then when a request came from Pinkerton, be gone for weeks or possibly months. No matter her feelings for him, her life would be better as an independent woman, making her own decisions and not relying on a man such as Luke.

She bolstered her courage and locked her gaze on his. "I don't see we have anything to talk about. It was just a kiss, a celebration of the news of Rachel being with child—nothing more." The calm conviction in her voice surprised Ginny. She believed nothing of the sort, yet had to make Luke think she did. His inconsistent actions were a threat to her heart and future.

His eyes narrowed on hers, and seeing the slightest flicker of doubt, he stepped closer. "I see. You felt nothing for me either time I held you, kissed you until your eyes glazed over and you couldn't catch a breath?" He stroked a finger down her cheek, letting the caress follow her jaw and down the soft column of her neck, feeling her tremor beneath his touch. "You're certain?"

She held his gaze as long as she could, her heart thundering in her chest, before looking away. Her tongue darted out to moisten her lips as she took a step back, finding herself trapped against the edge of the counter. "Yes, that's what I'm saying," she whispered, still not looking at him, knowing her trembling voice gave away the lie.

He moved his finger under her chin, lifting her face and seeing the confused determination in her eyes. "All right. I won't speak another word about it."

He leaned down and placed a soft kiss on her lips, then a second before covering her mouth with his, sending a unanticipated wave of heat through him. He felt her hands move to his arms in a steadying motion as he deepened the kiss, feeling her fingers tighten.

His tongue traced the outline of her mouth, then delved inside as she opened for him. He took his time, not rushing the pleasure jolting through him. She shivered in his arms, and he splayed his hands across her back, drawing her tight and feeling her softness against the taut muscles of his chest. She squirmed against him, trying to get closer as her body rubbed sensuously against his, sending waves of fire streaking through him.

He couldn't remember any woman causing such intense hunger to build within him. Her taste, unique scent, even her soft sighs combined to create a passion new to him. He realized he didn't want to let her go. The knowledge slammed into him, causing what was left of his sanity to return. He pulled back and took a step away, hearing her soft sigh as her eyes slowly opened, and immediately missing the feel of her against him.

The sound of brisk knocking drew Luke's attention, even as his gaze remained fixed on hers. "I suppose one of us should answer it," he said, a tinge of uncertainty in his voice as he turned toward the sound of renewed knocking.

Chapter Twenty-Four

Ginny remained rooted in place, unable to move as intense sensations ripped through her body, clouding her mind. She shook her head and closed her eyes, trying to clear her jumbled thoughts. She didn't know much about the feelings which swamped her, except that being near Luke posed a clear threat to her heart.

Rachel strolled into the kitchen, holding Mary's hand and nodding toward the room behind her, a bright smile lighting her face. "Gabe and Noah made it." The thrill in her words couldn't be missed. "I don't know how they got through the snow drifts, but they did. Is there any coffee left?"

Ginny pulled herself together, hating the fact Luke made her feel so vulnerable.

"Yes. I'll get it." She grabbed cups and filled them with coffee, glad she'd thought to start a new pot. "Mary, please give these to Mr. Evans and Mr. Brandt." She watched as her sister disappeared, took a calming breath, and followed her.

"Merry Christmas, Ginny," Gabe said as Mary handed him a cup.

"Merry Christmas, Sheriff. We weren't sure you'd be able to get here."

"Noah and I never had a doubt, right?" Gabe glanced at his friend.

"True enough. Merry Christmas, Ginny." Noah breathed in the aromas coming from the kitchen, feeling the stirrings of a growl coming from his stomach. He placed a hand over it, but not in time to stifle the familiar sound.

Ginny dashed into the kitchen, emerging a moment later with a platter filled with sliced cold cornbread and pickled vegetables. She set it and small serving plates on the decorated dining room table and glanced at the small gathering, keeping her eyes averted from Luke, who'd watched her since she walked into the room.

"This should hold you until supper is ready, which won't be long," she announced before leaving them to finish the final touches to the meal.

"How is she doing?" Gabe asked Rachel, nodding toward the kitchen.

"Ginny is wonderful. I still can't believe the amount of work she does for us."

"And takes care of her sister," Uncle Charles interjected. "Who, from what I hear, is a handful." He winked at his niece, knowing how much Rachel had grown to love Mary.

"Oh, she's not too bad now, but something tells me she's going to be as she grows older," Rachel replied.

"Is there anything we can help with before supper?" Noah asked, never comfortable standing around, doing nothing.

Rachel watched Noah nibble on the cornbread. The customs of the frontier differed significantly from those of the east. At her parent's home in Boston, a guest would never be allowed to help. Here, offers to lend a hand were frequent and accepted.

"Let me check with Ginny to see if she needs anything." Rachel stepped into the kitchen as Ginny drained the potatoes. Several covered dishes sat on the work counter, ready to be taken into the dining room, plus mince and apple pies, and the almond sponge cake Ginny made using her mother's recipe. It seemed like enough to feed an army, which was around the number of people who'd be crammed into the dining and living rooms for supper.

"Noah asked if you needed any help."

"Does he need something to fill his time?" Ginny asked, wiping an arm across her damp brow.

"Yes, I believe he does." Rachel's mouth curved into a tired smile.

"Why don't you lie down for a bit? I'll have Noah help me with the goose and roast, then come and get you when we're ready."

"Absolutely not. We have guests, and I won't miss a moment of the day." Rachel straightened, knowing if Ginny noticed her fatigue, others might also. "I'll get Noah." She didn't have to walk far as Noah came up to her the moment she left the kitchen. "She could use your help."

He nodded and stepped past her. "What shall I do?" he asked Ginny, marveling at all the dishes and pies sitting around the room.

Luke watched Noah join Ginny in the kitchen, a knot forming in his chest. His body still thrummed from holding her and feeling her passionate response. The thought of another man in a closed room with her felt wrong, yet he had no hold on her, and knew Noah would cross no lines of propriety.

Even if he denied it, the whole town knew Noah's feelings toward Abigail Tolbert, and believed she felt the same. Did they think the same of him and Ginny? From their behavior, the ranch hands seemed to believe Luke as smitten as Noah. Was he? He took a breath, knowing his feelings had become too strong to ignore. He didn't know if he loved her, but he sure as hell wanted her, and not just for one night. Fear gripped him as he accepted that once he had her, he'd never be able to let her go.

"You staying here now?" Gabe's question jerked him to the conversation they had been having about the raids.

"Uh...yes. I've closed up the house. If all goes as we hope, we'll lay our sights on the thieves real soon."

A knock had them turning toward the front door as it opened and Bull walked in, followed by all the men.

"Are we early?" Bull asked, a wide grin on his face.

"We were wondering where you all were." Dax shook his hand, as well as those of the other men, tossing out Christmas greetings, offering whiskey or coffee to each.

The room boomed with the sound of men's voices, laughing and relishing a celebration meant to take them through the anticipated long winter. Bull spotted Mary standing next to Rachel, eyes wide in a sea of adults. He knelt before her and took in the new red dress she wore.

"Your dress sure is pretty, Mary."

She moved her eyes to him and smiled. "Ginny made it for me."

"Well, she did a real good job."

He stood, turning at muffled sounds coming from the kitchen, then saw the door swing open and Noah emerge, carrying two large bowls. Bull followed him into the kitchen and within no time, the tables were covered with platters and serving dishes full of white butter beans, red cabbage, potatoes, lima beans, peaches, bread, sliced venison, and hearty chunks of roast beef.

"Looks to be time for everyone to find a seat," Rachel said.

They'd squeezed the two extra tables as close as they could to the existing table. Ginny had made decorations for all three, placing an abundance of candles on each.

Bull brought the last dish out, a large platter containing the goose he'd shot and Ginny had prepared, surrounded by brandied fruit. He stood behind an empty chair, then waited for Dax to seat Rachel as Luke pulled out Ginny's chair.

On most nights, Luke took a seat across the table from her. Tonight, he'd chosen the one next to Ginny, resting a thigh against hers, feeling the slight flinch as she tried to shift away. Luke hid a grin, knowing she sat wedged between him and Noah. He shot a quick glance at her, seeing a blush creep up her face.

"Dax," Rachel encouraged, looking at her husband.

He picked up his worn copy of the Soldier's Prayer Book he'd carried with him the last years of the war—a gift from a fallen comrade.

"I'd like to say a prayer." He opened the book, selecting a short one he'd read many times during the long campaigns, and bowed his head.

"Direct us, o Lord, in all our doings, with thy most gracious favor, and further us with thy continual help that in all our works begun, continued, and ended in thee, we may glorify thy holy Name and finally, by thy mercy, obtain everlasting life. Amen."

"Please, help yourselves." Rachel lifted a steaming bowl of potatoes and passed them to her uncle. "Ginny, did Hank come over for their supper?" Hank and Bernice had decided it'd be best to stay in their home near the bunkhouse. Even though the men had offered to carry her to the main house, Hank had refused, knowing Bernice's energy wouldn't last long in a large crowd.

"Bull and Noah carried their meal to them. Hank and Bernice were very grateful and wished us all a Merry Christmas."

Muffled sounds came from around the room as conversations continued between mouthfuls. Ginny thought she'd made plenty, then began to worry as one by one, the bowls emptied. She breathed a sigh of relief when the pace slowed and the men began to lean back in their chairs, satisfied.

Luke kept up with the various conversations while casting glances at Ginny, noticing she'd touched little of her own supper. He'd already had seconds of the roast and potatoes, while her food grew cold.

"You're not hungry?"

She pulled her eyes from the other side of the room to focus on Luke. "Just waiting to see if anyone topples over from the cooking," she responded with a cautious, self-deprecating grin.

Luke burst into a hearty laugh. It wasn't often Ginny joked with him anymore. She hadn't done it once since she'd moved into the house.

He glanced around the table. "It doesn't appear you need to worry about it. Go ahead and eat. You worked hard and it's all quite good."

Ginny took a few bites, believing the reason for her lack of appetite had nothing to do with the food. The man sitting next to her, letting his thigh rest against hers, seemed to push all rational thought from her mind. She could feel the warmth from his muscled leg seep through his trousers and her dress, creating a tingling sensation which made her shudder. She shifted, trying to gain distance, but Luke wouldn't have it. Each time he'd close the distance within seconds, at one point moving his hand under the table and resting it on her knee. Her involuntary jerk produced a slight smirk from Luke, which she chose to ignore as she took a few more bites.

"Sorry," he mumbled as he pulled his hand back above the table.

"No, you're not," she challenged in a low voice.

"You're right. I'm not." He leaned back in his chair and crossed his arms, keeping an eye on Ginny as she used her napkin to dab the dampness from her brow.

"I believe the heat from cooking all day has affected me." She took a deep breath and hoped that was the reason she felt waves of warmth moving through her body.

"Could be," Luke responded, knowing what she felt had nothing to do with the cooking.

When everyone finished and the plates had been cleared, Ginny brought out the pies, cake, and coffee. She offered generous slices to everyone. A couple of the men refused, then changed their minds upon hearing the satisfied groans of the others.

"Miss Ginny, that was the best Christmas supper I've ever had." Noah rested a hand on his stomach, craving another piece of her apple pie, but knowing he had no room for it. "May I help you clean up?"

"Certainly not," she scolded in a mild tone. "You go spend time with the other men. I'm sure you could use a whiskey or brandy."

"Perhaps." He offered a vague smile, his thoughts on Abby Tolbert and how much he'd wanted to spend time with her. When they'd had dinner at the boardinghouse, she invited him for Christmas supper, but he'd refused. Even though she'd insisted her father would welcome him, he knew different. Although King Tolbert might see him as a good blacksmith and a hard worker, he also considered him well beneath his daughter's social standing. In Noah's mind, the man had it right. Noah would never be good enough for Abby. He'd been fortunate to be able to offer her a truthful excuse—he'd already accepted Rachel's invitation. The slump in her shoulders and forced smile told him how much his answer had disappointed her. He'd have to find a way to make it up to her.

Suzanne blew out the last of the candles in the dining room, disappointment swelling within her at the way Christmas Day had come and gone. She'd declined the Pelletier's invitation to supper, as well as Gabe and Noah's last minute invitation to ride out with them.

She'd spent all morning preparing enough food for those she thought would come by—townsfolk who always made it a point to offer their greetings, even if they only picked up a pie or stayed for soup. The one boarder she had, other than Nick Barnett, left the day before, wanting to take advantage of the clearing weather to get over the mountains into Idaho before a new storm came through. Nick had already told her he planned to have supper at the saloon.

Amos Henderson came by for a minute, as did Horace Clausen, both apologizing for not being able to stay longer or take the time for dinner.

Suzanne stepped into the kitchen and eyed the roast she'd made, along with vegetables and an assortment of other dishes. She'd baked four pies, and not one had been touched.

"Oh, well," she sighed, grabbing a cup and pouring herself coffee from the full pot, then took a seat at the table. Her appetite had fled along with her customers. She set the cup down and rested her head in her hands, feeling alone and empty. Since her husband and daughter had died, she'd done her best to build a new life. Her friendships, along with her faith and work at the boardinghouse, had sustained her. For the first time in years, she felt like giving up.

"Any pie left?"

Suzanne glanced up at the sound of the masculine voice. Nick Barnett stood in the doorway, a bottle in his hand. She'd been so lost in her own self-pity, she hadn't heard anyone approach.

"Of course." She swept her hand toward the counter with the untouched pies. "Pick whichever one you want."

He didn't even look. "I'll take mince, if you have it. And two glasses."

She cut a large slice of mince for Nick and a slice of apple for herself, set them on the table, then grabbed glasses.

He walked around the table, pulled out Suzanne's chair, and made a slight bow. "Madame."

Suzanne couldn't help but smile at Nick's antics, deciding he'd already been enjoying some liquid cheer. He opened the bottle and poured a generous amount of whiskey in each, then took his own seat and lifted his glass.

"Merry Christmas, Suzanne." His broad, sincere smile meant more to her than any of the other greetings she'd received today.

Picking up her glass, she held it out, her hand shaking. "Merry Christmas, Nicholas."

"Come on upstairs, Noah. I'll show you where you and Gabe will be staying tonight." Rachel stopped next to him and wrapped her arm through his. "I hope the two of you don't mind sharing a room. It has a couple beds."

"We're grateful to have a place at all. I don't mind telling you, riding back to Splendor tonight doesn't appeal to me at all."

They'd just started upstairs when they heard shouts from outside. The men had left for the bunkhouse not long before, Bull staying a few extra minutes before following them.

Gabe shot Noah a look before dashing out the door and onto the porch, trying to see in the darkness. A moment later, Noah, Dax, Luke, Doc Worthington, and the women joined him, followed a minute later by Mary, who grabbed Ginny's hand.

"Settle down, you rascal." Bull's stern voice came from the direction of the chicken coop. A moment later, he walked toward them, dragging what appeared to be a squirming Indian boy by the collar.

"Don't fight me, boy, unless you want to take a ride over my shoulder," Bull warned, beginning to lose patience with the young Indian. He hauled him up the steps, bringing him to a halt in front of Gabe, the boy's long dark hair hanging in front of his face. "Here you go, Sheriff. I found him hiding in the shed. Guess I forgot to lock it when the boys and me moved the tables and benches."

Gabe stared at the boy, whose head was bent, appearing to be focused on the deerskin moccasins covering his feet. He stood well over five feet, his frame bone thin, clothes hanging off his shoulders and hips. Gabe guessed he weighed little more than a hundred pounds.

"Do you speak English?" Gabe knew little of the Blackfoot dialect Running Bear's tribe spoke. Bull knew some, perhaps enough to find out where the boy had been living.

He stayed silent, not looking at anyone.

A defiant jerk dislodged the finger Gabe placed under the boy's chin in an attempt to make eye contact. Gabe bent to look into his face, achieving nothing when the boy spun away from him. Bull grabbed his shoulders and spun him back around, holding him in place to face the sheriff.

"Where have you been living?" Gabe asked, then looked up at Bull, who did his best to translate the question into the Blackfoot language. Still, the boy remained silent.

"What's your name?" Bull asked, again in the Blackfoot language.

When the boy remained silent, Gabe stood and let out a breath. "Not much we can do except lock him up in the chicken coop until he decides to talk."

"Ginny..." Mary beseeched.

"It's not our place to interfere, Mary." She put a finger to her lips, indicating they needed to stay silent.

"Do you think we should tie him up?" Noah asked, eyeing the boy as he figured out Gabe's strategy.

"May not be a bad idea. In a few days, he might be willing to talk," Gabe answered.

The boy turned and tried to jump from the porch. Bull reacted quickly, grabbing his shirt and pulling him back toward them. This time he walked the boy to a chair and nudged him into it, then reached into his pocket, extracting a long, thin cord. He wrapped it around one wrist, then around the arm of the chair before stepping away and taking a good, long look at him.

No one spoke, each trying to figure out the best way to handle the boy and find the others involved. It took a couple minutes before the boy's head came up, his chin jutted out in a defiant gesture, his eyes blazing—angry blue eyes as clear as the Montana morning sky.

"My God, he's white," Rachel murmured, leaning into Dax.

Gabe stepped in front of Bull, believing the boy understood everything they'd said. "How long since you've eaten a regular meal?" When he didn't answer, Gabe grabbed the boy's chin between his thumb and fingers. "How long?"

For the first time, fear flashed in the boy's eyes. "Three days," he spat out, then closed his mouth tight.

"Ginny, would you mind getting him some food and water?" Dax asked.

She wasted no time filling a plate and grabbing utensils. "Here." She handed the food to Gabe.

"I'm telling you right now, if you throw this food or pull some other harebrained antic, I *will* tie you up and lock you in the chicken coop. Do we understand each other?"

The boy glared at him but nodded. "Yes."

Gabe handed him the plate and fork, keeping the knife in his hand, and untied the leather strap around the boy's wrist. The speed at which he devoured the food surprised everyone. Within minutes he handed the plate back to Gabe and wiped a sleeve across his mouth.

"Do you want more?" Gabe asked.

The boy shook his head, and for the first time, made eye contact with other others. The men had poured out of the bunkhouse at the sound of Bull's voice, and stood around, not ready to leave until they'd learned more about the boy.

"What's your name?" Bull asked again.

"Boy Who Runs Fast."

Bull decided it best to remember the name and what it implied. "What's your white name?"

"Billy."

Bull looked at Gabe, asking without words what the sheriff wanted to do next.

"Billy, let's go inside." Gabe reached out a hand, which Billy ignored as he stood and walked through the front door.

"We'll go in the study. Ginny, is there a place Billy can sleep tonight?" Dax asked.

"He'll sleep in the same room with Noah and me." Gabe planned to take no chances.

Luke, Dax, Bull, and Noah took seats in the study, followed by Gabe and Billy. There were still many questions needing answers, including the location of where he and the others lived.

"If you don't need me, I believe I'll turn in." Doc Worthington turned toward the hall.

"Will you be around tomorrow?" Gabe asked.

"I can stay another day, if you'd like."

"Thanks, Doc." Gabe turned toward the boy. "Now, Billy, tell us where you've been living, and how many more are hidden in the mountains."

Chapter Twenty-Five

The men questioned Billy until they'd grown weary of hearing the same story over and over. He told them he'd escaped a Crow village months before and worked his way across Montana, heading west until the bad weather started and he realized he couldn't go any further until spring. He decided to hole up in a cave above Luke's house.

The men believed the only truthful part of the tale was his escape from the Crow camp. Each thought the rest to be pure hogwash.

They decided to start again in the morning. The boy's fierce protection of the others gained the respect of the men, yet it also put Billy's friends in danger. If he didn't return, there'd be one less person to gather food and supplies.

The sun had begun to rise over the mountains in the east. Gabe sat at the kitchen table, watching over the rim of his coffee cup as Billy shoveled one spoonful of food after another into his mouth. He had told them he'd turned fifteen on his last birthday and had lived with the Crow Indians for almost three years.

"Why'd you decide to leave the Crow? Quite a decision for a lone boy to make. Seems you would've had others traveling with you." Gabe had never been a lawman before agreeing to take on the sheriff's job in Splendor. He'd been a colonel in the Union Army, making tough decisions and leading men into battle. The skills he learned during the war served him well in his new job—one he had no intention of keeping for long.

Billy continued to chew his food, ignoring Gabe's question, hoping the lawman would give up. The boy didn't know Gabe or his friends. When they had a goal, these men never quit.

"Is there anyone left to find food after we take you into town? You know, unless you lead us to the others, they'll be left to take care of themselves. I hope none of them gets sick." Gabe leaned forward, resting his forearms on the table and keeping his gaze trained on Billy. The last question caused the boy to squirm in his chair as his eyes darted around the room. Gabe knew the boy had decided to run.

The sound of chair legs scraping wood was the only warning as Billy jumped to his feet and ran toward the back door. Gabe let him go, knowing the others were ready to follow him into the woods. Last night they'd made the decision to allow him to escape, hoping he'd lead them to his friends.

"There he goes," Noah said as Billy took off at a fast pace, dashing around the bunkhouse and into the trees beyond. "It shouldn't take long for Luke and Dax to spot him."

Bull nodded, then nudged his horse into a gallop, determined not to the let the boy get away.

Gabe came out the front door and walked toward the barn where Blackheart stood saddled and waiting. "Let's go." Gabe swung into the saddle and they followed the path Bull set.

Most people thought tracking someone in the winter was harder than other times of the year. Dax and Luke believed otherwise. The decreased foliage allowed them to spot their prey easier. They'd taken away Billy's moccasins, providing him with boots he refused to wear. They hoped following bare footprints would be better than trying to track someone wearing moccasins. At least the lack of protection on his feet might slow him down.

Bull kept Billy in sight while staying as far back as he felt safe. He knew where Luke and Dax would be—on the exact path Billy had chosen to take.

"There he is." Luke pointed as he and Dax moved farther behind the boulder shielding them from Billy's view. "The boy sure can run."

They followed him as he crossed Wildfire Creek, not thirty yards from Luke's house. They noted the direction he took and waited for the others to join them.

"Fan out, fifteen yards apart, and follow him up the hill. One shot in the air when you spot the cave." Dax moved across the swelling creek, Hannibal not flinching at the frigid water. Luke and Bull spread out to his left, while Gabe and Noah rode to his right. The five kept a steady pace, listening and noting any changes as they pursued their prey.

Billy squatted and looked around. He knew the men followed him, yet he didn't dare stop. He had to warn the others before they were discovered and hauled into jail for stealing. His feet stung from the icy ground and freezing water, and Billy knew he'd made a mistake leaving without the boots.

As the wind swirled around him, he shivered and thought of Lydia, the woman who'd risked her life to help them escape. She'd been promised to a Crow brave, the one who'd pulled her from a burning cabin even as she fought him.

Her parents had died in the fire, which started over a disagreement between a neighboring Crow village and her father. A fire, Lydia had once told Billy, could've been avoided if her father hadn't fired on the small band of Crow who approached their house. He'd panicked, shooting and killing a young brave.

The enraged Crow killed her parents, taking Lydia and her younger sister and brother captive. They'd come to the tribe a year before, two years after Billy and his sister. She'd been given time to adjust, then was told the warrior who saved her would become her husband. Lydia had no desire to stay with the tribe, become the bride of a man she didn't love, and live her life away from the white world and the customs she knew.

Billy had learned of the plan to escape and confronted her, telling Lydia he and his sister would be going along. They'd snuck away from the village several months before while most of the warriors were away hunting. He still didn't know how they'd stayed hidden from the Crow party which hunted them, but they had.

Along the way, they'd been turned away more times than he could count by farmers and ranchers who didn't want to associate with whites who'd lived with the Crow. None would take the chance of sheltering the former captives or helping them back into the white world. Most gave them food and sent them on their way.

Billy now trusted few white men. He'd seen the pained expressions of the women, along with the disgust of the men, as they were turned away. They were relegated to a third world, one between the whites and the Indians.

He pushed away the painful memories and glanced behind him once more. Seeing nothing, Billy dashed up the hill, trying to stay below the tops of the sparse brush. The sound of a bird chirping had him crashing to the ground. The sound repeated a moment later, then stopped. He doubted it came from the men who followed him. He didn't believe they'd know how to make calls similar to the ones used by the Crow warriors. Convinced it was nothing, Billy stood and ran as fast as his bare feet would carry him, up the hill, around a thick stand of pine, and slipped through a tight opening in the rocks, which led to a hidden cavern deep within the mountain.

"Got him," Bull said, looking through the field glasses he always carried. "He disappeared into those rocks behind the stand of pine."

"You're certain he didn't go around them?" Luke signaled Dax with the bird call they'd perfected as children, then slid off Prince, receiving an answering call from his brother.

"I am. He's hidden in the rocks or in a cave we didn't spot." He slipped the glasses into his saddlebag, then dismounted as the others joined them.

The five spread out, approaching the rocks on foot, keeping watch around them. The sky remained clear and the bright sun now stood overhead, washing light through the tall pines.

"There's no way in from this side." Noah walked around from the right. "I checked as far as I could before the trail closed up."

"Come look at this." Bull's quiet voice drifted toward the others, who followed it to see him staring at an opening between the rocks. "I think he slipped through here."

Dax peeked through the slim gap. "There's a large cave, but Billy isn't in sight. I'm guessing there must be other tunnels. We won't know until we go inside." He looked at the others, knowing he, Luke, and Gabe were the only three who might fit through the opening.

Noah took a quick look and snorted. "I'll stay out here, make sure no one gets past you."

"I'll stay with Noah. There's no chance I'll get through the opening without tearing off an arm." Bull offered a slight grin as he took a position opposite Noah.

"You two ready?" Gabe asked just before he slipped inside, ripping a hole in the new shirt he'd bought for Christmas.

"Billy, we were so worried about you." Margaret, his younger sister, ran up and wrapped her arms around him. At seven, she was the youngest in the group, was devoted to him, and was the reason Billy had stayed in the Crow camp for three years. She'd just turned four when they were captured. Her age and small stature never would've allowed her to escape before now.

"Lydia is still sick. She's been vomiting, won't eat, and feels hot. I don't know what to do." Lydia's fourteen-year-old brother, Samuel, ran both hands through his long hair, then clasped them behind his neck. "Were you able to find anything to help her?"

Billy cast his gaze at Lydia. Her younger sister, Selina, sat cross-legged on the hard ground, gripping her sister's hand, eyes full of worry. He looked back at Sam. "No. They caught me. I wasn't able to get away until this morning." He took a few steps toward Lydia, noticing her red-rimmed eyes. He felt his stomach clench as he turned back toward Sam. "We have to leave. I'm sure they've followed me."

"Leave? Lydia can't move and won't eat. We can't take her out of here." Sam paced a few feet away, then swung back around. "What are we going to do?"

"You'll come with us. We'll help you."

The deep voice got everyone's attention as Dax walked into the cave, followed by Luke and Gabe. He didn't stop until he stood over Lydia, looking down at her prone form. He dropped to his knees, causing Selina to scoot away, although she didn't drop Lydia's hand. He placed a hand on her forehead and shot a look at Luke.

"She's holding her stomach and has a fever. We have to get her to Doc Worthington."

"You're not taking her anywhere." Billy stepped between Luke and Dax, daring them to interfere. "She's not leaving."

Gabe strode forward, fixing Billy with a hard look. "She's sick. Dax's wife is a nurse, her uncle is the town doctor. They won't hurt her, but you will if you insist on keeping her in this damp cave without adequate food and medical supplies."

Samuel stepped forward, grabbed Billy's arm and spun him around. "Lydia needs help. They're offering and I think we should accept it."

Billy scrubbed a hand over his face, his stomach knotting as his eyes settled on Lydia. He didn't want to count on help from the type of white men they'd encountered over the last few months, yet these men hadn't turned them away. They'd taken him into their home, fed him, and given him a place to sleep. Now they were offering their help again.

"You're right, Sam." Billy glared at Dax and took a step closer. "You'd better not hurt her."

"She'll be fine. You need to trust us." Dax wrapped the blanket edges around her, taking care to keep her feet and hands covered. "Does she have a bonnet?"

Selina jumped up and pulled an old, worn bonnet from a leather bag, handing it to Dax. He fitted it over her head and tied the strings under her chin, catching her watching him.

"Hello, Lydia. I'm Dax Pelletier. This is my brother, Luke, and our friend Gabe Evans. We're going to take you to a doctor."

She closed her eyes and swallowed, not making any effort to answer.

"Gather your belongings," Gabe said to the others while Dax prepared Lydia for the trip. "We have five horses, enough for everyone to ride double down the mountain." He waited a moment and when no one moved, he grabbed a nearby blanket and tossed it at Billy. "You take this and whatever else you can carry. Now. Everyone else pick up what you need. We're leaving as soon as Lydia is ready."

Samuel, Margaret, and Selina scrambled to do as Gabe asked, grabbing their meager belongings and stuffing them into grimy sacks.

"You, too, Billy." Gabe eyed the boy, not at all sure what to expect. He might leave with them or he might try to run. Gabe hoped he'd choose to leave. If he ran, they didn't have enough men to follow him. Their primary obligation was getting Lydia to Doc Worthington.

Billy fought conflicting emotions, knowing he had just one choice. He'd never leave Margaret, and he'd formed a strong bond with Sam, Selina, and Lydia. He swung away from Gabe and began to gather what he owned—an old hat, an extra pair of moccasins, and a few other items still inside his worn, leather sack.

"We're ready." Dax lifted Lydia into his arms and caught Luke's attention. "You go through the opening first, then I'll hand her to you." Both knew he'd never be able to make it through the slim gap holding her.

Gabe led the way through the tunnel, which opened into the first cave and passage to the outside. He glanced over his shoulder to make sure no one had stayed behind, and slipped through the opening.

"Noah, Bull..."

They appeared within seconds, both sets of eyes narrowing when they saw the group following Gabe.

"There are five, so we'll double up. Luke is carrying a woman who's ill. It might be best to have her ride with you, Bull."

Bull nodded. He owned the biggest of the five horses, an easy-going roan gelding named Abraham—Abe, for short.

"Selina, you ride with Luke. Margaret with Noah. Bull's going to take Lydia." Gabe glanced at Samuel and Billy. "Samuel, you'll ride with Dax, and Billy with me."

"I'll walk," Billy bit out.

Luke handed Lydia to Bull, then glanced down at Billy's bare feet, already bleeding from his trek up the mountain. "You'll ride behind Gabe, either seated or tied to the back. Your choice."

Billy shot Luke a killing look, then reached for Gabe's hand and swung up on the back of Blackheart.

They moved at a slow pace down the icy slope, stopping a few minutes at Luke's house, then onto the ranch. Every so often, Samuel would turn to look at Lydia nestled in Bull's broad lap. The thought of losing her terrified him. She'd been the one to hold them together over their last year of living with the Crow. Compared to stories they'd heard of other tribes, the Crow's treatment of them wasn't harsh. They were worked hard from before sunrise until late at night. Unlike Billy, who'd been allowed to train with the young warriors and men, Sam had been relegated to work alongside the women. He wanted to find a home in the world they'd been taken from and return to the customs of the whites.

Luke reined in next to Bull as they came to a stop by the barn. "I'll help you with Lydia." He swung a leg over Prince, helped Selina down, then reached up as Bull lowered Lydia into his arms.

"She sure doesn't weigh much." Bull slid from Abe and followed Luke up the steps to the house.

Doc Worthington opened the door and stepped aside to let the men pass. "Take her to the back bedroom where I've been staying." He'd almost closed the door when it was shoved open, Billy pushing past the doctor to follow Bull and Luke, behind him were Sam, Margaret, and Selina. "Wait up," he called before they disappeared down the hall. "You, too, Billy."

"I'm going with them." The hard edge of his voice almost broke.

"All of you will wait out here." Charles focused on Billy, already knowing the boy didn't back down easily. "I know you're worried, but I can't have anyone else in the room except for my nurse. Understand?"

"Her name's Lydia. She's my sister." A boy he didn't recognize spoke in a quiet, nervous tone. The slump of his shoulders told the doctor of the worry he'd been holding inside.

"What's your name, son?"

"Samuel. This is my other sister, Selina, and Billy's sister, Margaret."

"I'll do everything I can for her, Samuel. How long has she been sick?"

"It started last night after we ate the last of the food."

The doctor glanced up to see Ginny standing a few feet away. "Can you find something for them to eat while Rachel and I check on Lydia?"

"Yes, sir. Follow me and we'll get some food in you." She watched as each took a reluctant step toward her, then walked the rest of the way into the kitchen. She scooped generous portions of stew into bowls, setting one in front of each, then sliced thick pieces of cornbread. "There's more in the pot if this isn't enough."

They sat motionless, not picking up the spoons Ginny set next to the bowls.

"Sam?" Selina asked, looking at her older brother.

He knew they were starving and the smell of the stew was too tempting to pass up. Sam picked up his spoon and dug in. Before long, all the bowls were empty and only crumbs remained of the cornbread. Without a word, Ginny grabbed the bowls and ladled more stew into each. Except for Margaret, they devoured every bite.

"How are you doing in here?" Luke stood in the doorway, his gaze landing on Ginny first before noticing the satisfied faces at the table. Even Billy appeared to be somewhat relaxed, allowing his guard to slip a little.

"It was real good. Thank you." Sam wiped a sleeve across his mouth before carrying his bowl to the sink.

"Billy and Samuel, I'd like you to come with me so we can talk. Margaret and Selina can stay in here with Ginny." Luke shot a quick glance at Ginny before turning to follow the boys from the kitchen. "In here." He gestured to the study.

Dax walked around the desk, resting a hip against the edge and crossing his arms. "We want to know everything. How you came to live with the Crow, how you escaped, and where you were headed." His eyes bored into Billy's. "And we want the truth this time."

Chapter Twenty-Six

"What do you think it is, Uncle Charles?" Rachel continued to apply cold cloths to Lydia's forehead in an attempt to bring down the fever.

"With her fever, stomach cramps, and vomiting, I suspect she ate something tainted."

"I still have a little apple cider vinegar."

"Get it. She'll need to drink plenty of water, too."

Charles had Lydia sitting up when Rachel returned with the vinegar, a spoon, glass, and pitcher of water.

"Help me get a couple spoonfuls of vinegar down her, then we'll see if she'll drink some water." Charles put a hand behind her neck to help steady her. "Lydia, you need to drink this and not spit it out."

She did as the doctor asked, almost gagging at the taste of the vinegar, then drank a little water before Charles helped her settle back on the bed.

"We'll give her another spoonful in an hour. I need to speak with the other children to see what she may have eaten."

"I'll stay with her." Rachel lowered herself into a chair, watching as Lydia drifted off to sleep. She knew if the food poisoning were mild, the vinegar should help her improve within hours. Then they'd need to make a decision about what to do with them. She turned her head at the sound of the door opening.

"From what the two girls, Margaret and Selina, remember, Lydia ate the last of the chicken they'd cooked a few nights before. No one else ate it." He felt her forehead, which remained warm. "Appears she ate spoiled meat."

"Then she should pull through," Rachel said.

"How's she doing?" Dax stood in the doorway, looking at Lydia, then moving his gaze to Rachel and her tired features.

"Seems to be food poisoning. We've given her vinegar, and I expect she'll start feeling better within a few hours." Charles moved toward the window and peeked out at the darkening sky. "Clouds are moving in. I think I'll spend the night, then ask you to take me back to town tomorrow after I've made sure Lydia is doing better."

"I'd like both of you to come to the study. We need to talk about what to do next." Dax held out a hand for Rachel. "Then you need to take a nap."

Walking into the study, Dax closed the door behind them and motioned for them to sit down. "I've got Bull watching Samuel and Billy. I doubt either will try to take off as long as Lydia is sick." Dax sat next to Rachel and grabbed her hand. It took him little time to tell them about the group's journey across Montana. "From what the boys tell us, they don't have any relatives who could help. No aunts, uncles, or grandparents. The question is, what do we do with them now?"

"Do you think anyone in Splendor would take them in?" Rachel asked, already suspecting the answer.

"It's doubtful, but I'm willing to check." Gabe watched out the window, keeping an eye on the boys grooming the horses, Bull standing nearby.

"I wonder if the Frey brothers would take Billy and Margaret. They're always in need of help, and Billy says his sister can cook and clean." Luke crossed his arms.

"My understanding is she's only seven. I'm not sure she'd be much help. Maybe the Tolberts would take them in, give Billy a job and let Abby help with Margaret." Noah knew Abby needed something to keep her mind occupied. She'd grown tired of being relegated to the role of mistress of her father's house.

"I'd like to see the day King Tolbert volunteers to help someone who doesn't offer an immediate benefit to him." It was no secret neither Luke nor Dax had any use for the man and his tactics.

"It would be worth asking him." Rachel thought Abby would love to have Margaret live with them. "Billy would be a handful, though."

"He'll be a handful for anyone." Gabe turned from the window. "You ready to head back, Noah? Looks like a storm is building."

"You'll be okay with having them stay here until we work something out with the neighbors?" Noah asked. He had an uneasy feeling it would be much harder than anyone expected to find homes for the five.

"We'll get Sam and Billy on horses and out with the men. Can you find chores for Margaret and Selina?" Dax squeezed Rachel's hand.

"Of course. Plus, they can take lessons with Mary until they get settled in new homes."

"All right. Then it's settled. I'm headed out to the herd." Luke stood and moved toward the door.

"I'll ride with you." Dax leaned over and placed a kiss on Rachel's cheek. "Try to rest a while."

She nodded, knowing with three extra females in the house, there'd be little time to rest.

Big Pine, Montana

"What do you mean they moved up the date?" Dutch asked Tom, perplexed by the latest action by the citizens committee.

"They got wind the sheriff and a few of his deputies left for Moosejaw, and they want to take advantage of his absence to catch the outlaws."

"It makes no sense they'd want *less* lawmen around when the wagon moves. Who do you think made the decision?"

"Only one man could force a change at this point, and that's King Tolbert." Tom had never met the man, yet had grown to distrust him and the way he worked. His clear disdain for the law put him at odds with men trying to bring order and justice to the frontier. "There's nothing we can do. Three deputies and us remain—unless you can get approval to send for Luke."

"Let's go."

They walked the short distance to the telegraph office. Tom stood by the door as Dutch wrote a message to Pinkerton headquarters. Then he penned a message to Luke, giving him notice he'd sent a request for his services in Big Pine.

Dutch pulled up his collar as they stepped outside. "How does the committee expect to get word out about the change of date? The goal is to lure the outlaws out."

"They've identified an inside man, one they believe is providing details of gold shipments to the outlaws. He's already been given access to the records showing dates. The committee has no doubt the outlaws will know of the trip and attempt to rob it."

"When?" Dutch asked.

"From what I've heard, the first of next week."

Dutch let out a low whistle. "Four days. How long will Sheriff Sterling be gone?"

"He's not due back for another week."

Dutch studied Tom, knowing they felt the same regarding the committee's action. "I thought of sending a message to Sterling, but it's not our place. We've been hired by the committee. *They're* our client, not the sheriff. Although I have no hesitation requesting the help of his deputies. The committee can't stop them from getting involved."

Tom shoved his hands in his coat pockets, more out of frustration than the cold. "I hope we hear back from headquarters soon or Luke won't make it in time."

Redemption's Edge Ranch

Luke's temper had simmered for several days. Ginny's not-so-subtle tactics to avoid him since they'd discovered the cave were about to end.

"Where is she?" Still shedding his coat and gloves, he strode into the study where Dax sat at the desk.

Dax continued working, not looking up. "Who?"

Luke blew out a breath, not understanding the impatience he felt or the driving force behind his feelings. "Ginny. She's not in the kitchen or in her room."

"Is there something wrong?"

"You bet there is." Luke tossed his gloves on a chair, then rested his hands on his hips.

"You want to talk about it before you confront her?" Dax set his pen down and leaned back in his chair, hands clasped behind his head.

Luke glared at him, irritated he hadn't been able to vent the frustration he felt at Ginny's determination to put as much distance between them as she could. He knew why. He'd handled the confusion he felt at his own feelings so badly, she didn't know what to expect from him. Now she'd decided to put a wall up, protect herself from his attempts to get closer. He raked a hand through his damp hair and wiped the moisture from his face.

"Ah, hell. I'm not sure what I want to say to her. I just know I want her to talk to me." He slumped into a chair and stretched out his legs.

"I didn't know she wasn't."

"She's cordial. Says good morning, good evening…but nothing else. She keeps Margaret, Selina, or sometimes Lydia around her, as if they can shield her from me."

"And do they? Protect her from you, I mean?" Dax had a hard time believing Luke hadn't taken charge and asked the girls to leave him alone with Ginny.

Luke knew where Dax's comments were going and jumped to his feet. "No." He headed outside.

"I believe they're in the barn," Dax called after him.

Luke bounded down the porch steps and grabbed Prince's reins. The sound of laughter pierced the night air as he entered the barn to see Ginny, Margaret, and Selina huddled around the baby cradle he'd been fixing for

Rachel and Dax. He walked past them to a stall and led Prince inside, grabbing a bucket and brushes to wipe him down. He didn't say a word, just watched Ginny watch him through the corner of her eye, swinging her face away when he shifted toward her.

"It's time we went inside." She began to herd Margaret and Selina from the barn, then turned at Luke's voice.

"I'd like a word with you, Ginny."

"I can't—"

"Now."

She flinched at the hard tone, wrapping her arms around her waist as she turned toward him.

"Go into the house, girls, while Ginny and I talk." Luke tossed the brush into the bucket and closed the stall gate. His gaze locked on her before taking several purposeful strides, stopping within inches of her, crowding her space and causing her heart to beat in a wild rhythm.

Ginny lifted her face to his, trying to calm the knot forming in her stomach. She knew her actions the last few days were discourteous, but she could find no other way to protect herself from his confusing signals. One day, he'd act as though she meant something to him. The next, he'd barely acknowledge her. She'd had enough of not knowing what to expect. No matter what her heart felt, her head had to be the voice of reason and the path she took.

"Is there something you want to say?"

Hell yes, there's something I want to say, he thought. Instead, he let his gaze rake over her in a slow perusal, seeing the discomfort his close scrutiny caused. He slowly walked around her, as if checking an animal available for purchase, not stopping when she whipped her head around to glare at him.

"What *are* you doing?"

"Well, you look like the Ginny I've known for almost a year. Same face, clothes, voice, and hair. The problem is, you don't act anything like her. You see me and turn away, leave the room, or speak to someone else. Have I become invisible to you, or are you truly not the same Ginny I met months ago?" He finished circling around her to stand a mere foot away, his arms crossed in front of his chest, feet spread shoulder width apart.

She would've laughed if being so close to him didn't make her feel so defenseless. Her feelings for him had grown to an unrealistic degree, frightening her in a way she never expected. Ginny knew her lack of experience left her ill-prepared to defend herself from a man like Luke—charming, smart, handsome, and without a shred of desire to settle down with one woman. In her mind, she had no choice.

She dug deep inside to calm her voice and gripped her shaking hands in front of her. "I'm the same Ginny, except I've figured out what I want and what's best for Mary. A man like you doesn't fit our future, as I'm sure I don't fit yours." She saw his eyes narrow as his jaw tightened, and she knew she had to get out what needed to be said, and fast. "I have plans and you aren't a part of them."

Luke's heart thundered in his chest. He didn't believe a word of what she said. He needed to stay focused, keep his wits about him, and find a way to break through the wall she'd built between them. Knowing she'd never been able to resist his touch, he lifted a hand, intending to stroke his knuckles down her face, hoping she'd lean into him as she'd done in the past. Instead, she took a step away.

"Stop, please. I can't do this anymore, Luke."

"Can't do what?" The furrowed brow and stunned expression conveyed the confusion he felt.

"Let you muddle my mind by trifling with me." She crossed her arms under her chest and took a deep breath. "You're a handsome, charming rogue, Luke, and I realize flirting with me means nothing to you. You'll choose Pinkerton assignments and travel over a permanent life on the ranch." Her eyes darted around the barn as she searched for the right words.

"Oh, you'll fulfil your commitment to Dax. You aren't a man who'd ever shirk his duties. Yet you aren't the kind of man to ever settle down, fall in love with one woman, and feel as if your life is complete. The next telegram from Pinkerton will drag you away, forcing you to make a choice between the ranch and family, or an assignment. I'm a convenience for you, nothing more."

Her words stunned him into silence. He had no idea how to respond since most of what she said was true, or had been until he'd come to terms with his feelings for Ginny. He let his arms drop to his sides, then turned to pace a few steps away, hanging his head and trying to clear his mind. If he'd been able to sort through his feelings sooner, they may never have come to this place, where she felt pushing him from her life was her only choice. He turned around to face her, seeing the same pain he felt reflected in her face.

"You're wrong about me, Ginny. I've changed. So much about me is no longer the same. My feelings for you are much more than you believe." His soft, rough voice pierced her heart, even as she knew her decision had to be final.

She swallowed the lump in her throat, ready to end this when the sound of a horse and rider reining up outside drew their attention. They heard someone dismount and dash up the porch steps, then pound on the door.

"Is Luke around?"

Luke recognized Bernie Griggs' voice. He owned the Western Union and postal service in Splendor, and never rode out at night unless he held an urgent message.

"He's in the barn." Dax headed in that direction with Bernie.

Luke sent an apologetic look at Ginny. "I'd better go see what Bernie wants." He took a couple steps, then stopped. "We aren't done with this conversation. In fact, we're a long way from being done."

"Evening, Luke. Sorry to bother you so late, but I got an urgent message from Big Pine." Bernie handed the telegram over.

Luke held it in his hand, afraid he knew what it contained, and knowing it would add more confirmation to Ginny's concerns about him. He tore it open and read it twice, then looked up at Dax.

"I have to go to Big Pine. Dutch got approval for me to help with what they believe will be a raid on a gold wagon in a couple days." He saw reluctant acceptance on Dax's face and felt guilt rip through him. "If I hadn't already committed to helping them, believe me, I wouldn't leave." Luke shot a look at Ginny, wanting her to understand why he had to go. Instead, her face held no emotion at all. "Bernie, would you send a reply that I'm on my way?"

"Sure will, Luke."

He glanced back at Dax. "I'll be back as soon as I can."

Chapter Twenty-Seven

Big Pine, Montana

Rick startled at the sound of robust pounding on his door, tempted to ignore it. He'd just returned from Felicity's house, having spent the entire day with her. By next Christmas, if all went well, they'd be married and he'd be well out of the life he'd led the last few years.

The pounding started again. He reached into the drawer by the bed and pulled out his revolver, tucking it into the waistband of his trousers. There could only be one person who'd visit him this late, and he was no longer welcome. Rick walked down the stairs at a slow pace, hoping Flatnose would give up and leave, but knowing it wouldn't happen. He opened the door.

"What do you want?" Rick asked in a low voice as he looked around, making certain no one saw his visitor.

Flatnose pushed past him, glaring at Rick as the door closed. "They changed the date of the gold shipment. It goes out in two days and we want you with us."

Rick walked further into the room, standing so his back faced a solid wall with Flatnose several feet away. The news surprised him, but had no effect on his decision to stay out of the gang. "I gave you my answer the last time you came by. I'm out. You're welcome to the gold."

"That doesn't work for us. The men want you along and I told them I'd bring you back with me tonight." As he'd done before, Flatnose poured himself a drink and downed it in one swallow.

"I'm not going with you tonight or on the raid."

"I told the boys you'd say that."

He began to reach toward his holster, but Rick reacted faster, drawing his gun and pointing it at Flatnose. "It doesn't have to be like this. You can decide to leave, go after the gold, then ride from the territory. There's no point in either of us dying." He held the gun firm, prepared to fire if Flatnose forced him.

A mirthless laugh emerged from Flatnose, surprised Rick had figured out his intent. He held his hands out, palms up. "You're right. It's your choice to walk away or stay. If you change your mind, meet us at the ranch at sunup in two days. We'll hit the wagon at the same spot we held up the first one." He left, leaving a chill in the air, and making the decision Rick had been struggling with an easy one.

Rick grabbed paper and pen, scribbling a short note, then slipped into an old work coat and muffler before pulling back the curtains and looking outside. Neither Flatnose nor his horse were anywhere in sight. He walked out the back door and disappeared into the night, choosing not to take his horse. His destination lay a few blocks away in a business district still buzzing with the sound of piano music and laughter.

He pulled his collar up, wrapped the wool scarf around his face, and walked into the well-lit hotel lobby, stepping to the desk. Rick waited until the clerk acknowledged him.

"May I help you?"

"I need to leave a message for Dutch McFarlin."

"It's good to see you, Luke. Sorry to pull you away right after Christmas." Dutch extended his hand. "At least the weather stayed clear."

Luke missed the storms and made good time, considering the size of the snow drifts. "Let me get some coffee, then I want to hear about the gold shipment."

An hour later, Dutch, Tom, and Luke had finished supper and reviewed everything the agents knew about the gold shipment.

"The clerk has no idea who left the message for you?" Luke asked Dutch.

"He says the man wore a ragged coat with the collar up, and a wool scarf wrapped around his face. He'd pushed his hat down so the clerk couldn't see his eyes. He swears he's never seen the man before."

"Do you think the information is accurate, or could he be leading us off their trail?"

"The location makes sense, and it's where the gang hit the first wagon. It's also where both Dutch and I would plan a raid." Tom sipped the last of his coffee and leaned back in his chair.

"Besides the men from the committee who want to ride out, we have three deputies and the three of us. Plenty of men to take out the number mentioned in the message. It's interesting he included the names of each of the outlaws." Dutch still couldn't believe the note awaiting him when he'd left for breakfast. He and Tom had met with several committee members a few hours before Luke arrived, deciding too much information had been included to be a hoax. "Whoever the man is, he must know the gang. Which means he's putting himself in substantial danger."

"He may be one of them," Tom said.

"*Was* one of them. If they discover what he told us, my bet is he'll be dead within the week." Luke pushed up from his chair, ready to put another day behind him.

"Appears everyone is ready." Luke reined in beside Dutch, who checked his revolver, then looked around at the gathered men.

"Everyone circle up." Dutch waited for the riders to move closer. "The wagon is scheduled to be at the spot the outlaws will attack in four hours. We need to be in place and ready before then. We want to take them alive. However, if they draw on us, we shoot to kill. Any questions?" The men mumbled or shook their heads. "Let's get going."

The group rode through the cold weather until Dutch reined up at the location where they'd been told the raid would take place. "We'll ride up to the ridge above and wait. From there, we'll have our best chance of spotting the outlaws as they take positions. We'll disperse around them and come in from behind. Do not move forward until I give the order."

Although the men nodded their agreement, their expressions told a different story. Along with the eager anticipation on their faces, Dutch could see the temptation to act as they chose when the outlaws appeared. It would be a miracle if any of the raiders made it out of there alive.

Tom took a position ahead of Dutch and Luke, acting as a lookout. They hadn't been in place long before he signaled the others, indicating he'd spotted men approaching from the south. The wagon would come from the east. The riders he saw had to be Flatnose's gang.

He pulled out his field glasses, counting seven men, fewer than they'd anticipated. They rode straight toward the spot on the trail where the wagon would pass by, staying mounted and fanning out on both sides.

Dutch signaled the deputies, who got word to the committee members to hold their positions until the wagon came into sight. He still had concerns that some men might take it upon themselves to go after the outlaws before the gold appeared. They needed to catch the gang taking the gold if they had any hope of convicting them of the thefts. He had to let his concerns go. At this point, he could do nothing except the job he'd been hired to do.

Tom shifted his field glasses east. The snow and large load would slow the wagon down, although no one believed gold would be the actual cargo. The gold would be layered on top of dirt and rock, giving the impression of being full of ore.

Before he even saw the wagon, he spotted two guards on horseback, two more men sat on the bench seat, while four guards rode on either side and behind the wagon. He signaled Dutch and Luke, then took up his own position and waited. From his location, he could see the outlaws pull bandanas over their faces and draw their guns—they'd also spotted the wagon.

Luke reined Prince further behind the stand of trees and rocks where he hid. They'd already determined Dutch would cover Flatnose, while Luke, Tom, and the deputies would cover the other members of his gang. The committee members had agreed to hang back, coming forward only if the deputies and Pinkerton agents needed help. None of them believed the men would live up to the agreement. Their desire to eliminate the gang was too great.

The sound of the approaching wagon drew their attention.

"Hold up." Flatnose's loud voice bellowed as three of his men dashed in front of the wagon, causing the driver to pull up as the guards seated next to him began to raise their rifles.

"Don't do it," one of Flatnose's men said, cautioning the guards to lower their weapons as the other outlaws rode in from the back, guns pointed at the remaining guards.

When all seven outlaws came into sight, Dutch, Luke, Tom, and the deputies emerged, closing in around them, guns drawn.

Flatnose swiveled in the saddle, his first thought being that Rick had been right. The committee had set a trap and they'd ridden right into it. He acted without thinking, aiming his gun at Dutch, firing high as a bullet ripped through his shoulder. His horse bolted before charging down the trail, Flatnose slumped over the saddle horn. Luke watched Flatnose disappear down the trail, unable to go after him as shots whizzed past him.

What followed happened within the span of seconds. Bullets flew in all directions, followed by men dropping to the ground, moans coming from those injured or dying, and shouts from those still shooting.

"Dutch," Tom called from his position above.

"Here. Luke's beside me." He'd slid from his horse at the same time as Luke, taking cover while surveying the scene around the wagon.

"Six of them are down. I can't see Flatnose." Tom made his way down the slight incline, joining them as the deputies checked the fallen men. "Two guards were hit, but they're still alive." He spun around, trying to locate the missing outlaw.

"Flatnose caught a bullet and took off down the trail. Doubt he'll get far." Dutch joined the others, looking at the men who'd already robbed several gold wagons. This would be their last raid. Six lay dead and Flatnose was missing.

Ezra scanned the road ahead. "Guess I'll get the bodies loaded on horses or the wagon. I expect we'll find Flatnose's body on the trail."

Luke hoped so. He didn't want anyone else facing the wounded outlaw before they found him and made certain he wouldn't hurt anyone else.

"Take the injured guards to the doctor. I'll send a telegram to Sheriff Sterling and let him know what happened." The sun began to set as they arrived in town. Ezra left the other two deputies to take care of the wounded men while he walked to the telegraph office.

"Good work out there today, Duncan." Dutch and Luke caught up with him on their way to send a message to Pinkerton headquarters before Western Union closed for the day.

"The problem is we don't know where Flatnose went. I thought for sure we'd find his body along the trail. I hate having a man such as him loose. Who knows what he'll do." Ezra kept shifting his gaze around as he continued walking, expecting to see the outlaw show up seeking treatment for his wound. He needed to talk with the other deputies and set up patrols where Flatnose might look for help. He'd feel better once Sheriff Sterling returned from Moosejaw.

"Does he have anyone he visits in Big Pine, someone who might help him?" Luke asked, shifting his gaze around.

"Not that I know of. 'Course, I haven't been in town long." Ezra thought of the one other person he knew in Big Pine besides Sterling and his deputies—Frederick Marlowe. He'd seen him a few times in town and at church, but they hadn't spoken since that day at the restaurant. He knew Marlowe owned a big house in a nice section of town, and wondered how the man had come across the type of money needed to buy such a place. He'd let his curiosity go, believing he'd already caused the man enough pain.

Ezra wished he could turn back time, make a different decision regarding the gang who'd terrorized his town in Nebraska. He'd been so certain Marlowe had been involved, putting his faith in the testimony of the wrong man. His decision had caused the deaths of Marlowe's wife and son, resulted in the loss of Ezra's own family, and triggered years of nightmares.

"Can we buy you supper?" Dutch asked Ezra after they finished sending their telegrams.

"Thanks, but I want to start patrolling areas where Flatnose might look for help. I have an uneasy feeling about him still being out there, even with a bullet wound."

"You can never guess what a man like him will do. I'm afraid he'll be a threat until someone puts him in his grave." Luke glanced around once more before pulling his collar up against the chill. "I'll be heading back to Splendor tomorrow. It was good working with you."

"You, too, Luke. Hope we meet under different circumstances next time." Ezra shook his hand and turned toward the jail, ready to keep watch for a man he suspected would have vengeance on his mind.

Ezra and the other deputies had circled the streets the night before and into the early morning, watching for any sign of Flatnose. All of his instincts told him the man would seek help, then find vengeance.

Luke had taken off early for Splendor, leaving Dutch and Tom to await word from Pinkerton headquarters about their next assignment. Ezra refused their help to search for Flatnose, believing their work finished.

The sun peeked over the horizon as he rode through the main street and into a section of homes. Most were modest. A few stood out with their sheer size and elaborate trim. One of these had been purchased by Frederick Marlowe.

As Ezra approached Marlowe's two story home, he heard a horse whinny at the same time a dog raced from the yard. He rode closer, hearing a door open and close before spotting a horse tied along the side of Marlowe's house, saddled and ready to go—and it looked much like the horse Flatnose had ridden.

He slid to the ground and cautiously made his way toward the house, crouching under an open window, hearing an angry male voice he recognized as belonging to Flatnose.

"You're the one man outside the ranch, who knew the spot where we planned to take the wagon. No one else, Rick."

"Why would I tip them off to your plans?"

Ezra straightened enough to peer into the room where Flatnose held a gun on Frederick Marlowe...or Rick, as he'd called him.

"That's what I want you to tell me. 'Course, it doesn't matter. Either way, you'll still end up dead."

"I had no reason to tell anyone. What would I have to gain?" Marlowe asked.

Ezra watched as Rick inched toward his desk, keeping his eyes trained on Flatnose.

"Silence, that's what."

"Silence?" He edged another inch to his side.

"All the men, except me, are dead. There's no one else to tell the law how you were involved in all the raids in Idaho and here."

Ezra's eyes widened at the accusation, a part of him not surprised to learn of Marlowe's involvement. For a split second, he wondered what would drive a man to go from being a respected farmer to an outlaw, but in his heart, Ezra knew. Seeing a posse gun down your wife and son could do all kinds of things to a man, including push him into a life he wouldn't have imagined before the tragedy. A wave of guilt washed over Ezra.

"I'm sorry about the gang, but now you have no one left to testify against you. You can take their share of the gold and leave the territory." Marlowe's hand touched the side of the desk as he spoke.

"No one—except you."

"Why would I say anything? It would be the same as a confession if I came forward and told anyone what I knew."

Ezra had heard enough. He snuck to a side door and checked the knob. Locked. Next to it a window had been opened a few inches. He lifted it several more inches, holstered his gun, gripped the sill, and pulled himself up through the opening. He landed with a soft thud. He could still hear the voices as he drew his gun and crept forward. Ezra stopped outside the room, poking his head around the corner to see he stood behind Flatnose.

"Nothing you say matters, Rick. You've had your bit of fun and now it's over." Flatnose lifted his gun, stretching his arm out in front of him.

"Drop it, Flatnose."

The outlaw spun and fired, hitting Ezra, then turned back toward Rick, who now held the revolver he kept in his desk. A shot rang out, slamming into Flatnose, whose eyes widened in shock just before he crumbled to the floor.

Rick rushed to make sure Flatnose posed no further threat before kneeling next to Ezra. His chest wound didn't bode well for the deputy, who moaned as Rick pulled off his shirt and tried to stem the flow of blood.

"Hang in there, Ezra."

Ezra's eyes opened to slits, trying to focus on Marlowe. "It's no use."

"I need to get help."

"It won't do any good." He settled a hand on Rick's arm, gripping tight as he tried to get the last words out. "It's for the best. Now we're even." His eyes closed as his head rolled to the side.

A sadness Rick never thought he'd feel for the man washed over him. After all that happened between them, Ezra had saved his life. It would never make up for the loss of his wife and son, but perhaps, in some strange way, they truly were even. No longer would he have to run to hide his past. He and Felicity could marry, and no one would ever have to learn of the mistakes he'd made since leaving Nebraska.

Chapter Twenty-Eight

Redemption's Edge Ranch

"Do you mind if Mary and I ride into town with you?" Ginny stood on the front porch, bundled against the cold, surprised to see Travis leaving for Splendor this late. The hands not with the herd had eaten their midday meal and were occupied with their afternoon chores.

"I'd welcome the company, if you don't mind getting back just before sunset." Travis pulled the wagon to a stop, jumped down and helped Mary up, then Ginny. "With luck, the sky will stay clear."

Ginny knew little about Travis other than he stayed to himself and worked hard. Besides Bull, Ellis, and Rude, she knew Dax and Luke considered him one of their best men. It wasn't often he pulled duty picking up supplies. It's why Ginny dashed outside when she saw him with the wagon. He wouldn't ask questions. He would just go about his business and make sure she and Mary got to town and back safely.

As she suspected, he said little during the trip, while Mary chatted away, talking about

Margaret, Selina, and Lydia, who'd improved enough to help in the kitchen. As they passed the school and livery, Ginny asked him to let them out at the boardinghouse. She knew Suzanne would welcome a visit from Mary, which would allow Ginny to run the errands she had planned.

"Miss Suzanne," Mary called as she dashed inside, heading straight for the kitchen.

"Why, Mary, what a wonderful surprise." Suzanne caught Mary in her arms, giving her a squeeze before setting her down.

"I hope it's all right that we came by to visit." Ginny gave Suzanne a hug as she looked around the kitchen. "Something seems different."

"Not much. Noah built a few extra shelves and hooks for my pots. Now I have room for more dishes and serving bowls."

"You're keeping busy then?"

"I don't know why, but the morning after Christmas, the restaurant was full for every meal and has stayed that way since. With stores opening up and people moving in, everyone seems to be keeping busy." The week before Christmas, she'd despaired, knowing an entire winter with few customers would make it hard for her to survive. Now she felt optimistic.

"Have you had dinner?" Suzanne asked.

"We ate before leaving the ranch."

"How about some coffee and pie?" Suzanne began to pull down plates and cups.

"Would it be all right if I ran my errands first?"

"Of course. You can leave Mary with me while you're gone."

Ginny hoped Suzanne would offer, knowing she couldn't take Mary into the place she needed to visit.

"She'd love to stay with you. I won't be gone long." At least she hoped not.

Luke reined Prince to a stop under the protection of a large group of pines not far from Splendor. He'd made good time, leaving Big Pine early, and stopping twice.

He'd made the decision to decline any further requests from Pinkerton. The money provided extra cash the ranch could always use. The assignments, however, had lost their appeal.

He'd thought of little except the conversation between him and Ginny before he left. He knew she talked of independence, having her own life, and raising Mary. He felt certain a part of her also wanted to settle down and be loved.

This last job, and the risks it entailed, made it clear how much he wanted the life Dax had built with Rachel. He spent most of his time thinking of Ginny, wondering if she'd allow him an opportunity to express the decision he'd made and give them a chance. He loved her, probably had since the first day he'd set eyes on her at the Wild Rose. Now he knew the time had come to express his feelings and hope she felt the same.

He'd stop at the Rose for a drink or two, then head on to the ranch in time for supper. He wanted to speak with Ginny before she pushed him away with her excuses. And they would be excuses. He now realized how much he wanted her in his life. Her thoughts about him being incapable of settling down were dead wrong, and he meant to not just tell her, but show her.

Luke swung back up on Prince and turned toward Splendor, hoping his charm and persuasive abilities didn't elude him tonight.

"Is Mr. Barnett available?" Ginny almost hadn't gone through with her plan. She'd stood outside the Dixie, pacing back and forth before finding the courage to walk inside.

The bartender looked at her with narrowed eyes, then nodded once toward the back. "I'll go get him. What's your name, girl?"

She swallowed the lump in her throat. "Ginny Sorensen."

The man tossed down the towel he held and disappeared into the back.

"There's a girl out front to see you, Nick."

He didn't look up from the paperwork, which seemed to grow each day. "She'll have to come back another time."

"I'll tell Miss Sorensen that."

"Wait." Nick tossed down his pen. "What's her name?"

"Ginny Sorensen."

Nick's brow's knit together. The last he knew, she worked for the Pelletiers. Suzanne had told him how much she liked it out at their ranch.

"Tell her I'll be right out." He straightened his vest and tie before pushing open the door to the saloon. "Miss Sorensen. What a wonderful surprise." He stopped in front of her, noticing what seemed to be pure panic in her eyes. "I heard you wanted to see me."

She glanced around, not wanting anyone else to hear her request. "Uh...yes. Do you have time to talk in private?"

"Of course. Let's go into my office." He gestured to the back and followed her through the door, hoping she hadn't come to talk about working at the Dixie. "Please, have a seat and tell me why you came."

She took her time, gripping her hands together so tight, the knuckles began to turn white. She cleared her throat, not knowing where to start. "I wanted to talk to you about…" Her voice trailed off as her courage began to wane. Maybe this wasn't such a good idea.

"Yes?"

"Well… I wondered if, perhaps, you might have a job for me."

Nick leaned forward, keeping his expression blank as he rested his arms on the desk. He let his eyes narrow on hers, wondering what had prompted someone like her to seek work in a saloon. She knew he didn't hire serving girls, only those who were willing to work on their feet downstairs and their backs upstairs.

"Why don't you tell me the reason you want to leave the Pelletiers and make such a drastic change. Seems you have it good with them."

"Yes, they're good to me. The work is fair, as are the wages and living arrangements."

"But?"

"It's all changed since Luke arrived back from Denver. It's clear he doesn't want me there. The job is no longer what I thought it would be. I need to make enough to buy a house, raise Mary, and not be tied to anyone." She clamped her mouth shut, not wanting to divulge any more.

"I see. And what is it you propose to do here?"

"I thought I could do the same work as the other girls who work for you." She forced herself to look at Nick, even as she felt her body quake at the declaration.

He studied her, trying to figure out what had driven Ginny to seek money by using her body. "Are you certain you understand what the girls who work for me do? Have you spoken with them?"

"Well, no. I haven't met any of the people who work here, but I have spoken with Belle and some of the other girls at the Rose."

"What did they tell you?"

She licked her dry lips as her eyes darted around the room. She hadn't expected Nick to question her like this.

"Belle says it's not so bad. The same with the others. They have a place to stay, food, and save some money every month. Each plans to get out as soon as they save enough to find another job and a place to live."

"Have any of them given you the idea they're able to quit soon? From what I understand, everyone at the Rose has been with Amos for a good long time. Don't you think they could've saved enough to quit by now if that's what they wanted to do?"

Nick was right. The girls had settled into their chosen life and none seemed anxious to leave it. "I suppose so, but that doesn't mean I'd do the same."

He blew out a breath. Dissuading her might take longer than he anticipated. Perhaps he should see how far she'd go before he gave her a firm, gentle no.

"I'd rather have you work for me than Amos, or anyone else who opens a place in Splendor." He pushed from his chair and walked around the desk, leaning against the front edge and crossing his arms over his chest. "If you're determined to do this, show me what the paying customers will get."

Her eyes widened in shock. "What? Now? Here? You want me to...?" She couldn't finish for the tightness in her chest.

"Of course. I'm putting you on display for the men to see. I want to know they'll be satisfied with what they get for their money."

He waited a moment, letting his gaze trail up and down her body, seeing the discomfort grow, hoping it would have the desired effect. "Come now, Ginny. If you can't take your clothes off for me, how will you be able to do it for someone you don't know at all?"

He could see her lower lip and chin quiver as she stood. Her hands shook as she undid the buttons on her coat, letting it fall to the chair. Her arms dropped to her sides and she forced her gaze to his, waiting.

"All of it, Ginny." He relaxed against the desk, doing his best to remain expressionless, as if this were any other business deal. The agony he saw in her eyes tore a hole through his gut, yet he knew from experience this would be the only way to get her to see the flaws in her thinking. "Start with the front buttons of your dress."

She moved her hands up, her fingers shaking so much she couldn't seem to grip the small buttons. After a moment, she had success with the first one, then moved to the second, and third, trying to control the sick feeling in her stomach.

"Good evening, Luke. You just get back from Big Pine?" Al asked as he poured him a whiskey and slid it in front of him.

"I did. Thought I'd stop here before heading on to the ranch." He downed the liquid and held out the empty glass, indicating he wanted another. He'd just brought the glass to his lips when he felt a hand on his shoulder.

"Evening, Luke."

"Travis. You're in town late." Luke shook his hand and leaned his back against the bar. The sun still hadn't set and there remained at least a couple of hours before darkness fell.

"Dax needed supplies and I seemed the best person to come in. Miss Ginny and Mary rode in with me." Travis saw the brief surprise in Luke's face before he masked it.

"Where are they now?"

"That's what I came over to tell you. Mary is with Mrs. Briar at the boardinghouse. Ginny had some errands to run, and..." Travis stammered and glanced around the bar before finishing. "I saw her go into the Dixie not too long ago."

"What the hell?" Luke slammed down the glass and took off at a fast pace toward the Dixie.

Ginny got as far as the seventh button, her chemise and top of her breasts visible to Nick, then stopped. She swallowed again and shook her head before slowly lifting her face to his. The misery he saw broke his heart. He moved toward her, grasping her shoulders and forcing her to look at him.

"Ginny, both of us know this is a bad idea. Your background and circumstances don't compare to those of the girls who work here. You have choices they never did." He kept his voice calm, knowing she already felt a measure of humiliation. "Not one was a virgin when they started with me. They may have lost their virginity in another brothel, but not in one of my saloons." He turned her toward the door leading to the saloon and opened it. "Is this where you want to lose your virginity?"

Ginny clasped a hand to her mouth as tears began to form.

"Then give yourself to any man willing to pay until you're too worn down to do anything else?"

She looked at the floor and slowly shook her head.

Nick shut the door with a quick push and guided her back toward the desk.

"Look at me, Ginny." He put a finger under her chin and lifted her face up. "This isn't the place for you. Not because you aren't pretty enough, because you are. Any man would be a fool to turn you away, but that's what I'm doing."

The door slammed open, causing Ginny to spin around, her dress falling from her shoulders, allowing Luke to see what she'd already shown Nick.

The oath that emerged from Luke's mouth was foul and loud as he launched himself at Nick, landing a blow to the man's face, causing him to rock back on his heels.

"Luke, stop it!" She positioned herself in front of Nick, shielding him from more blows.

Nick gently moved her aside, looking at an irate Luke standing with his hands fisted, ready to throw another punch. "If you're certain you want to fight, I'll oblige you."

Luke could see amusement cross the man's face and held up. He glanced at Ginny, then back at Nick. "What the hell is going on here?"

His booming voice startled Ginny and she took a step away as she frantically tried to close the buttons on her dress.

Nick straightened and rubbed his jaw, glancing at Ginny. "Do you want to tell him, or should I?"

Luke swung his gaze to Ginny, pinning her with a hard, unyielding glare. He crossed his arms, waves of anger still rolling off him.

"I...uh..." The words died on her lips as humiliation won out over the horror she'd felt at seeing Luke. Her fingers trembled so badly, she couldn't close her dress. She looked up at Luke in alarm.

"Ah, hell." He reached down, grabbed her coat, and tossed it at her. "Put this on."

She slipped into the coat and closed the larger buttons in a few quick motions, then wrapped her arms tight around her waist.

"Ginny came here to talk to me about a job," Nick said in a flat voice, not wanting to cause her any more distress.

"What?" Luke bellowed. He had to get himself under control. He paced to the window and back, taking a couple of deep breaths and forcing his gaze away from Ginny until he'd calmed his features. "Why, Ginny?"

She licked her lips in a frantic attempt to clear her head and answer. "I... You... We..." She buried her face in her hands, rubbing her eyes and massaging her temples where a painful throbbing had begun the moment Luke burst into the room.

Luke shifted his gaze to Nick, who nodded toward the door. "Take her home. Give her some time and she'll explain everything."

"You and Ginny—"

"Don't insult me, Pelletier. Take your woman and go."

Chapter Twenty-Nine

Luke replayed the scene at the Dixie over and over on their way to the ranch with Ginny snuggled up against his chest. He tightened his arm around her waist, drawing her toward him, trying to make sense of what he'd seen. Luke sent word to Travis, saying Ginny would ride back with him on Prince, and asking the ranch hand to get Mary from the boardinghouse. Luke and Ginny needed time alone to sort through what had happened and understand if they had any future together.

He'd recovered from the initial shock. Now he needed to know why she'd acted the way she had. What woman would walk out of a secure, safe home, where she had a good job and plenty to eat, and ask for a job in a brothel? No one, as far as Luke believed. Not one woman he'd ever met would do what Ginny did. It made no sense and he sure as hell wanted to understand her reason.

She shifted in the saddle, causing him to groan, heat flaring through his body. He breathed in her clean scent, letting wisps of hair blow across his face until he couldn't resist her any longer. He buried his face in the side of her neck, placing kisses on her soft skin until she sighed, snuggling closer to him.

"You're going to tell me why you did this," he whispered as he pulled his head back and replaced the weak moment with the strength he knew he'd need once she told her side of the story.

He saw no movement around the ranch as he rode into the barn and slid from Prince. He helped Ginny down, then turned her to him. "Don't even consider going into the house and locking yourself in your bedroom. I swear, Ginny, I'll bust the door down if I need to."

She scowled, but nodded and walked toward the house as he took care of Prince. She disappeared long enough to fix her hair and wash the tears that had dried on her cheeks during the ride home. Luke didn't give any indication he'd noticed her damp face, although she felt certain he had. Ginny heard the front door open and close, followed by the sound of male voices before another door closed. She grabbed her shawl, making the decision to get their conversation over with now and face whatever consequences Luke and Dax doled out.

Luke could hear her coming down the hall. Hank walked out the back door to join Bernice, pointing to a full pot of coffee. Everyone else was out with the herd and not expected back until well past sunset. Doc Worthington had come by earlier to get Rachel as he'd gotten word Abby Tolbert wasn't well.

They were alone.

He looked up as she stopped just inside the kitchen. "Do you want some coffee?" he offered, grabbing two cups.

"I'd prefer water."

Her voice still shook and if he hadn't walked in on her and Nick, he might be able to feel sorry for her. He filled her cup with water and his with coffee, then took a seat at the table, nodding for her to do the same. She settled across from him, wrapping the shawl around her, tying the ends together, then grasping the cup with both hands.

Luke took a sip of the hot, strong brew and watched her over the rim of his cup, his eyes narrowed.

"Did you plan to let Nick take you to bed when you rode into town?"

She jumped up and slammed her hands flat on the table, eyes flashing. "No, of course not. And that is not what was happening when you almost busted down his door."

"Sit down, Ginny." The calm tone of his voice belied the rage he felt. Until he knew what had inspired her to go into the Dixie, he knew his stomach would be tied in knots and his chest would feel as if it were being squeezed in a vice. The faster he learned the truth, the sooner he'd be able to control his fury. "Why did you go there?"

Ginny lowered herself into the chair, focusing on her cup of water, clasping her hand in her lap. She let out a slow breath. "I thought it would be best for Mary and me."

"To work in a brothel?" His voice was low, steady, and disbelieving.

"To get away from you and the confusion I feel when you're around. I don't know what to expect from you, or what you want from me." She let her eyes look past him and to the window over the sink as she tried to get her jumbled thoughts in order.

The pain that flared with her words staggered Luke. She'd made the decision to work in a saloon to escape him. "You'd toss a life at the ranch and your reputation aside to get away from me?"

"You don't understand." She rubbed her eyes, needing to control her emotions.

He leaned forward, resting his arms on the table. "You're right. I don't."

She swallowed the lump in her throat, knowing he wouldn't let her leave the room until he understood why she'd gone to Nick. "When my parents died, I knew there would be hard choices if Mary and I were to survive. Few ways exist for a woman to make enough money to live. I didn't have a wagon to continue our journey to Oregon as my father had planned, so we stayed in Splendor. Suzanne provided a room and board in exchange for work. She spoke to Amos about hiring me. I'm not sure he wanted to, but he did, and I counted my blessings for the good fortune." She took a sip of water as her thoughts began to unfold.

"Then the Dixie opened and Amos didn't have the business to keep me. Suzanne also struggled when the new restaurant opened and I knew she would need the money from every room. Rachel offering me a job was a wonderful surprise...except for one problem."

"Me." Luke settled back in his chair.

Her gaze settled on his as a sad smile formed. "Yes, you. I'd made the decision to be independent, never marry, and find contentment raising Mary. The job at your ranch would fulfill all of these, except I'd have to deal with my feelings for you every day. You muddle my thoughts, make me doubt what I believe I should do to protect myself and Mary. I thought I could handle it, but you...well..."

"I wouldn't leave you alone, and couldn't explain how I felt," Luke murmured.

"You didn't need to explain. I already knew you'd chosen a life that included the ranch and jobs with Pinkerton. You have no use for building a family, yet I couldn't change the way I felt when you were around. I did everything I could to ignore you. I soon learned that wouldn't work."

Luke recalled his irritation at her obvious attempts to keep her distance, and his determination not to let her. Looking back, his actions seemed selfish.

"I realized I couldn't stay here, no matter how much I wanted to—not with you around. Even though Splendor is growing, there's little work for someone like me. Suzanne couldn't bring me back, and no one else needed help. The one place where a woman can find work, and good money, is in a saloon. I couldn't bring myself to go to Amos, so I went to Mr. Barnett." She fell silent, now knowing what a mistake she'd made by approaching Nick. She raised her eyes to Luke. "He turned me down."

Luke's eyes widened at the news. "It didn't appear as if he turned you down."

"Well, he did. He knew I wasn't meant for a life in a saloon, but I was determined to try. He pushed me to the point I understood what I'd be giving up." She stood and walked to the window, looking out at the darkening sky, her back to Luke. "I need this job. I'll just have to find some way of pushing aside my feelings for you."

She heard chair legs scrape across the floor a moment before he stepped behind her, wrapped his arms around her waist, and pulled her against his chest. He rested his chin on top of her head and closed his eyes.

"I would rather you not push aside your feelings for me, Ginny, as I feel the same for you." He tightened his hold as he felt her shift at his words. "Do you recall the day I received the telegram from Dutch, asking me to meet him in Big Pine?"

"Yes," she breathed out, her heart hammering in her chest.

"Do you remember what we were talking about when it arrived?"

"You mentioned your feelings for me had changed."

He placed a kiss on her temple, letting his warm lips glide to her ear, nipping at the lobe. "I love you, Ginny."

Her breath hitched at his words, wanting to believe them.

He brushed his lips down her neck, then retraced a path back up. He could feel shivers ripple through her and pulled her closer. "It took me a while to figure it all out, and I'm sorry if my actions caused you pain. There's no doubt in my mind that I want you. I'm through with Pinkerton. It's over." He turned her toward him, locking his gaze with hers. "Marry me, Ginny."

Her body shook so hard, she wouldn't have been able to stand without Luke's firm hold on her. She blinked, trying to hold back tears.

"You want to marry me?" Her voice broke as she felt her entire body tremble. She looked up into his eyes. "Are you certain?" Her trembling question gave away how much she wanted him to say yes.

"Quite certain." He offered a tender smile, lowered his head, capturing her mouth for a brief kiss, then pulling back. "Well?"

She smiled through the tears in her eyes. "Yes. I'll marry you."

He crushed her mouth with his as a joy he'd never felt swelled within him. His heart pounded, and the need to possess her gripped him. The kiss became insistent as he pulled back to trace the outline of her lips with his tongue. She made a low sound of pleasure and her lips parted, allowing him access, hungry for the taste of her.

His hands moved up her back, and he slid his fingers into her hair, pulling out the pins to let waves of golden brown curls drape around her shoulders. He broke the kiss long enough to see her eyes open, and a heated gleam appear before they fell closed and she drew him back down to her. A deep growl signaled his approval as a hand moved to the small of her back, aligning her body with his as fire streaked through him.

He broke the kiss and pulled back. "Ginny, we have to stop before this goes too far."

She drew him back down, whispering against his lips, "Not yet."

"But, Ginny..." His voice trailed off as she continued to hold him to her.

"I don't want you to stop," she breathed. "Please, Luke."

Common sense warred with passion as she melted against him, her hunger impossible to resist. He tightened his hold, then moved his hands up and down her body in almost frantic motions, capturing the hem of her dress and drawing it up until his hands rested on her bare thighs. A moan of pleasure escaped her lips, bursting the last shred of self-control Luke possessed. He lifted her into his arms, not breaking their kiss, and walked down the hall to her bedroom, pushing the door open, then kicking it closed.

He lay her on the bed, looking down at her, his heart swelling beyond reason, and giving her one more chance to change her mind. Instead, she smiled, causing his chest to tighten as she reached her arms up to him.

"I love you, Luke," she whispered as he lay down beside her and took her in his arms.

"I love you, too, Ginny."

Epilogue

Two weeks later...

"I have to hand it to you. When you make up your mind, you don't waste any time." Dax clasped Luke on the shoulder as they stood inside the church after the ceremony.

"I didn't have much choice when Rachel came home and caught me leaving Ginny's room, still buttoning my shirt. As I recall, she ordered me to stay away from Ginny until we got married. I'd have married her the next day if the women would've allowed it."

"Just feel fortunate Mary didn't get home earlier and surprise you." Dax glanced over at Rachel holding Mary's hand, laughing.

"Gabe told me he's had no success finding homes for the children. What are we going to do with them?" Luke watched as Billy and Sam spoke with a couple other boys close to their age.

"We won't worry about it for now. Today is for celebrating your marriage. How about I get us something to drink?" Dax walked off without waiting for Luke's answer, already knowing what it would be.

Luke kept his gaze trained on his bride as she accepted hugs and congratulations from those who'd been able to attend. He'd agreed to a big shindig in the spring, but made it clear he wasn't waiting months to marry her. He shifted his gaze when Nick Barnett walked up, offering a hand.

"Congratulations, Pelletier. You made the right decision."

"Guess I owe you an apology, Nick."

"None needed. It all turned out fine." He nodded toward Ginny, surrounded by Suzanne, Rachel, Lydia, and Abby.

"Uh, Nick—"

"Don't even ask. What happened stays between us." He shot a quick look at Luke before returning his gaze to Suzanne. "Guess I'll go break up the ladies and escort Suzanne to the refreshment table. She won't eat unless someone guides her toward the food."

Luke watched him walk away, wondering if there might be something brewing between the two.

"Congratulations, Pelletier." King Tolbert offered a hand, although his eyes scanned the room as if he were looking for someone.

"Thank you. I'm glad you and Abigail could attend."

"Abby refused to miss it, even though she still felt weak a few days ago from the sickness. She seems fine today." His eyes searched the room in an attempt to find her. "I also want to thank you for your services in Big Pine. You know, a deputy discovered the last outlaw and killed him."

Before leaving Big Pine, Dutch had sent Luke a message about the deaths of both Flatnose and Ezra Duncan. Sheriff Sterling didn't quite understand why the shooting took place in the home of a wealthy citizen. The committee seemed satisfied with Frederick Marlowe's explanation of the outlaw breaking into his home seeking shelter.

"Yes, I heard. Duncan was a good man. I'm sorry he lost his life over such a worthless human being as Flatnose." Luke saw Ginny glance his way and smile. "You'll have to excuse me. I should claim my bride." He strode across the room, his eyes never wavering from Ginny and the love he saw reflected back at him. It would be hard to wait through the reception and trip home to get her back in his bed. Two weeks had proven to be entirely too long. Although it had given him enough time to resupply his house on Wildfire Creek and get it ready for her and Mary. He hoped Ginny liked what he'd done.

"Hungry?" Luke asked as he came to stop next to her, grabbing her hand and squeezing.

"Starving."

"Let's eat, then head home. I can't wait much longer." He leaned down and placed a kiss on her lips. They'd just reached the table covered with food Suzanne had prepared when shouts erupted from the preacher's office at the back of the church. "Wait here."

Luke took off, followed by Dax and Gabe, toward the sound of the commotion.

"What's going on back here?" Luke asked, stopping in the doorway to see Noah, Abby, and King Tolbert.

"I want this man arrested, Sheriff." Tolbert's face glowed red.

"Father!" Abby placed herself between the two men glaring at each other.

"And just why would I arrest Noah?" Gabe asked as he glanced between the three people.

"He attempted to attack my daughter—"

"Noah did no such thing, and I won't have you accusing him of it." Abby moved in front of her father, her back to Noah.

"It's all right, Abby—"

"No, it isn't all right. He's trying to make a scene and I won't have it." She rested her fisted hands on her hips and glared at her father. "Tell Sheriff Evans you made a mistake."

"I made no mistake, Abigail. I saw his hands on you."

"I kissed him. All he did was try to set me aside."

Noah winced at the image she painted. If they'd been someplace else, he wouldn't have warned her off. He would've dragged her up to him and kissed her senseless.

"Abigail." Tolbert's hard, cold voice did nothing to cool her anger.

"It's true." She turned to Noah. "Tell him."

Noah's jaw worked as he tried to clear his mind. He couldn't blame her for something he'd wanted for a long time. "It's my fault, Mr. Tolbert. We never should've come back here."

"Noah..." Abby's response died on her lips as King grabbed her arm, escorting her from the room.

"You'll hear from me Brandt," Tolbert said as he disappeared with Abby.

Noah cursed under his breath and dragged a hand through his hair.

Gabe rested a hand on his shoulder. "It'll blow over. In a few days Tolbert will forget all about it."

Noah's gaze snapped to his friend. "Somehow, I don't believe he will."

The men began to leave when Rachel came storming toward them. "What happened in here?" she asked, a look of alarm on her face.

"It wasn't anything, Rachel," Dax said.

"It must have been something. King stormed past us with Abby, saying he'd had enough. He said he'd made up his mind and would be taking her to Big Pine, then putting her on the first train to Philadelphia."

Join me in the continuation of the Redemption Mountain series with the story of Noah and Abby in book three, Sunrise Ridge, due to release in 2015.

Thank you for taking the time to read Wildfire Creek. If you enjoyed it, please consider telling your friends or posting a short review. Word of mouth is an author's best friend and much appreciated.

Please join my reader's group to be notified of my New Releases at:
http://www.shirleendavies.com/contact-me.html

I care about quality, so if you find something in error, please contact me via email at
shirleen@shirleendavies.com

About the Author

Shirleen Davies writes romance—historical, contemporary, and romantic suspense. She grew up in Southern California, attended Oregon State University, and has degrees from San Diego State University and the University of Maryland. During the day she provides consulting services to small and mid-sized businesses. But her real passion is writing emotionally charged stories of flawed people who find redemption through love and acceptance. She now lives with her husband in a beautiful town in northern Arizona.

Shirleen loves to hear from her readers.

Write to her at: shirleen@shirleendavies.com
Visit her website:
http://www.shirleendavies.com
Sign up to be notified of New Releases:
http://www.shirleendavies.com/contact-me.html
Comment on her blog:
http://www.shirleendavies.com/blog.html
Facebook Fan Page:
https://www.facebook.com/ShirleenDaviesAuthor
Twitter: http://twitter.com/shirleendavies
Google+:
http://www.gplusid.com/shirleendavies

LinkedIn:
http://www.linkedin.com/in/shirleendaviesauthor
Pinterest:
http://www.pinterest.com/shirleendavies
Tsu: http://www.tsu.co/shirleendavies

Other Books by Shirleen Davies

Tougher than the Rest – Book One
MacLarens of Fire Mountain Historical Western Romance Series

"A passionate, fast-paced story set in the untamed western frontier by an exciting new voice in historical romance."

Niall MacLaren is the oldest of four brothers, and the undisputed leader of the family. A widower, and single father, his focus is on building the MacLaren ranch into the largest and most successful in northern Arizona. He is serious about two things—his responsibility to the family and his future marriage to the wealthy, well-connected widow who will secure his place in the territory's destiny.

Katherine is determined to live the life she's dreamed about. With a job waiting for her in the growing town of Los Angeles, California, the young teacher from Philadelphia begins a journey across the United States with only a couple of trunks and her spinster companion. Life is perfect for this adventurous, beautiful young woman, until an accident throws her into the arms of the one man who can destroy it all.

Fighting his growing attraction and strong desire for the beautiful stranger, Niall is more determined than ever to push emotions aside to focus on his goals of wealth and political gain. But looking into the clear, blue eyes of the woman who could ruin everything, Niall discovers he will have to harden his heart and be tougher than he's ever been in his life...Tougher than the Rest.

Faster than the Rest – Book Two
MacLarens of Fire Mountain Historical Western Romance Series

"Headstrong, brash, confident, and complex, the MacLarens of Fire Mountain will captivate you with strong characters set in the wild and rugged western frontier."

Handsome, ruthless, young U.S. Marshal Jamie MacLaren had lost everything—his parents, his family connections, and his childhood sweetheart—but now he's back in Fire Mountain and ready for another chance. Just as he successfully reconnects with his family and starts to rebuild his life, he gets the unexpected and unwanted assignment of rescuing the woman who broke his heart.

Beautiful, wealthy Victoria Wicklin chose money and power over love, but is now fighting for her life—or is she? Who has she become in the seven years since she left Fire Mountain to take up her life in San Francisco? Is she really as innocent as she says?

Marshal MacLaren struggles to learn the truth and do his job, but the past and present lead him in different directions as his heart and brain wage battle. Is Victoria a victim or a villain? Is life offering him another chance, or just another heartbreak?

As Jamie and Victoria struggle to uncover past secrets and come to grips with their shared passion, another danger arises. A life-altering danger that is out of their control and threatens to destroy any chance for a shared future.

Harder than the Rest – Book Three
MacLarens of Fire Mountain Historical Western Romance Series

"They are men you want on your side. Hard, confident, and loyal, the MacLarens of Fire Mountain will seize your attention from the first page."

Will MacLaren is a hardened, plain-speaking bounty hunter. His life centers on finding men guilty of horrendous crimes and making sure justice is done. There is no place in his world for the carefree attitude he carried years before when a tragic event destroyed his dreams.

Amanda is the daughter of a successful Colorado rancher. Determined and proud, she works hard to prove she is as capable as any man and worthy to be her father's heir. When a stranger arrives, her independent nature collides with the strong pull toward the handsome ranch hand. But is he what he seems and could his secrets endanger her as well as her family?

The last thing Will needs is to feel passion for another woman. But Amanda elicits feelings he thought were long buried. Can Will's desire for her change him? Or will the vengeance he seeks against the one man he wants to destroy—a dangerous opponent without a conscious—continue to control his life?

Stronger than the Rest – Book Four
MacLarens of Fire Mountain Historical Western Romance Series

"Smart, tough, and capable, the MacLarens protect their own no matter the odds. Set against America's rugged frontier, the stories of the men from Fire Mountain are complex, fast-paced, and a must read for anyone who enjoys non-stop action and romance."

Drew MacLaren is focused and strong. He has achieved all of his goals except one—to return to the MacLaren ranch and build the best horse breeding program in the west. His successful career as an attorney is about to give way to his ranching roots when a bullet changes everything.

Tess Taylor is the quiet, serious daughter of a Colorado ranch family with dreams of her own. Her shy nature keeps her from developing friendships outside of her close-knit family until Drew enters her life. Their relationship grows. Then a bullet, meant for another, leaves him paralyzed and determined to distance himself from the one woman he's come to love.

Convinced he is no longer the man Tess needs, Drew focuses on regaining the use of his legs and recapturing a life he thought lost. But danger of another kind threatens those he cares about—including Tess—forcing him to rethink his future.

Can Drew overcome the barriers that stand between him, the safety of his friends and family, and a life with the woman he loves? To do it all, he has to be strong. Stronger than the Rest.

Deadlier than the Rest – Book Five
MacLarens of Fire Mountain Historical Western Romance Series

"A passionate, heartwarming story of the iconic MacLarens of Fire Mountain. This captivating historical western romance grabs your attention from the start with an engrossing story encompassing two romances set against the rugged backdrop of the burgeoning western frontier."

Connor MacLaren's search has already stolen eight years of his life. Now he is close to finding what he seeks—Meggie, his missing sister. His quest leads him to the growing city of Salt Lake and an encounter with the most captivating woman he has ever met.

Grace is the third wife of a Mormon farmer, forced into a life far different from what she'd have chosen. Her independent spirit longs for choices governed only by her own heart and mind. To achieve her dreams, she must hide behind secrets and half-truths, even as her heart pulls her towards the ruggedly handsome Connor.

Known as cool and uncompromising, Connor MacLaren lives by a few, firm rules that have served him well and kept him alive. However, danger stalks Connor, even to the front range of the beautiful Wasatch Mountains, threatening those he cares about and impacting his ability to find his sister.

Can Connor protect himself from those who seek his death? Will his eight-year search lead him to his sister while unlocking the secrets he knows are held tight within Grace, the woman who has captured his heart?

Read this heartening story of duty, honor, passion, and love in book five of the MacLarens of Fire Mountain series.

Second Summer – Book One
MacLarens of Fire Mountain
Contemporary Romance Series

"In this passionate Contemporary Romance, author Shirleen Davies introduces her readers to the modern day MacLarens starting with Heath MacLaren, the head of the family."

The Chairman of both the MacLaren Cattle Co. and MacLaren Land Development, Heath MacLaren is a success professionally—his personal life is another matter.

Following a divorce after a long, loveless marriage, Heath spends his time with women who are beautiful and passionate, yet unable to provide what he longs for . . .

Heath has never experienced love even though he witnesses it every day between his younger brother, Jace, and wife, Caroline. He wants what they have, yet spends his time with women too young to understand what drives him and too focused on themselves to be true companions.

It's been two years since Annie's husband died, leaving her to build a new life. He was her soul mate and confidante. She has no desire to find a replacement, yet longs for male friendship.

Annie's closest friend in Fire Mountain, Caroline MacLaren, is determined to see Annie come out of her shell after almost two years of mourning. A chance meeting with Heath turns into an offer to be a part of the MacLaren Foundation Board and an opportunity for a life outside her home sanctuary which has also become her prison. The platonic friendship that builds between Annie and Heath points to a future where each may rely on the other without the bonds a romance would entail.

However, without consciously seeking it, each yearns for more . . .

The MacLaren Development Company is booming with Heath at the helm. His meetings at a partner company with the young, beautiful marketing director, who makes no secret of her desire for him, are a temptation. But is she the type of woman he truly wants?

Annie's acceptance of the deep, yet passionless, friendship with Heath sustains her, lulling her to believe it is all she needs. At least until Heath drops a bombshell, forcing Annie to realize that what she took for friendship is actually a deep, lasting love. One she doesn't want to lose.

Each must decide to settle—or fight for it all.

Hard Landing – Book Two
MacLarens of Fire Mountain
Contemporary Romance Series

Trey MacLaren is a confident, poised Navy pilot. He's focused, loyal, ethical, and a natural leader. He is also on his way to what he hopes will be a lasting relationship and marriage with fellow pilot, Jesse Evans.

Jesse has always been driven. Her graduation from the Naval Academy and acceptance into the pilot training program are all she thought she wanted—until she discovered love with Trey MacLaren

Trey and Jesse's lives are filled with fast flying, friends, and the demands of their military careers. Lives each has settled into with a passion. At least until the day Trey receives a letter that could change his and Jesse's lives forever.

It's been over two years since Trey has seen the woman in Pensacola. Her unexpected letter stuns him and pushes Jesse into a tailspin from which she might not pull back.

Each must make a choice. Will the choice Trey makes cause him to lose Jesse forever? Will she follow her heart or her head as she fights for a chance to save the love she's found? Will their independent decisions collide, forcing them to give up on a life together?

One More Day – Book Three
MacLarens of Fire Mountain
Contemporary Romance Series

Cameron "Cam" Sinclair is smart, driven, and dedicated, with an easygoing temperament that belies his strong will and the personal ambitions he holds close. Besides his family, his job as head of IT at the MacLaren Cattle Company and his position as a Search and Rescue volunteer are all he needs to make him happy. At least that's what he thinks until he meets, and is instantly drawn to, fellow SAR volunteer, Lainey Devlin.

Lainey is compassionate, independent, and ready to break away from her manipulative and controlling fiancé. Just as her decision is made, she's called into a major search and rescue effort, where once again, her path crosses with the intriguing, and much too handsome, Cam Sinclair. But Lainey's plans are set. An opportunity to buy a flourishing preschool in northern Arizona is her chance to make a fresh start, and nothing, not even her fierce attraction to Cam Sinclair, will impede her plans.

As Lainey begins to settle into her new life, an unexpected danger arises —threats from an unknown assailant—someone who doesn't believe she belongs in Fire Mountain. The more Lainey begins to love her new home, the greater the danger becomes. Can she accept the help and protection Cam offers while ignoring her consuming desire for him?

Even if Lainey accepts her attraction to Cam, will he ever be able to come to terms with his own driving ambition and allow himself to consider a different life than the one he's always pictured? A life with the one woman who offers more than he'd ever hoped to find?

All Your Nights – Book Four
MacLarens of Fire Mountain
Contemporary Romance Series

"Romance, adventure, cowboys, suspense—everything you want in a contemporary western romance novel."

Kade Taylor likes living on the edge. As an undercover agent for the DEA and a former Special Ops team member, his current assignment seems tame—keep tabs on a bookish Ph.D. candidate the agency believes is connected to a ruthless drug cartel.

Brooke Sinclair is weeks away from obtaining her goal of a doctoral degree. She spends time finalizing her presentation and relaxing with another student who seems to want nothing more than her friendship. That's fine with Brooke. Her last serious relationship ended in a broken engagement.

Her future is set, safe and peaceful, just as she's always planned—until Agent Taylor informs her she's under suspicion for illegal drug activities.

Kade and his DEA team obtain evidence which exonerates Brooke while placing her in danger from those who sought to use her. As Kade races to take down the drug cartel while protecting Brooke, he must also find common ground with the former suspect—a woman he desires with increasing intensity.

At odds with her better judgment, Brooke finds the more time she spends with Kade, the more she's attracted to the complex, multi-faceted agent. But Kade holds secrets he knows Brooke will never understand or accept.

Can Kade keep Brooke safe while coming to terms with his past, or will he stay silent, ruining any future with the woman his heart can't let go?

Always Love You– Book Five
MacLarens of Fire Mountain
Contemporary Romance Series

Eric and Amber's story – Releases Winter 2015

Redemption's Edge – Book One
Redemption Mountain – Historical
Western Romance Series

"A heartwarming, passionate story of loss, forgiveness, and redemption set in the untamed frontier during the tumultuous years following the Civil War. Ms. Davies' engaging and complex characters draw you in from the start, creating an exciting introduction to this new historical western romance series."

"Redemption's Edge is a strong and engaging introduction to her new historical western romance series."

Dax Pelletier is ready for a new life, far away from the one he left behind in Savannah following the South's devastating defeat in the Civil War. The ex-Confederate general wants nothing more to do with commanding men and confronting the tough truths of leadership.

Rachel Davenport possesses skills unlike those of her Boston socialite peers—skills honed as a nurse in field hospitals during the Civil War. Eschewing her northeastern suitors and changed by the carnage she's seen, Rachel decides to accept her uncle's invitation to assist him at his clinic in the dangerous and wild frontier of Montana.

Now a Texas Ranger, a promise to a friend takes Dax and his brother, Luke, to the untamed territory of Montana. He'll fulfill his oath and return to Austin, at least that's what he believes.

The small town of Splendor is what Rachel needs after life in a large city. In a few short months, she's grown to love the people as well as the majestic beauty of the untamed frontier. She's settled into a life unlike any she has ever thought possible.

Thinking his battle days are over, he now faces dangers of a different kind—one by those from his past who seek vengeance, and another from Rachel, the woman who's captured his heart.

Wildfire Creek – Book Two
Redemption Mountain – Historical Western Romance Series

"A passionate story of rebuilding lives, working to find a place in the wild frontier, and building new lives in the years following the American Civil War. A rugged, heartwarming story of choices and

love in the continuing saga of Redemption Mountain."

Luke Pelletier is settling into his new life as a rancher and occasional Pinkerton Agent, leaving his past as an ex-Confederate major and Texas Ranger far behind. He wants nothing more than to work the ranch, charm the ladies, and live a life of carefree bachelorhood.

Ginny Sorensen has accepted her responsibility as the sole provider for herself and her younger sister. The desire to continue their journey to Oregon is crushed when the need for food and shelter keeps them in the growing frontier town of Splendor, Montana, forcing Ginny to accept work as a server in the local saloon.

Luke has never met a woman as lovely and unspoiled as Ginny. He longs to know her, yet fears his wild ways and unsettled nature aren't what she deserves. She's a girl you marry, but that is nowhere in Luke's plans.

Complicating their tenuous friendship, a twist in circumstances forces Ginny closer to the man she most wants to avoid—the man who can destroy her dreams, and who's captured her heart.

Believing his bachelor status firm, Luke moves from danger to adventure, never

dreaming each step he takes brings him closer
to his true destiny and a life much different
from what he imagines.

www.ingramcontent.com/pod-product-compliance
Lightning Source LLC
Chambersburg PA
CBHW070339170726
48291CB00001B/111